Richelle Mead has an MA in Comparative Religion and a passion for all things wacky and humorous. She currently lives in Seattle and rarely gets up before noon. As well as writing the 'Succubus' series and the 'Dark Swan' novels, she is the author of the bestselling 'Vampire Academy' series.

Catch up on her late-night musings and updates about her next novel at: www.richellemead.com

Praise for Richelle Mead

'My kind of book – great characters, dark worlds, and just the right touch of humour. A great read'
Patricia Briggs, author of *Moon Called*

'Richelle Mead has a way of cutting through the clichés to get to the heart of her story. This is urban fantasy the way it's meant to be: smart, clever, magical, meaningful, with great characters and real heart'
Carrie Vaughn, author of *Kitty and the Midnight Hour*

'With sharp prose and a powerhouse voice, Richelle Mead took a death grip on my imagination and refused to let go. I, too, fell prey to the enchantments of her succubus, and couldn't stop thinking, wondering, and caring about her until I turned the final page'
Vicki Pettersson, author of *The Scent of Shadows*

'Deliciously wicked! Dysfunctional, funny, and sexy. I look forward to reading more tempting morsels about this succubus-with-a-heart-of gold'
Lilith Saintcrow, author of *Dead Man Rising*

'Take a beautiful, sassy immortal. Mix in suspense, murder and plenty of hot sex. Pour yourself a great read and enjoy the

M   s

D0238195

Also by Richelle Mead

SUCCUBUS BLUES
SUCCUBUS NIGHTS
(published in the US as *Succubus On Top*)
SUCCUBUS DREAMS
SUCCUBUS HEAT
SUCCUBUS SHADOWS

STORM BORN
THORN QUEEN
IRON CROWNED

and published by Bantam Books

www.transworldbooks.co.uk

Succubus Revealed

Richelle Mead

BANTAM BOOKS

LONDON • TORONTO • SYDNEY • AUCKLAND • JOHANNESBURG

TRANSWORLD PUBLISHERS
61–63 Uxbridge Road, London W5 5SA
A Random House Group Company
www.transworldbooks.co.uk

SUCCUBUS REVEALED
A BANTAM BOOK: 9780553826081

Originally published in the United States of America by Kensington Books
First publication in Great Britain
Bantam edition published 2011

A CIP catalogue record for this book
is available from the British Library.

Addresses for Random House Group Ltd companies outside the UK
can be found at: www.randomhouse.co.uk
The Random House Group Ltd Reg. No. 954009

The Random House Group Limited supports the Forest Stewardship Council
(FSC®), the leading international forest-certification organisation. Our books
carrying the FSC label are printed on FSC®-certified paper. FSC is the only
forest-certification scheme endorsed by the leading environmental
organisations, including Greenpeace. Our paper-procurement policy
can be found at www.randomhouse.co.uk/environment.

Typeset in Sabon
Printed and bound by CPI Group (UK) Ltd, Croydon, CR0 4YY

2 4 6 8 10 9 7 5 3 1

MIX
Paper from
responsible sources
FSC
www.fsc.org   FSC® C016897

For the man in my dream

Acknowledgments

Georgina's story has been a long time in telling and wouldn't have been possible without the help of countless people. Many thanks to all the family and friends who supported me from the very beginning of my career, especially Georgina's first reviewers—David, Christina, and Marcee—who probably never thought we'd make it this far when they were reading those early sample chapters. Thank you also to Jay for putting up with all the "feelings" along the way in these books! Your strength helps get me through the long days. And of course, thank you to the dream team behind the scenes: my agent, Jim McCarthy, of Dystel & Goderich Literary Management; and my editor, John Scognamiglio, of Kensington Publishing. The endless hours you guys have put in to help me have made writing this series a joy and have taken it to places I never dreamed.

Lastly, I'll always be grateful to the many readers around the world who have loved and cheered for Georgina throughout her tumultuous journey. Your enthusiasm and support continues to inspire me every day. Thank you.

Chapter 1

This wasn't the first time I'd worn a foil dress. It was, however, the first time I'd done so in a family-friendly setting.

"Vixen!"

Santa's voice rang out above the mall crowd, and I hurried away from where I'd been corralling a group of Burberry-clad kids. It wasn't actually Santa Claus calling me, of course. The man sitting in the holly-and-light-bedecked gazebo was named Walter something-or-other, but he asked that those of us working as his "elves" refer to him as Santa at all times. Conversely, he had christened all of us with either reindeer or Seven Dwarves names. He took this job very seriously and said the names helped him stay in character. If we questioned that, he'd start regaling us with tales of his extensive career as a Shakespearean actor, one that he claimed had come to an end because of his age. We elves had our own ideas about what might have cut his career short.

"Santa needs another drink," he told me in a stage whisper, once I reached his side. "Grumpy won't get me one." He inclined his head toward another woman dressed in a green foil dress. She was holding back a squirming boy while Santa and I conducted our conversation. I met her pained expression and then glanced down at my watch.

"Well, Santa," I said, "that's because it's only been an hour since the last one. You know the deal: one shot in your coffee every three hours."

"We made that deal a week ago!" he hissed. "Before the

crowds picked up. You have no idea what Santa endures." I didn't know if it was part of his acting method or just a personality quirk, but he also referred to himself in the third person a lot. "A girl just asked for SAT scores good enough to get her into Yale. I think she was nine."

I spared him a moment's sympathy. The mall where we were earning holiday pay was in one of Seattle's more affluent suburbs, and the requests he got sometimes went beyond footballs and ponies. The kids also tended to be better dressed than me (when I wasn't in elf-wear), which was no small feat.

"Sorry," I said. Tradition or not, I sometimes thought putting children on an old guy's lap was already creepy enough. We didn't need to mix alcohol into it. "The deal stands."

"Santa can't take much more of this!"

"Santa's got four hours left of his shift," I pointed out.

"I wish Comet was still here," he said petulantly. "She was much more lenient with the drinks."

"Yes. And I'm sure she's drinking alone right now, seeing as she's unemployed." Comet, a former elf, had been generous with Santa's shots and also partaken of them herself. Since she was half his weight, though, she hadn't held her liquor as well and had lost her job when mall officials caught her taking off her clothes in The Sharper Image. I gave a curt nod to Grumpy. "Go ahead."

The little boy hurried forward and climbed onto Santa's lap. To his credit, Santa switched into character and didn't pester me (or the boy) further about a drink. "Ho ho ho! What would you like for this nondenominational winter holiday season?" He even affected a slight British accent, which wasn't really necessary for the role but certainly made him seem more authoritative.

The boy regarded Santa solemnly. "I want my dad to move back home."

"Is that your father?" asked Santa, looking toward a couple standing near Grumpy. The woman was pretty and blond, with the look of someone in her thirties who'd been preemptively hitting the Botox. If the guy she was plastered all over was old enough to be out of college, I would have been very surprised.

"No," said the boy. "That's my mom and her friend Roger."

Santa was silent for a few moments. "Is there anything else you'd like?"

I left them to it and returned to my post near the line's start. Evening was wearing on, increasing the number of families turning out. Unlike Santa's, my shift ended in less than an hour. I could get in a little shopping time and miss the worst of the commuting traffic. As an official mall employee, I got a considerable discount, which made drunken Santas and foil dresses that much easier to bear. One of the greatest things about the happiest time of the year was that all the department stores had extensive cosmetics and fragrance gift sets out right now, gift sets that desperately needed a home in my bathroom.

"Georgina?"

My dreams of sugarplums and Christian Dior were interrupted by the sound of a familiar voice. I turned and felt my heart sink as I met the eyes of a pretty middle-aged woman with cropped hair.

"Janice, hey. How's it going?"

My former co-worker returned my stiff smile with a puzzled one. "Fine. I . . . I didn't expect to see you here."

I also hadn't expected to be seen here. It was one of the reasons I'd chosen to work outside the city, to specifically avoid anyone from my old job. "Likewise. Don't you live in Northgate?" I tried not to make it sound like an accusation.

She nodded and rested her hand on the shoulder of a small, dark-haired girl. "We do, but my sister lives over here, and we thought we'd visit her after Alicia talks to Santa."

"I see," I said, feeling mortified. Wonderful. Janice was going to go back to Emerald City Books and Café and tell everyone that she'd spotted me dressed as an elf. Not that that could make things worse, I supposed. Everyone there already thought I was the Whore of Babylon. It was why I'd quit a few weeks ago. What was an elf dress on top of that?

"Is this Santa any good?" asked Alicia impatiently. "The one I saw last year didn't get me what I wanted."

Over the buzzing of the crowd, I just barely heard Santa saying, "Well, Jessica, there's not much Santa can do about interest rates." I turned back to Alicia.

"It kind of depends on what you want," I said.

"How did you end up here?" asked Janice, with a small frown.

She actually sounded concerned, which I supposed was better than her gloating. I had a feeling there were a number of people at the bookstore who would have loved the idea of me suffering—not that this job was so bad.

"Well, this is just temporary, obviously," I explained. "It gives me something to do while I interview for others, and I get a mall discount. And really, it's just another form of customer service." I was trying hard not to sound defensive or desperate, but with each word, the intensity of how much I missed my old job hit me more and more.

"Oh, good," she said, looking slightly relieved. "I'm sure you'll find something soon. Looks like the line's moving."

"Wait, Janice?" I caught hold of her arm before she could walk away. "How . . . how's Doug?"

I'd left behind a lot of things at Emerald City: a position of power, a warm atmosphere, unlimited books and coffee . . . But as much as I missed all of those things, I didn't miss them as much as I missed a single person: my friend Doug Sato. He, more than anything, was what had spurred me to leave. I hadn't been able to handle working with him anymore. It had been terrible, seeing someone I care about so much regard me with such contempt and disappointment. I'd had to get away from that and felt I'd made the right choice, but it was still hard losing someone who'd been a part of my life for the last five years.

Janice's smile returned. Doug had that effect on people. "Oh, you know. He's Doug. The same, wacky Doug. Band's going strong. And I think he might get your job. Er, your old job. They're interviewing for it." Her smile faded, as though she suddenly realized that might cause me discomfort. It didn't. Not much.

"That's great," I said. "I'm happy for him."

She nodded and told me good-bye before hurrying forward in line. Behind her, a family of four paused in their frantic texting on identical cell phones to glare at me for the holdup. A moment later, they hunched back down again, no doubt telling all their Twitter friends about every inane detail of their holiday mall experience.

I put on a cheery smile that didn't reflect what I felt inside and continued helping with the line until Sneezy, my replacement, showed up. I got him up to speed on Santa's drinking schedule and then abandoned the holiday nexus for the mall's back offices. Once inside a bathroom, I shape-shifted out of the foil dress, trading it for a much more tasteful sweater and jeans combo. I even made the sweater blue so that there would be no confusion. I was off the holiday clock.

Of course, as I walked back through the mall, I couldn't help but notice I was never off the clock for my main job: being a succubus in the illustrious service of Hell. Centuries of corruption and seduction of souls had given me a sixth sense for spotting those most vulnerable to my charms. The holidays, while ostensibly being a time of cheer, also tended to bring out the worst in people. I could spot the desperation everywhere—those hoping to frantically find the perfect gifts to win over the ones they loved, those dissatisfied with their ability to provide for their loved ones, those dragged along on shopping trips to create a "perfect" holiday experience they had no interest in. . . . Yes, it was everywhere if you knew how to look for it: that sorrow and frustration tucked in amongst the joy. Those were exactly the kinds of souls that were ripe for the taking. I could have picked off any number of guys if I wanted to tonight and taken care of my quota for the week.

My brief exchange with Janice had left me feeling strange,

however, and I couldn't muster the energy to go strike up a conversation with some discontent suburban businessman. Instead, I consoled myself with impulse purchases for myself and even found a couple of much-needed gifts for others, proving that I wasn't totally and completely selfish. By the time I left, I felt confident traffic had died down and would give me an easy drive back to the city. As I walked past the center of the mall, I heard Santa ho-ho-ho-ing loudly while waving his arms energetically around, much to the terror of a small child on his lap. My guess was that someone had cracked and broken the drinking rule.

On the way home, I noticed I had three voice mail messages, all from my friend Peter. Before I could even attempt to listen to them, the phone rang.

"Hello?"

"Where are you?" Peter's frantic voice filled up the small space of my Passat.

"In my car. Where are you?"

"At my apartment. Where else? Everyone's here!"

"Everyone? What are you talking about?"

"Did you forget? Damn it, Georgina. You were a lot more punctual when you were unhappy and single."

I ignored the jab and scanned through my mental calendar. Peter was one of my best friends. He was also a neurotic, obsessive compulsive vampire who loved hosting dinners and parties. He usually managed to throw something together at least once a week, never for the same reason, so it was easy to lose track.

"It's fondue night," I said at last, proud of myself for remembering.

"Yes! And the cheese is getting cold. I'm not made of Sterno, you know."

"Why didn't you just start eating?"

"Because we're civilized."

"Debatable." I pondered whether I wanted to go or not. Part of me really just wanted to get home and snuggle with Seth, but I had a feeling he'd be working. I likely couldn't expect snuggling for a while, whereas I could appease Peter right now. "Fine. Start without me, and I'll be there soon. I'm just getting off the bridge now." Wistfully, I drove past Seth's exit and instead set my sights on the one that would take me to Peter's place.

"Did you remember to bring wine?" he asked.

"Peter, until a minute ago, I didn't even remember I was supposed to be at your place. Do you really need wine?" I'd seen Peter's wine cabinet. On any given day, he had a dozen each of reds and whites, both domestic and international.

"I don't want to run out of the good stuff," he said.

"I seriously doubt you're going to— wait. Is Carter there?"

"Yes."

"Okay. I'll pick up some wine."

I showed up at his apartment ten minutes later. His roommate and apprentice, Cody, opened the door and gave me a broad, fang-filled smile. Light, music, and the scent of fondue and potpourri washed over me. Their home put Santa's gazebo to shame and had decorations filling every square inch. And not just Christmas ones.

"Since when do you guys have a menorah?" I asked Cody. "Neither of you are Jewish."

"Well, we're not Christian either," he pointed out, leading me toward the dining room. "Peter wanted to take a multicultural slant this year. The guestroom is all done in Kwanza decorations, if you know someone looking for a truly tacky overnight experience."

"It is not tacky!" Peter stood up from a table where our other immortal friends sat around two tubs of melted cheese. "I can't believe you're so insensitive to other people's religious views. Jesus Christ! Is that boxed wine?"

"You said you wanted wine," I reminded him.

"I wanted good wine. Please tell me it's not blush."

"Of course it's blush. And you didn't tell me to bring good wine. You said you were worried Carter would drink all your good wine. So I brought this for him instead. Your wine is safe."

At the mention of his name, the only heavenly creature in the room looked up. "Sweet," he said, accepting the box from me. "Santa's little helper delivers." He opened up the box's dispenser and looked at Peter expectantly. "Do you have a straw?"

I sat in an empty seat beside my boss, Jerome, who was contentedly dipping a piece of bread in molten cheddar. He was the archdemon of all of Seattle and chose to walk the earth looking like a circa 1990 John Cusack, which made it easy to forget his true nature sometimes. Fortunately, his brimstone personality always came out the instant he opened his mouth. "You're here less than a minute, Georgie, and already you've made this get-together fifty percent less classy."

"You guys are eating fondue on a Tuesday night," I retorted. "You were well on your way without me."

Peter had settled himself back down and was trying to appear calm. "Fondue is very classy. It's all in the presentation. Hey! Where'd you get that?"

Carter had set the wine box on his lap, dispenser on top, and was now drinking from it with an enormous straw that I suspected had been literally conjured from thin air.

"At least he's not doing that with a bottle of Pinot Noir," I told Peter good-naturedly. I helped myself to a fondue fork and speared a piece of apple. On the other side of Jerome, Hugh busily typed away on his phone's keyboard, reminding me of the family at the mall. "Telling the world about this lowbrow party?" I teased. Hugh was an imp, a type of hellish administrative assistant, so he could have actually been buying or selling souls via his phone for all I knew.

"Of course," said Hugh, not looking up. "I'm updating Facebook. Do you know why Roman won't answer my friend request?"

"No clue," I said. "I've barely spoken to him in days."

"When I talked to him earlier, he said he had to work tonight," Peter explained, "but that we should go ahead and draw for him."

"Draw?" I asked uneasily. "Oh Lord. Tell me it's not Pictionary night too."

Peter sighed wearily. "Draw for Secret Santas. Do you even read the e-mails I send?"

"Secret Santas? Seems like we just did that," I said.

"Yeah, a year ago," said Peter. "Just like we do every Christmas."

I glanced over at Carter who was quietly drinking his wine. "Did you lose my hat? You look like you could use one." The angel's chin-length, blond hair was even more unkempt than usual.

"Tell us what you really think, Georgina," he replied. He ran a hand over his hair, but it somehow only made things worse. "I'm saving it for a special occasion."

"If I get your name again, I'll buy you two hats so you don't have to ration yourself."

"I wouldn't want you to go to the trouble."

"No trouble at all. I get a discount at the mall."

Jerome sighed and set down his fork. "Are you still doing that, Georgie? Don't I suffer enough without having to endure the humiliation of a succubus who moonlights as a Christmas elf?"

"You always said I should quit the bookstore and find something else to do," I reminded him.

"Yes, but that was because I thought you'd go on to do something respectable. Like become a stripper or the mayor's mistress."

"This is just temporary." I handed Carter the elegant crystal wineglass that had been sitting by my plate. He filled it with wine from the box and gave it back. Peter groaned and muttered something about despoiling Tiffany's.

"Georgina doesn't need material things anymore," teased Cody. "She's paid in love now."

Jerome fixed the young vampire with a cold stare. "Do *not* ever say anything that saccharine again."

"You're one to talk," I said to Cody, unable to hide my

smile. "I'm surprised you could drag yourself away from Gabrielle tonight." His face immediately grew dreamy at the mention of his ladylove.

"That makes two of us," observed Peter. He shook his head bitterly. "You guys and your perfect love lives."

"Hardly perfect," I said at the same time Cody said, "It *is* perfect."

All eyes fell on me. Hugh even looked up from his phone. "Trouble in paradise?"

"Why do you always assume that? And no, of course not," I scoffed, hating myself for the slip. "Things are fantastic with Seth."

And they were. Just speaking his name sent a flood of joy through me. Seth. Seth was what made everything worthwhile. My relationship with him was what had caused the rift between me and my former co-workers at the bookstore. They saw me as the reason for his breakup with Doug's sister. Which, I suppose, I was. But no matter how much I'd loved that job, giving it up was a small price to pay to be with Seth. I could endure being an elf. I could endure the quotas he and I put on our sex life, to ensure my succubus powers didn't suck him dry. With him, I could handle anything. Even a future of damnation.

There were just a couple of teeny-tiny things about my relationship with Seth that gave me pause. One had been eating at me for a while, one I kept trying to ignore. But now, suddenly, with my immortal friends watching me, I finally drummed up the courage to address it.

"It's just . . . I don't suppose any of you told Seth my name, did you?" Seeing Peter open his mouth in confusion, I immediately amended, "My real name."

"Why would that ever come up?" asked Hugh dismissively, returning to his texting.

"I don't even know your real name," said Cody. "Are you saying it's not Georgina?"

I regretted the words already. It was a stupid thing for me

to worry about, and their reactions were just proving that point.

"Do you *not* want him to know your name?" asked Hugh.

"No . . . it's fine. I just, well. It's just weird. A month or so ago, when he was half-asleep, he called me by it. Letha," I added, for Cody's benefit. I managed to say the name without tripping over it. It wasn't a name I welcomed. I'd shed it centuries ago, when I became a succubus, and had been taking assumed names ever since. In banishing that name, I'd banished that former life. I'd wanted to erase it so badly that I'd sold my soul in exchange for everyone I'd known forgetting I existed. That was why the conversation with Seth had totally blindsided me. There was no way he could've known that name.

You are the world, Letha . . . he had told me drowsily.

He hadn't even remembered saying it, let alone where he'd heard it. *Don't know,* he'd told me, when I questioned him about it later. *Greek myths, I guess. The River Lethe, where the dead go to wash away the memories from their souls . . . to forget the past. . . .*

"That's a pretty name," said Cody.

I shrugged noncommittally. "The point is, I never told it to Seth. But somehow, he knew it. He couldn't remember anything about it, though. Where he heard it."

"He must have heard it from you," said Hugh, ever practical.

"I never told him. I'd remember if I had."

"Well, with all the other immortals traipsing through here, I'm sure it came up from one of them. He probably overheard it." Peter frowned. "Don't you have an award with your name on it? Maybe he saw that."

"I don't really leave my 'Best Succubus' award lying around," I pointed out.

"Well, you should," said Hugh.

I eyed Carter carefully. "You're being awfully quiet."

He paused in drinking from the wine box. "I'm busy."

"Did *you* tell Seth my name? You've called me it before."
Carter, despite being an angel, seemed to have a genuine affection for us damned souls. And like an elementary school boy, he often thought the best way of showing that affection was by picking on us. Calling me Letha—when he knew I hated it—and other pet names was one such tactic he used.

Carter shook his head. "Sorry to disappoint you, Daughter of Lilith, but I never told him. You know me: model of discretion." There was a slurping sound as he neared the wine's end.

"Then how did Seth find out?" I demanded. "How'd he know the name? Someone must have told him."

Jerome sighed loudly. "Georgie, this conversation is even more ridiculous than the one about your job. You already got your answer: either you or someone else slipped up and doesn't remember. Why does everything have to be so dramatic for you? Are you just looking for something to be unhappy about?"

He had a point. And honestly, I didn't know why this had bugged me so much for so long. Everyone was right. There was no mystery here, nothing earth-shattering. Seth had overheard my name somewhere, end of story. There was no reason for me to overreact or assume the worst—only a tiny, nagging voice in my head that refused to forget about that night.

"It's just weird," I said lamely.

Jerome rolled his eyes. "If you want something to worry about, then I'll give you something."

All thoughts of Seth and names flew out of my head. Everyone at the table (except Carter, who was still slurping) froze and stared at Jerome. When my boss said he had something for you to worry about, there was a strong possibility it meant something fiery and terrifying. Hugh looked startled by this proclamation too, which was a bad sign. He usually knew about hellish mandates before Jerome did.

"What's going on?" I asked.

"I had a drink with Nanette the other night," he growled.

Nanette was Portland's archdemoness. "Bad enough she still won't let me forget the summoning. She was also going off on some bullshit about how her people were more competent than mine."

I glanced briefly at my friends. We weren't exactly model employees of Hell, so there was a very good chance that Nanette was right. Not that any of us would tell Jerome that.

"So," he continued, "when I denied it, she demanded we step up and prove what superior Hellish minions we are."

"How?" asked Hugh, looking mildly interested. "With a soul pledge drive?"

"Don't be ridiculous," said Jerome.

"Then with what?" I asked.

Jerome gave us a tight-lipped smile. "With bowling."

Chapter 2

It took me a moment to really comprehend that in thirty seconds, the conversation had gone from a deeply seriously mystery about my love life to bowling for demonic bragging rights. And yet, this wasn't a particularly unusual pattern in my world.

"And by 'we,' " added Jerome, "I mean you four." He nodded toward Peter, Cody, Hugh, and me.

"I'm sorry," I said. "Let me make sure I'm following this. You've signed us up for some sort of bowling league. One that you aren't even going to participate in. And this is somehow going to prove your employees' 'evilness' to the world."

"Don't be silly. I can't participate. Bowling teams only have four people." He didn't comment on the proving evilness part.

"Well, hey, I'll totally yield my spot to you," I said. "I'm not that great a bowler."

"You'd better become one." Jerome's voice grew cold. "All of you had, if you know what's good for you. Nanette will be impossible to live with at the next company meeting if you lot lose."

"Gee, Jerome. I love bowling," said Carter. "How come you never mentioned this to me before?"

Jerome and Carter held gazes for several heavy seconds. "Because, unless you're ready to take a *fall* for the team, you can't really compete with us."

A funny smile fell over Carter's face. His gray eyes glinted. "I see."

"I don't really like your use of 'us,' seeing as you've already written off any participation on your part," I pointed out to Jerome, imitating his earlier snide tone.

Peter sighed, looking rather woebegone. "Where on earth am I going to find tasteful bowling shoes?"

"What's our team name going to be?" asked Cody. That immediately degenerated into a conversation of truly terrible suggestions, such as Soulless in Seattle and Split Decision. After almost an hour, I couldn't handle any more.

"I think I'm going to go home," I said, standing up. I had kind of wanted dessert but was afraid I'd be drafted for beach volleyball and cricket if I stayed much longer. "I brought the wine. You guys don't really need me anymore."

"When you get home, tell my wayward offspring that I need him to coach you guys," said Jerome.

"By 'home,' I actually meant Seth's," I said. "But if I see Roman, I'll let him know you've found a good use for his formidable cosmic powers." Roman—Jerome's half-human son and my roommate—actually *was* a pretty good bowler, but I didn't want to encourage Jerome.

"Wait!" Peter sprang up after me. "You have to draw for Secret Santas first."

"Oh, come on—"

"No complaining," he argued. He hurried to the kitchen and returned with a ceramic cookie jar shaped like a snowman. He thrust it toward me. "Draw. Whatever name you get is who you're buying for, so don't try to get out of it."

I drew a piece of paper and opened it up. *Georgina.*

"I can't—"

Peter held up a hand to silence me. "You drew the name. That's who you've got. No arguments."

His stern look stopped me from any more protests. "Well," I pointed out pragmatically, "at least I have a few ideas."

To his credit, Peter sent me home with some chocolate fondue sauce and a Tupperware bowl filled with fruit and marshmallows. Hugh and Cody were running forward with the bowling team plan, trying to come up with a practice schedule. Jerome and Carter said little and instead kept watching each other in a speculative, knowing way that was typical of them. It was hard to read much on their faces, but for once, Jerome gave off the vibe of having the upper hand.

I left Capitol Hill for Seattle's University District and Seth's condo. All the windows were dark when I pulled up, and I couldn't help a smile. It was almost eleven. Seth must have called it an early night, something I'd been urging him to do for a while. Thinking of that, my smile faded as quickly as it had come. A few months ago, Seth's sister-in-law, Andrea, had been diagnosed with ovarian cancer. The disease had been pretty far advanced when caught, and although she'd almost immediately gone into treatment, the outcome still wasn't promising. Worse, the treatments had taken a huge physical toll on her, one that was testing the family's strength. Seth was frequently helping them out, especially when his brother Terry was working, since it was harder for Andrea to care for their five daughters now. Seth had been sacrificing both sleep and his writing career to look after them.

I knew it was necessary. I loved Seth's family and had helped them out as well. But I still hated seeing Seth run himself down and knew that it hurt him to put his work on hold. He claimed his writing was the least of his problems right now and had time before deadlines were an issue, particularly since his next two books were queued for printing next year. I couldn't argue against that, but the sleep issue? Yeah, I was on him a lot about that and glad to see my words had gotten through tonight.

I used my key to let myself in and slipped through the condo as silently as possible. I practically lived here lately and had no trouble finding my way around furniture in the darkness. When I reached his bedroom, I could just barely make out his form wrapped up in covers, softly outlined in the light of his alarm clock. I quietly took off my coat and then shape-shifted into a cotton babydoll nightgown. It was sexy but not blatantly so. I planned on sleeping with him tonight, for real.

I slid into bed and pressed myself up against his back, lightly tossing an arm over him. He stirred slightly, and I couldn't resist pressing a kiss against his bare shoulder. The scent of cinnamon and musk washed over me as he snuggled closer. Despite sternly chastising myself that he needed to sleep, I lightly ran my fingers along his arm and sneaked in another kiss.

"Mmm," he murmured, rolling over toward me. "That feels nice."

A few things hit me at once. First, Seth didn't wear any sort of cologne or aftershave that smelled like cinnamon. Second, Seth's voice didn't sound like that. Third, and perhaps most important, Seth wasn't in bed with me.

I didn't mean to scream as loudly as I did. It just kind of happened.

I was out of the bed in a flash, groping for the light switch on the wall while the intruder attempted to get up. He ended up getting tangled in the covers and falling off the bed with a loud *thump,* just as I found the light. I promptly reached for a weapon, but seeing as this was Seth's bedroom, my options were limited. The heaviest, most dangerous object I could readily grab ahold of was Seth's dictionary, a leather-bound monstrosity that he kept on hand because he "didn't trust the Internet."

I stood poised and ready to literally throw the book at the intruder as he scrambled to his feet. As he did and I got a good look at him, I noticed something crazy. He looked . . . familiar. Not only that, but he *kind of* looked like Seth.

"Who are you?" I demanded.

"Who are *you?*" he exclaimed. He seemed more confused than anything else. I don't think he found the threat of a five foot four woman with a dictionary all that frightening.

Before I could answer, a hand touched my arm. I yelped

and threw the dictionary out of instinct. The guy dodged, letting the book crash harmlessly against the wall. I spun around to see who'd touched me and found myself looking into the eyes of a white-haired woman with gold cat-eye glasses. She was wearing flowered pajama bottoms and a pink sweatshirt with a crossword puzzle on it. She was also wielding a baseball bat, which was pretty astonishing—not just because it was more dangerous than a dictionary but also because I hadn't known Seth owned one.

"What are you doing here?" she asked fiercely. She glanced over at the shirtless, dumbfounded guy. "Are you okay?"

For half a second, I actually toyed with the idea that I had somehow let myself into someone else's condo. Like, maybe I was just one door over. This scene was so ridiculous that a mix-up seemed far more likely. It was only the obvious evidence—like my key and Seth's University of Chicago teddy bear watching this spectacle—that drove home the fact that I was indeed where I was supposed to be.

Suddenly, the sound of the front door opening and closing rang through the condo. "Hello?" came a blessedly familiar voice.

"Seth!" exclaimed all three of us in unison.

Moments later, Seth appeared in the doorway. As usual, he looked adorable. His reddish brown hair was typically unkempt, and he was wearing a *Dirty Dancing* T-shirt that I'd never seen before. Despite my panic and confusion over this current situation, the concerned part of me still noted the little signs of fatigue on Seth's face, the dark circles and lines of weariness. He was thirty-six and usually looked younger than his age. Not today.

"Seth," said the bat-wielding woman. "This lady broke into your house."

He looked at each of us in turn before resting his gaze on her. "Mom," he said quietly, "that's my girlfriend. Please don't bludgeon her."

"Since when do you have a girlfriend?" asked the guy.

"Since when do you have a baseball bat?" I asked, recovering my composure.

Seth cut me a wry look before gently trying to remove the bat from the woman's hands. She didn't let go. "Georgina, this is my mom, Margaret Mortensen. And that's my brother Ian. Guys, this is Georgina."

"Hi," I said, feeling surprise of a different sort. I'd heard a lot about Seth's mother and younger brother but hadn't expected to meet them anytime soon. Seth's mother didn't like to fly, and Ian was . . . well, from the stories Seth and Terry told, Ian was just hard to track down in general. He was the wayward Mortensen brother.

Margaret relinquished the bat and put on a polite but wary smile. "It's very nice to meet you."

"Ditto," said Ian. I now understood why he looked familiar. Aside from the fact I'd probably seen a picture of him somewhere, he also shared some of Seth's and Terry's features. He was tall like Seth, but with Terry's thinner face. Ian's hair was all brown, with no coppery hint, but it had that same messy look that Seth's did. Except, on closer examination, I had the feeling Ian's had been purposely styled that way with the help of much time and product.

Seth suddenly did a double take between Ian and me. He didn't even have to say anything for me to guess the question on his mind. Or questions, perhaps. My nightgown and Ian's shirtlessness undoubtedly raised a number of them.

Ian's defense came swift and certain. "She got into bed with me."

"I thought he was you," I said.

Seth's mother made a strange noise in her throat.

"You were supposed to be on the couch," said Seth accusingly.

Ian shrugged. "It's uncomfortable. And you weren't home yet, so I figured there was no harm done. How was I supposed to know some woman was going to come manhandle me in my sleep?"

"I didn't manhandle you!" I cried.

Seth rubbed his eyes, again reminding me how exhausted he was. "Look, what's done is done. Why don't we all just go to bed—where we're supposed to—and then get to know each other in the morning, okay?"

Margaret eyed me. "She's going to sleep in here? With you?"

"Yes, Mom," he said patiently. "With me. Because I'm a grown man. And this is my home. And because in thirty-six years, this isn't the first woman to stay over with me."

His mother looked aghast, and I groped for a more comfortable topic. "Your shirt's great." Now that she wasn't threatening to strike me, I could see that the crossword spelled out her five granddaughters' names. "I love the girls."

"Thank you," she said. "Each one of them is a blessing, born within the holy confines of wedlock."

Before I could even fumble a response to that, Ian groaned. "Lord, Mom. Is that from that Web site I told you not to order from? You know their stuff's made in China. I know this woman who could have made you one out of sustainable organic fabric."

"Hemp is a drug, not a fabric," she told him.

"Good *night,* you guys," said Seth, pointing his brother to the door. "We'll talk in the morning."

Margaret and Ian murmured their good nights, and she paused to kiss Seth on the cheek—which I actually thought was pretty cute. When they were gone and the door was closed, Seth sat on his bed and buried his face in his hands.

"So," I said, coming to sit beside him. "Exactly how many women have stayed over in thirty-six years?"

He looked up. "None who were caught by my mother in so little clothing."

I plucked at the skirt of the nightgown. "This? This is tame."

"I'm sorry about that," he added, waving vaguely toward the door. "I should've called and warned you. They just drove into town tonight—unannounced, of course. Ian can't be expected to do what people expect. It would ruin his reputation. They showed up at Terry's, but there's no room for them there, so I sent them on ahead since they were so tired. I had no idea it would result in you trying to sleep with my brother."

"Seth!"

"Kidding, kidding." He picked up my hand and kissed the top of it. "How are you? How was your day?"

"Well, I tried my best to keep Santa from getting drunk and then found out Jerome signed us up for a Hellish bowling league."

"I see," said Seth. "So. The usual."

"Pretty much. What about you?"

The small smile that had been tugging at his lips fell. "Aside from unexpected family? The usual too. Terry was out late with work stuff, so I was there all night with the girls while Andrea rested. Kendall has to build a papier-mâché solar system, so that was fun for everyone." He held up his hands and wiggled fingers coated in white powder.

"And let me guess. No writing?"

He shrugged. "It's not important."

"You should've called me. I could've watched them while you wrote."

"You were working and then . . . what, it was fondue night, right?" He stood up and stripped off his shirt and jeans, getting down to green flannel boxers.

"How did you know that?" I asked. "I barely knew that."

"I was on Peter's e-mail list."

"Well, regardless, it doesn't matter. And that mall job is nothing. I could have been over here in a flash."

He stepped into his bathroom and returned a few moments later with a toothbrush in his mouth. "That job *is* nuffing. Haf any of your interfeews panned out?"

"No," I said, not adding that I hadn't gone on any other interviews. Everything paled compared to Emerald City.

The conversation was put on pause while he finished brushing his teeth. "You should be doing something better," he said, once he was done.

"I'm fine where I'm at. I don't mind it. But you . . . you

can't keep going on like this. You're not getting enough sleep or *working*."

"Don't worry about it," he said. He turned off the light and crawled into bed. In the dimness, I saw him pat the spot beside him. "Come over here. It's just me, I promise."

I smiled and curled up beside him. "Ian didn't smell right, you know. I mean, he smelled good, but not like you."

"I'm sure he spends gratuitous amounts of money to smell good," muttered Seth through a yawn.

"What's he do for a living?"

"Hard to say. He's always got new jobs. Or no job. What-ever money he's got goes toward carefully maintaining his hard-fought, effortless lifestyle. Have you seen his coat?"

"No. The only clothing of his I've seen is his boxers."

"Ah. Well, it must be in the living room. It looks like it came from a thrift store but probably cost four figures." He sighed. "Although, I shouldn't be too hard on him. I mean, yeah, he'll probably hit me up for money while he's here, but I can't knock him and Mom coming out to help. At the very least, they can help watch the kids now."

I wrapped my arms around Seth and breathed in his scent. It was the right one, and it was intoxicating. "And you can catch up on some writing."

"Maybe," he said. "We'll see how it goes. I just hope I'm not babysitting Mom and Ian more than the girls."

"How bad of an impression did I make on her?" I asked.

"Not that bad. I mean, no worse than any woman—scant-ily clad or otherwise—would've made who was spending the night with me." He kissed my forehead. "She's not so bad. Don't be fooled by her conservative Midwest grandma act. I think you guys will get along."

I wanted to ask if Maddie had met Margaret and, if so, how they'd gotten along. I bit my tongue on the question. It didn't matter. It was in the past, and Seth and I were the pre-sent. Sometimes, especially staying here as much as I did, I felt a little weird remembering that Maddie had lived with him too. There were still little touches here and there that bore the mark of her influence. For example, Margaret was most likely staying in Seth's office, which had a futon, courtesy of Maddie's ingenuity. She'd been the one to suggest he get it to help make the office double as a guestroom. Maddie had gone; the futon had stayed.

I tried not to think about those things very often, though. In the big picture, they didn't matter. Seth and I had come through too much for me to get hung up on something like that. We'd overcome the problems in our relationship. I'd accepted his mortality and his decision to risk his life by being physical with me. True, I still rationed our sex life, but the fact that I allowed it at all was a big concession for me. Meanwhile, he accepted the terrible truth that I was often out sleeping with other men in order to sustain my existence. They were difficult things for us both, but they were worth it for us to be together. Everything we'd gone through was worth it.

"I love you," I told him.

He placed a soft kiss on my lips and pulled me closer. "I love you too." Then, in an echo of my thoughts, he added, "You make it all worthwhile. All this stuff I'm dealing with. . . . I can do it because you're in my life, Thetis."

Thetis. That was his longtime nickname for me, coming from the shape-shifting goddess in Greek mythology who'd been won by a steadfast mortal. He called me that all the time—and Letha, only once. I thought again about that night. The troubled feelings it stirred never seemed to go away, but I once again tried to force them aside. It was another of those little things that I was trying not to let bug me. It was nothing compared to the greatness of our love, and like my friends had said, Seth had probably overheard the name.

I fell into a contented sleep, only to be awakened abruptly around dawn. My eyes flew open, and I sat upright. Seth shifted and rolled over but wasn't awakened by my sudden movement. I stared around the room, my heart racing. I'd been jolted out of sleep by an immortal presence, one I didn't know. It had felt demonic.

There was nothing here now, visible or invisible, but I knew for a fact some servant of Hell had just been in the room. This wasn't the first time I'd had unwelcome visitors in my sleep, often ones with nefarious intentions. Of course, I'd felt this demon just now, and demons—being higher immortals, not a lesser human-turned-immortal like me—could mask their immortal signature. If he or she had wanted to sneak around or hurt me unannounced, it could have done so. Whoever this was hadn't cared about discovery.

I slipped out of bed and continued studying the room, looking for some sign or reason for the demon's passage. I was certain there would be one. There. Out of the corner of my eye, I caught a flash of red—in my purse. There was a business envelope sitting on top of it. I hurried over and scooped up the envelope. It was warm to my touch, but as I quietly opened it, I began to feel cold. That feeling intensified as I pulled out a letter printed on official Hell stationery. No good could come of this.

Sunset had filtered more than enough light into the room to read by. The letter was addressed to Letha (alias: Georgina Kincaid), from Hell's HR:

This is the thirty-day notice for your transfer. Your new assignment will begin on January 15. Please make travel arrangements to leave Seattle and report to your new location in a timely manner.

Chapter 3

The crisp paper with its laser printing was a lot different from scrawling script on vellum, but I knew an official transfer letter when I saw one. I'd received dozens in the last millennia, in various forms, pointing me on to new assignments and locations. The last one had come to me while I was in London fifteen years ago. From there, I'd moved here to Seattle.

And now this one was telling me it was time to move on yet again.

To leave Seattle.

"No," I breathed, far too soft for Seth to hear. "No."

I knew this letter was legitimate. It wasn't a forgery. It wasn't a joke sent on Hell's stationery. What I was praying for was that this official transfer order had just been sent to me in error. The letter had no information about my next assignment because, per protocol, employees were usually briefed by their archdemons before a transfer. The letter then came afterward, to make the termination of the old job and start of the new one official.

I'd seen my archdemon less than twelve hours ago. Surely, *surely,* if this was real, Jerome could have brought himself to at least mention it. The transfer of a succubus would be a big deal for him. He'd have to juggle both the fallout of losing me and gaining someone else. But, no. Jerome hadn't behaved as though he had a major personnel change coming.

He'd said nothing to even hint about it. One would think this would have trumped his bowling league just a little.

I realized I was holding my breath and forced myself to start breathing again. A mistake. Whoever had sent this had clearly made a mistake. Lifting my eyes from the paper, I focused on Seth's sleeping form. He was sprawled in his usual way, with his limbs all over the bed. Light and shadow played across his face, and I felt tears spring to my eyes as I studied those beloved features.

Leaving Seattle. Leaving Seth.

No, no, no. I wouldn't cry. I wouldn't cry because there was nothing to cry about. This was a mistake. It had to be because there was no way the universe could be this cruel to me. I had already gone through too much. I was happy now. Seth and I had fought our battles to be together. We'd finally achieved our dream. That couldn't be taken away from me, not now.

Can't it? A nasty voice in my head pointed out the obvious. *You sold your soul. You're damned. Why should the universe owe you anything? You don't deserve happiness. You should have this taken away from you.*

Jerome. I had to talk to Jerome. He would sort this out.

I folded the letter four times and stuffed it into my purse. Grabbing my cell phone, I headed for the door and shape-shifted on a robe. I managed to slip out of the room without a sound, but my victory was short-lived. I'd hoped to be able to sneak outside, past Ian in the living room, and call Jerome in privacy. Unfortunately, I never made it that far. Both Ian and Margaret were up and awake, forcing me to stop mid-dial.

Margaret stood in the kitchen cooking something on the stove while he sat at the kitchen table. "Mom," he was saying, "it doesn't matter what the water-to-coffee ratio is. You can't make an Americano out of drip. Especially with that Starbucks crap Seth buys."

"Actually," I said, slipping the phone regretfully into my

robe's pocket, "I bought that coffee. It's not that bad. It's a Seattle institution, you know."

Ian didn't look as though he'd hit the shower yet, but at least he was dressed. He regarded me critically. "Starbucks? They might have been okay before they became mainstream, but now they're just another corporate monstrosity that all the sheep flock to." He swirled his coffee mug around. "Back in Chicago, I go to this really great hole-in-the-wall café that's run by this guy who used to be a bass player in an indie rock band you've probably never heard off. The espresso he serves is *so* authentic, it's mind-blowing. Of course, most people have no clue because it's not the kind of place mainstream people tend to frequent."

"So," I said, suspecting one could make a drinking game out of how many times Ian used "mainstream" in a conversation, "I guess that means there's plenty of Starbucks here for me."

Margaret nodded briefly toward Seth's coffeemaker. "Have a cup with us."

She turned around and continued cooking. The phone was burning in my pocket. I wanted to sprint toward the door and had to force myself to behave normally in front of Seth's family. I poured myself a cup of delicious corporate coffee and tried not to act like they were keeping me from a phone call that could change the rest of my life. *Soon,* I told myself. I'd have answers soon. Jerome probably wasn't even up. I could delay here briefly for the sake of politeness and then get my answers.

"You're up early," I said, taking my coffee over to a corner that gave me a good view of both Mortensens. And the door.

"Hardly," said Margaret. "It's nearly eight. Ten, where we come from."

"I suppose so," I murmured, sipping from my mug. Since signing up for Team North Pole, I hardly ever saw this side of noon anymore. Children didn't usually hit Santa up for Christmas requests so early, not even the ones at the mall I worked at.

"Are you a writer too?" asked Margaret, flipping over something with a flourish. "Is that why you pull such crazy hours?"

"Er, no. But I do usually work later in the day. I work, um, retail, so I'm on mall hours."

"The mall," scoffed Ian.

Margaret turned from the stove and glared at her son. "Don't act like you never go there. Half your wardrobe's from Fox Valley."

Ian actually turned pink. "That's not true!"

"Didn't you get your coat at Abernathy & Finch?" she prodded.

"It's Abercrombie & Fitch! And, no, of course I didn't."

Margaret's expression spoke legions. She took down two plates from the cupboard and stacked them high with pancakes. She delivered one to Ian and the other to me.

I started to hand it back. "Wait. Is this *your* breakfast? I can't eat this."

She fixed with me with a steely gaze and then looked me up and down. It gave me a good view of the quilted teddy bears on her sweatshirt. "Oh? Are you one of those girls who doesn't eat real food? Is your usual breakfast coffee and grapefruit?" She gave a calculated pause. "Or do you not trust my cooking?"

"What? No!" I hastily put my plate on the table and took a chair across from Ian. "This looks great."

"Usually I'm vegan," said Ian, pouring syrup on the pancakes. "But I make exceptions for Mom."

I really, really should have let it go but couldn't help saying, "I didn't think 'usually' and 'vegan' go together. You either are or you aren't. If you're making exceptions some of the time, then I don't think you get the title. I mean, sometimes I put cream in my coffee and sometimes I don't. I don't call myself vegan on black days."

He sighed in disgust. "I'm vegan *ironically*."

I returned to my pancakes. Margaret was back to cooking

again, presumably her own breakfast now, but still continued the conversation. "How long have you and Seth been seeing each other?"

"Well . . ." I used chewing as an excuse to formulate my thoughts. "That's kind of hard to answer. We've, um, dated off and on for the last year."

Ian frowned. "Wasn't Seth engaged for part of the last year?"

I was on the verge of saying, "He was engaged ironically," when Seth himself emerged from the bedroom. I was grateful for the distraction from explaining our relationship but not pleased to see Seth up.

"Hey!" I said. "Go back to bed. You need more sleep."

"Good morning to you too," he said. He brushed a kiss against his mother's cheek and the joined us at the table.

"I mean it," I said. "This is your chance to sleep in."

"I got all the sleep I need," he countered, stifling a yawn. "Besides, I promised to make cupcakes for the twins. Their class is having a holiday party today."

" 'Holiday,' " muttered Margaret. "Whatever happened to Christmas?"

"I can help you," I told Seth. "Well . . . that is, after I take care of a couple of things."

"I can make them." Margaret was already going through the cupboards, seeking ingredients. "I've been making cupcakes before any of you were born."

Seth and I exchanged glances at that.

"Actually," he said, "*I* can make them on my own. What would help the most, Mom, is if you could go to Kayla's school today. She's got a half day, and Andrea will need babysitting." He nodded at me. "You work tonight, right? Come help me with the twins. I know they can use more volunteers. Elf costume optional. And you . . ." He turned to Ian and trailed off, at a loss for how Ian could actually be helpful.

Ian straightened up importantly. "I'll go find an organic

bakery and pick up some stuff for the kids who want to eat baked goods that are made with free-range ingredients and don't contain animal products."

"What, like free-range flour?" I asked incredulously.

"Ian, they're seven," said Seth.

"What's your point?" asked Ian. "This is my way of helping out."

Seth sighed. "Fine. Go for it."

"Cool," said Ian. He paused eloquently. "Can I borrow some money?"

Margaret soon insisted that Seth have breakfast before attempting anything else, and I took advantage of his becoming the center of attention. I quickly put on casual clothes and made a polite exit, thanking her for breakfast and telling him that I would meet up with him at the twins' school for cupcake distribution. As soon as I'd cleared the condo, I began dialing the phone again.

Unsurprisingly, I got Jerome's voice mail. I left him a message and made no attempt to hide my urgency . . . or irritation. That kind of attitude wasn't going to endear me to him, but I was too pissed off to care. This transfer was a big deal. If there was any chance of its legitimacy, he really should have given me a greater heads-up.

Back at my place, my cats Aubrey and Godiva were happy to see me. Actually, I think they were just happy to see anyone who could feed them. They were lying in front of Roman's closed bedroom door when I walked in and immediately jumped up. They pranced over to me, snaking around my ankles and bombarding me with piteous meows until I refilled their food dishes. After that, I was old news.

I toyed with the idea of waking up Roman. I really, really wanted to talk out this transfer news with someone, and Seth hadn't been an option this morning. Roman, unfortunately, shared his father's "fondness" for mornings, and I wasn't entirely sure I'd have the most productive conversation if I woke him against his will. So, instead, I took my time showering and getting ready for the day, hoping that Roman would get up on his own. No such luck. When ten rolled around, I left another voice mail message for Jerome and finally gave up on Roman. A new idea had hit me, and I went to go check it out first, setting the mental condition that if Roman wasn't up when I returned, I'd wake him then.

The Cellar was a favorite bar for immortals, especially Jerome and Carter. It was an old dive of a place down in historic Pioneer Square. The bar didn't generally do a lot of business this time of day, but angels and demons were hardly the types to care about propriety. Jerome might not be answering his phone, but there was a very good chance he was out and about for a morning drink.

And, as I came down the steps that led into the establishment, I did indeed feel the wash of a greater immortal signature over me. Only, it wasn't Jerome's. It wasn't even demonic. Carter was sitting alone at the bar, nursing a glass of whiskey while the bartender punched in 1970s songs on the jukebox. Carter would've sensed me too, so there was no point in trying to sneak off. I sat on a stool beside him.

"Daughter of Lilith," he said, waving the bartender back. "Didn't expect to see you out and about so early."

"I've had kind of a weird morning," I told him. "Coffee, please." The bartender nodded and poured me a mug from a pot that had probably been sitting there since yesterday. I grimaced, recalling the espresso shops I'd passed on the way here. Of course, Ian would probably love this stuff for its "authenticity."

"Do you have any idea where Jerome's at?" I asked, once Carter and I were in relative privacy again.

"Probably in bed." Carter's gray gaze was focused on the glass as he spoke, carefully studying the play of light off of the amber liquid.

"I don't suppose you'd take me there?" I asked. Carter had teleported me once before in a crisis, but otherwise, I had no clue where my boss hung his boots.

Carter gave me a small smile. "I may be immortal, but there are still some things I fear. Showing up at Jerome's this early in the morning with you in tow is one of them. What's so important? Did you come up with a name for the bowling team?"

I held out the memo I'd received. Even before he looked at it closely, Carter's smile fell. I didn't doubt that the paper had some type of Hellish residue that my senses couldn't pick up. When he didn't take the note, I simply set it down in front of him to read.

"A transfer, huh?" His tone was odd, almost like he wasn't surprised.

"Allegedly. But I have to assume there's some kind of mistake. Jerome is supposed to meet with me first, you know? And you saw him last night. There was no indication that anything weird was going. Well. Weirder than usual." I tapped the paper angrily. "Someone in HR messed up and sent this on accident."

"You think so?" asked Carter sadly.

"Well, I certainly don't think Hell's infallible. And I don't see any reason why I would be transferred." Carter didn't answer, and I studied him carefully. "Why? Do *you* know of some reason?"

Carter still didn't reply right away and instead downed his drink. "I know Hell well enough to know they don't need a reason."

A strange feeling settled over me. "But you do know of one, don't you? You aren't that shocked by this."

"Hell doesn't really surprise me anymore either."

"Damn it, Carter!" I exclaimed. "You're not answering my questions. You're doing that stupid half-truth thing angels do."

"We can't lie, Georgina. But we can't always tell you everything either. There are rules in the universe that even we can't break. Can I have another?" he called to the bartender. "A double this time."

The bartender strolled over, arching an eyebrow at Carter's request. "Kind of early for that, don't you think?"

"It's turning into one of those days," said Carter.

The bartender nodded sagely and liberally refilled the glass before leaving us alone again.

"Carter," I hissed. "What do you know? Is this transfer real? Do you know why I got it?"

Carter pretended to be intrigued by the light sparkling on his whiskey again. But when he suddenly turned the full force of his gaze on me, I gasped. It was this thing he did sometimes, like he was peering into my soul. Only, there was more to it this time. It was as though for a brief moment, his eyes held all the sadness in the world.

"I don't know if it was a mistake," he said. "Maybe it is. Your people certainly get their wires crossed often enough. If it's legitimate . . . if it is, then no, I'm not surprised. I can think of a million reasons, some better than others, for why they would want to move you out of Seattle. None of which I can tell you," he added sharply, seeing me start to interrogate him. "Like I said, there are rules to this game, and I have to obey them."

"It's not a game!" I exclaimed. "It's my life."

A rueful smile played over the angel's lips. "Same difference, as far as Hell's concerned."

Within me, I began to feel an echo of that terrible sadness I'd briefly seen in his eyes. "What do I do?" I asked quietly.

That seemed to catch Carter off guard. I demanded answers from him all the time, clues to figuring out the many puzzles that seemed to follow me around. I was pretty sure, however, that this was the first time I'd simply asked for such open-ended life advice.

"Let me guess," I said, seeing him gape. "You can't tell me."

His expression softened. "Not in specifics, no. First, you need to find out if this was an error. If it was, then that'll make everyone's life easier."

"I need Jerome for that," I said. "Maybe Hugh or Mei would know."

"Maybe," said Carter, though it didn't sound like he believed it. "Eventually, Jerome will pick up his phone. Then you'll know."

"And if it is real?" I asked. "Then what?"

"Then, you may have to start packing."

"That's it? That's all I can do?" Even as I said the words, I knew they were true. You couldn't refuse something like this. I'd had dozens of transfers to prove it.

"Yes," said Carter. "We both know you don't have a choice there. The question is, how are you going to let this affect your future?"

I frowned, starting to get lost in angel logic. "What do you mean?"

He hesitated, as though reconsidering what he was about to say. At last, he rushed forward with it, leaning close to me. "Here's what I can tell you. If this is real, then there's a reason for it, absolutely. Not some random re-org. And if there's a reason, it's because you've been doing something Hell doesn't want you to do. So, the question becomes, Georgina, are you going to keep doing whatever it is they don't want you to do?"

Chapter 4

"But I don't know what it is I'm doing!" I cried. "Do you?"

"I've told you all I can for now," said Carter, that sadness returning. "The most I can do now is buy you a drink."

I shook my head. "I don't think there's enough whiskey in the world."

"There isn't," he said bleakly. "There isn't."

Despite Carter's pessimism, I still tried calling Hugh to see if he knew anything. He didn't, but his incredulity was so similar to mine that I took some comfort in it.

"What? That's ridiculous," he told me. "It was a mistake. It has to be."

"Will you try to get ahold of Jerome for me?" I asked. "I mean, I'll keep trying too, but maybe if we're both calling, he'll eventually notice the phone." Even though it was still early for the demon, I also had this strange feeling that he could very well be avoiding my calls if something was afoot. Hugh might sneak in where I couldn't.

I was fast approaching the time when I was supposed to meet Seth at the twins' school. I had wanted to run home and try talking to Roman about my potential transfer, but it didn't seem as important now, not until I had the story confirmed or denied by Jerome. So, after a few more errands that seemed hopelessly mundane compared to the greater supernatural workings of the universe, I drove up to Lake Forest Park and arrived at the school just as Seth did.

Ian got out of the car too, and Seth flashed me a quick look that said he wasn't thrilled about having brotherly company. Ian was wearing the jacket Seth had mentioned, a brown wool peacoat that fit him well enough to be tailored and had strategically placed patches meant to give it a vintage appearance. Ian completed the look with a carefully knotted striped scarf and fedora. He also had on glasses, which I'd seen no sign of at Seth's.

"I didn't know you wore glasses," I told him.

He sighed. "They go with the scarf."

Seth was carrying two huge containers of white-frosted cupcakes that were liberally and sloppily dusted with green and red sparkles. I took one batch from him and walked inside with the brothers, where we signed in and were given directions to the classroom.

"Looks like you were productive," I said with a smile.

"No thanks to Mom," Seth replied fondly. "It took her forever to leave. She kept offering to help and double-check my work, make sure the oven was set and all that. It was a boxed mix. There wasn't *that* much I could mess up."

Ian muttered something about preservatives and high fructose corn syrup.

The classroom was pleasant, organized chaos. Other parents and family friends were there to help with the party, distributing food and running games. The twins ran up to the three of us with quick, fierce hugs before scurrying off to play with their friends. I didn't see Morgan and McKenna outside of the family very often, so it was neat to watch them so active and outgoing with their peers. They charmed their friends as much as they charmed me, and it was clear the two girls were leaders of sorts. Tiny, adorable blond leaders. The knot I'd carried inside me since getting the HR memo began to soften as I allowed myself the small joy of observing them.

Seth slipped an arm around me, following my gaze as we maintained our post near the food table. He nodded toward where Ian was trying to pitch his own cupcakes—organic, vegan, gluten-free creations from a local bakery—to some of the twins' classmates. To be fair, the cupcakes were beautiful. They were vanilla, topped with elaborately swirled chocolate icing that was in turn adorned with perfect white frosting flowers. They made Seth's cupcakes look like something the girls might have made, but I knew better than to be fooled. When you made cupcakes without most of the ingredients found in traditional baked goods, the truth came out in the taste. Pretty or not, Ian wasn't doing so good a job moving them.

"These are so much better for you than all this other junk food," Ian was telling a wide-eyed boy named Kayden. Despite the fact we'd been inside the warm classroom for almost an hour, Ian was still completely clad in his scarf and wool coat ensemble. "They're made with brown rice flour and garbanzo bean flour and sweetened with maple syrup—none of that processed white sugar crap."

Kayden's eyes grew impossibly bigger. "Those have beans and rice in them?"

Ian faltered. "Well, yes . . . but, no, I mean. It's flour derived from those ingredients in a way that's totally fair trade and nutritious. Plus, I picked a brown and white color scheme, not only to save you from artificial dyes but also to show respect for all holidays and tradition, rather than giving into the mainstream domination of the Judeo-Christian machine."

Without another word, Kayden grabbed a red-frosted snowman cookie from the snack table and wandered off.

Ian gave us a long-suffering look. "I fear for today's youth. At least we can take the leftovers back to Terry's."

"We'd better," said Seth. "Those cost me a small fortune."

"You mean they cost *me* a small fortune," said Ian. "They're my contribution."

"I paid for them!"

"It was just a loan," said Ian imperiously. "I'll pay you back."

The party didn't last too much longer—seven-year-olds didn't need to slam drinks for hours like my friends did—but

I still kept checking my phone whenever Seth wasn't watching. I had it set to vibrate in my pocket but was afraid I would miss Jerome's call. But no matter how many times I looked, the phone's display remained the same. No incoming calls or texts.

With things winding down, McKenna made her way back to me and wrapped herself around my leg. "Georgina, are you going to come to our house tonight? Grammy's cooking. We're going to have lasagna."

"And cupcakes," piped in Ian, carefully packing up his goods. By my estimation, he'd given away exactly one cupcake, and that was to a boy who'd taken it on a dare from his friends.

I lifted McKenna up, surprised at how big she was getting. The years didn't alter my immortal friends or me, but mortals changed by leaps and bounds in such short time periods. She wrapped her arms around me, and I pressed a kiss into her blond curls.

"I wish I could, baby. But I have to work tonight."

"Are you still helping Santa?" she asked.

"Yes," I said solemnly. "And it's very important work. I can't miss it." Without me, there was no telling how sober Santa would stay.

McKenna sighed and leaned her head against my shoulder. "Maybe you'll come over when you're done."

"You'll be in bed," I said. "I'll see what I can do for tomorrow."

This earned me a tighter hug, and I felt my heart ache. The girls always had this effect on me, triggering a mix of emotion that was both love for them and regret for the children I myself would never have.

Children had been something I'd wanted as a mortal, something denied to me even then. The pain of that reality had been driven home last year when Nyx, a primordial chaos entity, had visited me in my sleep and used tantalizing dreams to distract me while she stole my energy. The one that had recurred the most had shown me with a little girl—my own daughter—stepping outside into a snowy night to greet her father. He'd been shadowy at first, later revealed as Seth. Nyx, in a desperate bid for help later, had sworn the dream was true, a prophecy of things to come. It had been a lie, however. An impossibility that could never be mine.

"Maybe you'll come by my house after you're done with work," Seth said to me in a low voice, once she'd wriggled away.

"That depends," I said. "Who's going to be in your bed?"

"We had a talk. He knows to stay out of my room."

I smiled and caught hold of Seth's hand. "I would, but I've got some things to do tonight. I've got to hunt down Jerome about . . . business."

"You're sure that's it?" he asked. "You're sure my family's not scaring you off?"

I'll admit, I didn't relish the thought of seeing Margaret Mortensen's disapproving gaze, but I also couldn't imagine I'd be very good company for Seth if I still didn't know what was going on with my transfer by tonight. The transfer. Looking into his kind, warm eyes, I felt a pit open in my stomach. Maybe I should be jumping at every chance I could get to be with him. Who knew how many more we had? *No, I scolded myself. Don't think like that. Tonight you'll find Jerome and clear up this mess. Then you and Seth can be happy.*

"Your family has nothing to do with it," I assured Seth. "Besides, now that you have extra help, you can use your free time to get some work done."

He rolled his eyes. "I thought self-employment meant not having a boss."

I grinned and kissed him on the cheek. "I'll come by to-morrow night."

Kayden, passing by for one last cookie, caught sight of my kiss and scowled disapprovingly. "Ew."

I parted ways with the Mortensens and headed off to the mall. It was often a surprise to mortals to learn immortals like me purposely chose to take day jobs, so to speak. If you were around for a few centuries and semiwise with your money, it wasn't that hard to eventually build up enough to comfortably live off of, making human employment unnecessary. Yet, most immortals I knew still worked. Correction—most lesser immortals I knew did. Greater ones, like Jerome and Carter, rarely did, but maybe they already had too concrete of a job with their employers. Or, maybe, lesser immortals just carried over the urge from when we were human.

Regardless, days like today were clear reminders of why I chose gainful employment. If I'd had nothing but free time on my hands, I would've spent the rest of the day ruminating about my fate and the potential transfer. Assisting Walter-as-Santa—as absurd as it was—at least gave me a distraction while I waited to hear from Jerome. Vocation gave purpose too, which I'd found was necessary to mark the long days of immortality. I'd met lesser immortals who had gone insane, and most of them had done nothing but drift aimlessly throughout their long lives.

A new elf—one whom Walter had christened Happy—had joined our ranks today, one who was certainly helping pass the time if only because of how much she was grating on my nerves.

"I don't think he should be drinking *at all*," she said, for what felt like the hundredth time. "I don't see why I have to learn this schedule."

Prancer, a veteran elf, exchanged glances with me. "None of us is saying it's right," he told Happy. "We're just saying it's reality. He's going to get a hold of liquor one way or another. If we deny him, he'll sneak it in the bathroom. He's done it before."

"If we're the ones giving it to him," I continued, "then we control the access and amount he gets. This?" I gestured to the schedule we'd drawn up. "This isn't much. Especially for a guy his size. It's not even enough to get buzzed."

"But they're children!" Happy cried. Her eyes drifted off toward the long line of families trailing through the mall. "Sweet, innocent, joyful children."

Another silent message passed between Prancer and me. "Tell you what," I finally said. "Why don't you make them your priority. Forget about the liquor schedule. We'll handle that. You go trade places with Bashful at the head of the line. She doesn't really like working with the public anyway." When Happy was out of earshot, I remarked, "One of these days, someone's going to report us all to the mall's HR office."

"Oh, they have plenty of times," said Prancer, smoothing out his green spandex pants. "I've worked with Walter for three years now, and Happy's not the first elf to have moral qualms about Santa getting lit. He's been reported lots."

That was news to me. "And they haven't fired him?"

"Nah. It's harder to fill these jobs than you might think. As long as Walter doesn't touch or say something inappropriate, the mall doesn't seem to care."

"Huh," I said. "Good to know."

"Georgina!"

Beyond the gates leading to Santa's pavilion, I saw someone waving at the edge of the crowd. Hugh. My heart rate sped up. This mall was actually right around the corner from his office, so he'd come by before for lunch. In light of recent events—and the look on his face—something told me he wasn't here for a casual meal today.

"Hey," I said to Prancer. "Can I take my break now?"

"Sure, go for it."

I cut through the crowd and met up with Hugh, trying not to feel self-conscious about wearing the foil dress. Hugh had come from the office and was dressed impeccably, playing up the role of successful plastic surgeon. I felt cheap beside him, especially as he and I walked farther from the holiday mayhem toward some of the mall's more upscale shops.

"I was on my way home from work and thought I'd stop by," he said. "I figured you weren't taking many calls while on the job."

"Not so much," I agreed, gesturing to the tight dress and

its lack of pockets. I caught hold of his arm. "Please tell me you heard something. The transfer's a mistake, right?"

"Well, *I* still think it is, but no, I haven't heard anything back yet—not from HR or Jerome." He frowned slightly, clearly not liking the lack of communication. Underneath that, I also sensed another emotion in him—nervousness. "I've got something else for you. Can we talk somewhere . . . kind of private? Is there a Sbarro or Orange Julius around here?"

I scoffed. "Not in this mall. There's a sandwich place we can go to."

"Sandwich place" wasn't entirely accurate. They also sold gourmet soups and salads, all of which were made fresh and packed with enough prissy ingredients to make Ian happy. Hugh and I snagged a table, my appearance gaining the attention of some children there with their parents. I ignored them as I leaned toward Hugh.

"What's up, then, if not the phantom transfer?"

He eyed the watchers uneasily and took several moments to begin speaking. "I was calling around today, trying to work connections and see if I could find out anything about you. Like I said, I couldn't. But I got caught up on all sorts of other gossip."

I was kind of surprised Hellish gossip was what he wanted to discuss, more surprised still that it had apparently warranted him coming in person. If he'd heard a rumor about a mutual friend, it seemed like a phone call would've sufficed to pass the news. Even e-mail or text.

"Do you remember Milton?" he asked.

"Milton?" I stared blankly. The name meant nothing to me.

"Nosferatu," he prompted.

Still nothing, and then—

"Oh. Yeah. Him. The vampire." A month or so ago, Milton had visited on vacation, much to Cody and Peter's dismay. Vampires were territorial and didn't like outsiders, although Cody had been able to use Milton's presence to impress his macabre loving girlfriend, Gabrielle. Or so I'd heard. "I never actually saw him. I just knew he was in town."

"Yup, and it turns out last week, he was in Boulder."

"So?"

"So, first of all, it's weird that he'd have two 'vacations' in that short time. I mean, you know how it is for vampires. You know how it is for all of us."

It was true. Hell didn't like to give us vacations very often. When your employers owned your soul, they really didn't feel any need to make your life pleasant. That wasn't to say we didn't occasionally get time off, but it certainly wasn't a priority for Hell. The business of souls never rested. For vampires, this was doubly true because they didn't like to leave their territory. They also had various complications with traveling, say, like with sunlight.

"Okay, so, it's weird. How does that affect us?"

Hugh dropped his voice low. "When he was in Boulder, a local dark shaman died under mysterious circumstances."

I felt my eyebrows rise. "And you think Milton was involved?"

"Well, like I said, I had time to make some calls and do some research today. And it turns out that even though he's based in Raleigh, Milton travels an awful lot for a vampire— and every place he goes, some mortal in the supernatural community ends up dead."

"You're saying he's an assassin," I said, intrigued but still not seeing the point. As part of "the great game" we all played, angels and demons weren't supposed to directly influence mortal lives. That's where lesser immortals came in, with our offers of sin and temptation. Now, we weren't really supposed to kill either, as far as the game went, and we certainly weren't supposed to do it on behalf of a greater immortal's instructions. We all knew it happened, however, and Milton wasn't the first assassin I'd heard of taking out inconvenient mortals.

"Exactly," said Hugh. He frowned. "He goes to places, and people disappear."

"How does that affect us?"

Hugh sighed. "Georgina, he was *here*."

"Yeah, but nobody—" I gasped, freezing a moment in shock. "Erik . . ."

The world reeled around me for a moment. I was no longer in an elite mall's food court but instead was looking down on the broken, bleeding body of one of the kindest men I knew. Erik had been a longtime friend in Seattle, using his many years of occult and supernatural knowledge to advise me on my problems. He'd been investigating my contract with Hell when a freak robbery at his store had resulted in his death by gunshot.

"Are you saying . . ." My voice was barely a whisper. "Are you saying Milton killed Erik?"

Hugh shook his head sadly. "I'm not. I'm just laying out the evidence for you, which is compelling—but not enough to form a hard link to Milton."

"Then why tell me at all?" I asked. "You don't like to get involved with anything that questions the status quo." It was true, and it had been a constant point of contention with Hugh and me.

"I don't," he said. I understood now why he was so uneasy. "Not at all. But I care about you, sweetheart. And I know you cared about Erik and wanted answers."

"Key word: *wanted*. I thought I had them." My heart still mourned Erik, but I had begun to heal from his loss, moving on with life the way we all must after losing a loved one. Knowing—or, well, thinking—he'd been killed in a robbery didn't exactly give me peace, but it did provide an explanation. If there was any shred of truth to Hugh's dangerous theory, that Milton—a potential assassin—might have been responsible, then my whole world was suddenly knocked off-kilter. And in that scenario, the big issue wasn't that Milton had done it. What became important was *why* he had done it. Because if he was one of those Hellish assassins lurking in the shadows, then someone higher up had given him his orders, meaning Hell had a reason to want Erik dead.

"You okay?" Hugh's hand on mine made me jump. "Jesus, Georgina. You're like ice."

"I'm kind of in shock," I said. "This is big, Hugh. Huge."

"I know," he said, not sounding happy at all. "Promise me you won't do anything foolish. I'm still not sure I should have told you."

"You should have," I said, squeezing his hand and making no such promises about the foolish part. "Thank you."

I had to leave shortly thereafter, returning to assist Happy. A little of her zeal about the pure, magical nature of children had faded in that time. I think it was the six-year-old who asked for a nose job that might have cracked her. As for me, I was in a daze, stunned over what Hugh had told me. Erik murdered. His dying words to me had implied something more was going on, but there'd been no evidence to prove it. Or wait . . . was there? I vaguely remembered the glass pattern of his broken window, the suspicion from the police that it had been broken from within. But what did I do with this theory? How did I get the answers I needed?

Equally amazing to me was the concession Hugh had made in telling me this. He valued his job and his comfortable position. He really wasn't the type to try to upset Hell or ask questions about things that didn't concern him. Yet he'd pursued his hunch about Milton and passed on the news to me, his friend. Hell made desperate, soulless creatures out of its employees—and most certainly liked it that way—but I doubted any of the higher-ups had imagined the levels of friendship we were still capable of managing.

Naturally, only one other thing could have distracted me from this new development, and that was Jerome's presence in my condo later that night. I was returning home after work and sensed his aura coming from within as soon as I put my key to the door. My fears and theorizing about Erik and Milton moved to one part of my brain, replaced by all the old speculation about the mystery transfer.

When I entered, I found Jerome sitting in the living room with Roman, both at their ease and barely acknowledging my presence.

"And so," Jerome was saying, "that's why you need to do this. As soon as possible. Nanette's people have been at it for a long time, so you've got a lot of ground to cover. Set up a schedule—I don't care how rigorous it is—and make those slackers start putting in their time at the alley."

I stared incredulously. "You're here about the bowling competition?"

Both men looked at me, Jerome seeming irritated at the interruption. "Of course. The sooner you start practicing, the better."

"You know what else might be better the sooner it happens?" I produced the well-worn HR memo with a flourish. "You telling me if I'm being transferred or not. My money's on it being a mistake because surely, *surely* you wouldn't put off telling me. Right?"

Several heartbeats of silence hung in the room. Jerome held me in his dark, dark gaze, and I refused to look away. At last, he said, "No. It's real. You're being transferred."

My jaw wanted to drop to the ground. "Then why . . . why am I only just now hearing about it?"

He sighed and made an impatient gesture. "Because *I* just found out about it. Someone jumped the gun and delivered the memo to you before telling me." His eyes glinted. "Don't worry, I wasn't too thrilled about that myself. I made sure they know my feelings on the matter."

"But I . . ." I swallowed. "I was so sure there was a mistake. . . ."

"There was," he agreed. "Just not the kind you were thinking of."

I wanted to sink to the floor and melt away but forced myself to stay strong. I had to ask the next most important question, the question that would shape the next phase of my life.

"Where . . . where am I going?"

Jerome studied me once again, this time I think just to drag out the suspense and agony. Bastard. At last, he spoke.

"You're going to Las Vegas, Georgie."

Chapter 5

I'd been bracing myself for "Cleveland" or "Guam." I was too much of a pessimist to think I might be offered something even moderately appealing. If I was already going through the trauma of leaving Seattle, then surely it would be for somewhere terrible.

"Did you say Las Vegas?" I asked, sinking down onto my couch. Immediately, I guessed the catch. "Ah. It's not Las Vegas, Nevada, right? It's a different Las Vegas. New Mexico? Or some other continent?"

"Sorry to disappoint you and your martyr fantasies, Georgie." Jerome lit a cigarette and inhaled deeply. "It's Las Vegas, Nevada. I think you even know the archdemon there—Luis. Isn't he a friend of yours?"

I blinked. "Luis? Yeah. I mean, in as much as an archdemon can be." That got a small smile from Jerome, though I only barely noticed. I had worked for Luis a long time ago, and if I had to be honest, he was probably my favorite boss of all time. That wasn't to say Jerome was a terrible one, but Luis—while strict—still had an easy way about him that could sometimes make you forget you were damned for all eternity. "So . . . my orders are to go to Las Vegas and work for Luis."

"Yes," said Jerome.

I looked back at him from where I'd been staring vacantly out the window. "Is there any way to change that? To stop it?

Isn't there anything I can do to just stay here? And are you *sure* it's not a mistake—what with the delivery mix-up?"

Jerome's dark eyebrows rose. It was one of those rare moments when he'd been caught off-guard enough to display surprise. "You don't want to go? I mean, I'm flattered you'd want to stay under my rule, but I'd think you would be pleased with this situation. Las Vegas is perfect for a half-ass succubus like you."

I ignored the jab—though he had a point. Las Vegas was such a breeding ground for sin and salvation that it was nearly packed to bursting with servants of both Heaven and Hell. It probably had one of the highest concentrations of succubi in the world, meaning it was easy to slide by with quotas. Here, I was the only succubus, so my number of corrupted souls was scrutinized heavily. In Las Vegas, there'd be plenty of go-getter succubi to cover for slackers like me.

"It's not about you," I said slowly. "It's about . . . Seth."

Jerome sighed loudly and stamped out his cigarette on my coffee table. I supposed I should be glad it wasn't my couch or carpet. "Of course it is. Because in the grand scheme of the universe, your boyfriend is important enough to make Hell's HR change their minds about a re-org. Come on, Georgie. How naive are you? How many transfers have you had over the years? Or perhaps I should ask, how many transfers do you know of that were cancelled because someone 'didn't feel like it'?"

"None," I admitted. At most, Hell would take unhappy employees into account and move them out of places they weren't being productive. I had requested transfers before and gotten a couple of them. But once HR made up its mind? That was it. The cold truth of this, that it wasn't a mistake and that I couldn't stop it, was beginning to wrap around me. I tried to make sense of it another way. "But why? Why did they decide to this? I've been a good employee. . . ." Yet, even as I spoke, I grew uncertain. Jerome looked at me knowingly.

"Have you?"

"I haven't been a bad employee," I amended. "Not exactly."

"This isn't a game. We don't want mediocre employees who can keep the status quo. We want souls. We want to *win*. And you've spent most of your time here being mediocre. Don't glare at me like that. You know I'm right. You've had fits and starts of productivity, the most notable being when you were under duress. Even that's been inconsistent." I'd made a bargain with Jerome a year ago, in which I'd behaved like a model succubus for a while. After I'd helped rescue him from summoning, there'd been an unspoken acceptance of me slacking off once again without getting any grief from him. "If you'd thrived here and turned over large amounts of souls, I doubt you'd be leaving. So, if you're looking for someone to blame, look in the mirror."

"You sure sound smug about this," I pointed out petulantly. "Like you're happy about it."

"Happy? Happy about the gamble of getting a new employee—or of inheriting Tawny permanently? Hardly. But unlike you, I accept that my happiness means nothing to my superiors. The only thing that matters is me following their orders." His tone and expression clearly said that the same was true for me.

I almost never held back from sparring with Jerome, but today I did. Why? Because there was nothing I could say, no bargain I could make with him. I'd negotiated a number of favors and allowances in my years with him, things specifically pertaining to my existence here within Seattle. That was his domain. But the rest of the world? That was out of his control. There was nothing he could do to change this reassignment, even if he wanted to. There was nothing I could do either. You just couldn't fight against some things. Hell was one of them. When I'd signed my soul away, I'd signed away control of my eternity to them as well.

"It's not fair." Guessing Jerome's snappy retort, I quickly added, "I know, you don't have to say it. Life isn't fair. I get it. But it's just . . . it's just cruel. Seth and I finally managed a working relationship. And now I have to leave him."

Jerome shook his head, and I could tell by his restless stance that he was ready to go. His patience with this conversation was running thin.

"You know, I might miss some of your witticisms when you're gone, but one thing I won't miss? Your overwhelming sense of melodrama and despair. It's too much even for me."

The sorrow and self-pity within me transformed to anger. "I'm sorry, but this is serious to me! How can I not be upset? I love Seth. I don't want to leave him."

"So don't. Take him with you. Or date long distance. I honestly don't give a fuck, so long as you stop your whining. How can you not see solutions here? You've apparently decided that you being immortal isn't a deterrent to your great love . . . but a two-hour plane ride is?"

I felt kind of cowed. Normally, I resented Jerome for mocking me when I was upset because I blamed it on his lack of empathy. But now, I had to admit that maybe he was onto something about me being overly melodramatic. Why couldn't I take Seth with me? If Seth really loved me, a move shouldn't be a problem. And of all the jobs in the world, he had one of the best suited for a change of venue. Unfortunately, it was a bit more complicated than that. I sighed.

"I don't know if he would. His family's here, and his sister-in-law's sick. He can't leave them anytime soon. . . ."

Jerome shrugged. "We're back to the part where I don't give a fuck. I do, however, care that you go there to visit sooner rather than later. Luis asked if I'd send you down in advance to scope out the area for a couple of days. Seeing as bowling practice doesn't start until Monday, I can't help but think this weekend would be an excellent time to get that out of the way. I'm happy to oblige him—but not at the cost of interfering with my team."

"Really?" I scoffed. "You expect me to care about bowling in light of all this?"

He gave me a thin-lipped smile. "Seeing as you're still my employee for the next four weeks, yes. I expect you to care about it immensely." He glanced over at Roman, who had observed all of this silently. "And I expect you to come up with an excellent training regimen for them. I'll see you both then."

Jerome vanished in a poof of smoke, further verifying how self-satisfied he felt about all of this. Losing me might be inconvenient for him, but I think his demon nature still took some delight in seeing the torment of others.

I covered my eyes and rolled over to lie flat on the couch. "Oh God. What am I going to do? This can't be happening."

Breaking up with Seth last year had torn my heart apart. I had wanted to die. Being reunited with him had felt like being born anew. I'd loved life, even my damned one. Now I was starting to feel that terrible, aching desperation again. It wasn't possible that someone could go through so many extreme ups and downs in so short a time span. *Welcome to being in love*, I thought.

I felt Roman sit down by my feet. A moment later, both cats joined us. I uncovered my eyes and found his sea green ones staring down at me. "He wasn't exactly tactful, but I have to admit he had a point. Why wouldn't Seth just move with you?"

"Under normal circumstances . . ." I had to pause in order to not start laughing. Our circumstances were *never* normal. "Under normal circumstances, he would. But like I was saying, with Andrea, I don't even think he can. And honestly, I wouldn't want him to." I didn't realize that was true until I spoke the words. If Seth dropped everything to run off with me, he would be hurting both himself and his family for my sake. I could never allow that. My heart sank. "I can't believe this. How could this have come about so quickly? I was so happy."

Roman scratched Aubrey's head and leaned back. "That's an excellent question. This was all kind of sudden. Is that how it normally is?"

"Well, I mean, we never get much warning of transfers. Sometimes you know a re-org is coming. Sometimes you get one after requesting a transfer. Usually, though, someone has a meeting, plans your fate, and you find out about it later. The only weird thing here was Jerome apparently having less notice than me."

Roman had been staring at the ceiling and then snapped his head back to look at me. I flinched under the intensity of his gaze. "Explain that again. What happened and what was unusual."

I started to tell him I'd just explained it but instead swallowed off any sharp retort, knowing he wasn't the true source of my irritation. "Normally, your archdemon meets with you to tell you the details, and then the letter with the transfer date follows. This happened so fast that I got the letter before Jerome had a chance to talk to me."

"Hell doesn't do things without a reason." He reconsidered. "Well, impromptu bowling competitions aside. But they like their bureaucracy, their paperwork, and all their details in order. Even if they quickly decided to do a transfer, they'd still follow all their inane procedures. For the letter to have jumped ahead of Jerome getting his instructions, things must have been seriously expedited. The question: why? Why such a rush to get you out of Seattle?"

I couldn't help a smile. "You're looking for a conspiracy here. I mean, don't get me wrong, I think this sucks. It's terrible. But I don't think there's anything more to it than what Jerome said about me skimping at my job. Which . . . well, which is my fault."

"Yes, but Hell deals with bad employees all the time. They go through reams of procedure to figure out the best way to deal with those people. Pop might be right that Hell can't tolerate mediocre workers, but it's not to the extent that they have to deal with it *right that second*. What's so special about you that someone would suddenly decide to initiate a hasty transfer?"

I appreciated that Roman was trying to help me, but I didn't want to get caught up in what could easily become an obsessive quest for him. Nephilim had serious grudges with Heaven and Hell and were always looking for ways to challenge and thwart them. Roman himself had once gone on a killing spree of higher immortals. There was something in his nature that wanted there to be more than bad luck here, but I just wasn't sure I believed there was.

Carter's words echoed in my head, no matter how much I tried to shrug them off: *If there's a reason, it's because you've been doing something Hell doesn't want you to do.*

"You should talk to Carter," I muttered. "He's certain there's a reason too." Seeing Roman's expectant look, I half-heartedly tried to humor him. "I don't know what it could be. Maybe because I got captured by Oneroi? Maybe they're worried I'm unstable or something. Or that this isn't a safe place for me."

Roman nodded along with my words. "That does make you special. However, if I was worried about an employee losing it, I'd want to keep them in a place where I knew they felt stable. I'm sure Hell knows you're happy here, and if anything, they might think that experience bound you to Jerome more closely. They'd want to encourage that loyalty."

"Hell doesn't need to encourage loyalty," I told him. "All they care about is that I signed my soul over to them. That's bigger than loyalty."

A startled look crossed his face. "That *is* all they care about. Georgina, when did this happen? Exactly when did this happen?"

"Er, the letter?"

There was a fanatic look in his eyes. No question. He was getting obsessed. "Yes."

"This morning. It showed up at Seth's. I sensed the courier and woke up to it."

"You were at Seth's. What were you doing at the time? What were you doing just before then?" He'd stopped petting Aubrey, and she slithered toward me in a huff, seeking a more attentive audience. "Walk me backward from that point."

"Well, like I said, I was sleeping. Before that . . ." I winced, remembering getting into bed with Ian. "I met Seth's mom and younger brother. Before that, I was at Peter's fondue party. Before that, I was at the mall—"

"Peter's. Tell me about Peter's. Did anything weird happen to you there?"

I cut him a look. "It was a fondue party at a vampire's. Everything about that is weird."

"I'm trying to help you!" There was a strained, agitated quality to his voice as he leaned toward me. "Just hold off on the jokes, okay? *Think*. What happened—to you specifically? What did you talk about? What did they say to you?"

I was growing increasingly uncomfortable at his intensity. "They were teasing me about my job," I said.

"Jerome too?"

"Of course. He said me being an elf was an embarrassment and that I should do something else." A shocking thought hit me. "Roman . . . you don't think Jerome requested the transfer, did you? Could he really be that upset with me? That embarrassed?"

"I don't know," admitted Roman. He absentmindedly ran a hand through his curling dark hair. "It's possible. Some of the weirdness might be explained away if Jerome was trying to hide that he initiated all this. But then, it's not like any of your other friends are exactly normal. If something was going to embarrass Jerome enough to get rid of an employee, I kind of feel like there would have been a lot of other opportunities before you. Anything else come up?"

"I asked them about—" I hesitated. The topic was still sensitive for me. It was hard to mention to Roman, and I could hardly believe I'd had the guts to bring it up to the gang that night. Roman caught my uncertainty and pounced. "What? What else? What did you ask them about?"

I waited a few more moments and then decided to tell him.

It couldn't hurt, and besides, for all I knew, Roman had mentioned my name to Seth.

"About a month ago, when we were in bed, Seth called me Letha when he was half-asleep. When I asked him how he knew that name, he couldn't remember. He couldn't even remember calling me that. So, I asked the group that night if any of them had told my name to Seth."

"And?"

"And they all said no. Cody didn't even know my name. I got berated for being melodramatic again, and the general consensus was that Seth had just overheard it from me or someone else and forgotten."

Roman was silent, which was almost more unnerving than him grilling me. I straightened up and nudged him.

"Hey, you didn't tell Seth, did you?"

"Huh? No." He frowned, caught up in his own thoughts. "What did Jerome think? Did he concur with that theory?"

"Yes. He thought me bringing it up was a total waste of time and didn't hesitate to tell me. He was so bored by it that he started talking about bowling instead."

"That's when he told you about the bowling team? The bowling team that came out of nowhere?"

"Yeah...." Now I was frowning. It was clear that Roman's thoughts were running off to a place I wasn't at or able to follow. "Why? What are you thinking? Is this related somehow?"

"I don't know," he said at last. He stood up and paced the living room a couple of times. "I need to think about this. I need to ask some questions. What are you going to do now?"

I rose as well and stretched, suddenly feeling weary. "I need to talk to Seth. I have to tell him what happened. And I suppose . . ." I made a face. "If I do have to go to Las Vegas, this weekend is the time to do it."

"So you don't miss bowling practice?" teased Roman.

"That, and I have it off from work. Seth's pretty tied up with his family in town, which makes it another good time to go. Although . . . it'd kind of be nice if he went with me. I mean, if he was going to think about moving, he could check it out too." Yet, again, that worry returned to me: how could I ask Seth to abandon Terry and Andrea?

"Actually," said Roman, humor vanishing, "I think it's best he doesn't go."

"Why not?"

"Because whatever the reasons, something's just not right about this. I don't know what's waiting for you in Las Vegas. Maybe nothing. But I just feel like there's a larger hand in all of this, guiding it, and that it's safest for Seth if you don't drag him into immortal drama." Roman's face softened. "I'm actually not thrilled about you facing it alone, but I'm not sure me walking into a hotbed of immortal activity is so smart either."

"I'll be fine," I said, trying to not be put off by his ominous words. "No matter how terrible a transfer is, I have to admit, I got kind of lucky with this one. I mean, I'm not saying I trust any demons, but if I had to, it would be Luis. He's really great, and Vegas is, well, Vegas. Like I said. I got lucky."

Roman grew thoughtful again. "Yes. Yes, you did."

The next day, I found Seth later at his brother's house. Andrea had had another treatment that day and was sleeping it off. Seth and Margaret were helping take care of the household as best they could, cooking a late dinner and watching the girls. I arrived at about the same time as Terry got home from work, and our double entrance was greeted with shouts and hugs. I scooped Kayla up in my arms and kissed her while Terry asked what I had been wondering.

"Where's Ian?"

Seth and Margaret exchanged looks. "Ian had some things to do," she said neutrally.

"Yeah," agreed Seth. "In the form of scoping out ironic parts of Seattle."

So much for Ian stepping up to help the family. No doubt he'd found new hipster friends at a coffee shop and was now hanging out with them somewhere, drinking PBR and regaling them with stories of all the obscure bands he knew.

Terry smiled good-naturedly. "Well, that's his loss because dinner smells great. More for us." He swung Kendall around and kissed his other daughters before going upstairs to check on Andrea. I felt a lump form in my throat as I watched him go. He put on such a good face for the kids, but I knew this had to be tearing his heart apart. My own petty concerns seemed exactly that: petty. Small. Inconsequential.

Nonetheless, news of the transfer weighed on my mind throughout dinner. I'd wanted to wait until Seth and I were alone at his place, but my face must have betrayed my feelings.

"Hey," he said gently, slipping an arm around me. The family was gathered in the living room, starting a movie, while Seth and I stood in the doorway to the kitchen. "Everything okay?" I hesitated, unsure about bringing it up here. Sensing that, he pulled me into the privacy of the kitchen. "Thetis, talk to me."

"I got some bad news today," I began. I tried to think of a clever or funny way to lead into it, but nothing came. So, I just blurted it all out, explaining the inarguable nature of transfers and the details of mine.

"Las Vegas," he said flatly. He looked as though he'd been slapped. "You're moving to Las Vegas."

"Not for a month," I said, clasping his hands. "And believe me, I don't want to. God, Seth. I still can't believe it. I'm sorry. I'm so, so sorry."

"Hey, don't apologize. Not for this." He drew me near, the kindness and compassion on his face nearly making me cry. "This isn't your fault. You have nothing to be sorry about."

I shook my head. "I know, but . . . it's just so crazy. I thought this was it. Our chance to be together. And now I don't know what to do. I can't ask you to . . ."

"Ask me to what?"

I leaned my head against his chest. "Come with me."

He was quiet for a few moments. "Would they let me? I always thought . . . I mean, whenever you've talked about your past, it always sounded like you reinvented yourself. New name, new appearance. I thought you had to leave your past life behind."

"I have, but that was always just my choice. For you . . . I mean, of course I wouldn't do that. I'd stay Georgina Kincaid, just as you know her. But you can't leave them." I gestured to the living room. "It's not worth it."

Seth moved his hands to my head, tilting my face up so I could look him in the eye. "Georgina," he said softly. "I love you. You're worth it. You're everything to me. I'd follow you to the ends of the earth. And beyond."

"That doesn't make sense." I smiled sadly. "And I'm not *everything*. You love them too. And you'd hate yourself for running off with me while they need you so much."

"So, what? You've made my choice for me?" he asked. There was a playful note to his voice, despite the deadly seriousness of the topic. "Are we breaking up?"

"No! Of course not. I just . . . I just want you to know that I don't expect you to come with me. Do I want to be with you? Yes, of course. But I love your family, Seth. I love all of them. My happiness . . ." It was strange, speaking those words. *My happiness.* For so long, I'd been miserable. Happiness wasn't even a concept I'd imagined for myself in ages. "My happiness isn't worth theirs."

He leaned down and brushed his lips against mine. "What about mine?"

I stared in astonishment. "Are you saying you'd abandon them and run off to Las Vegas?"

"No," he said firmly. "I would never abandon them. But there must be some middle ground here. Some way that doesn't involve sacrificing us or them. We just have to figure it out. What we have is too important. Don't give up on us yet, okay?"

I hugged him, losing myself in the sweetness of his warmth and scent. My heart had lightened a little at his words, but I still didn't want to get my hopes up. There was too much at stake, still too much that could go wrong.

"I love you," I told him.

"I love you too." He squeezed me tight and then kissed me again before pulling apart. "Now. Let's go watch that movie and pretend to be social so that we can leave early."

"Why?"

"Because if you're going to Vegas this weekend, then I want to get you home and get some quality time in tonight."

I grinned and put my arm around him. "Does 'quality time' mean what I think it does?"

"Yes," he said, as we walked back to the living room. "Yes, it does."

"Well, then, you know that's against the rules."

"Rules that you made up," he pointed out.

"Rules that are for your own good," I corrected. "It's not time yet. Remember, we have to ration ourselves."

It was part of the conditions of us getting back together. Keeping strictly platonic before had strained us, so this time, I'd agreed that some sex was okay . . . even though I cringed at the thought of how each act, no matter how small, would take away some of his life. Seth had told me he didn't care, that he'd take any risk to be with me. I was still cautious, and he'd yielded to me to set the schedule for our rationed sex life. I still wasn't entirely sure what constituted proper rationing in this situation, but something in my head said we should have sex only every few months. I hadn't told Seth that, though. It had been one month since the last—and only—time we'd had sex since getting back together as a mortal and a succubus, and I knew he was getting restless. It was especially difficult for him because although he respected me, he also didn't think such caution was needed when he was the one who faced the dangers—dangers he swore he didn't mind.

"Not tonight," I continued.

"It's practically a special occasion, though," he told me. "A big send-off."

"Hey, I didn't say we couldn't do anything," I replied. "Just not as much as you'd like to do." One thing we'd inherited from our chaste days was a set of several creative workarounds, mostly involving doing unto ourselves what we couldn't do unto each other. "The question is, is there going to be a problem with your houseguests?"

"Not if we're quiet," Seth said. After a moment, he shrugged. "Scratch that. I don't care. Let them hear."

I scoffed. "Oh, yeah. So that your mom can come break down your door with her baseball bat."

"Don't worry," he said, kissing my cheek. "She's no match for you and that dictionary."

Chapter 6

Fortunately, no dictionaries or bats ever came into play, and Seth and I spent a pleasant night together. He sent me off that weekend in a good mood, and during the time I was with him, it was easy to believe this might all end well. Once I began the tedious parts of travel by myself, the doubts began to set in.

The ride to the airport, security, safety instructions . . . all little things in and of themselves, but each one began to weigh on me. I just couldn't see Seth moving to Las Vegas—not anytime soon, at least. That left long-distance dating, and it was hard to imagine us going through a trip like this every . . . hell, I didn't know how often. And that was another problem. What exactly did long-distance dating mean? Visits every week? Every month? Too-frequent visits meant the irritation of travel. Too few put us in danger of out-of-sight, out-of-mind complications.

So, naturally, I was all worked up by the time my flight landed in Las Vegas. And strangely, I took comfort remembering Jerome's words, of all things. If Seth and I had survived the huge problem of immortal–mortal dating, then really, what was a two-hour plane ride compared to that?

We could make this work. We had to.

"There she is!"

A familiar, booming voice startled me as I was waiting at the baggage claim. I spun around and found myself looking up at the tanned good looks of Luis, Archdemon of Las

Vegas. I let him wrap me up in a giant hug, something he managed with remarkable delicacy, considering what a bear of a man he was.

"What are you doing here?" I asked, once those muscled arms had released me. Realization hit me. "You're not here to pick me up, are you? I mean, don't you have people who have people to do that kind of thing?"

Luis grinned at me, his dark eyes sparkling. "Sure, but I couldn't trust an underling to pick up my favorite succubus."

"Oh, stop," I groaned. My bag came around the carousel, but when I went for it, Luis brushed me aside and easily lifted it up. As I followed him toward the parking garage, I couldn't even begin to picture Jerome doing something like this.

"You scoff, but most of the succubi around here bore me to tears. Hell, most of our staff here does," Luis said. "You get a full range of personalities and talent levels with so many. The exceptional and the unexceptional. You, my dear, are exceptional."

"You don't have to try to sweet-talk me into the job," I said, smiling in spite of myself. "Not like I have a choice."

"True," he agreed. "But I want you to be happy here. I want everyone who works for me carrying stories about how awesome I am. It ups my cred at the annual company conference."

"Jerome's trying to up his by having us beat Nanette's employees in bowling."

Luis laughed at that and led us out to a gleaming black Jaguar double-parked in the handicapped zone. Once he'd stowed my suitcase, he even went so far as to open the door for me. Before starting the car, he leaned over conspiratorially and whispered loudly, "If you want to shape-shift into something else, now's your chance while we're still inside."

"Shape-shift into what?"

He shrugged. "You're in Vegas. Live the lifestyle. No need to resign yourself to jeans and sensible shoes. Give yourself a cocktail dress. Sequins. A corset. I mean, look at me."

Luis gestured grandly at himself, just in case it was possible to miss the gorgeous and undoubtedly custom Italian suit he was wearing.

"It's barely noon," I pointed out.

"Doesn't matter. I dress like this the instant I get out of bed."

With a self-conscious look around the garage outside, I quickly shape-shifted out of my travel clothes and into a one-shoulder minidress that wrapped around me like a Grecian gown. The fabric glittered silvery when it caught the light just right. My long, light brown hair turned equally glam. Luis nodded in approval.

"Now you're ready for the Bellagio."

"The Bellagio?" I asked, impressed. "I figured I'd be shoved off to some crappy motel ten miles from the Strip." I amped up my makeup for good measure.

"Well," he said, backing the car out, "that *is* actually what the normal budget allows for when it comes to new employee visits. I was able to pull some extra funds—and dip into my own pockets—to upgrade you a bit."

"You didn't have to do that," I exclaimed. "I could have paid for my own room somewhere." Yet, even as I said it, I knew that if accruing funds over the centuries was easy for someone like me, it was a million times easier for someone with Luis's lifespan. The car and his suit were probably bought with pocket change from his income. He waved off my concerns.

"It's nothing. Besides, my car would probably get stolen if I parked it at one of the 'budget-friendly' places."

The car's readout told me the outside temperature wasn't that far off from Seattle's in December. The difference was in the light.

"Oh my God," I said, squinting out the window. "I haven't seen the sun in two months."

Luis chuckled. "Ah, just you wait until high summer, when the temps hit triple digits. It cooks most people alive, but for someone like you, you'll love it. Hot and dry. Doesn't get below eighty at night."

I loved Seattle. Even without Seth in the picture, I could have been happy there for many, many years. But, I had to admit, my one weakness with the region was the weather. Relative to the extremes of the East Coast, Seattle was a very mild climate to live in. That meant it didn't get very anything. Not very cold, and certainly not very warm. The hot weather we got in midsummer was fleeting, and then the mildness of the winter was marred with rain and clouds. By February, I was usually ready to start consuming entire bottles of vitamin D. I'd grown up on the beaches of the Mediterranean and still missed them.

"This is great," I said. "I wish I were visiting while it was warmer."

"Oh, you don't have long to wait," he told me. "Another month like this, and then the temperature will start going up. You can break out your bikini by March." I thought that might be kind of an exaggeration but returned his grin nonetheless.

We were approaching the Strip and all its glory. The buildings became more flamboyant and expensive looking. Sidewalks and streets grew more crowded. Billboards advertised every form of entertainment imaginable. It was like an adult-oriented theme park.

"You seem pretty happy here," I said.

"Yup," Luis agreed. "I lucked out. Not only is the place great, but I command one of the largest groups of Hellish servants in the world. When I saw your name come up, I thought, 'I've got to get her in on this.' "

Something in his words put a crack in the rose-colored glasses I was viewing the wondrous sights around me through. "When my name came up?"

"Sure. We get e-mails all the time about transfers, job openings, whatever. When I saw you were being moved out of Seattle, I tossed my hat into the ring."

I turned toward the side window so he couldn't see my face. "How long ago was that?"

"Oh, I don't know. A while ago." He chuckled. "You know how long these things take."

"Yeah," I said, trying to keep my voice light. "I do."

It was exactly what Roman and I had talked about: the painstakingly long time Hell took with personnel decisions. Roman swore the circumstances surrounding this transfer were suspicious and implied a rush. Yet Luis was behaving as though everything had gone along according to perfect procedure. Was it possible there really had just been some oversight with Jerome's notification about my transfer?

It was also possible, I knew, that Luis was lying. I didn't want to believe that of him, but I knew that no matter how friendly and likable he seemed, he was still a demon at the end of the day. I couldn't allow myself to be lulled into complete trust by his charm. We had a favorite saying among my friends: *How can you tell if a demon is lying? His lips are moving.*

"I was surprised to be transferred at all," I said. "I've been happy in Seattle. Jerome said . . . well, he said it was because I was a slacker employee. That I was being moved for bad behavior."

Luis snorted and pulled into the driveway for the Bellagio. "He did, huh? Well, don't beat yourself up, honey. If you want a reason for them pulling you out, my guess is that it has something to do with Jerome getting himself summoned and letting nephilim and dream creatures run rampant with his succubus."

I had nothing to say to that, but fortunately, we reached the hotel's entrance and yielded the car to a valet driver who seemed familiar with Luis and his generous tips. Entering the Bellagio, I was soon awash in stimuli—color and sound and life. A lot of the people moving in and out were dressed as glamorously as us, but plenty of average "everyday" people walked through as well. It was a mixing of all social classes and cultures, all here and united in search of enjoyment.

Equally overwhelming was the intense wave of human emotion. I didn't have any magic power to let me "see" emotion, exactly, but I was very good at reading faces and expressions. It was that same knack that had let me pick out the desperate and hopeless at the mall. This was the same, except magnified a hundred times. People swung the full gamut of hope and excitement. Some were joyous and eager, either high off of triumph or ready to risk it all for triumph to come. Others had clearly attempted it—and failed. Their faces were full of despair, disbelief at how they'd ended up in this situation and sorrow over their inability to fix things.

Just as obvious were the good marks. Some guys were so blatantly trolling for a hookup that I could have propositioned them then and there. Others were ideal succubus bait, guys who had come here saying they were going to keep themselves in line—but who could easily step off the edge of temptation with the right finessing. Even with my heart tied up with Seth, I couldn't help but take in and thrive under all the admiring looks I got. I was suddenly glad I'd taken Luis up on his shape-shifting suggestion.

"So easy," I murmured, staring around as we waited for an elevator. "They're just there like . . ."

"Cattle?" suggested Luis.

I made a face. "Not quite the word I wanted."

"Not much difference."

An elevator opened, and a cute twenty-something guy gestured me forward. I smiled winningly at him, loving the effect I had. After he exited on his floor, Luis winked at me and leaned over to whisper in my ear.

"Easy to get used to, huh?"

Our floor came next, and Luis nodded to our right when the door opened. A few steps down the hall, I realized something. "I have a suite?" I asked, startled. "That's a little much, even to make a good impression."

"Ah, well, that's what I didn't get a chance to tell you yet. You have a suite because it has more room. You have to share it with another new employee."

I nearly came screeching to a halt. Here it was, the catch in what was otherwise a sugar-coated fantasy. I envisioned myself rooming with another succubus and immediately knew I'd be seeking other accommodations. Succubi forced into close proximity put reality show drama to shame.

"I don't want to impose on anyone's privacy," I said delicately, wondering how I could get out of this.

Luis reached a door and took out a keycard. "Nah, the place is huge. Two bedrooms and a living room and kitchen that go on forever." He unlocked the door and opened it. "You could avoid each other all weekend if you wanted to. But somehow, I don't think you will."

I was about to question that, but suddenly, there was no need. We'd stepped into a living room as expansive as Luis had promised, all sleek lines and modern furniture, colored in shades of gold and green with dark wood trim. A long window offered a sweeping view of the city, and a man stood in front of it, admiring the panorama.

I couldn't see his face, and something told me that even if I could, I probably wouldn't recognize it. That didn't matter. I knew him by his immortal signature, the unique sensory markers that distinguished him from everyone else. I could scarcely believe it, even as he turned around and smiled at me.

"Bastien?" I exclaimed.

Chapter 7

No matter what shape he wore, Bastien always managed the same kind of smile—warm and infectious. I was grinning as I hugged him, too overwhelmed to form any other logical greeting or even ask why he was here.

The last time I'd seen Bastien had been in Seattle last fall. He'd come to town to help discredit a conservative radio host and had succeeded (thanks to me), earning him accolades from our superiors. I'd lost touch with him shortly thereafter and had thought he'd been transferred to Europe or the East Coast. Maybe he had been, but he was here now. The full impact of Luis's earlier words came back to me as I stepped away from Bastien.

"Wait. *You're* the other new employee?"

Bastien's grin widened. He loved being able to shock and surprise me. "Afraid so, Fleur. I moved here a week ago, and our employer was kind enough to put me up here while I look for a place of my own." He swept Luis a gallant bow.

Luis nodded back, clearly enjoying the scenario he'd created. "Which, hopefully, you'll do soon. Accounting isn't going to let me get away with this place forever."

Bastien nodded gravely. "I've already scouted a couple of potential locations."

"And," I teased, "Bastien doesn't even really need to find his own place. He could go out tonight, smile at the right people, and have a dozen rich women more than happy to give him a place to stay." His current body looked to be in its late twenties, with sun-streaked brown hair and hazel eyes. It was pretty cute, but even if he'd looked hideous, he could still have talked himself into someone's heart. He was just that good.

"Is that an invitation?" Bastien asked. "Because I have no plans for tonight."

"Well, you do now," said Luis. "I figured you and Georgina would want to catch up, and you can give her your impressions of the city so far—which are all good, of course."

"Of course," Bastien and I said in unison.

"Also, I'd like her to meet Phoebe and maybe some of the other succubi," Luis continued.

"Ah, Mademoiselle Phoebe." Bastien nodded his head approvingly. "An exquisite creature. You'll adore her."

"You apparently do," I said. Succubi and incubi hooked up sometimes but generally stuck to humans for romantic liaisons. Bastien, however, had a particular penchant for my kind.

He made a face. "None of my charms seem to be working on her. She says that I'll never be as infatuated with anyone else as much as I am with myself, so there's no point in her getting involved."

I laughed. "I like her already."

"Then it's settled." Luis moved toward the door. "I have some business to take care of, but I'll see you before you leave. In the meantime, I trust Bastien will show you a good time. Don't hesitate to call me if you need anything."

Luis snapped his fingers, and a small business card appeared in his hand. He handed it to me. It was still warm.

"Thanks, Luis," I said, giving him a quick hug. "I appreciate everything you've done."

Luis nodded gravely. "I know you're not thrilled about this transfer, but I really, really would like for you to be happy here."

He left, and Bastien and I stood there in silence for a few moments. "You know," I said at last, "in the years I've been in Seattle, I don't think Jerome has ever told me to call him if I needed anything."

Bastien chuckled as he walked over to a small but well-stocked bar. "Luis is quite exceptional from what I've seen so far. I was lucky to end up here. You too."

"Yeah. We're all lucky, aren't we?" I crossed my arms and leaned against the wall by the war. "How *did* you end up here?"

"The same way any of us end up anywhere. I was living in Newark until I got the transfer order a couple days ago. Here I am."

I frowned. "I thought you said you'd been here a week?"

"Week, a few days. I don't know. I admit, I've been kind of intoxicated since I arrived. It was recent, that's all. And a surprise."

"So was mine," I murmured. "Astonishingly so. And now you're here too. It's kind of weird."

"Is it?" He emptied a martini shaker into two glasses. "We've worked together before. Figures that it would happen again."

I accepted the glass he offered me. "I suppose so. But still . . . the number of times we've ended up together has been pretty amazing. For it to happen again is a huge coincidence." I took a sip and nodded approvingly. He'd used Grey Goose.

"Maybe it's not a coincidence. They keep track of our performance records. They probably know we work well together."

I hadn't considered that. "You think they'd actually place us together because of that? To get results? I mean, I'm still trying to figure out why I was even transferred at all."

"There doesn't have to be a reason, not with them."

"I know. One theory about me being here is that I haven't been all that great of a succubus."

"Ah, then there you are. They sent you to me because they know what a good influence I am on you."

"Bad, you mean."

His eyes twinkled. "This is going to be a *lot* of fun having you here. I haven't even gambled yet, and already I feel like I hit the jackpot." He knocked back his drink. "Finish that, and let's go have some fun. I know a great place for lunch. We'll go there and then hit some games of chance."

It felt weird going out on the town, especially so early in the day. I'd become too subdued in my Seattle life, I realized. I'd done such a good job at playing human that I'd forgotten what it was like to think like a succubus. Why not live it up in daylight? This was technically a business trip, but the point was to scope out the place of my future employment. I'd been here lots of times before, but this was the first time I really and truly studied the city through the eyes of an "on the clock" succubus. Again, I was struck by that earlier, heady sense: easy, so amazingly easy.

We caught a cab, and Bastien gave instructions for us to go to Sparkles. I ran through my mental list of Las Vegas attractions and came up empty.

"I've never heard of that," I said. "It sounds like a strip club."

"Nah, it's a brand-new hotel and casino," Bastien told me. "So shiny and new, in fact, that it just opened a couple of weeks ago, and already it's a hit."

"Why's it called Sparkles?" I asked.

He grinned. "You'll see."

The answer was obvious once we got there. Everything was, well, sparkly. The exterior sign was a riot of glittering, chasing lights that should've had a seizure warning affixed to it. Everyone who worked in the hotel and casino wore elaborately sequined outfits, and all the décor was done in brightly colored metallic and glittering surfaces. Paired with the flood of flashing lights already found in a casino, the entire spectacle was hard on my eyes at first. Yet, despite what could've easily degenerated into tackiness, there was still something in the feel of the place that radiated luxury. Sparkles was over the top, yes, but in a good way.

"Here," said Bastien, leading me through the maze of the casino. "There's a little less sensory overload where we're going."

Opposite the side we'd entered in was a doorway dominated by a sign reading DIAMOND LOUNGE. With a name like that, I expected strippers and more glitz but instead found myself in a quiet and much more tastefully subdued establishment. Crystal chandeliers and wineglasses provide the only sparkle here. Everything else in the restaurant was warm, honey-colored wood and red velvet. When we were seated at our table, Bastien said to the waitress, "Can you tell Phoebe that Bastien is here?"

I gave him a wry look once we were alone. "I see how it is. Here I thought you were going out of your way to take me somewhere nice. You're just here to visit your crush."

"That's merely a perk," he told me easily. "The food here really is excellent. And Luis wants you to meet Phoebe too, remember? Don't worry, you'll like her."

I made no effort to hide my skepticism. "I don't know, Bastien. I can count on one hand how many succubi I've actually liked over the years. At best, they're tolerable and semiamusing, like Tawny." At worst—and more often than not—succubi were raving bitches. Me excluded, of course.

"Just wait and see," he said.

We didn't have to wait long because a couple minutes later, I felt the wash of a succubus aura come over me, one reminiscent of orange blossoms and honey. A tall, willowy woman in a black and white uniform appeared, carrying a tray with our cocktails on it. The employees here didn't have to match the glitzy attire of their hotel brethren. She set the cocktails before each of us with a grace and fluidity that was almost too much for this establishment. It reminded me of something more suited to the serving halls of kings from long ago—which, I suspected, she had probably known very well.

"Ah, Phoebe," Bastien sighed dreamily. "You are a vision, as always. Come meet our newest colleague."

She gave him the look one has when indulging a ridiculous child and sat down in one of our table's empty chairs. Her dark blond hair was pulled back into a neat ponytail, revealing high cheekbones and long-lashed green eyes. "Oh, Bastien, don't start in on the vision stuff. It's far too early in the day." She extended a polite hand to me. "Hello, I'm Phoebe."

"Georgina," I said, shaking the offered hand.

"Whatever Bastien's told you, only believe half of it." She reconsidered, eyeing him carefully. "Make that a third."

"Hey," exclaimed Bastien, with mock incredulity. "I resent that. As if I would ever lie to two such treasures as yourselves!"

"Bastien," said Phoebe dryly. "You'll lie to anything female if you think it'll get you in their pants faster."

I laughed in spite of myself, earning me another wounded look from Bastien. "Fleur, you know that's not true. You've known me longer than anyone."

"Which is exactly why I know it is true," I replied solemnly.

Bastien muttered something uncomplimentary in French and was saved further indignation when Phoebe's colleague returned to take our order. Phoebe, with our permission, ordered for us, requesting some "specials" that weren't on the menu.

"Are you a cook here?" I asked her.

"Bartender," she replied, clasping her hands and resting her chin on them. "Gives me something to do until the show starts."

"Show?"

Bastien's earlier dismay was gone, replaced with an expression of supreme smugness. "You see, Fleur? I told you I had a good reason for coming here. My lady Phoebe here is a . . ."

He paused delicately. "Is it still polite to say 'showgirl'? I can never keep track of what's PC anymore. It took me ages to figure out why I kept getting in trouble for calling career women 'working girls.' "

Phoebe laughed. "Yes, 'showgirl' is fine."

I felt myself sitting up straighter. "You're a dancer? Where do you perform?"

"Here," she said. "Or, well, I will in a couple months. It hasn't opened yet."

"What kind is it?" I asked. "I mean, is there a theme?"

"It's a full-fledged Vegas music-dance extravaganza. Exactly what you'd expect from a place called Sparkles. Rhinestones everywhere. Scanty, but not topless." She tilted her head, regarding me with interest. "Are you a dancer?"

"I dance," I said modestly. "I haven't done full stage performances in a very long time, though. I'm out of practice."

Bastien scoffed. "That's nonsense. Fleur can pick up any routine. She used to bring the dance halls of Paris to their knees."

"Yeah," I said. "A long time ago."

"Are you interested in being in it?" asked Phoebe, face serious. "They're still scouting. I can get you an audition. Although . . . you might want to make yourself taller."

"I . . . I don't know," I said, suddenly feeling overwhelmed. "I mean, my transfer doesn't take place until next month. . . ."

Phoebe was unconcerned. "I don't think Matthias would mind. He's the company manager. In fact . . ." She glanced at her watch. "He'll be around in another hour or so. I can take you to meet him."

"She'd be happy to," said Bastien.

"I'm sure she can answer for herself, monsieur," replied Phoebe tartly.

I chuckled at seeing Bastien dressed down again. "I'd love it. That'd be great."

Phoebe left us as our food began arriving, promising to return at the end of our meal. Everything she'd ordered for us was amazing, and I fretted over eating so much since I wasn't entirely sure if this meeting with the company manager would turn into a full-fledged audition.

"Lovely, isn't she?" asked Bastien.

"She is," I agreed. "You were right." What I found more astonishing than having the chance to dance in a Las Vegas show was that Phoebe was responsible for orchestrating it— and had seemed genuinely happy to do so. In my experience, succubi would jealously guard those kinds of positions, keeping out the competition.

"I have no doubt you'll dance your way right into this Matthias's heart," Bastien mused. He gave a mournful sigh. "Would that I could dance so easily into Phoebe's heart."

"She's too smart for you," I said. "She knows your tricks."

"Of course she does. I'd think that would be half the appeal." He paused to finish off the last of his cocktail. "Speaking of bizarre attractions . . . I'm totally behind in what's transpiring in your Northwestern world. Are you still joined at the hip with that introverted mortal?"

"Literally and figuratively," I told him. Thinking of Seth diminished some of my earlier good mood. "This transfer . . . it was kind of a shock. I don't know how it's going to affect our relationship."

Bastien shrugged. "Bring him here."

"It's a little more complicated than that."

"Not if he wants you badly enough. Here." Bastien waved to get the waitress's attention. "Have another round with me. That'll fix everything."

"Not when I might have to dance soon!"

But I shared the round anyway and found my cheerfulness returning. It was hard not to with Bastien. I'd known him for a long time, and there was something so easy and comforting about being in his presence. We swapped stories and gossip on immortals we knew, and I got the scoop on some of the more colorful ones I'd eventually be meeting here in Las Vegas.

Phoebe returned just as we were paying the bill, having swapped her work attire for casual dance clothing. She led us back through the labyrinthine glitz of the casino and into the quieter and much more subdued back halls of the building. They in turn led to a backstage door to the casino's theatre, which wasn't yet open to the public. We found the vast space empty, save a couple guys installing tables in the seating area. The pounding of their hammers echoed through the room. A moment later, I did a double take when I saw a man sitting off to the side of the stage, so still I'd hardly noticed him. He glanced up from a sheaf of papers at our approach.

"Phoebe," he said. "You're early."

"I wanted to introduce you to someone," she said. "Matthias, these are my friends Bastien and Georgina. Georgina's moving here next month."

Matthias looked like he was in his late twenties, early thirties at most, and had sandy blond hair in need of a haircut. There was something cute about its disheveled state, and he took off wire-rimmed glasses to peer up at me. I couldn't help but think Ian would've liked those glasses, but unlike Ian, Matthias probably needed them. Matthias blinked a couple of times, and then his eyebrows rose in surprise.

"You're a dancer," he said to me.

"Er, yeah, I am. How'd you know?" Per Phoebe's suggestion, I'd made myself put on some height while we were walking down the back halls, but that was hardly enough to tip him off.

Matthias got to his feet and studied me up and down, not in a leering kind of way . . . but more like how someone assesses the value of a piece of art. "It's in how you walk and stand. There's a grace to it. An energy. It's exactly what she does." He nodded toward Phoebe. "Are you guys sisters?"

"No," said Phoebe. "But we've taken some of the same classes."

Bastien choked on a laugh.

Matthias was nodding, completely enraptured. He picked up his papers and flipped through the pages. "Yes . . . yes . . .

we could definitely use you here and here." He paused, checking a few more places. "And here. Maybe even here." He jerked his head up, blue eyes alight and excited. "Let's see what you can do. Phoebe—do the opening part of the second number."

Phoebe responded instantly, springing to center stage and instantly falling into line as Matthias began counting off beats. When they finished, he looked at me expectantly. "Now you do it."

I started to point out that I was in heels and a dress but then realized showgirl attire probably wouldn't be too different. I took a spot near Phoebe and mirrored her as Matthias counted again. We repeated the combination, and by the third time, I hardly had to look at her to get the steps. He directed her to a different number, slightly more complicated, and a similar performance ensued as I sought to match her. When we finished, he clicked his tongue in approval.

"Amazing," he said. "You guys need to tell me where you trained so that I can recruit all your classmates." Turning back to his papers, he began scribbling notes. "Phoebe, can you lend her some clothes for practice? Not that it'll affect her performance, of course, but I imagine she'd be more comfortable in something else for two hours of rehearsal."

Phoebe winked at me. "I'm pretty sure we can get her a change of clothes."

I glanced between her and Matthias. "Rehearsal?"

"Sure," said Matthias, still not looking up. "That's what we do to get ready for performances around here."

"You want to be in the show, don't you, Lucy?" teased Bastien.

"I understand . . . but I'm not moving to Las Vegas until January," I explained. "I have to go home tomorrow night."

Matthias finally glanced up briefly from his beloved notes, seeming as pained as Seth often was when interrupted while writing a book. "You're here right now, aren't you? Might as well get started. Unless you've got something else going on?"

I looked helplessly at Bastien and Phoebe, who were grinning like idiots. The incubus slung a friendly arm around me. "Of course she doesn't."

After a moment's hesitation, I gave a slow nod, still a little overwhelmed at how fast things were moving here. "I . . . I'd love to rehearse."

Chapter 8

It was hard to believe that in only a couple of days I'd gone from doubting my transfer was real to suddenly signing on to be in a Las Vegas stage production. Things happened so fast that it was easy to get swept along, and Bastien and Phoebe's gleeful encouragement just made things happen that much more quickly.

Shape-shifting took care of my clothing problem, and Bastien soon left us, allegedly to go get a drink and try his hand at the blackjack table. Once he left the theatre, though, Phoebe leaned over to me conspiratorially and whispered, "Here's a wager for you. How much do you want to bet he comes back with a glow?"

I laughed and whispered back, "I won't take that bet. Are you sure you haven't worked with him before?" Admittedly, an incubus looking to get laid wasn't that far of a stretch, but I liked how adeptly Phoebe was able to pick up on my old friend's personality quirks.

"Nah," she said with a smile. "I've just known his type."

Other dancers began trickling in. Phoebe introduced us as they arrived, and most were friendly and excited to have someone new in the group. They weren't yet at their full number needed for the show, so everyone was anxious for that to happen. I brought them one step closer, though it surprised me they were still short. From my experiences, there were always groups of girls lined up to try to make it in show business. Phoebe confirmed as much.

"Oh, yeah, tons have tried out. And you should have seen them at the beginning, when they first did the open casting. Matthias is just really selective, that's all. Cornelia—the head choreographer—is just as bad."

"And yet he took me on a five-minute audition," I pointed out.

Phoebe grinned. "Sweetie, he just knows talent when he sees it. Besides, he's in charge of this gig. If he says you're in, you're in."

Matthias wasn't the only one running the show, of course. Along with the dancers came other management and staff, like the aforementioned Cornelia. Everyone had a part to play. The rehearsal was fast-paced and aggressive—but also lots of fun. Phoebe hadn't been joking. The other dancers were good—really good. It had been a very long time since I'd danced with any sort of group, even longer since I was with one of such caliber. I was used to being the standout at anything dance related, and it was a surprise—a good one— to find myself surrounded by so many equals. I had to work to keep up with them on the first day, and even if I didn't walk out as an instant star, I left confident that I'd held my own.

Before I could go, one of the show's costumers asked to take my measurements backstage. Phoebe told me she'd go hunt down Bastien and meet me at the casino's central bar. The seamstress appeared with her tape measure, and I made a mental note of my height for future shape-shifting. Matthias came by, carrying his notes, and paused when he saw us.

"You did really well today," he told me. "It's like you've been with us from the first day."

"Hardly," I said. "I've still got a lot to learn. Especially in the fourth song. The steps are deceptively simple . . . but there's a certain attitude you've got to hold to pull them off. No, maybe not attitude. Grace? Vibe? I can't explain it, but the simplicity's what makes it so genius. It seems like such a basic pattern, but how it's executed is what truly brings out the beauty." I was thinking aloud, just sort of rambling, and realized that I sounded kind of ridiculous. "Sorry. That probably doesn't make any sense."

"No, no." Matthias stared at me wonderingly. "That's exactly it. That's how I intended it. I was inspired by watching classical ballet, how all the moves are amplified by the emotion put into the routines. Cornelia said it was crazy to try to think that deep for a show like this, but it just felt right."

"It's beautiful," I said honestly. "I can absolutely see where you were going with it. Reminds me of something from *La Bayadère.*"

"You know *La Bayadère?*" he asked, wide-eyed.

"Of course," I said. "It's a classic. Who doesn't?"

"You'd be surprised."

I realized then that the seamstress had left, having achieved her goal. Matthias was still regarding me in amazement. Now that they weren't focused on the clipboard, I was able to see how blue his eyes were. They were like the sky on a clear, crisp day.

"Are you busy tonight?" he asked a few moments later. "Would you . . . would you like to go get dinner? Or even just a drink? I'd love to talk dance more with you."

For a succubus, I could be surprisingly naïve sometimes. Because for half an instant, I almost accepted. I was so keyed up after the rehearsal and so excited to talk more about the show that I actually briefly thought that was all he wanted to go out for. Now, I don't mean to imply that his motives were totally base either. He wasn't using this as a ruse to simply get me into bed. But he also wasn't treating this as a meeting of colleagues. Bottom line: he liked me. I'd peaked his interest, and he wanted to go out on a date.

Normally, that wouldn't have been a problem . . . except, there was something I sincerely liked about him. He was cute, and I found his passion for his work endearing. I loved how he kept getting wrapped up in it, totally consumed and distracted like—Seth.

And there was the problem. This guy was the choreographer version of Seth. A one-night fling with some sleazy guy who meant nothing wasn't cheating in the eyes of our relationship. But for me to go out with a guy I liked, that I found intriguing and attractive in the same way I found Seth . . . well. That was wrong, especially since Matthias was obviously interested in me. It was a strange situation to be in, one I hadn't expected.

"Oh, that would be great, but my friends and I already have plans," I told him. "We're trying to make the most of my trip since it's so short."

"Oh." His face fell a little, then brightened. "But you'll be back for tomorrow's rehearsal, right? It'd be great if you were able to get in the steps one more time before you left town. You know, give you something to practice."

"Sure," I said. "That'd be great."

The rest of the evening went by in a blur of activity. Phoebe joined Bastien and me in a whirlwind tour of Vegas highlights, which included a lot of casino and club hopping. Phoebe and I both donned skimpy, glamorous dresses, playing up our succubus sex appeal to its maximum. We draped ourselves on Bastien's arms, and he swaggered around even more than usual, smug with the envy he got over showing us off.

After hours of this, I was ready for some downtime. Phoebe and Bastien had a quick consultation and decided that if we hurried we could make the late performance of a magic show they knew.

"Magic?" I asked, more than a little tipsy from vodka gimlets. "Don't we *live* a magic show?"

"Damn near," said Bastien. He was ostensibly still being gallant in offering me his arm, but it was unclear who was really holding whom up. "There's something special about this show, I've heard." There was a mischievous glint in his eyes.

The three of us made our way to a modest, off-Strip hotel I'd never heard of. It still had alcohol and slot machines in its casino, which was probably all that mattered to most of its customers. Bastien bought us tickets to see The Great Jambini, and we hurried into the small theater—which was about half-full—just as the lights went down. A mediocre comedian did the warm-up act, and soon the star attraction himself came out. He had graying hair and a bright purple silk turban, along with a sequined cape that could have come straight from the wardrobe department at Sparkles. He kept tripping over its hem, which led to my first observation: he was totally drunk. A second observation soon followed, once I realized there were more immortal signatures in here than just mine, Phoebe's, and Bastien's. The Great Jambini was an imp.

He started off with some standard card tricks, receiving half-hearted applause from the audience. These were followed by juggling, which I found remarkable simply because of the concentration it required from someone so obviously intoxicated. He didn't miss a move. I think the other members of the audience shared my opinion because their applause warmed up. Inspired by this, Jambini then made a great show of setting his juggling pins on fire. This brought the applause to a standstill, and some of the people in the front rows shifted uneasily.

"Is that a good idea?" I murmured to my friends.

"It never is," remarked Phoebe.

"What do you mean nev—"

Within thirty seconds after lighting the pins, Jambini had begun juggling . . . and promptly set his cape on fire. People gasped and screamed as he flung it off him onto the stage. Considering its cheap material, I was kind of surprised the cape hadn't ignited faster. He stomped on it until the flames were out, and I saw a few stagehands on the periphery ready with fire extinguishers, just in case. Once the cape was a black, smoldering mess, he lifted it up. A dove emerged from underneath it, flying up into the air, much to the awe and delight of the spectators.

"It was part of the show," I breathed, equally impressed.

"Yup," said Phoebe.

Jambini reached for the dove, which just barely slipped past him. It circled around the room, then swooped low into the audience. Along the way, it sideswiped a woman whose hair was elaborately French braided. The dove's foot got tangled in her hair, and it soon became trapped, beating its wings frantically to escape as she leaped up and began screaming.

"Was *that* part of the show?" I asked.

"No," said Phoebe in awe. "But it really should be."

Within seconds, the stagehands were out in the audience, where they were able to remove and confine the dove. They escorted the woman off as well, heads bent low as they murmured apologies. The Great Jambini made a flourish-filled bow, much to the delight of the crowd. Everyone loves a wacky mishap.

He performed a few scarf tricks, most of which went off without a hitch, and then came to stand in the center of the stage, face grave. "For my next trick, I need a volunteer." His eyes fell on our corner. "A lovely volunteer."

"Oh, he noticed us," said Phoebe, with a sigh. She raised her hand, along with others in the audience. When I did nothing, she elbowed me until I raised my hand as well.

After a great show of examining all the volunteers, Jambini strode up to our table and extended his hand to me. Bastien and Phoebe whistled and cheered, urging me up. I was a little nervous about being set on fire or attacked by birds, but it was hard for me to refuse an audience. I accepted Jambini's hand and let him lead me up to the stage, while thunderous applause rang out around us.

"Just shape-shift into any outfit that comes to mind," he muttered in my ear, his breath heavy with the scent of gin.

Once we were on center stage, he took the microphone and kicked into showman mode. "Now, my lovely assistant here . . . what is your name, lovely assistant?"

I leaned toward the microphone. "Georgina."

"Georgina. What a lovely name. And so, lovely Georgina, all you have to do is allow yourself to be receptive to the awe-inspiring, truly mystical powers of my magic. If you do, wondrous transformations will occur." I nodded in agreement, and more cheering ensued.

Jambini walked over to his prop table and returned with a curtain attached to a hoop and a handle. When he held it up by the handle, the curtain hung down in a way that created an enclosed cylinder, completely concealing the person inside. I obligingly stepped forward, letting the folds of fabric hide me while Jambini gave a "magical countdown." In those brief seconds, I shape-shifted my sparkly cocktail dress to the first thing that came to mind: my green foil elf dress.

Jambini whipped the curtain away dramatically, revealing me in my new attire. People gasped and clapped with delight, and I gave a bow almost as showy as his. Encouraged by the response, Jambini declared, "One more time." I stepped back into the curtained enclosure and changed this time into black jeans, a silver-sequined top, and a woman's tuxedo jacket. When he pulled back the curtain, the applause faltered a little bit before increasing to a frenzy. I'd seen these types of tricks performed before among those not gifted with shape-shifting, and usually performers simply shifted between loose dresses, items easy to get on and off. My choice of clothing kind of defied the logic of those familiar with how the trick worked. But, hey. This was magic, right?

"Show-off," Bastien told me when I returned to my seat.

"Hey," I whispered back, watching Jambini attempt to swallow a knife. He'd gotten about a third of the way there before he started coughing. With a shrug, he finally gave up and simply bowed to delayed applause. "These people deserve something for their money."

Jambini—or Jamie, as I later learned he was really named—was much more appreciative of my performance. My group met up with him in the hotel's drab bar after the show.

"Switching to pants was genius," he told me, knocking

back a glass of gin. I had a sneaking suspicion that the show's actual performance was the longest he went without a drink on a given day. "People are going to be scratching their heads over that one for days."

"Maybe too much," warned Bastien. "You'll make mortals suspicious."

I shrugged, unconcerned. "This is Vegas, baby. No one'll question it. Besides, weirder things happen all the time."

Jamie was nodding along eagerly. "And that tacky holiday dress too? That was great. Really god-awful. You know, if you're moving here, I could totally hook you up with a job as my assistant." He chuckled. "People would probably get more out of seeing you than my tricks."

"That wouldn't surprise me in the least," said Bastien, straight-faced.

"Well, thanks," I said, "but I think I've got more jobs than I need. Phoebe already set me up with something."

"Poacher," said Jamie.

The other succubus laughed as she stirred cherries around in her cocktail. "Hey, I can't help it if I—"

A familiar aura spread through the room, and Phoebe fell silent. We all turned as one, watching as Luis entered the bar. Even mortals, who couldn't feel him like we could, paused and watched him stride through the room. There was just something that powerful and compelling about his dark presence.

"Boss man," said Jamie, holding up his glass in a mock toast. "You just missed my amazing performance."

"I've seen your shows before," said Luis, sitting down and beckoning the bartender over. "I don't think I really *missed* anything."

"Georgina was his 'lovely assistant,' " teased Phoebe.

"Oh?" Luis paused to place his order and then turned toward me. "Pray tell, what did you do to wow them? Set some scarves on fire?"

"Just some run-of-the-mill shape-shifting," I said modestly.

Jamie started in on his second gin glass. He'd ordered two when we sat down. I guess he didn't want to risk waiting the extra few minutes it would take to pour another. "That trick is always best with succubi. Even with a plant and a prepped costume, it never goes off quite as well. I used to have this girl who worked with me when I lived in Raleigh, and she did okay, but you could tell people knew how the whole get-up worked."

Alcohol was buzzing through me pleasantly, and I'd slowed down my consumption so as not to lose my head. Somewhere in that warm haze, Jamie's words tickled a memory. "Raleigh . . . when were you in Raleigh?"

"I moved from there a few years ago. I was there about . . . oh, I don't know." He took a sip of gin, perhaps to help his math skills. "Not that long. Twenty years. I did some good soul brokering, but really, my talents were better appreciated here, you know?"

"When you were there, did you know a vampire named Milton?" I asked. Remembering my conversation with Hugh while I was in the middle of a cheap Vegas bar was weird— but no weirder than hearing Raleigh mentioned twice this week.

"Milton?" Jamie's eyebrows rose, and some of his good humor dimmed. "Yeah, I know him. Scary son of a bitch. Looks like—"

"Nosferatu?" I suggested.

Jamie nodded solemnly. "How anyone as blatantly *vampire* as him got by as a covert operative is beyond me."

Phoebe frowned. "Did you say 'covert operative'?"

The waiter appeared then with Luis's drink. Luis motioned for him to stay and glanced around at the rest of us. "Refills? Another gimlet or cosmo? Jamie? You're drinking Tanqueray, right?"

Jamie looked offended. "Beefeater."

Luis rolled his eyes. "That's ridiculous and disgusting. Bring him some Tanqueray."

"No!" exclaimed Jamie. "Beefeater. I'm a purist."

"You have no discrimination," countered Luis. He looked back at the confused waiter. "Bring one of each. We'll have a taste test." The waiter looked relieved and hurried off before someone else contradicted the orders.

"It's a waste of time," said Jamie. "No offense, boss man. You'll see."

Luis was unmoved. "Beefeater's for peasants."

"Jamie," I tried, "about Milton—"

"Peasants!" I don't think Luis could've insulted Jamie more if he'd called his mother names. "Beefeater is a refined drink, for a refined palate. You know I have infinite respect for you, but clearly, despite your years of worldly experience . . . well . . ." Jamie drunkenly groped for an eloquent way to finish his speech. "You're wrong."

Luis laughed, something I couldn't help but think Jerome most definitely wouldn't have done if one of his subordinates said he was wrong. "We'll see, my friend. It's a complex matter really, coming down to an analysis of both base ingredients and the distillation process."

"Jamie—" I attempted again.

"That," declared Jamie, "we can both agree on. And Beefeater is vastly superior in both."

"Give it up, Fleur," Bastien told me in a low voice, eyes twinkling. "You can't compete with gin. Better luck tomorrow."

I started to protest, but further listening to Luis and Jamie's debate told me Bastien was right. Jamie was so fixated on defending his gin's honor that I doubt he would've even remembered me asking about Milton.

"Will he be sober tomorrow?" I asked skeptically.

"No," said Phoebe. "But he's usually a little less drunk during the first half of the day."

The gin arrived, and Luis and Jamie became totally consumed with conducting "scientific" examinations on it, involving scent and surface tension. I didn't really see how the latter made that much of a difference in a taste test, but they seemed to think it was a pretty serious matter.

"Dear God," I murmured, amazed.

Bastien finished off his cocktail. "When things turn serious, it's time for me to leave. What do you say, ladies? Would you like to go search out the clubs for some companionship?"

"I've got an early day tomorrow," Phoebe said with regret. "I should probably just go home now. But you'll be at practice tomorrow, right?"

"I guess so," I said. "I told Matthias I would."

Despite ostensibly being involved in liquor analysis, Luis glanced over at the sound of the company manager's name. "Oh? Did you arrange the introduction?"

I nodded. "Phoebe got me signed on."

Luis looked pleased. "Excellent. Are you happy with it?"

The question surprised me, but then I remembered his earlier comment upon my arrival, about how he wanted happy employees. "I think so. I think it'll be a lot of fun."

"Good. And what did you think of Matthias?"

That one was *really* a surprise. "I thought he was nice. Do you know him?"

"Only by reputation," said Luis. I was about to use the interruption to ask Jamie about Milton again, but before I could, Luis effortlessly slipped back to gin science, effectively blocking me from the imp's attention. Tomorrow, I decided.

"You know," said Phoebe slyly. "I could help you find Matthias if you wanted to see him tonight."

Even afloat on vodka gimlets, I still knew the right and wrong surrounding any sort of casual romance with Matthias. If I was going to hook up with anyone while I was here, it wasn't going to be anybody I would ever consider seriously.

I flashed her and Bastien my best saucy succubus smile. "Nah, too tame. I'm not here to settle down yet. Let's find something wilder and do this Vegas weekend right."

Bastien whooped with joy and caught hold of my hand. As he led me away, telling me about "this perfect dance club," I caught sight of Luis's face. He was nodding at Jamie, still seemingly interested in their debate . . . but there was something about the satisfied, knowing smile on Luis's lips that made me think it wasn't just the gin he was so happy about.

Chapter 9

It wasn't until I landed in Seattle on Sunday evening that the full surreal nature of my weekend in Las Vegas hit me. Being there had felt so . . . natural. I suppose part of that was just having old friends like Bastien and Luis around. Yet I'd been pleasantly surprised at how easily I got along with my newer acquaintances, like Phoebe and Matthias. I'd even grown to like Jamie, though I never did see him after that night. Despite my efforts to find him and ask him about Milton, the imp had remained elusive for the rest of my trip.

And the show . . . how had that happened? I couldn't even get a solid job here in my current hometown, yet hours after walking off the plane in a strange city, I'd landed what was, in many ways, my dream job. By the time we'd finished our second practice, Matthias was already talking about a special part he planned on creating for me, and several of the other dancers were so disappointed at me leaving for a month, you'd think we'd known each other for years.

It had, in spite of my misgivings, been a fantastic weekend.

Reality set in when I walked into my condo. Roman was out, with only a note reading *Bowling practice tomorrow night* to mark his passage. Naturally, the cats were as happy to see me as always. Scratching their heads in turn, I began to think about the logistics of moving both of them with me across state lines. I'd be taking them away from Roman, whom they loved, but there was nothing to be done for that.

He couldn't come with us. As a nephilim, he was in constant danger of being hunted down by other immortals, and it was only Jerome's protection that allowed him to have a semi-normal life in Seattle. Roman certainly wasn't going to give that up, and besides, Las Vegas was probably the worst place in the world for him to attempt to hide out.

A vase of pink-tipped white roses sat on the kitchen table, filling the air with sweetness. I opened up the card and read Seth's scrawled writing:

Welcome home. I've been counting the minutes.
—S

I texted him that I was back and received an answer urging me to come over to Terry and Andrea's for dinner. After leaving a note for Roman assuring him I'd be at practice, I headed out, my mind still spinning with more of the consequences of moving. The condo. I'd have to sell it. Unless I wanted to rent it to Roman? Hell would likely compensate any moving costs, but it'd be up to me to start making the actual arrangements now for things like movers and what-not.

I was good at making plans and organizing things, but all of my skills were useless against the one thing I wanted to bring with me to Las Vegas the most: Seth. I still had no solution for what to do with him.

I was met with the usual outpouring of love from his nieces when I arrived, just in time for a chaotic family dinner. With the additional family members, they'd given up any pretense of eating at the kitchen table and had simply taken their paper plates and homemade pizza off to the living room. The casualties of food and furniture were ones Terry and Andrea were long since used to, but Margaret couldn't focus on her dinner for fear of constantly watching the girls and what she perceived as imminent tomato-stained disaster.

I was happy to see Andrea out with the family, which wasn't something that happened very often lately. She looked tired but was in good spirits, and from the way the girls vied for position next to her, it was clear they were delighted to have her up and around too.

"Seth says you were out of town," she told me. "Anywhere fun?"

"Las Vegas," I replied. "Visiting friends."

"Man," said Ian. "I wish I had friends in Las Vegas."

"I figured it'd be too commercial for you," said Seth, deadpan.

Ian swallowed a bite of his pizza—it apparently wasn't a vegan day—before responding. "Only if you stay on the Strip and their overpriced luxury hotels. If you poke around in some of the out-of-the-way places, you could find some really cool and obscure dives."

It took nine-year-old Kendall to say what the rest of us were thinking. "I'd rather stay in luxury. Why would you want to stay in a dive, Uncle Ian?"

"Because it's nonmainstream," he told her. "Everyone stays at the nice places."

"But I like nice things," she argued. "Don't you?"

"Well, yes," he said, frowning. "But that's not the point—"

"Then why would you want to stay at bad places?" she pressed.

"You're too young to understand," he said.

Seth chuckled. "Actually, I think she understands perfectly."

Andrea decided to rest shortly after that, but not before extracting a promise that someone deliver her dessert later on. After doing dishes (which was pretty easy with paper plates), our group dispersed into separate activities. Kendall, Brandy, Margaret, and Terry started up a game of Monopoly while Kayla and the twins settled down to watch *The Little Mermaid*. Ian joined them, excited for the chance to show how the movie was an example of capitalism destroying America. Seth and I curled up on a nearby loveseat, ostensibly to watch the movie, but instead used the time to catch up.

"How was it, really?" he asked me in a low voice. "I've been worried about you. Was it as bad as you thought?"

"No," I said, leaning my head against his chest. "It was actually . . . pretty good. Would you believe I have a job already? Like . . . one that's not on Hell's payroll."

"You can't even get one of those here," remarked Seth.

"Yeah, the irony's not lost on me. I'm going to be a Vegas showgirl, complete with sequins."

Seth trailed his fingers through my hair. "That's actually kind of awesome. And hot. If you want to practice, I'd be more than happy to give you some constructive criticism."

I smiled. "We'll see."

There was a long pause. "So . . . it's real. This whole thing."

"Yeah," I said in a small voice. "It's real." I felt him tense and sensed the worry radiating off of him. "It's okay. We'll figure this out. It's still a month away."

"I know we will," he said. "You and I have overcome crazier things than this, right?"

"Crazier doesn't always mean harder," I pointed out. "I mean, when Peter tried to make a 'retro candle sconce' out of a Pringles can last month, that was pretty crazy—but it was also pretty easy to deal with once we found his fire extinguisher."

"You see?" said Seth. "This is what I love about you. I don't even consider that crazy. I consider that ordinary life with you, Georgina. You change all the definitions."

He pressed a kiss to my forehead. We fell silent and watched the movie, though I suspected Seth was paying as little attention as I was. We were both lost in our own thoughts, and I didn't really snap out of it until I heard Ian telling Morgan, "I like the original fairy tale better. It's pretty alternative, so you've probably never heard of it."

I glanced at the clock and sat up. "I'm going to go check on Andrea and see if she wants her dessert." Both Margaret and Terry were quick to offer to do it instead, but I waved them off, assuring them I was fine and that they should return to their game.

Andrea was awake, propped up on pillows and reading a book when I came in with the pie. "You didn't have to do that," she told me. "You should've asked Terry."

"He's busy buying and selling property," I told her, helping her settle the plate on her lap. "I couldn't ask him to interrupt that. Besides, he does plenty."

"He does," she agreed, smiling wistfully. "They all do. Even you. It's so strange, having others take care of me. I'm too used to looking after everyone else."

I settled down on a chair near her bed, wondering how often it must be filled lately. Andrea always had someone watching over her. "It's just for a little while longer," I said.

That got me another smile as she chewed a bite of pie. "You're very optimistic."

"Hey, why shouldn't I be? You look great today."

"Great 'ironically,' as Ian would say." She ran a hand through her limp blond hair. "But I do feel better than I have for a while. I don't know. It's deceptive, Georgina. There are days I feel confident I've beat every cancer cell in my body and others when I can't believe I'm still managing to walk this earth."

"Andrea—"

"No, no, it's true." She paused for more pie, but her eyes took on a vast, knowing look that reminded me eerily of Carter. "I've accepted it, come to terms with the fact that there's still a good chance I'll die. No one else has. No one else will talk about it. I'm okay with that. If that's what God wills for me, then so be it."

I felt a knot clench in my stomach. I couldn't say much about God, but I'd seen enough of Heaven and Hell to get angry when I heard humans accept their fate as part of some higher purpose. Half the time, it seemed to me the divine powers were making up this game as they went along.

"I'm not worried about me," Andrea continued. "But I am

worried about them." That serenity faded, replaced by very real human concern, a mother's fear for her children. "Terry's strong. So wonderfully strong. But this is hard on him. He can't do it alone, which is why I'm so glad Seth's here. I don't know what we would have done without him. He's the rock supporting us all right now."

The anxiety inside me eased for a few moments, replaced by a spreading warmth as I thought about Seth. "He's wonderful."

Andrea set down the fork, finished, and extended her hand to me. "So are you. I'm glad you're part of our family, Georgina. If something happens to me—"

"Stop—"

"No, listen. I mean it. If something happens to me, I'll rest easy knowing the girls have you in their lives. Seth and Terry are great, but the girls still need a strong woman role model. Someone to help them through growing up."

"I'm not that good of a role model," I said, not meeting her eyes. I was a creature of Hell, someone full of weakness and fear. What could I possibly have to offer such bright, promise-filled creatures like the Mortensen girls?

"You are," said Andrea adamantly, squeezing my hand. "They love you and admire you so much. I know they're in good hands."

I swallowed back tears that were threatening to overwhelm me. "Well," I said. "They're in even better hands with you, since we all know you're going to get well soon."

Andrea nodded, giving me an indulgent smile that I suspected she'd perfected after weeks of listening to others insist she was on the verge of recovery. A yawn soon betrayed her, and I carefully took the plate away and asked if she needed anything else. She assured me she didn't.

I crept back downstairs and returned the plate to the kitchen, where I found Brandy and Margaret eating pie of their own. I did a double take back toward the living room. "What happened to Monopoly?"

"Kendall bought us out," said Margaret.

"Man, I hate playing with her," grumbled Brandy. "No one her age should be that good."

"Don't knock it," said Seth, strolling in. "She's going to be supporting us all in fifteen years." He rested a hand on Brandy's shoulder. "Did you ask Georgina?"

Brandy looked at her feet. "No."

"Ask me what?"

"It's nothing," she said.

"Clearly it's something," I replied, exchanging looks with Seth. "What's up?"

"Is this the Christmas dance you were talking about before?" asked Margaret.

Brandy flushed. "A holiday dance. It's nothing."

"No way," I said. "I'm a big fan of dances. But isn't school out?"

"Yeah, but this is at church. It's a formal they have every year." She was using a *It's no big deal* tone, but her expression betrayed how interested she was.

The church part surprised me, since last I knew, the Mortensens didn't attend one. But obviously that had changed. Maybe Andrea's illness had played a role. Whatever it was, I could see faith wasn't on the line here, so much as a teenage girl's simple desire to participate in something fun with other people her age. It was a normal rite of passage, one I was guessing she didn't feel worthy of, in light of everything else going on right now with her family. No wonder she was hesitant to mention it. I wondered if maybe there was a boy involved too but certainly wasn't going to ask. She looked mortified enough to be having this discussion in front of her uncle and grandmother.

"You need to shop for a dress?" I guessed. People always called me for shopping. I used to be bothered by that but then figured I should accept what I'm good at. Brandy nodded, still looking embarrassed. "When is it?"

"Tuesday."

"Tuesday . . ." I frowned, thinking of my schedule. Tomorrow, Monday, was taken up with work and bowling practice. That didn't leave a lot of time. "We might be cutting it close."

"If you don't have time, it's fine," Brandy assured me. "Really."

"No way," I told her. "We can do it Tuesday morning."

Brandy looked down again. "My dad can pay you back. . . . I'll ask him how much we can spend."

"Forget it," said Seth, rustling her hair. She squirmed out of his reach. "Send the bill to me. You know where I live."

Brandy protested this, but Seth was firm in his offer—as well as his urging that Brandy not mention it to her father. But once Brandy and Seth were in the other room, Margaret caught hold of my sleeve and pulled me back into the kitchen before I could follow. Our interactions hadn't exactly been antagonistic (aside from our initial meeting with the baseball bat), but they hadn't always been pleasant either. I braced myself for some admonishment about dressing Brandy like a whore.

"Here," said Margaret, shoving some cash into my hands. I looked down and found two fifty-dollar bills. "Seth's not the only with income around here. He can't keep funding the whole family. Is that enough for what she needs?"

"Er, yes," I said, trying to hand it back. I'd actually planned on cutting Seth out as well and carrying the bill myself. "Definitely. You don't have to do this."

Margaret's response was to give me another bill. "Get her shoes too." She closed my hand around the cash. "I don't know what girls her age need when it comes to clothes, but I know you do. The money I can provide. The rest I rely on you for."

That sentiment—that faith in me—was too much, too fast on the heels of the conversation I'd just had with Andrea. "It's not enough," I blurted out. "What I'm doing, compared to everyone else. They're all giving so much. What's a shopping trip next to that?"

Margaret fixed me with a piercing gaze that bore no re-
semblance to the conservative, sweatshirt-wearing matron
I'd categorized her as. "For a girl growing up too fast, whose
life is crumbling around her? Everything."

"I hate this," I said. "I hate that this is happening to
them."

"God only gives us what we have the strength to endure,"
she said. I'd always hated that saying, largely because it too
seemed to go along with the idea of a universe having a plan
for everyone, something I'd seen no evidence of. "They have
the strength to get through this. *And* they have our strength
to help them."

I smiled at that. "You're a remarkable woman, Margaret.
They're lucky you're here." I meant it. She and I might have
different philosophies about premarital sex, but her love for
them was undiminished. I wasn't the only role model in the
girls' lives.

She shrugged, looking both flattered and embarrassed by
my praise. "Like you, I'm just trying to do enough—without
wearing out my welcome at Seth's."

"He loves having you," I said promptly.

She rolled her eyes. "I'm not stupid. I want to keep helping, but I know I can't stay with him forever. He's a grown
man, no matter how much I'd like to pretend otherwise."

That made me smile even more. "Don't worry. I won't tell
him you said so."

Nonetheless, I went home with a heavy heart that night.
Seth expected to be up late and hadn't wanted me waiting
around for him. We were both conscious of how little time
we'd had together recently, though, so he told me he'd join
me for tomorrow night's bowling practice. As a general rule,
he tried to avoid immortal goings-on, but I think he had a
morbid fascination with the idea of bowling for Hellish
honor.

"Thank God," said Roman, when I walked in the door. "I
thought you were going to stay at Seth's. There's soup on the
stove."

"No, thanks," I said. "I already ate."

"Your loss," he said. Judging from the way the cats were circling him for handouts as he settled down on the couch with a bowl, I guess they agreed with him. "How was it?"

My mind was still on the Mortensens, and for a moment, I thought that's what he meant. Then I remembered his single-minded focus and knew he was referring to Las Vegas.

"Surprisingly good," I told him, sitting down in an armchair.

His eyebrows rose. He hadn't expected that answer. "Oh? Tell me about it."

I did, and he listened attentively while eating his soup. When I'd finished the weekend's recap, he grilled me on nearly everyone I'd met there, immortal and mortal alike. In two days, I didn't have that much life history to report but gave him what I could.

"Well," he said, "isn't that lovely." He made no effort to hide his sarcasm.

I sighed. "You still think this was part of some greater conspiracy?"

"I think it's terribly convenient that this seemingly routine transfer is fulfilling every possible wish you might have."

I scoffed. "Aside from the fact that I'm being transferred in the first place. That's hardly something I wanted."

Roman straightened up, and the cats ran for his abandoned bowl. He ticked off points on his right hand. "Well, let's do a tally, shall we? When I first met you, I asked what your dream job would be. What did you say? A Vegas dancer. And wow! Look what conveniently falls into your lap. And who put it there? In a city full of conniving, backstabbing succubi, you were fortunate to find one as level-headed as you, complete with the same sense of humor and interests. Funny thing . . . did you even run into any other succubi that entire weekend? In a city packed with them?"

"Roman—"

"No, no, wait. There's more. How'd you meet this wonder succubus anyway? Through your closest immortal friend, who just happened to have been coincidentally transferred to Las Vegas, hired on by your favorite boss of all time. Are you following this fantasy so far?"

"But why would—"

"And," he continued, "lest you grow homesick for the wacky idiosyncrasies of your friends back here, Vegas is ready to supply you with new ones. A zany drunken imp. Seth 2.0. If you'd stayed longer, they probably would have unearthed an angel and a couple of vampires for you. And let's not discount the fact that you're going to Las Vegas in the first place! The single easiest place for a succubus to get by."

"Okay, I get what you're saying." I threw up my hands in exasperation. "It is perfect. Maybe too perfect. But you're missing one fundamental point. Supposing this is true, that someone has set up the most perfect scenario for me ever, a situation designed to keep me happy, why would they do it at all when the thing that would make me the most happy is to stay in Seattle? Why bother with this alternative? Why not leave me as I am?"

Roman's eyes gleamed. "Because that's the one thing they don't want you to have. They want you out of Seattle, Georgina. They want you out, and they don't want you to complain or look back."

"But why?" I protested. "That's what I can't figure out."

"Give me something else to work with," he said. "Hell's not that good. Even the most picture perfect setup has to have a flaw. Was there anything, anything at all this weekend, that felt disingenuous? That smacked of a lie?"

I gave him a wry look. "I was in Las Vegas, hanging out with servants of Hell. Everything was disingenuous."

"Georgina, think! Anything that seemed legitimately odd. Any contradiction."

I started to deny it but then paused. "The timeline."

He leaned forward even more. "Yes? What about it?"

I thought back to my first hours in Las Vegas. "Luis and

Bastien both went out of their way to act as though my transfer and Bastien's had been in the works for a while—like
Jerome said. But once, Bastien slipped. He sounded like he
hadn't been there for very long at all—not nearly as long as
they'd said before."

"Like that maybe he was suddenly pulled in on a moment's notice—to coincide with your transfer?"

"I don't know," I said, not liking the thought of Bastien
being part of some potential conspiracy centered around me.
"He corrected himself, said he misspoke."

"I'm sure he would say that." Roman leaned back now,
letting all of this sink in.

"Bastien wouldn't lie to me," I snapped. "He's my friend. I
trust him. He cares about me."

"I believe you," said Roman. "And I believe that he
wouldn't lie to you about something that he thought might
harm you. But if his higher-ups asked him to tell a white lie—
fudge a few days here and there—don't you think he would?"

I nearly denied it—but then had to wonder. Bastien had
been in trouble off and on with our superiors, his Seattle venture last year a desperate attempt to restore status. If he were
pressured enough—threatened, even—to tell me he'd been
transferred longer than he actually had, would he? Especially
if he thought it was harmless and knew of no nefarious reason behind it?

"But what nefarious reason would be behind all this?" I
muttered, not realizing I'd spoken my thoughts aloud until
Roman straightened up again.

"That's what we have to figure out. We have to figure out
what's happened to you that would've gotten someone's attention—and that happened recently, to spur such a fast response. We know about your slacker record. And we know
about Erik looking into your contract."

I blinked. "Milton."

I quickly told Roman about Hugh's information, about
Milton's secret assassin status and trip to Seattle lining up

with Erik's death. I also told him about briefly mentioning Milton to Jamie. Roman leaped to his feet.

"Jesus Christ! Why didn't you tell me about this sooner? I could've investigated Milton while you were gone. Shit. Now I'm trapped here under bowling duty." Nephilim had the same travel limitations as lesser immortals. They had to physically travel to places. No teleportation like greater immortals.

"I'm sorry," I said. "I wasn't thinking. I didn't connect it. And I didn't get a chance to ask Jamie more about Milton. He wasn't around the rest of the time I was in town."

Roman was nodding along with me as he paced. "Of course he wasn't. I'm sure they made certain he was unavailable before he could tell you any more. And explain again why your initial conversation with him didn't go that far?"

I shrugged. "He was drunk. He got distracted by a debate over gin with Luis."

"One that Luis initiated, no doubt."

"I—" I thought about it. "Yeah. I guess he did. But you're not saying . . . I mean, that's idiotic. Using gin as a distraction to cover up some plot?"

Roman's sea green eyes were gazing off in the distance, thoughtful. "It's not the most ridiculous distraction I've known a demon to use. He could've brought up bowling."

"Not that again."

Roman snapped his attention back to me, frustration all over his face. "Georgina, how can you be in denial about this? How can you refuse to believe that Hell is playing some larger game here? After all you've seen and been a part of?"

I shot up, angry at the insinuation that had been creeping along here, that I was too oblivious to see what was going on. "I know! I know they're capable of it. I know they can use means both ingenuous and simple—like gin and bowling—to get what they want. I'm not denying that, Roman. What I just can't grasp yet is the *why*. Show me that, and I'll get on board with any crazy scheme you want. I need to know why."

Roman came to stand in front of me, resting his hands on my shoulders as he leaned close. "That is exactly what I intend to find out. And when we do, I have a feeling we'll have blown the lid off of the biggest conspiracy Hell's had in centuries."

Chapter 10

In centuries? I thought that was kind of an exaggeration. But I wasn't going to argue any further with him, not when he had that zealous look in his eyes. It was one I knew all too well, which in its mildest form resulted in recipe experimentation and in its severest led to immortal killing sprees.

With all the schools on winter vacation now, Santa was no longer just doing evening duty at the mall. I had drawn a day shift for Monday and finally left Roman for bed so that I could get an early start. He acknowledged my good night with a nod, lost in his own brooding. Despite how hard he'd grilled me, I knew he was thinking about the same question I'd demanded of him: why would Hell want me out of Seattle so badly that they were willing to create a dream scenario for me?

I had no answers for it that night or the next morning. I arrived at the mall bright and early, in my foil dress, only to find a mob of parents and kids already lined up there waiting for us to open shop. Walter-Santa, I was pleased to see, was actually drinking straight coffee this morning, with no mention of alcohol. Of course, he was most likely getting rid of a hangover from last night, and I didn't doubt that the requests for "something harder" would start by noon.

"Santa wishes his pavilion wasn't under the mall's skylight," he remarked, furthering my hangover suspicions. He settled himself into his chair—much to the gathered children's delight—and winced unhappily up at the sunlight spilling through the latticed roof of the "holiday gazebo." He turned back to me and Grumpy. "I don't suppose we could get a tarp for that?"

Grumpy and I exchanged looks. "I don't think they sell tarps at this mall, Walt—Santa," I told him. "But maybe on my break I can score some sheets from Pottery Barn for you."

"Yeah," said Grumpy, repressing an eye roll. "I'm sure we can find something very tasteful."

Santa nodded solemnly. "Santa is grateful to have such dutiful elves."

We opened the floodgates. I was working right next to Santa today, meaning I got a front row seat for some of the more outlandish requests. I was also the one who got to remove screaming children, despite parental protests and pleadings to "just keep her there until I get the picture!" All the while, I kept thinking that instead of doing this, I could be in Las Vegas right now, working through Matthias's routines and listening to Phoebe's jokes along the way.

Of course, that isn't to say I was entirely scornful of the whole experience. I liked Christmas, and I liked children. I wouldn't have signed on for this job if either of those weren't true. But in watching these families—especially little girls with their mothers—I just couldn't shake my worries for the Mortensens. If I thought too much about them, I started to tear up. So . . . yeah. Cynicism was preferable at times. It kept me from getting lost in my own despair.

When my shift ended later in the day, I discovered I wasn't the only one going home. Grumpy put up a SANTA ON 10-MIN-UTE BREAK sign, much to the dismay of those waiting in line, and Walter followed me as I headed out to the mall offices. It was hard not to smile at the reaction of kids who just happened to be out shopping with parents and hadn't come to specifically see Santa. Children came to a standstill, mouths gaping and fingers pointing.

"You've been pretty good today," I told Walter.

"It's easier when Santa knows he can go out for a drink at dinnertime," he told me.

I frowned. "Are you going home? Oh. Of course you are. You've been here as long as me." Elves had always moved in and out of shifts, but Santa had stayed constant. Now, with us pulling longer hours, Walter couldn't be on the clock all the time. "Do you have a replacement?"

He put a finger to his lips and winked at me, refusing to say anything while we were in public. Once we were out of sight, in the administrative offices, I got my answer when we found another Santa sitting in a chair, leafing through a Victoria's Secret catalog. He looked up at our approach and set the magazine down.

"Is it time?"

Walter nodded and turned to me. "Vixen, do we look the same?"

"Of course," I said. "You're both men in red suits and white beards."

"Look closely," he scolded. The other Santa rose, and they stood side by side. "Details matter. Anything a child waiting in line might notice when Bob goes out to take my place. Beard alignment, glasses, fit of the coat . . . it all matters. One small detail is all it takes for those kids to realize they've been played, that there are two of us."

"And if they realize that," added Bob, using the same British accent Walter always did, "then the illusion is over. They'll know they've been tricked, that there is no one, true Santa."

"Wow, you guys take this seriously," I said, a little astonished. So, I did a closer assessment, making a few minor adjustments. I straightened Bob's hat and fixed the way some of his beard's curls were arranged. At last, I nodded. "You're good to go."

Bob looked at Walter expectantly. Walter took off his hat, beard, and glasses, revealing an ordinary-looking man with thinning salt-and-pepper hair. "Only one Santa can exist outside this room," explained Walter mysteriously, watching Bob go. "It's part of the magic."

"This was kind of sweet," I remarked. Off the clock now, Walter immediately produced a flask from his locker and began guzzling it. I wondered if the two Santas shared the same addiction. "Creepy, but sweet."

After a wardrobe change of my own and a brief stop home, I eventually made my way to Burt's Bowling Alley. Roman had chosen it for our immortal league practice. It was also the site of a date he and I had had way back when, during our ill-fated romance. Living with him day to day, coping with the mundane absurdities of roommate life, it was easy to forget about that part of our history. There had been a time when I thought I was falling in love with Roman, though eventually my feelings for Seth had won out. Learning Roman's true nature—and about his plot to kill Carter—hadn't helped our fledgling relationship. He'd given all that up, thankfully, but there were times I wondered just how much Roman still cared for me.

There was no sign of our illustrious teacher yet, but Seth was already there, along with Cody, Peter, and Hugh. Seeing me enter, Seth shot me a desperate, grateful look. I could only imagine what conversation he'd been subjected to while trapped with them. As I approached, the four guys' shirts instantly caught my eye. Seth was wearing a *Say Anything* T-shirt. That was typical of him. What wasn't so typical was that my three immortal friends were all wearing identical light blue shirts. Before I could get a good look at them, Cody leaped up and thrust a folded-up blue shirt toward me.

"Here," he said. "I can't wait to see what all four of us look like together in these."

The shirt was a standard bowling style, short-sleeved and button-down. My name was embroidered on the front. Flipping it over, I found THE UNHOLY ROLLERS done in elaborate, flaming letters. I arched an eyebrow.

"Really?" I said. "This is what we're going with?"

"It's clever on so many levels," Peter said excitedly. "It's a take on 'holy rollers,' and then when you think about the fact that we're *rolling* balls—"

"Yeah, yeah," I said, putting the bowling shirt on over my turtleneck. The size was off a little, and I shape-shifted to adjust it. "I know what the definition of a pun is, Peter. I just didn't realize we were going with something so . . . blatant."

"It was either that or the Sinsationals," said Hugh.

I made a face and settled into the crook of Seth's arm. "I think you went with the right choice. And at least they're in a tasteful color."

Hugh and Cody exchanged pleased, triumphant looks. Peter scowled.

"There's nothing wrong with pink," he said. "I think it would have made a statement."

"Yeah," said Hugh. "A statement that we're pansy-asses that Nanette's team could clean the floor with."

Peter gave a long-suffering sigh. "Why must you be so insecure about your masculinity? If Georgina had been around when we voted, I bet she would've gone with pink too."

At once, his words reminded all of them of why I'd been gone. Their faces fell. "Is it true then?" said Cody. "You're leaving?"

"Afraid so," I told him, attempting cheerfulness I didn't feel. "Next month, I'm Vegas-bound."

"But that's not fair," Cody protested. "We need you here."

Hugh gave him a rueful smile. "You haven't been in this business long enough, kid. 'Fair' doesn't enter into it."

Cody didn't like the reference to his lack of experience, but Hugh was right. Cody hadn't been immortal long enough to go through a transfer or the organizational machinations of HR. Peter and Hugh had, and while they might be sad at the thought of leaving me, they also knew that there were some things you just can't fight.

"Don't feel too bad for me," I said breezily. "Bastien's working there now. And I've already got a job as a dancer."

"You can't even get a job here," pointed out Peter.

"Like a topless dancer?" asked Hugh.

"No," I said. "But scantily clad in sequins."

Hugh nodded in approval. "That'll work."

Cody was still wearing his heart on his sleeve. His gaze fell on Seth. "Well. I guess one good thing is that with your job, you can live anywhere. Easy enough relocation."

I didn't know what Seth's thoughts on that were exactly, but he managed a brave smile. "We'll see." Suddenly all I could think about was my last conversation with Andrea, when we were talking about Seth. *He's the rock supporting us all right now.*

An uncomfortably warm feeling spread over me, tinged with the scent of brimstone. The other immortals and I looked up as Jerome entered, trailed by a pensive-looking Roman. I saw my surprise mirrored on my friends' faces.

"I didn't know you were coming," I said to Jerome, when the father-and-son duo reached us. "I thought you'd made it clear you weren't part of the team."

"I'm not," he said, eyeing the worn leather chairs with disgust. "But seeing as my honor is riding on this so-called team, I figured I'd best make sure you're on the right track."

"Thanks for the vote of confidence in my abilities," said Roman, entering our names into the lane's computer.

"I don't doubt your abilities," said Jerome, deigning to sit at last. "But I also know a little *encouragement* can sometimes go a long way in furthering success."

"I assume by 'encouragement,' you're referring to your extreme displeasure if we fail," I noted.

Jerome's lips twitched. "Exactly, Georgie. Besides, I also wanted to hear—"

Jerome fell silent as his gaze rested on Seth's T-shirt, depicting John Cusack's iconic stance with the boom box over his head.

"Nice shirt," said Jerome at last.

"Um, thanks," said Seth.

Jerome turned back to me, like nothing had happened.

"As I was saying, I wanted to hear about your Las Vegas weekend."

"How considerate," I said. Beside me, I felt Seth shift restlessly. I knew my other immortal friends made him uncomfortable in just a *weird* sort of way, but Jerome unnerved Seth in a whole other way. No, it was more than unnerving. Jerome *scared* Seth, which made sense because half the time, Jerome scared us too. "I'm sure you have enough eyes and ears to tell you exactly how my weekend went."

"True," said Jerome. "But that doesn't mean I don't enjoy getting your insight."

"Right," I said. "Because my happiness means so much to you."

Roman crossed his arms over his chest and fixed us with an irritated look. "Sorry to interrupt, but do you want to practice or not?" He gave no indication that he'd grilled me on every detail of the aforementioned weekend. From his expression now, you'd think that was the last thing on his mind.

"Certainly," said Jerome magnanimously. He gesture toward the lane, like some monarch kicking off a celebration. "Begin."

Roman rolled his eyes and then turned to us Unholy Rollers. "Okay, first, let's see what level you're all at."

Roman's lessons hadn't stuck with me over the last year, though I acquitted myself well with six pins on my first roll and two on the next. Cody surprised everyone with a spare, and Hugh, after first rolling a gutter ball, matched my eight. Peter created a perfect split on his first roll and hit nothing on the second. Seth, in a rare moment of bravery, leaned toward Jerome.

"Are there going to be handicaps in this tournament?"

"That," said Jerome, dark eyes on the gaping hole Peter had made, "is an excellent question."

Even Roman seemed a little surprised at how all over the map we were. He jumped into his role as coach, helping each of us with our own specific problems. Cody was the only one of us who needed little assistance and threw strikes and spares pretty regularly. I proved surprisingly correctable and was soon throwing spares about two-thirds of the time, which I thought was a decent rate. No amount of instruction seemed to help Peter, whose rolls were increasingly bizarre and erratic. Hugh improved slightly but still had a tendency to always throw right, which he just couldn't shake.

"Here," said Seth, standing up as Hugh was about to finish a frame. "Can I do it? I used to roll exactly like you do."

Hugh relinquished the ball willingly, and Seth stepped up to the line. I sat up with interest, never having seen Seth bowl. He showed Hugh his technique first, miming a throw that curved slightly left. Then Seth threw for real, releasing a fast, neat ball that cleaned up Hugh's leftover pins.

"Jesus Christ," said Jerome in disgust. "I'm going to have to see if Nanette will let me put mortals on the team. It's the only way I'm going to save face."

"Hey," said Roman. "Give them a chance. I can work miracles in a week."

Jerome stood up. "Miracles generally aren't in our repertoire. I've seen all I need to. I'm going to go drink now in a futile effort to wipe away the memory of this debacle. When I show up for your next practice, I expect to see significant improvement in *all* of you. If I don't, you're all going to learn a new definition of teamwork through your shared misery and suffering." He turned abruptly on his heels and nearly ran into a waitress approaching us. She yelped in surprise when she saw the furious look on his face. "Do *not* serve them alcohol," he warned her. "We can't risk any chance of this getting worse—not that that's probably possible."

We watched them both hurry away. Once Jerome left the bowling alley, Roman exhaled in relief and sat down with us. "Okay, now that he's gone, can we dispense with this bowling nonsense and get down to business? Cody, we need to talk to you about Milton."

"Whoa, whoa," said Peter. "Was I the only one who heard that part about 'shared misery and suffering'? We need to practice."

Roman waved a dismissive hand. "We'll get back to that."

"What about Milton?" asked Cody, looking puzzled for any number of reasons.

"You told him," said Hugh. "Shit."

"What'd you expect?" I asked. "You had to have known I'd do something about it."

"Milton's a hit man for Hell," said Roman.

"Milton . . . not Milton that asshole vampire that was here a while ago?" asked Peter incredulously. "A hit man? Come on. He was a fashion nightmare, but that's about it."

"We have good reason to think he really is an assassin," I said slowly. "He travels a lot, and when he's in town . . . people die. Like Erik."

"Erik was killed by a robber," said Cody. "There was no sign of a vampire."

"Well, of course not," said Roman. "Hell doesn't want its murders to look obvious."

"Yeah," said Peter, "but that implies Hell had a reason for killing Erik."

"Hell did," said Roman. He nodded toward me. "Her. Erik was investigating Georgina's contract when he was killed."

I swallowed, taking a moment to find my voice. There was a small, small comfort in thinking there was a reason for Erik's death and not just some random chance of the universe. But that comfort was negated by the fact that *I* was the reason.

"Roman thinks there's some nefarious explanation for me being transferred. Some larger plot. And that Erik's death was part of it," I said at last.

Seth stared at me in astonishment. "I thought you said this was routine."

I shrugged, unable to meet his eyes. "I don't know. Maybe it is. Maybe it isn't."

"It isn't," said Roman fiercely. "There are too many things going on, too many things that don't add up. Erik got too close to something, and Hell got rid of him. Which brings me back to my original point. Cody. You and Gabrielle followed Milton around, right?"

"I . . . yeah . . ." Cody was still in shock. "But I mean, we didn't see him kill Erik! We didn't see anything like that."

"Did you ever see him in Lake City?" I asked. That was where Erik's store had been.

Cody shook his head. "Never that far out. We just followed him mostly to some clubs. It was a game, that's all. She wanted to see a vampire, so we watched him for a while. We never followed him outside of downtown."

"I did."

Everyone turned to stare at Peter.

"Why are you looking at me like that?" he demanded.

"I didn't know about that," said Cody. "Why did *you* follow him?"

Peter snorted. "Why do you think? He was in our territory. I was seeing if he was really just on vacation like he claimed. I had to make sure he wasn't out hunting victims."

I grew so complacent sometimes with the idea of my silly, laid-back friends that it was easy to forget their true natures. Peter and Cody were the most deceptive of all sometimes. They were goofy and absurd in most of their normal living, but at the end of the day, they *were* vampires.

"And?" asked Roman, getting that zealous look again. "Did you see him in Lake City?"

"No. I followed him once to the Eastside and once to West Seattle."

A chill ran down my spine. "West Seattle? What was he doing there?"

"Nothing," said Peter. "He drove though some neighborhoods, sat in his car for a while. I figured he was stalking prey but saw me and gave up. Which he was smart to do."

"He might very well have been stalking prey," I murmured. "Erik lived in West Seattle. Do you remember the neighborhood?"

"If I saw it, maybe," said Peter. "But I couldn't lead you back there. I'm sorry."

"It doesn't matter," said Roman. "This is all we need. This is enough proof."

"It's circumstantial at best," argued Hugh. "Which I told Georgina initially. And it doesn't explain why Hell would want him killed—especially after he helped Jerome. I know, I know." Both Roman and I had started to protest, and Hugh held up a silencing hand. "The contract. But remember, Kristin checked it for you. She said there was nothing wrong with your contract."

Kristin was an imp who worked in Vancouver. I'd done her a favor, and in return, she'd dared to look in Hell's archives and review my contract for me, back when I'd clung to the hope that there might be an error. The imp who'd brokered my contract, Niphon, had been in town behaving suspiciously, and I'd been certain we'd learn that the contract was faulty. Kristin had come back with disappointing news: everything was in order.

"Erik said it wasn't mine that was the problem, though. He said it was a different one," I said.

"What other contract? And how is this connected to your transfer?" asked Hugh. When none of us had an answer, he sighed. "Look, sweetie. I'm as much for a good caper as any of you, but not at the expense of being stupid." He glared at Roman. "You've been around for a while, I'll give you credit for that, but you haven't lived our lives. You haven't had to answer to the system. We do. Don't fuck things up for her with some far-fetched, crazy-ass theory."

"What if it's more than a theory?" asked Roman. "What if it's true?"

Hugh met his gaze squarely. "Then make damned sure uncovering it is worth the consequences."

Silence fell over us. At long last, Cody said, "How much

do you think Jerome scared that waitress? Because I could really use a drink."

Roman resumed his coaching, but a weird mood had descended upon us in the wake of the Milton and Erik revelation. We went through the motions, but it was clear no one's heart was really in bowling. When we finally called it a night, Roman declared that we'd all improved but were still in need of more practice. Since that wasn't a mystery to any of us, we set up a schedule for the rest of the week before dispersing. Roman caught a hold of my arm as I was walking out.

"I won't be home tonight," he said. "I've got some . . . things to do."

"Things that are going to get you in trouble?" I asked warily.

"No more than I already am. Just figured I'd let you know in case . . ." He glanced at Seth, then me. "You know, just in case you wanted to know."

"Thanks," I said. Taking the hint, I turned to Seth once we were alone in the parking lot. "What do you think? Do you want to come have a sleepover? Or do you have to go back to Terry's?"

Seth put his hands around my waist and drew me close. "Actually, I have the night off. Andrea was having a good day today."

I remembered yesterday, how, despite her fatigue, it had been clear she'd significantly improved. I felt a flutter of hope in my chest and rejoiced at finally having something that was clear-cut and good in the world for a change. "Do you think she's really healing? That the treatment's working?"

"I don't know," he said wistfully. "I'd like to believe it. It would be . . . amazing. More than I could hope for."

My heart ached for him and for the whole family. I didn't know what to say, so I simply brushed a light kiss across his lips. They were warm in the chill air.

"Georgina," he said, when I'd pulled back. "All this other stuff . . . about your contract and the transfer. This is the first I'm hearing about it."

"I know," I said. "I'm sorry. I wasn't trying to keep anything from you. It's just . . . so much is still unknown. I didn't want to bring it up when I don't even fully understand what's happening."

"And I understand even less than you," said Seth.

I nodded. "I didn't want you to worry."

He gazed down at me, eyes honest and full of affection. "You have to stop that. I'm not going to break. You can always talk to me about anything. We won't get anywhere without things being open between us. We're in this together, Thetis. What happens to you affects me. I want to be there for you."

"I know," I said. "It's a hard habit to break . . . wanting to protect you."

"One thing struck me . . . what Hugh said. Are you doing something dangerous? He's right about Roman, isn't he? That Roman doesn't face the same consequences as the rest of you? I hate the thought . . . I hate the thought of you getting caught up in one of his schemes, that you might suffer for his rash actions."

"I'm not sure they're so rash," I said. "At first, I did. But now, I think he really might be onto something. About Erik. About my transfer."

"And if he is? What is there for you to gain? I mean, from what I know about Roman and nephilim, it'll be enough for him if he can catch Hell in a cover-up. That's what he gets his kicks from. But you . . . you answer to Hell. What do you get for uncovering some grand plan of theirs? Unhappy employers."

I leaned against his chest, staring off into the night. The sky was clear, but we were too close to downtown to see much in the way of stars.

"I get the truth," I said at last. "I don't know how my transfer plays into Erik's death—or if it even does—but if it's true that Erik wasn't killed by being in the wrong place at the wrong time, then yeah. I need to know that. I need to know the truth."

"It's worth it?" He squeezed me tight. "Worth the risk to yourself?"

"Yes," I whispered. "It's worth it."

Yet, even as I spoke, I thought of Erik—kind and wise Erik who did so much for others, with little regard for himself. Generous, wonderful Erik who had done so much for me and possibly lost his life for it. Finding out the truth of that, what he'd died for . . . yes, I'd meant what I said. It was worth any risk to me, but that didn't negate the terribleness of it all. It couldn't change what had happened to Erik. He was still dead, and the intrigue around us was only growing thicker and thicker.

"What's the matter?" asked Seth. Without even thinking about it, I'd closed my eyes and buried my face closer to his chest, perhaps in some subconscious effort to hide from the storm I felt was brewing around me and my immortal world.

I opened my eyes and sighed. "Nothing. Everything. I don't . . . I don't want to think about any of it. At least for a little while. Tomorrow . . . this is all going to be waiting, I know. But please . . ." I pressed myself even closer to him, keeping my lips only a couple inches away. "Let's go home. Help me to forget about this . . . just for tonight."

Seth didn't need to be told twice. His lips found mine, and we locked in a kiss that was both hungry and desperate. Heat and electricity coursed through me, making me oblivious to the winter night. When we broke away, both breathless, I just barely managed to say, "Meet you at my place."

We each headed off for our own cars, which was a good thing since we probably would have been hazardous together if attempting to drive home in the same vehicle. As it was, I was kind of amazed at my ability to get back to my condo on Alki Beach without breaking any traffic laws. But once we reached my place, pulling into the lot at almost the same moment, that was it. We were all over each other and just barely had the sense to make it through my door before letting go completely.

I'd tried to put up a good front about resisting sex, but the truth was, I'd missed it as badly as Seth. All the flings in the world couldn't make up for not doing it with *him,* the one I loved. My succubus duties were becoming even emptier and more hollow than usual. I still believed rationing our sex life was the smart and safe thing to do, but right now, I was willing to bend the rules.

He swept me into his arms as soon as we stepped inside my condo, still managing to kiss me at the same time. The cats, normally ready to pounce with love on anyone who came through the door, had enough sense to give us our space as we stumbled back toward the bedroom. Seth lost his balance while carrying me and only barely managed to make it to my bed when he stumbled, depositing us both in an unceremonious heap.

Had it really only been a month? As my mouth tasted his and my hands grew reacquainted with his body, I couldn't help but think it felt more like years. I'd been in a drought. I'd been starving for him. I couldn't get his T-shirt off fast enough and luxuriated in the feel of his bare skin under my fingertips. Seth was busy working on my shirt, which was a little difficult. The Unholy Rollers shirt didn't go over my head so well, meaning each button had to be undone individually. He did it with infinite patience and skill, soon making quick work of the shirt underneath.

Once I was stripped, he gazed at me with the same longing and hunger I felt for him. He ran his hands over the length of my body, reverently tracing the curve of my hips and breasts. "So beautiful," he murmured, drawing me on top of him. He then stretched back and shifted so that my breasts hung over his face, allowing him to take one of my nipples into his mouth. I gasped, not just because of the touch of his tongue—which was exquisite—but because it was *Seth*.

His lips and tongue teased my nipple until it was aching and tender. Then, he switched breasts, giving my other nipple the same adoration. Fire flared through me again, along with the silvery sweet high of his life energy. With it came his feelings—his love and passion for me—and the combination of it all was intoxicating. I cried out softly, and he slid me down so that our mouths could meet again, this time in a kiss so deep and crushing, it made the parking lot seem chaste.

As we kissed, I felt him slide a hand down the side of my body, moving toward my inner thighs. His fingers moved deftly as they explored me, slowly moving farther and farther until they slid inside of me. I exclaimed again, but the cry was swallowed in the kiss, which was so deep I felt as though I could hardly breathe. Patiently, those fingers danced around, testing me until he found the place that got the biggest reaction. Starting slowly, he stroked me over and over, playing with how wet I was, while intense pleasure lit all my nerve endings. I could easily put off my own climax as long as I needed, but there was no need tonight. I wanted to lose myself in him and let my body do whatever it wanted. What it wanted, as it turned out, was to come quickly. Seth and I had been apart too long, and my body has missed his touch.

A few more skillful touches, and I felt my lower body explode with bliss, the sensation so overwhelming that I wasn't certain I could handle being touched anymore . . . even though I craved it. Seth continued teasing me until my orgasm finally subsided, and only then did he remove his fingers. He finally broke the kiss too, and we both gasped for breath, our eyes locked on each other.

"Come here," I said, pulling him back toward me. Like me, Seth could've easily dragged out more foreplay . . . and like me, he didn't want to. I guess this was the cost of "rationing." It didn't leave much room for patience.

His body pressed against mine, and I felt him push inside me, hard and ready. I wrapped my arms around his neck and kissed him again as he began to thrust in and out of me. I wanted as much of him as I could get, wanted to make contact with as much of his body as I could. As we made love, though, I had the same sense I always did: even with him in me, pushing as hard as he could, he would never be close enough to me. I always wanted more of him. Our bodies were meant to be together, I decided. There was something so wonderfully, agonizingly right about the feel of him inside of me.

"Georgina," he gasped, as his motions grew faster and more intense. "You're amazing. Beyond amazing. . . ."

If any more sentiments were there, I never found out. His face transformed as his orgasm seized him, his body surging forward into mine with a new intensity. He let out a soft groan as he came, still thrusting as he took every last bit of pleasure that he could. And as he came, I felt the full surge of his stolen life force. It was glorious and heady, and I tried to accept it as part of the rest of the experience. I didn't want to ruin this moment with guilt.

When Seth's body finally slowed, he collapsed onto me, resting his head on my chest. He exhaled heavily and planted a kiss between my breasts. "Did I mention that you're amazing?" he asked.

I sighed contentedly and ran my hand through his hair, which was now even more messed up than usual. "Not that amazing," I remarked. "I feel like you did all the work."

He kissed me again. "That's what's great about you, Thetis. You don't even know when you're being amazing."

I felt a smile creeping over my face, and it had nothing to do with the compliments. *Georgina. Thetis.* The old, familiar nicknames. After the last time we'd had sex, some frightened part of me had worried I was in for a repeat and that he'd call me Letha again. But, no. That memory, that name . . . they were all gone, just like the person I used to be.

"I love you," I said, because it seemed the only adequate response.

"Mmm." He snuggled closer. "Let's not wait so long next time, okay?"

I laughed softly. "We're going to wait even longer. I don't think monthly sex is going to work if we ration for a lifetime. It's still too frequent."

He groaned. "Come on. I don't mind the risks. It's worth

it. I could be content with biweekly sex. Tonight was proof you can't hold out very long either."

"Biweekly! That's definitely too frequent. You only got it tonight because I suddenly had a moment of crisis."

He chuckled, though it was soon lost in a yawn. "If I got sex every time you had 'a moment of crisis,' then I'd probably be getting it every night."

I gently elbowed him. "That's not true." I thought about it. "Much."

He laughed again and wrapped his arms around me, keeping us close. "Oh, Georgina. You make everything we go through worthwhile. Everything."

Chapter 11

It was hard leaving Seth's side in the morning. We'd had too few nights together recently, and each day that passed only served to remind me I was that much closer to the transfer. Lying in his arms, watching him sleep in the early sunlight, I thought back to what he'd said about Andrea getting better. If that was true, if she was healing, then there was a chance the ties keeping Seth here might lessen. I felt selfish even thinking that way, but surely it wasn't too terrible a thing to wish we could all get a happy ending.

After a leisurely breakfast, Seth and I went over to the Mortensens'. He was on babysitting duty while Andrea went to a doctor's appointment, and I was there to pick up Brandy. Chaos met us at the door, and Brandy practically flew outside, breathless and laughing.

"Don't go in there," she warned me, after I gave Seth a quick kiss good-bye. She and I headed toward my car. "It's crazy. Mom and Dad slept in, and Grandma let Kendall and the twins 'help' with breakfast."

"What are they making?"

"Waffles," she said. "From scratch. I don't know which was scarier: Kendall mixing the batter or Morgan and McKenna on duty with the waffle iron. They set the smoke detector off twice."

I couldn't help but laugh as I pulled out of the driveway. "And you and Kayla didn't help?"

"No way," Brandy replied. "I stayed away from that mess, and Kayla was in one of her silent moods today."

"Aw." I kind of wished now that I'd taken a moment to go inside. Tiny Kayla had a special place in my heart. Though she was better than she used to be, she still had a tendency to simply watch her world without a word, and it could be difficult coaxing conversation from her. Some of this was shyness, and some of this—I suspected—was from the fact that Kayla was psychic. Her skills were still undeveloped, but she was sensitive to the workings of the supernatural world, which I had to imagine would make anyone of any age silent at times.

"She'll be fine. She loves waffles." Brandy smiled, and I was happy to see her so upbeat for a change. She shouldered just as much stress as the adults. "If any actually get made."

We drove downtown, and I quizzed Brandy about what she was looking for in a dress. She had little to offer, which was both charming and kind of heartbreaking. Brandy wasn't a tomboy, but with all of her family drama, dresses had been understandably off her radar. In fact, when her face lit up at all the downtown lights and decorations, it became clear that family had really been the only thing in her life recently.

"I haven't seen any of the holiday stuff this year," she told me, gazing out the windows. A pang in my heart reminded me that this would be my last year to see Seattle in all its holiday finery. "We usually always come down here so that the girls can see Santa. There's been no time."

"The girls haven't seen Santa?" I asked, snapping out of my moment of self-pity. "That's not fair, especially considering I see a little too much of him." It made me wonder how many drinks it would take to coax Walter into a house call. It also convinced me more than ever to make this a special day for Brandy. I couldn't expect her not to worry about her mom, but today, with Andrea on the mend and Seattle's shopping wonderland ready to explore, Brandy was entitled to worry just a *little* less than usual. She deserved to think about herself.

I took her on a whirlwind tour of designer stores, chastising her for looking at price tags. I wanted this to be about more than the dress itself. I wanted her to have an experience, to feel like a princess. I made sure the salespeople were falling all over themselves to help her, which wasn't always so easy to do at such a busy time of the year. Brandy's radiant expression told me it was worth the effort, and we finally hit gold at our third store, finding what was unquestionably *the* dress. It was made of dark pink satin wrapped around to create a sheath silhouette that could still show off her figure without being pornographically tight. Satin flowers near the top added a whimsical edge, and the straps and knee-length made me feel it wouldn't get her kicked out of a church function. We spent the next hour finding the perfect shoes and jewelry for it, and although each new purchase clearly made her uneasy, she stopped questioning me about the cost. She didn't know about Margaret's funding, but it had long since been spent.

Exhausted and triumphant with our purchases, we went to lunch at an Italian restaurant frequented by other ladies of leisure. It was inside a larger, elegant shopping complex, and just as we were about to enter the restaurant, I saw a familiar face emerge from a nearby store. Something in my chest clenched, and I spoke before I could help myself.

"Doug!"

It took him a moment to figure out who'd called to him. When he did, a series of emotions played over his face. I wondered then how the encounter would have been different if Brandy hadn't been there. Would he have even acknowledged me? Maybe. Maybe not. But Brandy's presence guaranteed politeness. No matter how angry Doug might be at me, he wouldn't snub her.

"Kincaid," he said, strolling over to us. "And little Brandy. How's it going?"

"Good," she said cheerfully. The two of them, I realized,

could have been related if Seth and Maddie had ended up getting married. The weird fallout from their breakup hadn't had as big an effect on Brandy as the rest of us, though, and she was genuinely happy to see him. "We're shopping."

He favored her with a smile, and I wondered if he was avoiding eye contact with me. "Last minute Christmas gifts?" he asked.

"Not a chance," I said. "This is all for Brandy. She's going to a dance tonight."

"Oh, I see how it is," he said. "Getting ready to break some hearts for the holidays, huh?"

She turned bright red. "No! It's at my church!"

Teasing girls was familiar and easy territory for Doug. "Yeah?" he said, forcibly keeping a straight face. "Then why are you blushing? Church boys' hearts break just as easily as us sinners', you know. I'm sure you'll leave a trail of hundreds in your wake."

"No," she protested. "Not hundreds—"

"Just one?" he asked slyly.

Brandy looked to me for help, and I laughed. "I knew there was someone."

"You guys are terrible," she said, though she didn't look *that* upset. "Can I go put our name on the list?"

"Sure," I said, still laughing. But the instant she was inside the restaurant, Doug's playful manner vanished.

"Well, I've got to go," he said, starting to turn away.

"Wait, Doug, I . . ." He looked back at me, but I was at a loss. What could I say? That I was sorry for sleeping with his sister's fiancé? That I was sorry for lying to all of them and breaking her heart? How could you apologize for something like that? "It . . . it was good to see you," I said at last.

"You too," he said, though he didn't sound convincing. He nodded toward the restaurant. "And her. I hope she has fun."

"Me too. She deserves it, what with everything else going on."

He had attempted to leave again, but my words made him pause. "How's her mom?"

I shrugged. "Good days and bad days. It's up and down. . . . sometimes it seems hopeless, sometimes it's like everything's fixed. Wreaks havoc on everyone. . . . you just can't assume anything, you know? She's having some good days right now, but it's been a hard road for all of them. We just never know what's going to happen next and have to hang in there as best we can. I'm trying to help, but I don't know. . . . I don't feel like it's enough. But what could be?" I promptly shut up, realizing I was rambling.

Doug said nothing, his dark eyes studying me for several heavy seconds. Then, his gaze shifted to Brandy, speaking to the hostess, for a few more moments before returning to me.

"You're a good person, Kincaid," he said softly. And this time, he did leave.

Nothing else he might have said could have surprised me more. In all the imagined conversations I'd had with Doug, I'd expected frigid politeness at best—and that had seemed like a long shot. More often than not, I'd envisioned him telling me terrible, hurtful things, things I deserved. As much as a secret part of me yearned for him to forgive me so that we could be friends again, I really didn't think I deserved that forgiveness. I watched him walk away until Brandy stuck her head out from the restaurant door and called that they had a table.

Despite how pensive my meeting with Doug left me, I was still able to enjoy the rest of the afternoon with Brandy. We were both in good spirits when we arrived back at the Mortensen home, and mine soared even higher when I saw Seth's car in the driveway. I hurried inside, eager to see him, only to have my mood shatter when I saw his face. Margaret and Terry wore similar expressions. Brandy, normally so observant, was too keyed up over her purchases to notice that there had been a significant mood shift in the house, compared to the bubbly chaos of this morning.

"We had such a great time," Brandy told them, face shining. "I got the best dress."

Margaret gave her a tight smile. "Why don't you try it on for us?"

Brandy didn't need to be told twice, and Kendall and the twins followed her uproariously to the bedroom, offering to "help." The instant they were gone, I turned to the adults. "What happened?"

"Bad prognosis at the doctor's," said Seth, when no one else spoke right away.

"But she was improving," I argued. I looked at them all for confirmation. "Right?"

"We thought so," said Terry. "At the very least, she seemed to be feeling better. But in these situations . . . well, cancer tricks you that way. It's why people go so long without ever knowing they have it. She woke up feeling bad this morning, and the doctor confirmed our fears." I was kind of in awe at how calmly he managed to deliver that. I wasn't sure I could have without breaking down. Honestly, I didn't know how he'd been able to handle any of this with as much strength and determination as he had. If this were happening to the love of my life, I was pretty sure I'd crawl into in a corner and cry.

Or would I?

Looking at Seth, at those beloved features and compassionate expression, I suddenly knew that wasn't true. If the one I loved needed my strength, then I would give all I had within me.

"We're not telling Brandy yet," said Seth. "We're not going to keep it from her, but we figured it would be best to wait until after tonight."

I nodded slowly, having no words. I was usually so quick with a quip or soothing line, but what response could I make to that? Especially when, moments later, Brandy came bounding back down the stairs in the pink dress. Each twin held a shoe, and Kendall carried the glittering chandelier earrings we'd found just before lunch. I was reminded of Cinderella's mouse retainers.

Brandy's tastes had been foremost in my mind while shopping, but I'd also had half an eye on what I thought her family would approve of in fashion. As she spun around for them, however, I realized it didn't matter. I could've brought her home in rags, and they would've loved it so long as she wore the look of radiance on her face that she did now. That was what sold it, one spot of pure joy in the dark cloud that kept hanging over this family. The adults were too overcome with emotion to speak, so Kendall did it for us.

"Doesn't she look like a princess?" She kept trying to smooth nonexistent wrinkles out of the skirt, much to Brandy's dismay. "I want a dress like this."

Morgan sat down on the floor and tried to forcibly push the shoe on Brandy's foot while she still stood, furthering my Cinderella images. McKenna joined in as well, and both nearly succeeded in knocking their older sister over.

"Well?" Brandy laughed. "What do you think?"

"It's beautiful," said Margaret.

"You're beautiful," said Terry.

Having successfully dislodged the twins, Brandy stepped into the shoes, flushing under the praise of her family. "I hope I don't fall in these. How stupid would that look?"

"I don't think anything could make you look stupid," said Seth. "You're perfect from head to toe."

"Okay, you guys," said Brandy, growing embarrassed. "Now you're just pushing it."

The "head to toe" comment suddenly reminded me of something. "Oh. I won't be here to do your hair. I have to go to work soon." At that moment, calling in sick seemed like a reasonable idea. Nothing seemed more important than giving her a perfect night.

"That's okay," said Brandy. "I can do it. Or maybe Mom can."

"She's been kind of tired today," said Terry neutrally. "But I know she'll want to see you before you leave."

"I can do a French twist," said Margaret, surprising us all. "If you want to wear it up."

"Will you show me?" asked Brandy.

Margaret nodded. "Sure, let's go upstairs."

Before they did, Brandy paused to give me a giant hug. "Thank you so much, Georgina. For everything."

They went upstairs, followed by the littler girls, all of whom thought there was nothing so wonderful as dressing up their older sister. Actually, I realized, that wasn't entirely true. Not *all* of them felt that way.

"Where's Kayla?" I asked. She hadn't been in the entourage.

Terry sighed and ran a hand through his hair, in a way similar to what I'd often seen Seth do. "In the living room, I think. She's been out of sorts today. Sometimes I think she can figure out what's going on, even when we don't tell her."

With Kayla's abilities, I didn't doubt it was true. I remembered Brandy saying Kayla had been in a "silent mood" since this morning and wondered just how much of her mother's illness the little girl was in tune with. I left the brothers to seek her out and found her curled up in a corner of the overstuffed sofa, making herself so small that she was almost lost in the cushions.

"Hey, you," I said, sitting down beside her. "How's it going? Don't you want to see Brandy's dress?"

Kayla shifted her face, looking at me with huge blue eyes. "Georgina," she said. "You have to make it stay away."

My thoughts were on the dress, so it took a moment for me to follow what she was saying. "Make what stay away, honey?"

"The Darkness."

There was something in the way she said the word that let me know she wasn't referring to shadows. When she said "Darkness," I could feel the personification in her word, the looming threat of something—or someone—tangible. With a pang, I remembered that Kayla had been able to sense Nyx when she'd escaped her angelic captors.

I leaned toward Kayla, glad Seth and Terry were preoccupied. "Kayla, are you talking about . . . about the creature you felt before? The one you could sense on me?" Nyx's return would be a complication I most certainly didn't need in my life right now.

She shook her head. "A different one. The Darkness comes *here,* to my house. To see my mommy. Will you make it go away?"

"Is it here now?" I asked uneasily.

"No. Just sometimes."

"How many times?"

Kayla thought about it. "Two."

A cold feeling crept over me. "Was last night one of those times?"

She nodded.

"Have you seen it?" I asked her.

"No. But I feel it. I can tell where it's at when it's here." She peered at me beseechingly. "Will you make it stop?"

I had no clue what this Darkness was or what I could do to stop it, but theories were running wild in my head. I kissed her forehead. "I'll do what I can, baby. I promise. I've got to leave now, but I'll see what I can find out for you, okay? We'll make sure the Darkness doesn't come back."

Like the flip of a switch, Kayla's whole demeanor changed. Whereas she'd been sad and withdrawn moments ago, she was now beaming and hopeful. All that faith—in me. With my empty assurance to take on something I didn't understand, she was able to put aside all of her fears and worries. All was right in her world now, thanks to me. She put her arms around me and kissed me back, and I felt like my heart would break when I finally untangled myself from her.

Holiday cheer was calling, as well as a burning need to suddenly talk to Roman. Seeing as how we kept missing each other lately, I sent him a text with a reminder of when I'd be home tonight and that I had important information for him. He was so caught up in his conspiracy theories that I wasn't sure if he'd want to make time for what he'd probably see as a little girl's fantasies. Kayla's perceptions—despite her difficulties in articulating them—had proven accurate before. I didn't know what she was sensing this time, but if there was a force inside the Mortensen household, I intended to stop it.

Chapter 12

My brief conversation with Kayla tormented me for the rest of the evening as I corralled kids at the mall. I couldn't shake the image of her eyes as she told me about "the Darkness." It was one of those times I both blessed and cursed her psychic abilities. If she hadn't had them at all, I never would've known anything was amiss in the Mortensen household. But with her imprecise understanding of her powers, I was left with too many questions about what she might have sensed. Erik would've known instantly.

There was another thing for me to worry about.

Erik. Murdered because of me.

And if we were operating on the assumption that Hell had directly acted against him, then what was I supposed to think about Kayla? In the past, any unusual supernatural activity in the area had been the result of rogue forces outside of the Heaven and Hell system. After all, Heaven and Hell had certain rules they were supposed to follow. Milton was proof, however, that Hell wasn't above breaking those. So was it possible someone from my own side had been visiting Andrea Mortensen—coincidentally during the times her condition worsened? And if so, why?

That, as Roman had pointed out, was a question with an answer that would crack all of this wide open.

My only pause in ruminating on immortal affairs came when I tried to coax Walter into doing a house call to the Mortensens. Two mothers had gotten in a fight in line, so we were all on an impromptu break while mall security sorted matters out.

"Santa doesn't do house calls," Walter told me.

"Last time I checked, that's *exactly* what Santa does," I countered. "Every Christmas Eve."

"Santa can't just be hired out for entertainment. Children must either wait until Christmas morning or come visit the retail wonderland Santa's gazebo is in. Those are the rules."

"Of course you can be hired out," I said. "It's why you're working here to begin with! Come on, I'll pay you. I'll buy you a drink. Both, if you want. These are little girls who need to see Santa. Their mother has cancer, for God's sake. How can you not be moved by that?"

He peered at me through his spectacles. "I'm very sorry for their plight, but I can't do it. Taking on this role is a commitment for the holiday season, a vow to stay true to the spirit of Santa. If I'm outside this mall while playing this role, and Bob is here playing the same role, then what does that say to the children?"

I stared at him incredulously. "Well, unless these children are capable of breaking the rules of time and space, none of them would know there's a Santa here, in Lake Forest Park, or in any of the other thousands of malls in this country."

"*I* would know. I can't be Santa while Bob is playing Santa. It would break our sacred pact."

" 'Sacred pact?' It's just a job!" I was seriously considering breaking the drinking rule. If I got him tipsy enough, surely he'd agree to what I wanted.

"Not to us, it isn't," he told me solemnly. Security finished up their intervention, and the line began moving again, bringing the discussion to a halt before I could point out that last I'd checked, liters of whiskey weren't part of the "spirit of Santa" either.

I might as well have been Grumpy for the rest of my shift. I appreciated Walter's dedication to the role, but honestly, it was kind of pushing absurdity.

I stayed at Seth's place that night, in spite of my earlier

plans to talk to Roman about what Kayla had told me. But when I called Seth on my way home, there was just something so sad and strained in his voice that I knew it was more important to be with him. Andrea's worsening condition had hit him hard. He and I spent the night chastely, but there was a desperation in the way he held me, a sense that I was all that was keeping him going in this madness.

"Oh, Thetis," he whispered, kissing my cheek as we snuggled in bed. "What am I going to do without you?"

"Don't worry about it," I said automatically. "I'm still here for a while."

"I know," he said. "But then . . ."

Silence. My heart lurched.

"I know," I said at last. "I know you can't leave them. It's okay."

"At least until she gets better. . . ."

His words faltered for a moment. I could guess his emotions because I shared them. We were both worried about that looming, unspoken fear. That maybe Andrea wouldn't get better. And the really, really awful thing was that if she didn't, then eventually, Seth might be able to come to me in Las Vegas. But how could I live with myself knowing what the price of my happiness was?

He finally managed to find his words again. "I understand why you get so frustrated with the universe," he said. "I've never wanted anything so much as I've wanted to be with you. I finally got you . . . and now this happens. People talk about throwing everything away for love, but reality doesn't work out that way. And honestly, if I was the kind of guy who could ignore his family for his own selfish wants . . . well, then, I don't think I'd be worthy of you. So here we are."

"It's okay," I repeated, forcing more bravery than I felt. "We'll be fine. They need you. Do what you have to do."

"Georgina."

"Seth." I brushed my lips against his. "This is more important right now."

"Than us?" he asked.

It took me a long time to answer. But I did.

"Yes."

The next day I had an early shift at the mall, working with Bob. I attempted the same bargain I had with Walter, in the hopes of arranging a visit to the Mortensen girls, only to be met with the same response. I'd kind of hoped that since Bob wasn't a blatant alcoholic, he'd be more reasonable. No such luck. He was full of the same nonsense about the magic and integrity of the Santa role.

Fortunately, things improved when I found Roman at home afterward. We had bowling practice that night, but I'd wanted to talk to him in private. My other immortal friends could be coaxed on board with a lot, but as Hell's hand became more obvious in all of this, I was hesitant to get them involved. Roman didn't face the same repercussions, and I didn't mind exposing myself to the wrath of my employers. I was less excited about subjecting my immortal friends to that same wrath on my behalf.

"Did she say anything else about this 'Darkness'?" Roman wanted to know, once I'd recapped everything for him. "Greater immortal, lesser immortal, outside deity?"

"She doesn't understand what any of that is," I said. "She's only four. Five now, I guess."

"She needs to understand it," he said darkly. "You should train her up."

"With everything else going on in her life? I think that's the last thing she needs."

"Not if some supernatural creature is making her mom sick!" Roman perched on the edge of the couch, his sea green eyes both thoughtful and angry. "And let's face it, Georgina. If something is, I really can't imagine it's because the powers that be have singled out that family by random. If something's targeting Andrea Mortensen, it's because of her connection to you."

I felt ill. More consequences, laid at my feet.

"So Andrea suffers because of me," I said, sinking into a chair. "Wonderful."

"It's Hell," said Roman. "What do you expect? If they want back at you for something, then they're going to find creative ways to do it."

"Seems like there are more direct ways to make me 'pay,' " I noted. "Especially seeing as they own the contract on my soul. We're assuming a lot that this *is* Hell."

Roman shrugged. "Not really. We already know they're interfering with your life. And healing and injuring are specific powers given to angels and demons."

"Do you think Carter could tell what visited her?" I asked. "If he looked at Andrea?"

"I think he *could*." Roman considered for a few moments. "The question is if he would get involved with it at all. You know how he is. Heaven, at least, makes a pretense of playing by the rules."

I nodded slowly, remembering my last conversation and how reluctant Carter had been to intervene. "True," I murmured.

"Well," said Roman, straightening. "You can ask him right now."

"Huh? How?"

"He's coming to practice. I overheard him and Jerome talking about it yesterday."

Apparently, Seth wasn't the only one with a perverse interest in watching Jerome's misfits bowl for his honor. I stood up as well.

"Then let's go. I'll drive."

As we headed downstairs, I gave Roman a sidelong look. "Have you ever wondered how you'd look in a white beard and Santa hat?"

Roman returned my look warily. "No, I have not."

I quickly explained how the Mortensen girls hadn't seen Santa yet this year. He was already shaking his head before I finished the story.

"Come on, Roman. They need to see Santa. And I know

you don't have any of those hang-ups like Walter does about multiple Santas existing together."

"Nope," agreed Roman. "My hang-up is about preserving my dignity, no matter how good the cause. Besides, I don't feel that guilty. If you really wanted them to see Santa, you could shape-shift and put us all to shame."

I scowled. It was annoying because it was true.

Roman and I were the last to arrive at the bowling alley, much to my dismay. I'd hoped to speak with Carter privately, but he and Jerome were already deep in conversation (and in their cups). The rest of the Unholy Rollers were waiting anxiously for their leader and gave me no end of grief for not wearing my shirt.

"I forgot," I said. "It's no big deal. I'll wear it for the real game."

Peter sighed. "But it helps build team solidarity now. And that sense of bonding and closeness will make us better."

"Actually," said Jerome, "hitting more pins would make you better."

"Look," I told Peter. "If I have to use the bathroom at some point, I'll shape-shift the shirt on."

"It's not the same," he grumbled.

Fortunately, Jerome's impatience allowed little time for further debate on the matter. He hadn't seen how our last practice had ended and was anxious to know if we'd improved. We *had*, to be fair, but I think Jerome was expecting us to all be throwing strikes every time. When it was clear that wasn't the case, he grew impatient and angry.

"How can you do that?" he demanded, after Cody made an impressive 9-1 spare. "Why can't you just hit them all the first time?" He glared at Roman. "Do something."

Roman eyed his father irritably, not liking his teaching skills questioned, especially since Cody was the best of us. "Why don't you? Why don't you give it a shot, Pop?" Jerome had been up pacing by the lane but wouldn't deign to actually touch a ball himself.

"Because it's not my job," Jerome retorted.

Roman rolled his eyes. "Then let me do mine."

While they bickered, I leaned over to Carter. "I need to talk to you. In private. Can you stick around after this?"

Carter had been watching the father–son exchange, but his eyes flicked briefly toward me when I spoke. He gave a small, barely perceptible nod. And when Jerome returned to his seat a few moments later, saying he wanted to leave and drink off his annoyance at the Cellar, Carter declined the offer.

"Nah," he said lazily, stretching. "I think I'll see how this pans out. There's no way Peter can keep throwing splits like that every time. It defies all the rules of physics."

Peter looked torn on whether he should be flattered or not by that.

"Fine," said Jerome. "If you've got any miracles you can work to help them, now's the time to cash them in."

"Noted," said Carter, waving as Jerome left.

My lesser immortal friends were agitated by our boss's disapproval, so I focused on the game and didn't bring anything up with Carter until we finished our practice. Jerome could criticize all he wanted, but Roman really was a good teacher. I think our greatest triumph was when Peter went four frames in a row without a split, thus returning the laws of physics back to their rightful state. True, he didn't get any strikes or spares either, but by that point, we were all so exhausted that we were willing to take what victories we could.

Roman, Carter, and I let the others leave ahead of us— once I'd promised I would definitely wear my team shirt next time, of course. As soon as we had relative privacy, I explained my problem to Carter. His face grew graver and graver as he listened.

"Daughter of Lilith," he said when I was done, "you know I can't interfere."

"I'm not asking you to," I said. "Not exactly. I just want to know if you could tell if someone—like a demon—had made Andrea Mortensen sick."

Carter's gray eyes were unreadable. "Yes. I can tell."

"Will you go see her with me and tell me what you sense?

That's it. I'm not asking you to break any rules." Well, I didn't
think I was. Honestly, I didn't understand half of these
"rules" he was always talking about. "I just need the information."

"Okay," he said, after what felt like forever. "I'll go with
you. Giving you that information doesn't violate anything."

"I don't suppose," said Roman, "that telling us *why* Hell
would do this wouldn't violate anything either?"

I answered before Carter could. "We already know. To get
to me. I've pissed somebody off, and they're going to make
me suffer by making those I love suffer."

"Yeah, but why Andrea?" asked Roman. "I mean, no offense, but there are other ways to hurt you more. Why not
make Seth suffer?"

I couldn't help but scoff. "Well. With this transfer, I kind
of feel like he already—" I came to a screeching halt, once I
realized what I'd been about to say. Roman was sitting opposite me in one of the worn leather chairs, and from the rabid
look in his eyes, I thought he was going to reach over and
shake me.

"What?" he demanded. "What did you just think of?"

"Andrea's sickness is terrible," I said slowly. "A horrible,
unfair thing that could hurt her whole family. But there's
something else. As long as she's sick, as long as the whole
family needs help . . . Seth has to stay with them. He can't go
to Las Vegas with me."

"And there it is," said Roman, wonder lighting his eyes.
"That's what this transfer is about. To get you out of Seattle,
away from Seth, and to make sure he can't follow."

"Eventually . . ." My stomach was twisting again, just like
it always did when I thought of people being affected because
of me. "Eventually he'd be able to. Andrea will either get better, or . . . or she won't."

"Yes, but how long?" demanded Roman. "How long will
that take? Long enough for you to fall even more in love with
your picture-perfect scenario—the one that they handcrafted
for you? Long enough for you to move on with some other

artsy introverted mortal? By the time he's free, it won't matter."

I was staring off at Roman but not really seeing him. Jerome had always been annoyed at my relationship with Seth, chastising me for being too attached to a mortal and letting it affect my job. Carter himself had said I was doing something that Hell didn't like. Was it possible *this* was it? That all of these forces were moving to keep Seth and me apart?

"If Hell wants me away from Seth, then why not just forbid it?" I asked. "Jerome's given me a hard time before. Or why not just drop me somewhere . . . anywhere . . . that isn't here? Why should they care that it's a place I'll fall in love with?"

"So that you'll forget him," said Roman. "So that you won't look back. If they ordered you apart, a teenage forbidden romance complex would kick in like that." He snapped his fingers. "You'd never stop pining for him. But this . . . this is more subtle. And effective."

"It is," I agreed, still reeling. "Even after all of Jerome's criticism, I never thought . . . I never thought Hell would be *this* upset over me being with a human."

Roman had no answer for me but lifted his eyes to Carter. "You're being awfully quiet."

Carter shrugged, face neutral. "You two have plenty to say. No need for me to chime in."

"Are we right?" I asked the angel.

"Of course we are," said Roman. "You've always known Hell thought you were too distracted by Seth. This explains everything."

"Doesn't explain Erik," I said.

"Are you *sure* you have nothing to add?" asked Roman, gaze still on Carter.

"I think we should get to the Mortensens' before it gets much later," said Carter mildly. "I'm sure those girls have respectable bedtimes."

I stood up, knowing we'd get nothing else from him. "I

have to drop Roman off at home first. Then we can go over there."

"How are you going to get me in to see her?" asked Carter. "It'll be a little weird bringing in a stranger to a sick woman's bedroom. Do you want me to go invisibly?"

I'd been about to suggest that very thing when a new idea struck me. I gave Carter a once-over. "Have you ever wanted to put on a Santa suit?"

"I have *always* wanted to do that," said Carter gravely.

Roman groaned.

Once I explained the situation to Carter, however, he was totally on board. In fact, he told me not to worry about the costume arrangements and promised to meet me at Terry's in an hour, once I'd had a chance to drop Roman off. As soon as we were in the privacy of the parking lot, Carter vanished into thin air.

"I hope he doesn't get an outfit from wherever it is he normally does his shopping," I mused to Roman as we drove. "We don't want a hobo Santa. Although, if Ian's there, he'd probably approve and say we were breaking out of the mainstream's iron grip."

"Goddamned hipsters," said Roman. He leaned his head against the car's window. "You're rolling the dice a little with Carter, but something tells me he won't mess this up, not for a bunch of girls with a sick mother. He's an angel, after all. He's got to earn his keep somehow."

"And thank goodness he doesn't have any hang-ups about Santa being at more than one place at the same time," I joked. "No space–time contradictions there."

Roman jerked up so fast, I nearly slammed on the brakes, thinking I was about to hit something. Half a second later, I realized whatever had startled him was in his own head.

"Oh God," he said.

"What?" I asked, acting like him earlier. "What did you just think of?"

"I think . . . I think I've figured this out." There was awe in his voice.

"What? This mystery we've been beating our heads against? We already figured it out."

Roman shook his head, wide-eyed. "No . . . oh, Jesus. Georgina, if I'm right . . . how do I even prove if I am?" He leaned back in dismay. "How do I get proof?"

"Tell me what you're thinking," I demanded.

"No. Not yet. Just drop me off, and we'll talk when you're done. I have to figure this out."

There wasn't much that was more infuriating than that. I hated having the lure of a secret being dangled before me. I hated the "I'll tell you later" stance. But no matter how much I badgered him, he refused to say any more. With Carter on his way to Terry's, I couldn't linger long over Roman. I had to get to Lake Forest Park first. With much grumbling, I left Roman to his machinations, after first warning him that he'd better be ready to spill when I got home later.

When I arrived at the Mortensens' soon thereafter, I was relieved to see that Seth was around and that all the girls were still awake. Recalling Carter's joke, I'd worried on my drive over that it might be past the littler ones' bedtime. Most of them were in their pajamas, but it was clear from their excited reaction to me that sleep was the farthest thing from their mind. Returning their hugs, I couldn't help but imagine their response when the real act showed up.

Only Brandy stayed on the couch when the others hugged me. She still smiled and nodded in greeting, but there was a haunted, hollow look that hadn't been there yesterday during our outing. My heart ached for her. After letting her have her night out, they must have told her the truth today about her mom. I sat down on the other end of the couch.

"Did you have fun last night?"

"Yeah," she said. "It was okay."

"Do you want to see the pictures?" asked Kendall excitedly. She nudged Brandy. "Show her!"

Smiling at her sister's enthusiasm, Brandy produced her cell phone and gave it to me to scroll through. It was filled with the kinds of pictures girls her age like to take, group shots of her and her friends crowded in, some with silly faces. I was pleased to see that it looked like any other school dance. I hadn't been sure what to expect from a church. The shots of her in particular were stunning. Margaret had done a good job with the French twist. One picture showed Brandy grinning next to a cute boy with sandy blond hair. He looked like a smart surfer. I glanced over at her and raised a questioning eyebrow. She nodded.

"Nice," I said.

A knock at the door brought everyone's excited chatter to a halt. Terry looked up in surprise from where he'd been leafing through a picture book with McKenna. "Who on earth is that?" He glanced around the room, as though doing a head count to make sure anyone who might possibly stop by was already here. I suppose with that many daughters, there was always the risk of losing track of one. Ian, Margaret, Seth, and I were also accounted for. There weren't too many others who would drop in unannounced.

"I don't know," I said cheerfully. "Seth, why don't you answer the door and see?"

Seth immediately picked up on the tone in my voice. He shot me a questioning look but walked over to the door anyway. He turned the knob and leaped back in astonishment when Carter burst in through the door.

Well, I was taking it on faith that it was Carter, based on our earlier conversation. Because really, the man who entered the living room looked nothing like the disreputable angel I knew. In fact, he didn't look like any of the Santas I knew. He looked better. There was magic in the way he moved his round frame. His red suit seemed to shimmer, and his rosy cheeks looked like he'd just come in from the North Pole, not a dreary Seattle winter.

He had out-Santa'ed Santa.

"Ho ho ho!" he bellowed, in a voice that filled the entire house. "Merry Christmas!"

Dead silence and wide eyes met him for a few moments. Then Kendall and the twins began squealing in delight as they ran over to him. "Santa! Santa!"

"What are you doing here?" demanded Kendall. "You aren't contractually obligated to come here until Christmas Eve."

"True," he said in a booming voice that I still couldn't believe was Carter's. "But I have to find out what you want for Christmas, don't I?"

This was met with more oohs and ahhs, and the twins urged him to sit down on the couch. Brandy scrambled out of the way, and Kendall immediately took her turn first, claiming Santa's lap.

Margaret and Terry looked like they were going to burst into tears. Ian looked dumbfounded. Seth caught my arm and pulled me to the side.

"Is that one of the guys you work with?" he whispered.

I grinned. "In a manner of speaking. It's Carter."

Seth did a double take, wearing the amazement I'd felt earlier. "Really? But how . . . I mean . . . even his body . . ."

"Mysterious ways," I replied.

Kendall was rattling off a list of board games and economics books. Nearby, the twins stood quivering with excitement, eager for their turn but too well bred to show bad manners in front of Santa. After a few subscriptions to prominent business magazines and newspapers, Terry gently cut Kendall off and suggested she let her sisters take a turn. Kendall agreed eagerly, but not before throwing her arms around Carter and thanking him.

"Okay," said Seth, drawing me near. "This was kind of amazing. Not that I should be surprised by anything you do anymore." He kissed my forehead. "We definitely have to make the most out of your last month. If we're going to be apart for a long time, then we have to find a way to work around my schedule here."

I started to protest and tell him not to change his plans with the family because of me but stayed silent instead. Some desperate part of me wondered, what did any of it matter? If Hell wanted us apart, then we couldn't stand against that. "A long time" would become "never." Maybe I really should be trying harder to maximize these last precious days. And yet if I did . . . would that make Hell work harder against us?

Glancing up, I saw Morgan had now replaced McKenna on Carter's lap. They were having a discussion on the virtues of two different kinds of pony action figures. Morgan wasn't sure what kind she wanted.

"Princess Ponies come in more colors," she told him seriously.

"True," he said. "But some of the Power Prism Ponies are unicorns. And you can do more stuff with their hair."

Across the room, I saw Kayla curled up in a chair, watching Carter raptly but making no moves to talk to him. Slipping away from Seth, I walked over and knelt beside her.

"Are you going to tell Santa what you want?" I asked in a very soft voice.

It took Kayla several moments to tear her gaze from him. "He's not Santa," she said. I was grateful she spoke as quietly as me. No one else heard.

"Of course he is," I said. "Who else would he be?"

"He's not Santa." She smiled and studied him again. "He's beautiful. He's more beautiful than anything."

No human could see an angel in his or her true form, unless the angel revealed it. Even then, a human would be destroyed by it. No, Kayla wasn't seeing Carter's true form, not exactly, but she was seeing *something*. Some piece of his true nature. I felt a moment of envy, wondering what it was she saw, what her senses allowed her that mine didn't. Whatever it was, I'd never know, but the enchanted look on her face made it clear it was wonderful.

"Beautiful," she repeated. She looked back at me. "Can he stop the Darkness?"

"He'll try," I said. Not the entire truth, but it would have to suffice. "Can you pretend he's Santa? Tell him what you want for Christmas?"

She nodded solemnly, just as Morgan finished and Carter beckoned toward us. I walked Kayla over. I helped her onto his lap, and he glanced up at me with twinkling gray eyes. Those, if nothing else, were definitely Carter's. I stepped back and let them talk. Kayla continued staring adoringly at him, but no one except me knew what truly captivated her. She looked like any other child starstruck by Santa as she related her list, making no mention of his beauty or supernatural creatures prowling through her home at night.

Leaving them to it, I quietly went upstairs and peered in Andrea's room. She was awake, reading a book. Dark circles hung under her eyes, and her face looked gaunter than last time. She nonetheless gave me a cheery smile.

"Georgina," she said. "I should've known you were the source of all that commotion."

I laughed. "Not all of that. A friend of mine is here, playing Santa for the girls. He's taking their Christmas orders right now."

Her expression softened, resembling the near tears I'd seen on the others' faces. "That's very sweet of him. And of you."

"Would you like to meet him before he leaves?" I asked.

Andrea grimaced and absentmindedly patted her hair. "Yes, in theory . . . but Lord. I look terrible."

"Believe me," I said. "He doesn't care."

When I went back downstairs, Kayla had finished, and Carter was trying to get a list out of Brandy who told him point-blank there was no way she was getting on his lap.

"I think you have plenty to work on with their orders," she told him good-naturedly.

"And there's nothing you want?" he asked in his best echoing Santa voice.

"Nothing you can give, I'm afraid," she said. Her smile faltered. "But thanks."

Carter peered at her with that piercing look he sometimes used on me, the one that seemed to look right inside me. "No," he agreed. "You're right. But I can give you all my prayers. And my hopes for the best."

Brandy stared at him, caught up in that gaze, and simply nodded. I don't think she knew what a powerful thing it was, for an angel to offer all of his prayers, but she most certainly sensed the sincerity and intention in his words. "Thanks," she repeated.

I caught hold of Carter's arm. "Their mom wants to meet you, Santa."

He stood up and followed me to the stairs. We passed Ian along the way, who watched us condescendingly. "Aren't you going to ask what *I* want?"

Carter paused and looked him over from head to toe. "Sorry. My workshop doesn't do shabby chic." Carter continued following me, despite Ian's protest that his style was "vintage" and that "shabby chic is for wannabes."

If Andrea felt insecure at the thought of meeting a stranger, she did a good job of hiding it. Indeed, when Carter walked into her bedroom, a little awe passed over her face, reminding me of Kayla. Andrea couldn't see what her daughter had, but I think she sensed some of Carter's grace. He came to a halt at the foot of her bed and took of his red hat in a genteel style, revealing rows of white curls.

"This is my friend Carter," I said, after first making sure no one small had followed us.

"Mrs. Mortensen," he said, dropping the showmanship. "It's very nice to meet you."

She smiled, and the joy in it made her beautiful, despite her weary state. "Nice to meet you too. Thank you for coming over and seeing the girls."

Their exchange was brief. He said something nice or funny about each girl, making Andrea's smile grow and grow. She in turn couldn't stop thanking him. When the pleasantries were finally done, I bid her farewell and stepped outside the room with Carter. I closed the door and was about to head downstairs when he caught my hand.

"Did you see what you needed to?" I asked quietly.

He nodded, face grave, looking more like Carter than ever.

"You were right. Her condition was made worse—by a demon."

"Can you tell which demon?" I asked. I knew Jerome didn't have my best interests at heart, but it was a hard thing to think of him purposely harming those I cared about.

"No," said Carter. "But it probably wasn't Jerome. It's the kind of dirty work a minor demon would do. I can also tell you that her illness, originally, was natural. Nothing gave this to her."

"They just made her relapse when she was starting to get better." *To get to me. To keep Seth busy.*

Carter nodded.

"Okay. Thank you for coming here tonight. I appreciate it." I started to turn, and he again stopped me.

"Georgina . . ." There was an odd, troubled note in his voice, one I didn't usually associate with confident, laconic Carter. "Georgina, I've told you over and over that there are rules about what I can and can't do, how much I can be involved. As a general rule, I'm really not supposed to do too much active interference in mortal lives."

"I understand," I said.

"But what happened to her . . ." He frowned slightly. "That was another breaking of the rules, something that shouldn't have happened. And in this situation, two wrongs can make a right."

I stared up at him in amazement. "What are you saying?"

"I'm saying that I can heal her. I can't completely eradicate the cancer, but I can take it back to the level it was at before she was harmed this week. I can undo what *they* did to her and clean the slate."

My jaw wanted to drop. "That . . . that would be amazing!" Carter still looked sad, and I couldn't figure out why. Did he feel like he was violating a rule, even if he was righting a wrong? "What's the matter?"

He sighed. "What you and Roman said earlier . . . about Hell wanting to keep you and Seth apart? About how her condition keeps him here? Well . . . it's possible, this is exactly what they want. She got better, then they made her worse again. Then, if she gets better on her own—or because of me—then everyone gets hopeful again, until they come back and make her worse. I'm not saying they will come back. But that they could. A limbo state like this ensures Seth stays around. If I heal her now—and I will if you want—I might be perpetuating that."

There were two key things I pulled out of that. One was a very, very subtle acknowledgment that Roman and I were right. Oh, Carter wasn't saying for sure that Hell was after Seth and me, but he certainly wasn't denying it either. It was all part of that careful angel way of his. The other thing—the most startling one—was the implication that thwarting Hell meant keeping Andrea out of the limbo they wanted her in. Seth would always be tied to his family if she moved in and out of health. If she completely recovered, he would be free. And if she died . . .

"No," I said. "It doesn't matter. Heal her. I don't care if he stays here forever, so long as it keeps her alive."

Carter nodded, and something shone in his eyes, something a little like pride . . . and sadness. "I thought you'd say that."

He knocked gently on Andrea's door before stepping back inside. "Sorry to bother you," he said. "But I forgot to ask what *you* wanted for Christmas."

Andrea laughed, eventually degenerating into coughing. Reaching for a glass of water beside her bed, she finally recovered herself. "That's nice of you, but I'm too old."

"Never," said Carter. "There must be something."

Andrea was still smiling, but it grew a little wistful. "There is something," she said. I wondered if she'd ask to be cured, which was obviously what Brandy had wanted as well. "I want . . . I want my girls to be happy. No matter what happens to me, I want them looked after and cared for."

Carter-as-Santa studied her with that soul-searching gaze,

and it was as though something passed between them, something I wasn't part of. At long last, he said, "I swear, it will be so."

He walked over to her bedside and extended his hand to her. A chill ran down my spine as he did. *I swear.* Those weren't words an angel could say lightly. I'd thought what he'd said earlier to Brandy was powerful, but it was nothing compared to this. Tentatively, Andrea took Carter's hand. I saw nothing blatant, no blinding flash of light or anything like that. I didn't even feel anything with my immortal senses. But Andrea's face transformed, growing radiant and dreamy, as though she were seeing and hearing the most beautiful things in the world. When Carter released her hand, she smiled at him and closed her eyes, drifting into sleep.

"You healed her?" I asked, deciding not to mention the promise.

"Yes," he said. "She won't remember much of my visit."

"Probably just as—"

My cell phone rang, and I hurried out of the room to answer it before Andrea woke up. It was Roman.

"Hey," I said.

"Hey, are you still with the Mortensens?"

"Yeah, why?"

"Because I think I've figured out how to prove my theory," he said, voice stern and strained.

"I still don't even know what your theory is," I said.

"You will soon enough. Ask Seth how he feels about hypnosis."

Chapter 13

Roman was impossible to live with after that.

He refused to tell me any more details, only that Seth needed to undergo hypnosis and that more would be revealed once that happened.

"But don't you think I should know now?" I demanded, for what felt like the hundredth time the following day.

"I don't want to influence either of you," came the response. "Just in case I'm wrong."

"I thought you said you'd figured it out! You're saying now that there's a chance you might be wrong?"

"There's always a chance," he said pragmatically. "But I don't think I'm wrong."

And with that infuriating response, there was nothing I could do except wait and speculate. I couldn't figure out what exactly Roman planned on doing with hypnosis, but at least it seemed relatively safe. I wouldn't have put it past Roman to say, "Let's stage a trap for some demons and use Seth as bait." There were worse things than being hypnotized into clucking like a chicken, I supposed.

It took a number of days to get an answer. The delay came from finding a time when both Seth and Hugh were available. Despite his many formidable skills, hypnosis apparently wasn't in Roman's repertoire. It was, however, in Hugh's, which I found kind of surprising. When I asked him about it, he explained that he'd once been at a medical conference, during which participants were required to take a certain number of seminars. He'd chosen hypnosis because he thought it would be a blow-off class.

"It was actually harder than it seemed," he remarked. "I did some more follow-up on it after the conference. Dabbled here and there. Haven't put it to much use since then, aside from an ill-fated date last year."

"Are you going to be able to do what Roman needs you to today?"

I nodded toward my living room, where Roman was pacing like a caged animal. We were all waiting on Seth to show up, and Roman kept obsessing over small details necessary to create "the perfect hypnotic environment." He was constantly adjusting the lighting and moving the recliner. Sometimes he'd put it in the center of the room. Other times, he'd drag it to the side, where there were more shadows. We'd given up on trying to advise him. He was too irritable and wound up.

Hugh frowned, watching Roman. "I don't know. What he asked me to do . . . well, it's pretty basic, as far as technique goes. It's what he wants me to do with it that's kind of wacky. I've read up on it a little this week, and honestly . . . I don't know if it's going to work."

I still didn't know what "it" was and had resigned myself to patience. Seth arrived shortly thereafter, mood bright and optimistic. Andrea's improvement after Carter's visit had been remarkable, and it was affecting everyone in the household. I crossed my fingers every day that Hell wouldn't send someone back to undo what Carter had done. Seth gave me a half hug and kissed me on the lips, a further sign of his good mood since he was usually so reserved in front of others.

"You missed a good time," he told me. He was wearing a *Princess Bride* shirt today. "I took Kendall and the twins Christmas shopping. They got Ian some used copies of *The Metamorphosis* and *Candide*."

"He's into those?" I asked. "I mean, they're great books, but I just never thought of them as his thing."

"Well, they aren't mainstream best sellers—like *some people's* sellout books—so he's into the elitist appeal. He likes to go to coffee shops—obscure ones that you've never been to, naturally—and pretend to read counterculture literature. He'll be glad to have the new material."

Seth's amusement faded as he took in the living room, with all its drawn shades and Roman carefully arranging the recliner (again). Noticing our attention, Roman paused and glanced between the three of us. "I wasn't sure what background noise would work best, so I loaded a few different things onto my iPod. I've got ocean waves, wind chimes, and white noise."

Hugh shrugged. "Makes no difference to me. I'm not the one being hypnotized."

"I'm still not sure I *can* be hypnotized," said Seth. "But if it doesn't matter . . . hmm, are there seagulls with the ocean waves?"

"Yes," said Roman.

"Then let's go white noise."

Roman obligingly started it up, filling the room with what sounded more like faulty radio reception than soothing neutral sounds. "Maybe you should keep it at a low volume," I suggested delicately. "You know, you don't want it to be so soothing that Seth falls asleep."

Roman looked dubious, but at a nod from Seth, the volume decreased. I might not understand how hypnotizing Seth was going to play into Hell's greater plans, but so long as Roman believed it was necessary, Seth got to call the shots. Seth gave me a quick hand squeeze and a smile that was meant to be reassuring. He didn't like immortal affairs but had accepted this crazy venture for me. Following Roman's direction, Seth settled himself into the recliner and eased it back. Hugh pulled up a stool near Seth, but Roman and I sat on the periphery of the living room. Hypnosis required a minimum of distractions, which we clearly were. I'd even had to lock the cats up in my bedroom earlier, to make sure

Aubrey and Godiva didn't decide to jump on Seth's lap mid-session.

"Okay," said Hugh, after clearing his throat. "Are you ready?" He took out a small notepad, filled with his illegible writing. It was the most low-tech thing I'd seen him use in a while.

"Ready as I'll ever be," said Seth.

Hugh glanced at Roman and me briefly, perhaps in case we had a last-minute change of heart, and then returned to the notepad. "Okay, close your eyes and take a deep breath. . . ."

I was familiar with some of the basics of hypnosis, and the exercises that Hugh began with were pretty standard. Although Seth had been joking, I too honestly wondered if he could be hypnotized. Part of his nature as a writer was to focus on all the details of the world, making it difficult to hone in on one thing sometimes. Of course, he could also show single-mindedness for his work, and that was the attribute that soon came out. After a few minutes of guided breathing, it became clear that Seth was definitely growing more and more relaxed. I almost thought he'd actually fallen asleep, until Hugh began asking him questions. Seth responded, eyes closed, voice perfectly steady.

"I want you to go back," said Hugh. "Back in your memories. Go past your thirties, into your twenties. From there, think about your college years. Then high school." He allowed a pause. "Are you thinking about high school?"

"Yes," said Seth.

"Okay. Go further back in time, back to middle school. Then elementary school. Can you remember a time before then? Before you started school?"

There was a slight delay before Seth spoke. Then: "Yes."

"What is your earliest memory?"

"In a boat, with my father and Terry. We're on a lake."

"What are they doing?"

"Fishing."

"What are you doing?"

"Watching. Sometimes I get to help hold a pole. But mostly I just watch."

I felt a knot form in my stomach. I didn't fully understand Roman's strategy here, but there was something terribly personal and vulnerable about what we were doing, listening to these memories. Seth rarely spoke of his father, who had passed away when Seth was in his early teens, and it seemed wrong to "make" him do it in this state.

"Go back even further. Can you remember anything before that? Any earlier memories?" asked Hugh. He seemed uneasy, a sharp contrast to Seth's utter calmness.

"No."

"Try," said Hugh. "Try to go back further."

"I . . . I'm in a kitchen. The kitchen at our first house, in a high chair. My mom's feeding me, and Terry's walking through the door. He runs to her and hugs her. He's been gone all day, and I don't understand where he's been."

School, if I had to guess. I tried to put an age on this memory, using what I knew of the age difference between the brothers. How long did kids stay in high chairs? And how young would he have to be to not understand the concept of school? Three? Two?

"That's great," said Hugh. "That's really great. Now keep going even more. Go back to something even earlier."

I frowned, thinking they were kind of pushing it now. I was no expert in human memory, but I thought I'd once read about how two was the age when memories really began forming. Seth seemed to struggle with this as well, frowning despite his otherwise calm exterior.

"Okay," he said. "I've got one."

"Where are you?" said Hugh.

"I don't know."

"What do you see?"

"My mother's face."

"Anything else?"

"No. That's all I remember of that."

"That's okay," said Hugh. "Now find something else before that. Any memory. Any image or sensation."

"There's nothing," said Seth.

"Try," said Hugh, not looking nearly as confident as he sounded. "It doesn't matter how vague it is. Anything you can remember. Anything at all."

"I . . . there's nothing," said Seth, the frown deepening. "I can't remember anything before that."

"Try," repeated Hugh. "Go further back."

This was getting ridiculous. I opened my mouth to protest, but Roman caught hold of my arm, silencing me. I glared at him, hoping I could convey all my frustrations at what they were doing to Seth in one look. Roman simply shook his head and mouthed *Wait.*

"I remember . . . I remember faces. Faces looking at me. Everyone's so much bigger than me. But they're mostly shadows and light. I can't see . . . can't comprehend much detail." Seth paused. "That's it. That's all there is."

"You're doing good," said Hugh. "You're doing great. Just listen to the sound of my voice, and keep breathing. We need to go back even earlier. What do you remember before that? Before the faces?"

"Nothing," said Seth. "There's nothing there. Just blackness."

Roman shifted in his chair, going rigid. He leaned forward, eyes bright and excited. Hugh glanced over questioningly, and Roman gave an eager nod. Swallowing, Hugh turned back to Seth.

"I need you . . . to go past the blackness. Go to the other side of it."

"I can't," said Seth. "It's a wall. I can't cross it."

"You can," said Hugh. "Listen to my voice. I'm telling you, you can. Push back in your memories, past the memories of this life, to the other side of the blackness. You can do it."

"I . . . I can't—" Seth cut himself off. For a moment, there was no other sound save the white noise on Roman's iPod, though it was a wonder I couldn't hear the pounding of my own heart. The frown that had been intensifying on Seth's face abruptly smoothed out. "I'm there."

Hugh shifted awkwardly, disbelief registering on his face. "You are? What are you doing? Where are you?"

"I . . ." The frown returned, but it was different in nature. It was distress from the memory itself, not the effort. "I'm bleeding. In an alley."

"Are you . . . are you Seth Mortensen?" Hugh's voice was a whisper.

"No."

"What's your name?"

"Luc." The frown smoothed again. "And now I'm dead."

"Go back to the alley," said Hugh, regaining his courage. "Before you . . . before, um, Luc died. How did it happen? Why were you bleeding?"

"I was stabbed," said Seth. "I was trying to defend a woman. A woman I loved. She said we couldn't be together, but I know she didn't mean it. Even if she didn't, I still would've died for her. I had to protect her."

It was about that point that I stopped breathing.

"Where are you?" Hugh reconsidered his question. "Do you know the year?"

"It's 1942. I live in Paris."

Roman reached across me to a stray catalog on a chair. Producing a pen, he scrawled something on the catalog's cover and then handed it to Hugh. Hugh read it and then gently placed it on the floor.

"Tell me about the woman," he said to Seth. "What's her name?"

"Her name is Suzette."

Someone let out a strangled gasp. Me. I stood up then, and Roman jerked me back down. A million protests sprang to my lips, and he actually had the audacity to clamp a hand over my mouth. He shook his head sharply and hissed in my ear, "Listen."

Listen? *Listen?* He had no idea what he was asking. He had no idea what he was hearing. For that matter, I wasn't sure either. All I knew was that there was no way this could be happening. Much like the night I'd gotten into bed with Ian, I had the surreal feeling that the only way any of this could be real was if I'd accidentally stumbled into someone else's life.

"Tell me about Suzette," said Hugh.

"She has blond hair and blue eyes," said Seth levelly. "She moves like music, but none of the music I make can compare to her. She's so beautiful . . . but so cruel. Not that I think she means to be. I think she believes she's helping."

"Go back now," said Hugh. "Back to your childhood, Seth—I mean, Luc. Go back to your earliest memories as Luc. Are you there?"

"Yes," said Seth.

"What do you see?"

"My mother's funeral, though I don't understand it. She was sick."

"Okay. I need you to go back again, younger and younger, back until you hit more blackness. Can you do that? Can you find it again?"

Again, the rest of us held our breath, waiting for Seth to respond. "Yes," he said.

Hugh exhaled. "Go to the other side of that blackness, back before Luc. You can cross it. You did it before."

"Yes. I'm there."

"What is your name now?"

"My name is Etienne. I live in Paris . . . but it's a different Paris. An earlier Paris. There are no Germans here."

"What do you do for a living?"

"I'm an artist. I paint."

"Is there a woman in your life? Girlfriend? Wife?"

"There's a woman, but she's none of those. I pay to be with her. She's a dancer named Josephine."

I began to feel ill. The world was spinning, and I lowered my head, willing everything to settle back to its rightful order. I didn't need to hear Seth next describe Josephine. I could've done it down to the last curl.

"Do you love her?" Hugh asked Seth.

"Yes. But she doesn't love me back."

"What happens to her?"

"I don't know. I ask her to marry me, but she says she won't. That she can't. She tells me to find someone else, but there *is* no one else. How can there be?"

Hugh had no answer for that, but he had his rhythm now. He kept repeating the pattern, pushing Seth back further and further through impossible memories, always crossing that black wall, always asking Seth's name and location, where he was, and if there was a woman who'd broken his heart.

"My name is Robert. I live in Philadelphia, the first of my family born in the New World. We run a newspaper, and I love a woman who works for us. Her name is Abigail, and I think she loves me too . . . but she disappears one night without a word."

"My name is Niccolò. I'm an artist in Florence. It's 1497 . . . and there's this woman . . . this amazing woman. Her name is Bianca, but . . . she betrays me."

"My name is Andrew. I'm a priest in southern England. There's a woman named Cecily, but I can't allow myself to love her, not even when the plague takes me . . ."

On and on it went, and with each step Hugh helped Seth take back, part of my heart broke. All of this was impossible. Seth couldn't have lived all these lives and times he was describing—and not just because of the obvious problems of life and death as we knew them. Seth wasn't just describing his lives.

He was describing *mine*.

I had lived every one of these lives that Seth described. I had been Suzette, Josephine, Abigail, Bianca, Cecily . . . They were all identities I'd assumed, people I'd become when Hell had transferred me to new places over the centuries. I would reinvent myself, take on a new name, appearance, and vocation. For every one of my identities Seth mentioned, I had lived a dozen more. But the ones he talked about . . . the ones he claimed to know as well, they were the ones that stuck out to me. Because although I'd had countless lovers, in countless places, there were a handful who had struck some part of my soul, a handful whom I had truly loved, despite the impossibility of our situations.

And Seth was touching upon every one of them, checking them off like items on a grocery list. Only, he wasn't just talking about these men I'd loved. He was talking about *being* them. Whereas I had created these lives, he was acting as though he'd been born into them, born as these lovers I'd had, only to die and be reborn again in some other place with me. . . .

It was impossible.

It was terrifying.

And eventually, it stopped.

"That's it," said Seth at last. "I can't go back further."

"You know you can," said Hugh. "You've done it before. Are you at the blackness again?"

"Yes . . . but it's different than before. It's not like the others. It's more solid. Harder to cross. Impossible to cross."

"Not impossible," said Hugh. "You've already proven that. Cross back to the next life."

"I can't."

The thing was, I was beginning to agree with Seth. I didn't think there was anything else he could go back to, not if he was paralleling my lives. I'd jumped ahead of him at one point and made some educated guesses on what he would say, and I'd been right each time. I knew how many great loves I'd had as a succubus, and there were none left. Before Seth, there had been eight.

"Push through," urged Hugh.

"I can't," said Seth. "They won't let me. I'm not supposed to remember."

"Remember what?"

"That life. The first life."

"Why not?"

"It's part of the bargain. My bargain. No, wait. Not mine. Hers, I think. I'm not supposed to remember her. But how can I not?"

It was another of those rhetorical questions, and Hugh looked to Roman and me for help. The imp had been confident there for a while, once the lives began rolling off so easily, but this was something different. Seth wasn't making a lot of sense, not that this had all been particularly crystal clear so far. Roman made gestures that seemed to be both encouraging and impatient, with a general notion that Hugh should improvise.

"Who's this bargain with?" asked Hugh.

"I . . . I don't know. They're just there, waiting for me in the blackness. After the first life. I'm supposed to go on to the light, but I can't. There's something missing. I'm incomplete. My life has been incomplete . . . but I can't remember why. . . ." Seth furrowed his brow, straining with the effort of remembering. "I just know I can't move on. So they make a bargain."

"What's the bargain?"

"I can't remember."

"Yes, you can," said Hugh, surprisingly gentle. "You were just talking about it."

"I don't remember the details."

"You said it was about you being incomplete. Something was missing."

"No . . . someone. My soul mate." Seth's breathing, which had been so steady throughout all of this, grew a little shaky. "I'm supposed to go on with her, into the light. I can *feel* it. I wasn't supposed to live that life alone. I wasn't supposed to go to the light afterward alone. But she's not there. She's not anywhere I can get to now. They say they'll give me a chance to find her, a chance to find her and remember. They say I can have ten lives to be with her again but that one is used up. Then I have to go with them forever."

"This life that you can't remember," prompted Hugh. "You said it's your first life, right? The one that's on the other side of this, uh, extra thick wall of blackness? The life they say you've already used?"

"Yes," said Seth. "That's the first. The one I'm supposed to forget."

"You can remember it," said Hugh. "You're already remembering parts of it, things you aren't supposed to. Go to the other side of the blackness, before the bargain, before your death. What do you remember?"

"Nothing."

"Do you remember a woman? Think about the bargain. The soul mate. Can you remember her?"

Seth's silence stretched into eternity. "I . . . yes. Kind of. I feel her absence, though I don't understand it at the time."

"Have you made it back yet?" asked Hugh. "To the first life?"

"Yes."

"What is your name?"

"Kyriakos."

"Do you know where you are? Where you live?"

"I live south of Pafos."

The name meant nothing to Hugh, but it meant everything to me. I began to slowly shake my head, and Roman gripped hold of my arm again. I'm not sure what he was afraid I'd do. It seemed to be an all-purpose attempt to keep me from interrupting the nightmare unfolding before me, either with word or movement. He needn't have worried. The rest of me was frozen.

"Do you know the year?" asked Hugh.

"No," said Seth.

"What do you do?" Hugh asked. "What's your job?"

"I'm a musician. Unofficially. Mostly I work for my father. He's a merchant."

"Is there a woman in your life?"

"No."

"You just said there was. Your soul mate."

Seth considered. "Yes . . . but she's not there. She was, and then she wasn't."

"If she was, then you must be able to remember her. What's her name?"

He shook his head. "I can't. I'm not supposed to remember her."

"But you can. You're already doing it. Tell me about her."

"I don't remember," said Seth, the faintest touch of frustration in his voice. "I *can't.*"

Hugh tried a new tactic. "How do you feel? How do you feel when you think of her?"

"I feel . . . wonderful. Complete. Happier than I ever believed possible. And yet . . . at the same time, I feel despair. I feel horrible. I want to die."

"Why? Why do you feel both happiness and despair?"

"I don't know," said Seth. "I don't remember."

"You do. You can remember."

"Roman," I breathed, finding my voice at last. "Make this stop."

He only shook his head, eyes riveted on Seth. Roman's entire body was filled with tension and eagerness, anxiously straining forward for the last pieces of info to fill out the theory he'd put together.

"She . . . I loved her. She was my world. But she betrayed me. She betrayed me and tore my heart out."

"Her name," said Hugh, catching some of Roman's excitement. "What was her name?"

"I can't remember," said Seth, shifting uncomfortably. "It's too terrible. They made me forget. I *want* to forget."

"But you didn't," said Roman, suddenly standing up. "You didn't forget it. What is it? *What is the woman's name?*"

Seth's eyes flew open, either because of his own inner turmoil or from Roman breaking the trance. Either way, the calm state of relaxation was gone. Raw emotions played over Seth's features: shock, sorrow, hate. And as he gazed around and reoriented himself to his surroundings, his eyes—and all of those dark, terrible feelings—focused on me.

"Letha," he gasped. "Her name is Letha."

Chapter 14

Seth shot up from the chair, face filled with hurt and fury. It was surreal. For a moment, he looked like a stranger . . . and yet, he also looked like everyone I'd ever known. Everyone I'd loved. Everyone I'd hurt.

"You," he exclaimed, striding toward me. "How could you do that to me? *How could you do that to me?*"

I had never heard Seth yell like that. I cringed against my chair, too stunned to react. Meanwhile, Hugh seemed to come to life. He had been as shocked by Seth's initial reaction as me, particularly since Hugh understood even less than I did about what was going on. He was still undoubtedly confused, but some instinct spurred him to action when he saw Seth advance. I didn't think Seth would've hurt me, but he was kind of scary just then. Hugh grabbed a hold of Seth's arm.

"Whoa, whoa," said Hugh. "Easy there. Everyone calm down."

Roman likewise seemed to suddenly realize something was wrong here. He'd been so excited by the developments, his face aglow as all his theories fell into place. Now events were moving in a direction he hadn't foreseen. He rose, mirroring Hugh's fighter's stance. Only, Roman was doing it defensively, coming to stand in front of me, in case Seth broke Hugh's hold. That didn't seem very likely. The imp was strong.

"How could you do that to me?" repeated Seth, voice still

roaring with fury. "I trusted you! I trusted you and I loved you!"

I had witnessed all of this unfolding but hadn't dared allow myself to really and truly accept it. I had seen the impossible. I had seen Seth relive the lives of men he hadn't known—men he *couldn't* have known—walking back through the centuries of my long existence. Some voice inside of me kept saying, *No, no, this isn't happening. This can't be real. It's some trick of Hell's.* I was working hard not to process what I'd heard because processing it meant accepting it. But with those last words, Seth penetrated something inside of my numb self. He broke through, and I snapped.

"I didn't! I didn't do anything to you!" I cried. I had to peer around Roman to meet Seth's eyes and almost wished I hadn't. They were cold. So terribly cold and hurt.

"You cheated on me," said Seth, straining against Hugh. "Cheated on me with my best friend. . . ." Yet, even as he spoke, I could see him falter. The feelings he'd felt as Kyriakos were real, but he was examining it now as Seth Mortensen. The mixed realities were confusing him. It was understandable. They confused me.

"Seth," I said desperately. "I didn't do that to *you*. Think about it. I love you. I love you so much."

Seth stopped struggling, though Hugh didn't relinquish his grip. Seth's features were still filled with hurt and confusion. "Not to me . . . to him. But I *am* him. I'm all of them." Seth closed his eyes and took a deep breath. What had been reasonable and clear under hypnosis was becoming more difficult to grasp. "How? How is that possible?"

"Past lives," said Roman. "You're right. You were all of them. You lived all of those lives, long before you were born into this one."

"Reincarnation? That . . . that's impossible," said Seth.

"Is it?" asked Roman, regaining some of his confidence now that the situation was no longer escalating. "How do you know? Do you have a direct line into the way the universe works?"

"So, wait . . . what about you guys?" asked Seth. "Are Heaven and Hell not real?"

"Oh," said Hugh wryly, "they're real."

"*All* of it is real," said Roman. "And vastly more complex than any faulty human system can understand." He turned to me, expression softening. I must have looked terrified. "What Seth saw . . . what he lived through. You knew all of them, didn't you? All of those identities?"

I focused on Roman, afraid I'd lose my nerve if I looked at Seth again. I nodded. "Yes . . . they were all people . . . all men I knew in my life."

Hugh frowned. "How is that possible? I can get on board with reincarnation. I've seen enough to believe it can happen. But him always being reborn around you? You running into him—what was it, ten times? That's statistically impossible."

"The things we're dealing with aren't really governed by statistics and probability," said Roman. "There are other forces at work here, forces that guide his rebirth. It was part of his contract, the deal you made as Kyriakos. What can you tell us about it?"

"I don't know what you're talking about. . . . I don't remember . . . I . . . ." Seth shook his head, the anger returning. "I don't want to talk about this anymore. Let me go. I need to get out of here. I need to get away from *her!*"

"Seth . . ." I said.

"But you're the key!" exclaimed Roman. "The key to unlocking Georgina's problems. *You're* the other contract, the one Erik was talking about. You're tied to her, tied to everything that's been going on with her."

"I don't care," said Seth. He seemed to just barely be able to keep his emotions in check. "I don't care about your various and sundry plots! Do you have any idea what I just saw? What I just went through? I'm still not even sure I understand any of it! I don't understand who I am! All I know is her—and what she did to me."

"Seth," I tried again. Or should I address him as Kyriakos?

I didn't know. "Please . . . I love you. I've always loved you. What happened . . . it was . . . it was an accident. . . ."

The look Seth gave me was dark and wary. "It sure didn't seem like an accident when I walked in on you."

"I never meant to . . ."

"To rip my heart out?" he cried. "To destroy my world? My life?"

"Roman," said Hugh carefully. "Maybe we should give him some time to process this."

"We don't have time," said Roman. "Hell can move fast—especially if they find out what we know. If we're going to save Georgina—"

"I don't care!" said Seth again, this time with more vehemence. "I don't care what happens to any of you, and I certainly don't care about what happens to *her*. It's probably less than she deserves."

"She didn't do anything to you," said Roman. "She's been a pretty solid girlfriend, from what I've seen."

"Seth," I pleaded, knowing Roman wasn't quite getting it yet. "I . . . I'm sorry. It was a long time ago." My words were terribly, terribly inadequate, but Seth was tapping into things I'd forced myself to block out—because they were too painful.

"For you, maybe," said Seth. "It happened over the course of centuries. One life for you. But for me . . . whatever you guys did with the hypnosis, it's all here now. All of those lives . . . those memories. Here in my head at the same time. It didn't happen 'a long time ago' for me. It's like it just happened yesterday! All those feelings, all that pain . . ."

"It'll fade," said Hugh, not sounding as though he was certain. "What you regressed through is still fresh, and you weren't brought out of the trance properly. Give it time. Or . . . if you want, I can put you back under and make you forget this."

"And forget *her?*" demanded Seth. "So I can forget what a faithless, conniving bitch she's been to me?"

"Seth . . ." I could feel tears forming in my eyes. "I'm sorry. I'm so sorry. If I could take it back, I would."

"Which part?" he asked. "The part where you proved our marriage meant nothing to you? Or the countless other times you lied to me and broke my heart? Do you have any idea how I feel? What it feels like to be experiencing *all* of that at the same time? Maybe you've moved past it all and don't care anymore, but it's real for me!"

"It is for me too. I . . . I love you." They were the only words I managed to get out, and they still weren't enough. Where was all my usual glib charm? My ability to talk my way out of anything? I was still too choked up on my emotions, still reeling from the fact that looking into Seth's eyes meant looking into the eyes of every man I'd ever loved. I wanted to convince him how sorry I was and explain that having a long life hadn't dulled the feelings inside me. If anything, it had only provided more time for those feelings to sink in and punish me. I wanted to explain to him how I'd felt during that first transgression and how it had been a poor reaction to feelings I didn't know how to process as a scared young woman. I wanted to explain that most of my actions since then, especially the times I'd pushed away other lovers, had been weak attempts at protecting them.

There was so much I wanted to say, but I just didn't have the words—or courage—to get any of it out. So, I remained silent, and the tears spilled out of my eyes.

Seth took a deep breath, forcing. "Let me go, Hugh. I won't hurt her. I don't want anything to do with her. I just want to go home. I need to get out of here."

"Don't," said Roman. "We need him. We need more answers, so that we can understand the contracts."

"Hugh, let him go." I barely recognized the voice as my own. Roman looked at me incredulously.

"We need him," he repeated.

"He's done enough," I said flatly. In my head, Seth's words echoed: *I don't want anything to do with her.* "We've done enough *to* him." When nobody reacted, I met Hugh's gaze squarely. "Do it. Let him go."

Hugh glanced between Roman and me and then made a decision. Still keeping hold of Seth's arm, Hugh steered him away from us and walked him to the door. Roman made more protests and took a few steps toward them, but I remained frozen where I was. I didn't look behind me, not even when I heard the door slam. Hugh returned, and Roman slumped back into his chair, sighing with frustration.

"Well," he said. "Once he calms down, we'll get him back and talk things out."

"I don't think he's going to calm down," I said, staring off at nothing. *I don't want anything to do with her.*

"He's just in shock," said Roman.

I didn't answer. Roman didn't know. Roman didn't understand the full scope of our history together. He hadn't seen Kyriakos's face after my betrayal, the grief that had been so deep it had nearly driven him to suicide. That was part of why I'd become a succubus, using my soul to purchase peace for him in the form of forgetfulness. It was the only way to save him. But if he remembered everything now, if he really was Kyriakos reborn . . . then, no. He wasn't "just in shock." I had done a terrible, terrible thing to him, and his outrage wasn't unfounded.

A shiver ran through me as I thought about the instant connection I'd had with Seth, the feeling like I'd always known him. It was because I *had* always known him. Life after life. I'd always felt like we were bound into something greater than ourselves . . . and we were. Something great and terrible.

Hugh dragged up a chair and sat across from me. He caught hold of one of my hands. "Sweetie, I swear to you, I had no clue any of that would happen."

I gave him a halfhearted squeeze back. "What . . . what did you think would happen?"

Hugh glanced at Roman. "He asked me if I could hypnotize Seth and attempt some past life regression. I had no idea what it was for. Fuck, I had no idea it would really work, let alone walk us through *nine* emotionally damaged lives. Ten, since we now seemed to have fucked up this one."

I felt hollow inside, hollow and aching. I turned to Roman, astonished I could manage any sort of reasonable discussion when my world had just been destroyed. "How did you know it would happen? How did you figure all of this out?"

"I only figured some of it out," said Roman. "It was actually your stupid Santa stuff that tipped me off. About how that guy was worried about Santa being in two places at once?" He scoffed and raked a hand through his hair. "I started thinking about how everyone says your contract is fine and how Erik had mentioned a second contract. We'd already deduced Hell wanted you and Seth apart, but why? And I thought, what if it's like the Santa thing? There's nothing wrong with your contract or Seth's in and of themselves, but together, something goes wrong."

"How did you even know Seth had a contract?" asked Hugh.

"Well, that's the thing. I didn't. And since Seth had never mentioned it before, it seemed he didn't know he had one either. And how could that be? I started thinking maybe it was because he hadn't made the contract in this life. I thought maybe Hell had a long game going on with him across lives, and hence . . . the hypnosis."

"Jesus Christ," said Hugh, shaking his head. "You made a fuckload of deductions there."

"And they were right," said Roman. "Georgina and Seth both have contracts with Hell. And those contracts don't work together."

"Why not?" I asked.

That zealous gleam was back in Roman's eye. "What were we able to deduce about Seth's contract? What did he get?"

The only thing I'd deduced was that Seth was never going to speak to me again. When I refused to answer, Hugh obligingly played student to Roman's teacher. "He got ten lives instead of one. The gift of reincarnation."

"Why?" asked Roman.

"To find Georgina," said Hugh. He paused, and I guessed he was replaying what Seth had described. "It sounds like he died in that first life, and when the time came for his soul to move on, he was aware of missing her. I'm guessing Hell wouldn't have gotten his soul then, so they made the deal to give him nine more chances to find Georgina and be reunited with her."

"He did find me," I said flatly. "Over and over." *Betrayal after betrayal.*

"Yes," said Roman. "And you were drawn to him without even realizing it. He certainly seemed to fit your dreamy artistic type each time. But you never made it work out."

"Which Hell was probably hoping for," said Hugh. The imp in him was coming out, puzzling over how a contract like this would have been designed. "Hell has to be fair, but they always want an advantage. So, they probably went into the deal thinking a guy hoping to make amends with his soul mate could never do it if she was a succubus. Seth—or who-ever—certainly didn't know that. He only knew that he was supposed to have forgotten her." He thought about it a few moments more. "There's nothing wrong with that, though. That's hedging your bets on a contract. There's no violation."

"You're right," said Roman. "And that's not the problem." He focused back on me. "What was your deal? What was your contract for becoming a succubus?"

"You already know it," I said wearily. I was tired of the scheming and fallout. I want to crawl off, curl up in my bed, and sleep for the next five centuries. I wanted to renegotiate my contract and have my memory and heart purged of all pain.

"Humor me," he said. "Just tell me the basics again. The deal Niphon made with you."

"Roman, leave her alone," said Hugh.

I waved him off. "Fine. I sold my soul and became a succubus in exchange for everyone I knew as a mortal forgetting about me."

Roman looked so supremely satisfied and triumphant that I wanted to punch him just then. He nodded to Hugh. "And tell me Seth's again, to the best of your guessing."

"At a guess? He gets to live ten lives, all of which will put him near her, giving him the chance to find her and make amends with her. Hell gets his soul at the end of the tenth life."

"And why did Seth make the deal?" prompted Roman, practically trembling with excitement.

"Because he remembered that—" Hugh cut himself off, eyes widening.

"Exactly," said Roman. He shook me in his excitement when I didn't react right away. "Don't you get it? Your contracts contradict each other! In fact, Seth's should never have even been written! He *remembered* you. He knew that you were gone from his life."

"He knew his 'soul mate' was gone," I said bitterly. "I don't think he remembered specifics. You saw how much trouble he had."

Roman shook his head. "Doesn't matter. I'm guessing your contract specifies forgetting you entirely. He remembered. By that happening, Hell violated your contract. Then, they wrote an impossible contract for him, claiming he'd have the chance to reunite with you—which again, implies a degree of remembering you."

"We don't know that exactly," warned Hugh. "We haven't seen the contract and didn't get all the details from him. I couldn't follow if he got anything for patching things up with her or not."

"We know enough," said Roman. "Seth wanted to be reunited with her and make amends. For that to happen, it would contradict Georgina's contract—specifying he forget her."

"I'd want to see the wording," said Hugh. "I'm not trying to dash your hopes. I just know how these things work."

"Fair enough," said Roman. "But can you deny that when Seth called her 'Letha' last month, that was most definitely in violation of her contract? *He remembered*. Not consciously. But some part of him, deep inside, remembered her."

My thoughts were still moving sluggishly, but something clicked into place. "The transfer . . . the transfer came through the morning after I told Jerome about Seth calling me Letha."

"Yes," said Roman. "That's why things were mucked up with it. I guarantee my dear father has always known about your contracts and has accepted them grudgingly, especially if Seth's contract allows for you two to keep running into each other. But, when you told the gang about the name, Jerome had a serious problem. He recognized the violation and tattled to his superiors as fast as he could, making them panic and act quickly—too quickly—to get you out of here."

"But . . . it already happened. Seth remembered. The violation took place," I said, scarcely able to believe it.

"It's like a tree in the woods," remarked Hugh. "It only happens if they're called on it. Neither you nor Seth would have known about the contracts or any violation. You were oblivious. Jerome needed to keep it that way, get you guys apart and kill any chance of you figuring out what had happened."

"Hence the Vegas dream job," said Roman. "It's like we talked about before. Forbidding you guys to be together would've drawn too much attention. A run-of-the-mill transfer, however, would've seemed like business as usual—if not for the screwup. Hell was so anxious to get it going that they sent you the memo before Jerome had a chance to meet with you. I guarantee everything you saw in Vegas was thrown together on a day's notice."

I drew my hand back from Hugh's and buried my face in my palm. "Oh God."

Roman patted my shoulder in a way that was probably supposed to be comforting but mostly made me grit my teeth. "God's not the one you've got to look to right now. Do

you realize what you've got here, Georgina? A once in a millennium opportunity to thwart Hell! You can challenge
them, call your contract into dispute. *And* Seth's. All you
need to do is talk to him, get the exact details of—"

I jumped up from my chair, finally giving way to all my
own grief and fury. "No! Didn't you see his face? Didn't you
hear him? He won't talk to me! Not now, not ever. And don't
say he's just in shock again," I warned, seeing Roman about
to speak. "You don't know what I did, what it was like for
him . . . back then. There's a reason I made him forget! He's
not going to forgive me for this. Never. He didn't then and
isn't going to now. Oh Lord. Why did we have to do this?
Why did we have to make him remember? We should've just
let him forget. . . . Everything was fine. . . ." My frantic pacing led me over to the living room window, where I drew
back the curtains. It was late in the day now, the sunset turning the clouds orange.

"Fine?" asked Roman, coming to stand beside me. "Hell
was creating elaborate ploys to separate you and cover their
asses! And they were killing his sister-in-law to do it. That is
not fine. You and Seth have done nothing but play into Hell's
hands all these centuries. Over and over, you find each other
and lose each other, you bicker and fight, throw it all away
on mistrust and lack of communication. Are you going to let
that continue? Especially when they didn't even give you
what you were promised?"

I rested my cheek against the glass, taking comfort in the
coolness, refusing to listen to Roman's logic. "But Seth didn't
remember until *we* made him."

"Not true. He remembered before that," said Roman.
"On his own, when he called you Letha. That's how this all
started. Nothing we did here changed that."

"He hates me," I said, fully aware of how whiny I sounded.

Roman didn't try to deny it. "People forgive."

I scoffed. "Do they?"

"They do," said Hugh, coming to stand on my other side.
"Seth must have—or whomever he used to be. Your hus-

band. Why else would he have made that bargain in the first place to find you?"

"Because he didn't remember what I'd done," I said. I met Hugh's eyes. "He only knew that I was missing from his life."

"You answered your own question, sweetie. His love for you was stronger than his hate, if he was able to remember the one and not the other."

I wanted to argue with that but didn't know how. "I can't . . . I can't face him. You don't know what this is like. It's . . ." My lifelong fear? My greatest sin? "I just can't."

"We need to know about the rest of his contract," said Roman. "We need all the details if we're going to see this through."

Hugh sniffed. "You keep saying 'we,' but somehow I don't see you being the one filing the paperwork with Hell to challenge her contract." When Roman didn't answer, Hugh added, "Which, by my estimate, we don't need any more of Seth's information for. We already have enough to question her contract's integrity."

"Question its integrity?" exclaimed Roman. "We have enough evidence to blow it wide open." There was that metaphor again. Roman loved the dramatic. "Hell failed to hold up their end of the bargain. They told you they'd make everyone forget. Obviously, they didn't."

"It may not be quite that simple. Hell will question what you call evidence," said Hugh.

"But it can be done, right?" asked Roman. "You know how to do it—to file the necessary paperwork?"

"Well, I've never done it before," said Hugh. "Jesus. I don't know anyone who's done it."

I dragged my gaze from the window. "Don't," I told Hugh. "It's not worth it. You don't know anyone who's done it because no imp who values his job or his life would ever try to get a contract revoked. I don't want you doing that for me."

"Hugh," said Roman, looking over me like I wasn't even

there. "You could free her. You could get her soul back for her. You could end this life she has—sleeping with strangers for eternity."

"Stop it," I snapped. "Stop trying to guilt him into it. *I* made this choice. No one tricked me into being a succubus. They told me what it entailed and what I'd get."

"And you didn't get it," said Hugh quietly.

"It doesn't matter," I said. If I didn't have Seth, one form of Hell was as bad as another.

"I would do it for you," said Hugh. "I'll file the paperwork. Maybe you knew what you were getting into, but that doesn't mean you don't have the right to change your mind—especially if you were played. If you want it, I'll help you do it."

"Why?" I asked, recalling all the times Hugh had become uneasy whenever we'd talked of challenging the status quo. "Why would you risk it?"

"Because you're my friend," Hugh said, his lips twisting into a bitter half smile. "And that still means something to me. Besides, give your pal Hugh some credit here. I might be able to pull this off with minimal punishment for myself."

A strange feeling welled within my chest, tight at first and then loosening. This day had become one impossible thing after another. Somehow, hearing Hugh say it made it more real. I was so used to Roman's ideas and dreams for undermining Hell that at times, it was easy to ignore them. But to hear Hugh saying this might actually work . . .

I swallowed, feeling more tears were on the way. "I can't even imagine that. A world where I don't belong to Hell. I don't know what my life would look like."

"Like anything you want it to," said Hugh, wrapping me in a hug. Behind me, I heard Roman sigh.

"Well, I'll settle for one contract blowing up in Hell's face. I mean, Seth was already Hell-bound anyways, wasn't he? With or without any of this?"

I winced. It was true. Seth's soul—once so bright and shining—had darkened when he cheated on Maddie with me.

He'd come to my bed out of love but had still felt guilty over what he'd done. The mark of sin had tainted his soul enough that were he to die right now, Seth would go to Hell.

Hugh cleared his throat and let go of me, suddenly looking uncomfortable. "It's funny you mention that. . . ."

"Why?" I asked.

"I hadn't seen him in a while and nearly didn't notice . . . but today when he was here, his soul . . ." Hugh shook his head. "I don't know what all he's done, but it's lightened. It's not the spotlight it used to be, but something's changed. Enough of the taint's gone now that I don't think he's marked for Hell anymore."

"Except, he is because of his contract," I realized. "That was the price for all those lives. It doesn't matter how good he is." I felt my legs grow weak again and had to struggle to stay up. Seth had redeemed himself for his sin. How? Probably through the sacrifices he'd made for his family. He'd given up the things he loved most for them—writing, even me. It was a remarkable feat, something few humans were able to rebound from. Usually, those who were damned stayed damned.

But it didn't matter. Seth's soul could shine like a supernova and he would still go to Hell, because it was the same soul he'd had as Kyriakos, the one that had made the bargain to come and find me.

"We don't know for sure," I said. "He didn't make it clear if he definitely signed his soul over or if there was a wager, like he'd get to keep it if he made amends with me."

"Which doesn't really seem like it's going to happen at the moment," said Roman. "So either way, he's damned."

"Unless we can break his contract too," I said. "And we need his help for it."

Hugh gave me a sympathetic look. "Do you want me to try to talk to him?"

I had hated myself for what I'd done to Kyriakos all those years ago, hated myself so much that I'd paid the ultimate price to be wiped from his memory. And after seeing the look in Seth's eyes earlier . . . well, honestly, if given the chance, I might very well have asked to be erased again. I couldn't stand seeing that hate, that disappointment in the eyes of someone I'd loved. I'd hurt him. I'd let him down. I wanted to hide and never see him again because if I faced him, I would have to face the failings within myself.

That had always been a problem for me, I realized. I hated confrontation—especially when I was the one at fault. I'd continually run away from that my entire life.

I forced a weak smile for Hugh, who stood there offering me a cowardly way out. No, I decided. If we were going to get Seth's help, it would be better coming from me. Would he talk to me? I didn't know, but I had to try. For nothing else would I have risked facing that hate and sorrow again . . . but for Seth's soul, I would.

"I'll go to him," I said.

Chapter 15

It was easier said than done, and once Hugh and Roman gave me some space, the full impact of what had taken place really and truly hit me.

Seth was Kyriakos.

Kyriakos was Seth.

Even after witnessing what I had with my own eyes, I don't think I would have believed it if something inside me . . . some gut instinct . . . hadn't told me it was all true. Not that I'd ever suspected it. Not that I'd ever dreamed it. The draw that I'd felt to Seth had been strong, no question, just as the draw to his other incarnations had been. I'd always felt there was something special about Seth in particular, though, and wondered now what might have set this life apart from the rest. Did some part of me—or some part of him?—recognize that this was the last chance for us to be together? Was that where the urgency was coming from? Or was it more about the passage of time and whom I had become? Recent years had made me more jaded about life as a succubus, and I wondered if perhaps that was what made him and our love so precious to me at this point in time.

Our love, which had just blown up before my eyes.

I called in sick to work the next day, something that didn't really go over all that well. It was Christmas Eve, one of the busiest days for Santa and his mall team, but I didn't care. There was no way I could face that chaos, not after what had

happened with Seth. I was told curtly that if I didn't come
into work, then I shouldn't expect to be rehired next year. I
almost laughed and only barely managed to cling to some
shred of professionalism, as I gravely informed my manager
that I'd take that risk. Next Christmas, I'd most likely be in
Las Vegas. Even if I wasn't, I was pretty sure I could manage
to get by without minimum wage and my foil dress.

Finding Seth proved trickier. He didn't answer my phone
calls, and when I went to his condo, no one answered. Neither his nor Margaret's car was parked out front, leading me
to believe they were either doing last-minute Christmas shopping or visiting Terry and Andrea. If it was the former, I had
no way of locating Seth easily. If it was the latter, I certainly
wasn't going to barge into Terry's house and demand Seth
speak to me. The situation might be dire, but I still had my
boundaries.

It would've been so easy to use these obstacles as the
means to dodge talking to Seth altogether. Despite my assur-
ances to Hugh and Roman, I really didn't want to see Seth.
Well, the part of me that was in love with him did. That part
was in agony every moment we weren't together. But the rest
of me didn't want to face that expression again, that terrible
hurt on his face. I didn't want to confront the reality of what
I was.

Despite agreeing to see Seth, I really hadn't been able to
truly convey to Roman and Hugh just how agonizing the
thought of facing up to my sins was. I hadn't been able to
handle the wrongness of what I'd done then; I could barely
do it now. I'd sold my soul, blighted away the memories of all
those I'd loved . . . all because I didn't want to accept the responsibility of what a terrible thing I'd done. You'd think
after almost a millennium and a half, that fear and self-
preservation would have changed. I guess it hadn't.

Or maybe it had. The fact that I was trying to find Seth
now was proof that I had changed a little, enough to attempt
another conversation after his adamant rejection of me.

"Kincaid?"

I glanced behind me. I was standing in line at a coffee shop Seth occasionally patronized to sit and write. Coming here had been a long shot, and I hadn't been all that surprised to see he wasn't around. Last I knew, he hadn't been here in ages, especially with everything going on in his family. Apparently, this place had other patrons I hadn't known about.

"Doug," I said in surprise. I quickly placed my order for a white chocolate mocha and then waved as Doug strolled over to me. He'd just come in, and fine drops of water covered his black hair. "What are you having?" I gestured to the barista. Doug looked a little surprised but only hesitated a moment before ordering an inhumanly sized cup of drip.

"Thanks," he told me, when I handed it over to him.

"You want to sit a minute?" I asked. My original intention had been to grab the mocha and go. I didn't know what Doug's plan was, but some perverse urge made me want to try to get a moment with him.

"Sure," he said, looking a little uncertain. "But just for a minute. I've got to be at work in an hour."

"We don't want you to be late for that," I agreed, settling down at a small table that gave us a fine view of the sleet outside. Seattle wasn't really known for white Christmases. "All those last-minute shoppers trying to get their boxed sets."

The ghost of a smile crossed his face. "You know it. I'm surprised you aren't at work. Is it true? I heard you were, uh, working elf duty at a mall on the Eastside."

I grimaced. "Painfully true. But I quit today."

His eyebrows rose. "On Christmas Eve? That's cold, Kincaid. Think of the children."

"I know. But, well, something came up. . . ." I glanced away, unable to meet his eyes as all my troubled feelings threatened to surface.

"Yeah, I can tell," he said.

I dared a look back. "What do you mean?"

Doug shrugged. "I don't know. Just this vibe I always got off of you when you were feeling blue. You put on a good face for most of the world, but when something hurts you, your energy changes. Christ." He took a big drink of coffee. "Now I'm sounding all New Agey and shit."

"Well, whatever it is, your instincts are right." I reconsidered. "Though 'blue' is kind of an understatement. More like navy. Or even black."

"Mortensen?" he guessed.

I shook my head and glanced away again. "You don't want to hear about that." Although, perhaps some part of him would be glad to know Seth and I were through. It'd be vindication after what we did to Maddie.

"Try me," said Doug. When I didn't answer, he sighed. "Kincaid, I don't hate you. I'm not happy about what went down, but in some weird, twisted way, I do still care about you. If something's wrong, you can tell me. Did Mortensen hurt you?"

"No," I said. Then: "Well, yes, but not without cause. I hurt him first."

"Ah."

I dragged my gaze back to Doug. His eyes were dark and serious, no trace of enjoyment in my suffering. "I've been trying to find him today . . . trying to get a hold of him. But I think he's avoiding me. No, I *know* he's avoiding me."

"You'll patch it up," said Doug.

"I don't know. I don't think we can this time."

" 'This time,' " he scoffed. "Kincaid, the first moment I saw you and Mortensen together, there was something there. I don't know how to describe it. I was always surprised you guys never went out. I *was* surprised when he started going out with Maddie, though they seemed happy enough until . . . well, you know. Until he figured out he should be going out with you." He paused, thinking. "Anyway, I talk a good talk about love in my songs but really don't know shit about it in real life. From what I do know, though, I feel like it's going to take more than whatever argument this is to keep you guys apart."

"Thanks," I said. "That's nice of you . . . but you don't know. What I did was pretty terrible."

"What you guys did to Maddie was pretty terrible," said Doug. "But I've forgiven you."

"You have?" I asked, startled.

"Yeah." He seemed a little surprised by the admission. "I mean, it helps that this neurosurgeon asked her out last week. I can forgive a lot if it means having a doctor brother-in-law. But in all seriousness? I know you guys didn't mean to hurt her, just like you didn't mean to hurt Mortensen here. What you did do is screw up majorly in the forthcomingness department."

"Forthcomingness?" I repeated.

He waved me off. "Whatever. It's a word. If you guys had been honest with yourselves and with her, you could've saved everyone a world of hurt. Keep that in mind now."

"You're a regular relationship guru," I said, earning me another scoff. Yet, as wise as his words sounded, I still didn't think there was any way to fix this thousand-year-old hurt. Before I could muster another comment, my phone rang. I looked down at the display in surprise. "It's Seth."

"You better answer it, then," said Doug.

With a gulp, I did.

"Hello? Yeah. Uh-huh . . . sure. Okay . . . I understand. Okay. Bye."

I disconnected and Doug gave me a questioning look. "That didn't sound all that warm and fuzzy."

"Seth wants me to come to Christmas dinner tomorrow," I said disbelievingly.

"Well, that's a good sign," said Doug.

I shook my head. "I don't think it is. He said he doesn't want to create more upset in the girls' lives and just wants me there for appearances, to make them happy. He made it clear that nothing's changed, nor does he expect it to."

"I guess it's more of a lukewarm sign, then," said Doug.

I sighed, and Doug gently chucked my chin.

"Cheer up, Kincaid. You wanted to talk to him. Here's your chance, no matter what he said. Don't waste it."

I mustered a smile. "How'd you get so wise, Doug?"

He finished his coffee in a gulp. "Fuck if I know."

Doug's words were the kind that you hear in movies and books, the kind that power the against-all-odds comeback we love to see. It was my one chance, my chance to break through Seth's walls and surmount the insurmountable problems between us.

But Seth made sure I never had the chance.

I arrived on my own, laden with presents, and was immediately directed to entertain the girls. Seth made the request, since he and most of the other adults (except Ian, who only marginally counted as an adult anyway) were dug in inside the kitchen, and it seemed very reasonable. Normally, I wouldn't have minded either, except I had the gut feeling Seth was purposely keeping us far apart and constantly surrounded by people.

So, I played with the girls, only half-listening as they excitedly told me about what they'd gotten for Christmas. The only time my brooding thoughts shifted from Seth was when Brandy remarked about how more presents had shown up under their tree this morning than could be accounted for.

"No one will own up to having gotten some of the presents. Mom and Dad think Uncle Seth did it. He thinks Grandma did it," Brandy said in a soft voice, so the littler ones wouldn't overhear her.

"What kind of presents?" I asked.

She shrugged. "Just toys . . . but lots of them. Like, Mom and Dad got Morgan some Princess Ponies. But this morning? There were some Power Prism Ponies there too."

I vaguely remembered Carter and Morgan discussing those very ponies. "Maybe Santa came by," I said.

Brandy rolled her eyes, looking skeptical. "Maybe."

When dinner came, there was no avoiding being near Seth.

Everyone expected us to sit together, and he could hardly ask to move somewhere else. But again, with so many people around, it didn't matter. I wasn't going to bring up any dangerous topics in the middle of Christmas dinner, and Seth knew that. Both of us were silent, simply listening as the others talked excitedly about the day and how happy they were that Andrea was feeling better.

When dinner ended, Seth was the first one up and made a big deal about how all the guys should do dishes tonight while the ladies of the household retired to the living room. Everyone was pleased with this idea, except for Ian and me.

"What is it with you guys and Christmas?" asked Andrea conspiratorially.

I was sitting with her on the loveseat watching as Kendall directed Morgan's ponies into an epic battle to the death. "Huh?" I asked, glancing away from the battlefield.

"You and Seth," said Andrea. "I remember last Christmas, you guys were the same. Isn't this supposed to be the happiest day of the year?"

I repressed a grimace. Last Christmas, I'd found out that Seth had slept with Maddie in an effort to "protect me" from a relationship with him. Yeah. That hadn't been a great holiday either.

"We've got nothing against Christmas," I said bleakly. "Just . . . some issues to sort out."

She frowned. "Is it about his tour? I figured you'd be for that."

"What tour?"

"His publisher wants him to go traveling right after New Year's. Seth had originally refused because of . . . well, me. But I've felt so good lately, I told him he shouldn't waste the chance."

I hadn't known about that. I wondered if it was something that had just come up in the last day or if Seth simply hadn't told me beforehand. The tour would fall before my Las Vegas transfer, and I wouldn't have put it past Seth to decline it in order to maximize his time with me. Well, at least before things went bad.

"That's not it," I said after several seconds, when I realized she was expecting an answer from me. "It's . . . complicated."

"It always is," she said wisely.

I looked past her, toward the kitchen, where I could just barely see the Mortensen men moving around with the dishes. "For now, I'd just settle for a few moments alone."

She made no comment about that, but later, when the guys returned to the living room, she said very casually, "Seth, would you mind going upstairs to get my red cardigan? I left it on the foot of the bed."

Seth was about to sit down—far away from me, of course—but sprang up instantly at the request. As soon as he'd disappeared up the stairs, Andrea nudged me with her elbow. I turned to her, startled, and she jerked her head toward the stairs.

Go, she mouthed. I glanced around, saw no one was paying much attention to me, and hurried after Seth.

I found him in the bedroom, staring around curiously for the sweater that most likely didn't even exist. When he saw me in the doorway, he sighed heavily, realizing he'd been tricked.

"I don't have time for this," he said, attempting to move past me.

I put out my arm to block the door. "Seth, please. Just listen to me. Just for a few minutes."

He stood there, only a few inches away, and then backed up. Since he apparently didn't want to push past and risk touching me, he must have decided distance was better, even at the risk of being trapped in the room. "Georgina, there is nothing you can say. Nothing that can change what happened between us."

"I know that," I said. "I'm not going to try."

He eyed me suspiciously. "You aren't?"

I swallowed, all words and thoughts fading from me as I stared into his eyes. There it was—that look. That same look of hurt and utter devastation that Kyriakos had worn so many centuries ago. It was looking out at me through Seth's eyes.

I nodded. "We need to know about your contract. We just want to know some details."

"To help you?" he asked.

"To help both of us. From what we've gathered, Hell violated my contract when it wrote yours. And that makes the conditions of yours contradictory. We might be able to get them both invalidated . . . but we need to understand yours better."

Seth leaned against the wall, eyes staring vacantly ahead as his thoughts turned inward. "I don't even understand the details of my contract. I barely remember it. . . . I mean, I do and don't. What went down . . . with the hypnosis . . . it's real and it's not."

I started to take a step forward, wanting badly to touch him and comfort him since he was clearly distraught. Caution held me back. "You have to try. Right now, if you don't, then you're going to go to Hell when you die. Doesn't matter if you become a saint before then. That contract brands your soul . . . unless, well . . . we're not sure if there was some condition that if you and I got back together, then you'd be free. That's what we need to know."

"Does it matter?" he asked. "Seeing as that doesn't look like it's going to happen—doesn't look like it was ever going to happen, if all those lives were any indication."

"Well, I mean, yeah . . . it matters in that the more information we have, the better our case."

"Can't you just have Hugh look it up?"

I shook my head. "Not without raising attention. It'd be better if we can get the details from you."

"Well, sorry, then. I don't remember anything more than what I told you. And honestly? I don't care."

"How can you not care?" I asked incredulously. "It's your *soul* we're talking about!"

"I'll take my chances," he said.

A spark of anger permeated the sorrow that had clung to me these last couple days. "There are no 'chances.' It's a done deal. Your soul belongs to Hell. Nothing's going to change it."

"Does it really matter? You *gave* your soul to Hell."

"For you!" I cried. "I did it for you. To save you. I would do it a hundred times over if I had to."

Seth scoffed. "Why didn't you just *not* cheat on me one time?"

"I was young, and I was stupid," I said, amazed at how levelly I could acknowledge that. "I was scared, and I felt like you were so far away from me. Like I wasn't part of your priorities anymore. It was all about work and music for you."

"And you never thought about talking to me about any of that first? You know you can always bring anything up to me."

I sighed. "To *you*, maybe. Not to Kyriakos. He . . . you . . . may have meant well but wasn't always so easy to get through to."

"But I *am* him," argued Seth, though he sound a little unsure. "Er, was."

"Yes and no," I said. "Look, I'm no expert on reincarnation, but from what I know, even though the soul and some parts of the character are constant, there's still, like . . . evolving taking place. You grow and change. That's the point of reincarnation. You're the same person, but you aren't. You weren't perfect back then. Hell, you aren't now. Maybe you—Seth—can handle talking about this . . . maybe after ten lives, you've developed enough relationship maturity. Back then? I'm not so sure. I obviously didn't have it either."

"Obviously," he repeated. His gaze held me for a long time, and this time, I couldn't tell what he was feeling. At least there was no overt hate or anything. Either that, or he'd simply learned to conceal it. Finally, he said, "I meant it. I don't remember the contract details. . . . Just that I would be allowed to keep finding you."

"That's it?" I said. "Nothing else? If there's anything more . . . I mean, the stakes here are huge, Seth. I know you said you'd take your chances, but remember when we're talking about your soul, we're looking beyond the scope of one human life. We're looking at eternity."

"There you go again," he said, with a small, rueful smile. "Making an argument for the sanctity of the soul, a soul you threw away."

"And I told you before, I'd do it again."

"So you wouldn't have to face me and look me in the eye after what you'd done."

"In part," I said. "But also to save your life. To give you a chance at happiness. Because at that moment . . . that was more important than my eternity."

Seth took a long time to answer, and I again wished I knew what was happening behind those brown eyes. Whose thoughts were stirring in there? His or Kyriakos's? Or any of the other men I'd had turbulent romances with?

"You didn't want to face me then," he said at last. "But here you are. Why? To save your own soul?"

"To save both our souls," I said.

Seth straightened up from his slouch against the wall and moved toward the door. "I can't help you. I mean it—I don't remember anything else. Now. If you'd please make some polite excuse to the others and leave, I'd really appreciate it."

He came to stand in front of me in the doorway, and for a half a second, time stood still as we studied each other, only a few inches apart. A thousand feelings warred within me, powered by a thousand years' worth of lifetimes. With a slow nod, I yielded and let him walk past me.

He didn't look back.

Chapter 16

The next week was one of the longest in my life. Every moment that passed was a moment without Seth and another reminder that I'd lost my one great love.

Even if I hadn't quit as Santa's helper, that job would've been done now anyway, so my days were made even longer by their emptiness. Hugh was over a lot that week, and sometimes he and Roman tried to cheer me up or at least distract me. Mostly, they were holed up together, working on my appeal to Hell. They occasionally consulted me on it, but Hugh had most of the info he needed and simply had to put it all together in the appropriate manner. The two of them discussed other things too, mostly having to do with Hell's legal system in general. I didn't entirely understand why, but Roman was very adamant about learning every detail of it. It was like he was trying to pass the bar exam or something.

I tried to preoccupy myself with packing for Las Vegas. Even with my appeal, I couldn't count on anything changing with my current Hellish status. So, I had to go forward with life as though Vegas were definitely in my future. Packing was mindless enough, however, that it didn't distract me so much as just provide more time for me to ruminate and agonize over being apart from Seth.

Packing also had its own pitfalls because I kept running into things that reminded me of him. The worst was when I unearthed a box of keepsakes collected from over the centuries. The most recent addition was a ring Seth had given me last Christmas, just before we broke up. It was a modern twist on a Byzantine wedding ring, decorated with dolphins and sapphires. Even when we'd gotten back together, I'd left it in the box. Little did he know that I also had—in the same box—my actual wedding ring from the fifth century. It was worn with age but hadn't entirely lost its gleam. Looking at them both gave me a weird moment of disorientation as I tried to grasp the idea that they'd technically been given to me by the same person.

During that week, I also received a fair amount of e-mail from the Las Vegas crew. Phoebe, Bastien, Luis, and even Matthias had stayed in touch since my visit, and all seemed to have increased their excitement over my pending move. Messages I would have found so witty and touching a week ago now left a bad taste in my mouth, now that I knew the truth about the transfer. Luis was simply helping to orchestrate Hell's grand plan to keep me and Seth apart, and I didn't trust a single word he said. Still, he *was* a demon, and one could expect a certain amount of insincerity from him. Phoebe and especially Bastien hurt more because they were operating under the pretense of friendship. I didn't doubt Bastien was still my friend, but everything he sent me seemed forced, since it was coming from the orders of those above him.

Matthias was kind of a mystery. I didn't know what role he played here, if he was just a convenient mortal they'd found to take me on or if he was in league with Hell. Many humans knowingly were, in the hopes of grandiose rewards someday. For all I knew, he could be an innocent in all this, just an ordinary guy who thought he'd lucked out in finding a dancer. Without being able to say for sure, I took no joy in his e-mails either.

Notably missing from the Las Vegas gang's correspondence was Jamie. I'd received no friendly "Can't wait to see you!" messages at all from him, something I suspected was also a direct result of Hell's orders. They wouldn't want to risk the topic of Milton again. When I mentioned this to Roman and Hugh, they told me it would be surprising if Jamie was even still in Las Vegas. If Hell saw him as a liability that might inadvertently expose the double-contract snafu, Hugh felt the odds were good they'd simply removed him to prevent me from finding him. If so, I hoped it was simply a matter of a transfer and that the imp hadn't been punished for drunkenly revealing information he didn't realize was dangerous.

On New Year's Eve, Hugh and Roman told me my petition was finished. They presented it to me, a staggeringly huge stack of paper filled with legalese, and showed me where to sign. There was an air of both gravity and pride around them, like they'd just created a painstakingly crafted work of art. Considering how rare this type of event was, perhaps that wasn't such a bad assessment.

I gave the ream back to Hugh, once I'd signed it about fifteen times. "Now what?" I asked.

"Now I take it to Mei and say you gave it to me to submit to Hell. I also claim ignorance about what this is in regard to, but the fact that it went through me tips her off that there's a witness to it all. Not that she'd probably 'lose it' or anything, but . . . well, with demons, it's best to be cautious."

"Are they really going to believe you're a hapless messenger?" I asked.

Hugh crooked me a smile and gestured to the paperwork. "Well, they certainly aren't going to believe you did this on your own. But there's no real way to prove my involvement, and anyway, I haven't technically done anything wrong. I'm an imp. I conduct business for Hell. That's what this is."

Too many days of pent-up emotion took hold of me, and I flung my arms around Hugh. "Thank you," I said. "Thank you so much."

It was all kind of awkward since he was trying to juggle the papers, but he still managed to pat me on the back. "It's nothing, sweetie," he said, seeming a bit flustered. "I just hope it actually accomplishes something."

I stepped back and attempted to get myself under control. "How will we know if it does?"

"When you're summoned to Hell," he said.

"Oh." My heart lurched with fear. "I actually . . . actually have to go there?"

Roman leaned against the wall and crossed his arms. "How else do you think this is going to get resolved?"

"I'd kind of just hoped they'd send me a letter," I said. "You know, like a college acceptance."

Hugh snorted. "Afraid not. If they respond to it, they'll summon you to Hell and hold a hearing to examine the contract, your complaints, and whatever evidence either side can muster."

I wrapped my arms around myself, trying to picture what that hearing would be like. "I've never been to Hell. Have either of you?"

They shook their heads, which wasn't a surprise. Lesser immortals were recruited on Earth, where they then served. We had no reason to visit the realm of our employers, not even an imp like Hugh. Roman, as a nephilim, was on Heaven and Hell's hit list. Walking into Hell would be like showing up in a lion's den and presenting yourself on a platter.

"I always kind of pictured Hell as a cross between waiting in line at the DMV and watching a marathon of *Perfect Strangers,*" remarked Hugh.

Roman shot him a sharp look. "What's wrong with that show?"

Overcome, I hugged Hugh again and then Roman. "Thanks, you guys. I mean it. I owe you . . . more than I can ever pay back."

"Just win," said Roman fiercely. "That's all the payback I need."

Hugh put the papers into his briefcase and slipped on his coat. "I'm going to get these over to Mei now, then head off to a party and drink away the memories of wading through all that legalese."

"You're going to Peter's?" I asked. Unsurprisingly, our vampire friend was holding a shindig to ring in the New Year.

"Nah," said Hugh. "Not much chance of getting laid there. I'm going to a party one of my nurses is hosting."

We wished him a happy new year and bid him farewell. As soon as he was gone, Roman turned to me. "What about you?" he asked. "Are you going to Peter's?"

I knew Peter was counting on it, but it was hard to make myself feel like celebrating. "No. I'm not in the mood. Besides, I'm not sure I want to risk running into Jerome since I'm sure Mei's going to tell him about the appeal. I'll just keep packing."

"Come on," Roman said. "You can't just sit around tonight. It's a new year . . . new opportunities. Maybe even the chance to break free of Hell."

I nodded, though it was still hard for me to imagine what "breaking free" would even look like. It was something we kept talking about, but I really couldn't *feel* it yet. And even though I'd talked a good talk to Seth about how the integrity of the soul and eternity were so much more important than any earthly concerns, it all seemed lackluster without him in my life. "I know," I told Roman. "But any celebrating I do is going to be forced. If I'm going to be unhappy, I'd rather do it in a place where I feel comfortable."

He glanced at the clock. "Let's at least go out to dinner. Dress up and get a good meal. Then we'll come back and watch all the New Year's shows."

I didn't have much of an appetite but suspected if I said no, Roman would consign himself to the same self-imprisonment as me. I didn't want his night ruined because of me, especially after everything he'd done this week. One problem presented itself.

"It's almost five," I said. "We'll never get in anywhere on such short notice. Unless we want to dress up for Taco Bell. Which I'm actually not averse to."

Roman was already reaching for his cell phone. "I know

someone who's a chef at this Italian place in Green Lake. We'll get a table."

Sure enough. One mysterious phone call, and we were on our way an hour later. I hadn't been up for elaborate styling and simply shape-shifted myself into New Year's finery, with an off-the-shoulder satin dress and my hair cascading in perfect waves. Roman had warned me "no black," so the dress was dark purple, which still seemed appropriate for my mood. I paired it with a glittering necklace of white gold and amethysts that had been my Secret Santa gift to myself. I had great taste.

"Have you made any moves to put your condo on the market?" asked Roman as he drove us through the city. "Contacted a real estate agent?"

I gazed out at the bright lights of the downtown skyline. This time of year, darkness came early. "No. I need to. Unless . . ." I glanced over at him. "Do you want to keep staying there? I'll keep it and rent if you want."

He shook his head, a wry smile playing over his lips. "No. It wouldn't be the same without you and those furballs. I'll get another place. Sell it or rent it to someone else."

"Easier to sell," I mused. "Well, in theory. But I'm not concerned with profit, and it saves the hassle of screening and dealing with—" I stopped as a startling thought suddenly came to me. "Hey. Do we have time for a, oh, fifteen-minute stop? Will your friend get rid of our table?"

"Not if I call. Where do you need to go?"

"The U District. Seth's place. Don't worry," I added, seeing his look of alarm. "I'm not going to do anything crazy or lovestruck. I'm not even going to see Seth. Please? Just a quick stop?"

Roman concurred, though his expression said this was against his better judgment. I almost told him his fears were unfounded because I was only going to actually stop if Margaret was home and Seth wasn't. The odds against that possibility seemed slim, particularly with the way my luck tended to run.

The universe apparently owed me a favor because when we reached Seth's condo, I saw her car there but not his. A light inside gave me hope that they hadn't just all carpooled off together.

"Do you need me to come in?" asked Roman, as he pulled into my parking spot.

"No, but thanks. I'll be right back."

I left the car and walked up to the door, hoping some wacky happenstance wouldn't actually put me face to face with Seth. Not that I wouldn't have loved to see him. God, I missed him so, so much. But I knew no good could come of an encounter between us. I rang the bell and waited anxiously. A few moments later, Margaret answered.

"Georgina," she said, clearly surprised. "What are you doing here?" She took in my appearance. "Are you supposed to meet Seth?"

"No, can I come in for a minute? I'll be fast, I promise." She had on a coat, making me think she'd been about to leave. Either that or she was trying to save Seth money on his heating bills.

She gestured me inside and shut the door. "I was about to go to Terry's. Seth's already there." I didn't bother asking where Ian was. He probably celebrated New Year's on January third or something, just to be contrary. "You haven't been around in a while."

I wondered what Seth had told his family about us, if he'd even told them anything at all. Maybe he was just going to say nothing until one of them noticed my absence.

"Ah, well," I said. "Seth and I are having a disagreement."

She clucked her tongue disapprovingly. "You two need to sit down and fix it then."

How I wished it was that easy. I forced a neutral smile. "We'll see," I said. "But the thing is . . . I may be moving. No, I *am* moving. I have a new job . . . and I was wondering if you'd like to stay in my condo when I leave. I remember you saying you didn't want to impose on Seth's space but that you wished you could stick around more to help. Well, now you can. You can have your own place. Mine."

"I can't afford to keep my place in Chicago and pay rent somewhere here, though," she said sadly. "That's been the problem."

"You don't have to pay rent," I said. "You can stay there for free."

She eyed me curiously. "How will you afford your mortgage?"

Yes, how indeed would a poor retail-bound girl like me be able to swing that? "The condo's paid off," I explained. Let her think it was passed down through the family or something. "And my new job pays well. Look, I really don't mind you staying. It'd be worth it to me to know that the girls have you close by to help. I mean, they're going to need a strong woman around, right?"

Margaret took a few moments to answer. "Right. I just thought you'd be that woman."

"Fate has other plans," I said. Wasn't that the damned truth.

"Is that why you and Seth aren't getting along? Because you're moving? I'm surprised he doesn't just go with you. . . ."

"No, no, it's not that at all," I assured her. "It's . . . complicated. If it was as simple as moving, he would when he was able to . . . you know, when Andrea's better." I hesitated, afraid of the answer to the next question, but it was one I had to know. With no contact from Seth, the status of the Mortensens had been a mystery. "How *is* Andrea? Is she still doing well?"

"Yes, she's doing great. We won't know the details for sure until she sees the doctor in a couple weeks, but on the outside, things look wonderful. We're all praying."

I found myself smiling, unable to help my joy and relief. Andrea had looked good at Christmas, but I'd worried ever since then that whatever demon had made her sick before would return one of these days. Again, a doctor would have the ultimate answer, but I took Margaret's own observation as a good sign.

"Thank you," I said. "You have no idea how much that makes my night. I've needed some good news."

"Well, thank you for the housing offer. Can I let you know my answer later?"

"Of course," I said.

I wished her a happy new year and told her good night. Then, I hurried off before I cracked and asked her to deliver some sentimental message to Seth. I liked Roman's company, but I still couldn't shake the wrongness of being out with him instead of Seth tonight. After last year's miserable New Year's Eve, I'd hoped this one would be better.

"That was nice of you," Roman said, when I explained what I discussed with Margaret.

"It's an easy thing for me to do that can help a lot of people," I said. "No reason not to."

He shook his head, incredulous. "You shouldn't even need a technicality to escape Hell's reach. They should fire you out of principle."

The restaurant was tiny but elegant—and packed. I seriously doubted any connections Roman had would get us in, but through some magic, the hostess beckoned us through the crowd and led us back to a cozy candlelit corner. In it was a table covered with an old-fashioned lace cloth, as well as crystal and china place settings—for three.

I looked at her in surprise. "But there's only—"

"Hey, hope I'm not late." Carter suddenly emerged from the crowd, wearing his usual grunge wear. The hostess didn't even blink an eye. Seeing us about to sit down, he smiled. "I guess not."

"What are you doing here?" I asked. I looked to Roman, who appeared just as perplexed as I was.

"I didn't tell him any details. He called while you were inside Seth's to see if we were going to Peter's, and I told him we were going to dinner instead. That's it."

Carter waved it off. "That's as good as a homing beacon. I *love* this place. You're getting wine, right?"

It wasn't that I was unhappy to see Carter. It was just that when Carter appeared, there was usually a reason.

"So you heard?" I said, once we'd placed our orders and dispensed with small talk.

Carter swirled the wine in his glass. We'd ordered a nice vintage that would probably be wasted on him at the rate he drank. "That you're skipping Peter's party? Yeah, I did. Man, he's going to be pissed."

I rolled my eyes. "That's not what I mean. Are you here about the appeal we filed?"

"I'm here to have dinner with friends," said Carter demurely. "But now that you mention it . . ."

"Word gets around fast, huh?" I asked. It had been a couple hours since we'd seen Hugh, more than enough time for him to deliver the paperwork to Mei and enough for her to have told Jerome.

"Oh, I found out from him," said Carter, nodding toward Roman.

"He asked when he called me earlier," explained Roman. "He knew we'd been working on it."

"How?" I asked, startled.

"Hugh and I have had to consult him on a couple of things this week," said Roman. "Nothing that breaks any rules, of course." Carter gave him a mock toast to that. "But enough to clarify a couple points about Hell's fucked-up legal system."

I wondered what they had needed to consult Carter on but doubted they'd tell me. I was also kind of amazed that I'd been so out of it this week that I hadn't even known my legal team had been in touch with the angel. No, on second thought, I wasn't that surprised. My misery had been pretty all-consuming.

"So what do you think our odds are?" I asked.

Carter shook his head. "I can't answer that."

"Because it breaks a rule?"

"Because it's too tempting for me to answer with a joke about a snowball's chance in Hell."

I sighed. "That's not very comforting."

"You're awfully grim about this," said Carter. "I figured there'd be a little more excitement from someone trying to win back their soul."

"It doesn't mean much without Seth," I said.

"Oh, for God's sake," said Roman. He reached for the wine bottle. "You're on the verge of getting your soul and your life back . . . and he's *still* what determines your happiness? You don't need a relationship to be happy, Georgina."

"No," I agreed. "But Seth's not just any relationship. He's tied to my soul. He found me in the world of dreams. We've come together, life after life. I'm not just some girl who needs a guy around. Seth and I are connected. We both have done terrible things to each other . . . but also made great sacrifices for each other. It just seems like only half a victory to get my soul back but not be with the person who's affected it so much."

Roman surprised me by acknowledging the point. "Okay. I can see where you're coming from there."

"And," added Carter gently, "you need to replay your own words there. You and Seth have come back together, life after life. What makes you think you won't again?"

"Well, his recent actions for one," I remarked bitterly. "That and . . . I don't know. Just the look in his eyes."

"Seth had a lot thrown at him all at once. Whose idea was the hypnosis anyway?"

"Mine," said Roman. "And get that accusing tone out of your voice. It was the fastest and easiest way we had to get the information we needed."

"Perhaps," said Carter. "But there's a reason reborn mortals forget their past lives. It's a lot to process, and that kind of regression brings on too much, too fast."

"Hugh kind of said something like that too," I said.

Carter nodded, gray eyes kind. "Don't give up on Seth yet. I think he might surprise you once he's settled down. He loved you enough to always come back to you. He loved you enough to remember you, even when Hell tried to erase you from his mind. That's powerful stuff, Daughter of Lilith."

It was, and I suddenly questioned how fairly I'd been approaching this situation. My old fears had held me back from truly fighting for Seth. I also hadn't really tried to imagine what it must be like for him to have ten people in one mind.

"It could take a while," I said, unable to meet Carter's eyes. "For him to come around, I mean. And it could take a while for Hell to respond to my appeal too, right?" Both men nodded. "What do I do then? What do I do with all that time?"

"You live," said Carter. "You go on with the life you have, with the opportunities you have. You want your soul. You want Seth. If it's within your power to achieve those things, do it. If it's not, accept it and figure out what else you want."

I muddled over his words. "Part of my immediate life is dictated for me. I have to go to Las Vegas."

"What do you want to do there?" prompted Carter.

"Be happy . . . if it's possible." I knew I was being melodramatic but couldn't help it. "If I have to be there, I'd like some sort of chance at a happy life that *I* created. Not a fake one Hell fashioned for me." I thought about it some more. "I'd like to find out if Bastien is my friend first and Hell's servant second."

"There you go," said Carter. "Start there. Focus on what you can control."

"I'd like to help Seth's family too," I added, kind of on a roll now. "I'm already trying to do something for his mom, but before I leave them, I want to do whatever I can. Even if Hell leaves Andrea alone, we don't know how things will turn out. Even if Seth decides he never wants to see me again, I still care about them. And there are still things they need."

"Indeed. That pony collection isn't nearly complete," Carter mused. When I dared a look back at him, I saw that the angel was smiling at me. "You see? You aren't lost. No matter what happens to you, you have a plan. There's still hope."

"You told me that once . . . that no matter what happens, there's always hope. Do you really still believe that?" I asked.

Carter topped off all of our wineglasses. "I'm an angel, Georgina. I wouldn't have said it if I didn't."

"And even though you're counseling contingency plans, you still think I can pull it all off, don't you?" I pushed. "What do you know that I don't?"

"At this point?" he admitted. "Nothing more than you do. The only difference is that I think I have more faith in you than you do."

"You're an angel," I pointed out, throwing his words back at him. "Don't you have to have faith in everyone?"

"You'd be surprised." He chuckled. "I have faith in some more than others. And you? I've always been one of your biggest fans. If you believe nothing else, believe that."

"Here, here," said Roman, raising his glass. "To faith and a new year."

I clinked glasses with them and caught Carter's eye. He winked. Was it enough? His faith? I'd noted before that having him pull for the Mortensens was a powerful thing. Having an angel say he believed in you was equally monumental. But I wasn't fighting an ordinary adversary. I was fighting Hell, the only force that could stand against Heaven.

I've always been one of your biggest fans.

I would find out soon if it was enough. For now, I drank up and tried to have hope.

Chapter 17

In spite of my sorrow over Seth, I was still ready for a storm. It hadn't really registered at the time, but when I woke up on New Year's Day with a wine-induced headache, I accepted the startling truth: I was challenging Hell.

Who did that? No one, that's who. My friends had hinted as much, and I certainly had plenty of myths and pop culture to enlighten me about the futile human dream of thwarting Hell's will. I had my own experience to go on too. I'd signed away my soul *for all eternity*. There wasn't much wiggle room with that. And yet, in spite of all the things I'd seen and all the people Hell had crushed, here I was, daring to say Hell had no claim on either my soul or Seth's.

I expected to hear about it immediately. I expected a huge uproar, perhaps in the form of Jerome showing up in my condo in all his brimstone glory, threatening me for my impertinence. At the very least, I expected a letter of acknowledgment from Hell, something along the lines of, *Thank you very much for your inquiry. We will respond to you within 4–6 weeks.*

Nothing. New Year's Day passed quietly. So did the next. I continued my pattern of packing and making Las Vegas preparations, all the while holding my breath for The Next Big Thing.

I thought something would surely happen a week later, when the long-awaited bowling tournament came around. Jerome and Nanette had flipped for it, and he'd won, meaning we got to hold the match here in Seattle. It saved us from making a trip to Portland, but for the sake of fairness, Nanette got to pick the bowling alley. Rather than our dive at Burt's, she chose a more upscale place, not far from the mall I'd worked at.

I hadn't seen Jerome since I'd filed the petition and was ready now to face his wrath. I didn't know if Nanette's lesser immortals would know about the request, but I felt certain she would by now. She and Jerome might be rivals of sorts, but at the end of the day, they were both committed to Hell winning. I was trying to thwart that and wouldn't have been surprised to find her sharing in Jerome's outrage.

"Good luck," Roman told me, as I prepared to leave the condo. "Remember to watch your footing."

I sighed. "I wish you were coming with me."

He offered me a small smile. "Me too. All that work, and I won't even get to see my students' final exam."

Roman could hide his nephilim signature from greater immortals, but considering the way his kind were hunted, we'd decided it would be best if he steered clear of Nanette while she was in town. Jerome's agreement to let Roman stay was both highly unusual and dangerous. If another archdemon discovered the truth, both Roman and Jerome would be in a lot of trouble.

"I'm afraid of what I'll face from Jerome," I said.

"Don't be." Roman came forward and rested his hand on my shoulder. "You're not doing anything wrong. They did. You're strong, Georgina. Stronger than them, stronger than Hell."

I leaned my head against him. "Why are you so nice to me?"

"Because Carter's not your only fan." When I looked back up, I saw Roman's green eyes were deadly serious. "You're a remarkable woman, just by your own nature. Smart. Funny. Compassionate. But what's really great is that you're so easy to underestimate. I did when we first met, you know. And Hell is now. No matter what their reaction to your appeal is,

I guarantee most of them doubt you have a chance. You're going to prove them wrong. You're going to break the unbreakable. And I'll be there helping you, as much as I can."

"You've done enough," I told him. "More than enough. More than I could have ever asked. Now you get to sit back and let me do . . . well, whatever I have to do now."

"Georgina, there's something you need to know. . . ." His face grew troubled.

"What?" I asked. "Oh God. You haven't heard something from Jerome that I haven't, have you?"

"I—" He bit his lip as he paused, then shook his head. His features smoothed out. "Forget it. I'm just going to worry you over nothing. You focus on bowling tonight, okay? Show those Portlandians that . . . fuck, I don't know. That you're a force to be reckoned with in the bowling alley."

I laughed and gave him a quick hug. "I'll see what I can do. How about we talk when I get back, okay? We'll grab a drink." I knew there was something big here he wasn't telling me, no matter how easily he'd tried to brush it off.

"I'd like that. Good luck."

When I arrived at the bowling alley, Peter nearly sank in relief when he saw me. I think he'd been afraid I'd show up without my Unholy Rollers shirt. Through whatever means Hell possessed, all the other patrons in the alley were playing on one side. The other half was empty, save for two lanes occupied by my colleagues. I was the last to arrive and approached with trepidation, unsure of my welcome.

Jerome was sprawled comfortably in a chair, and while it was in better shape than the ones at Burt's, I'm not really sure it deserved the thronelike airs he was putting on. Nanette sat across from him, looking equally regal. Her pale blond hair was rolled into an elegant coif, giving her kind of a Grace Kelly look. Her dress was a pale blue shift with a fuzzy gray cardigan over it, the innocence of the look clashing with the unnecessary vampish sunglasses she was wearing.

"Ah, Georgie," said Jerome. "Right on time and in team

colors." He favored Nanette with a lazy smile. "Ready for some humility?"

"Yours?" she asked him. "Always."

Neither gave me much more attention than was due for the last person to fill a team spot. No mention of the contract, no mention of my petition. Glancing around and taking in the full roster here, I saw that Mei had also come to watch the spectacle. The demoness was dressed in corporate black, matching her bluntly cut black hair and heavy eyeliner. Only her red lips provided color to the palette. She most certainly knew about my situation, but like her superiors, she barely glanced my way.

Carter was there, which I had not expected. Nanette and her cronies were clearly uneasy about this. Although all greater immortals, be they angels or demons, shared a certain world weariness with immortality and the Great Game, few were able to bond over it so well as Carter and Jerome. Their relationship was unique, and Nanette clearly felt no camaraderie with the angel. Whereas I received little of her attention simply because I was an underling, Carter she ignored as though he didn't even exist.

He gave me a small smile as I sat down, his gray eyes full of amusement. He was sitting with my friends, perfectly at ease, while Nanette's bowling team regarded him warily. I hoped maybe his presence would throw off their game. There were four of them, just like us, though they'd actually drafted Nanette's lieutenant demon, Malachi, to play for them. Rounding them out were a succubus named Tiara, an imp named Roger, and a vampire named V.

"What's the V stand for?" I asked.

He just stared at me, face blank.

They were an impressive-looking bunch, with deep red bowling shirts and sparkling black embroidery that read DEVIL MAY CARE on the back.

"That's not even a real team name," Peter whispered to me disapprovingly. "And those sparkles are just tacky."

Like ours, their shirts were standard button-ups with their names on the front. Only Malachi's was different, with a small designation declaring him *Captain*. I guess he needed to make sure his status was asserted over that of the lesser immortals. There was something lean and sinister about them, and in our baby blues, I felt downright cute and cuddly.

A waitress came by with drinks, and once Jerome had a glass of scotch in hand, he deemed proceedings fit to start. There was a part of me that wouldn't have minded a gimlet or two, but I didn't think alcohol was the best call just now. It had nothing to do with team solidarity or messing up my game. When surrounded by unknown and possibly untrustworthy immortals, it was always a good idea to keep your wits about you. And when you were possibly on Hell's radar for dissension, it was an *excellent* idea.

In my usual lucky way, I ended up having to go first. With all my worries about Seth and the contracts, my mind wasn't exactly focused on all of Roman's good instructions, but I nonetheless did my best to recall his training. I ended up hitting seven and then two pins. Not the greatest, but certainly not the worst. My teammates cheered me voraciously, both because Peter had sent us all a lengthy e-mail earlier in the day about "pep" and because with our track record, nine wasn't that bad.

Tiara went after me, and as she retrieved her ball, Cody whispered to me how she'd gotten in a fight with management earlier because she'd wanted to wear stilettos on the lanes. She'd apparently conceded to wear proper bowling shoes in the end, but unless there'd been a significant trend change in the industry, she'd ended up using her shape-shifting powers to make the shoes more to her liking. They were gold and encrusted with jewels.

Yet those weren't the worst part of her attire. That came in the form of her Devil May Care shirt, which I was pretty sure had shrunk about three sizes since I arrived. The buttons that were still actually fastened looked like they were about to burst. I winced as all that cleavage walked past me, and I wanted to cover my eyes when she reached the lane and bent over unnecessarily far, in order to give everyone a solid view of her ass. Her jeans were nearly as tight as the shirt.

"That is not a regulation stance," declared Peter. He studied her critically for a few moments. "I believe she's trying to distract us."

I scoffed. "Oh, you think?"

"Hey!" Peter elbowed Cody and Hugh who—judging by their gaping mouths—were not catching on to Tiara's ruse as easily as the rest of us. "Focus. Remember what you're playing for: Jerome's good will."

"Nothing wrong with looking," said Hugh. "Besides, there's no way she can hit anything with that—"

His words cut off as Tiara threw. Her ball blasted into the pins and knocked all ten over. With a little smirk and a lot of hip swaying, she strutted back proudly to her seat.

"Shit," said Hugh.

"Ready to focus yet?" asked Peter.

The imp shook his head, still in awe. "I don't think it's going to matter, not if they all bowl like that."

"They can't *all* bowl like that," countered Cody. But he didn't sound so sure.

Noticing our consternation, Tiara favored us all with a glossy-lipped smile. "We can call it quits right now if you want. We can go back to my hotel and have a party." She tossed her highlighted curls over one shoulder, and her gaze rested on me. "I can also give you some styling advice if you want."

"Oh my God," I muttered. "This is why I hate other succubi." I could almost give Hell credit for finding me the only appealing one in Vegas, even if it had been part of a more elaborate scheme.

Tiara soon became the least of our worries as her teammates took their turns. Strikes and spares all around, quickly surpassing our mix of erratic spares and . . . whatever it was Peter threw. As we moved further into the game, I glanced over at Jerome and saw that his smile had vanished, as had his cocky good mood. At least I could feel confident it had nothing to do with my contract.

V proved to be the most startling of the bowlers. Whenever his turn came, he walked up unhesitatingly, didn't even pause or aim, and threw strikes every time. *Every time*. He also never spoke a single world.

"How is he doing that?" exclaimed Cody. He glanced at Carter, who was watching everything with quiet amusement. "Is he using some kind of power?"

"No illicit ones," said Carter. "Just his own God-given . . . er, Hell-given abilities."

I hadn't really been worried about the other team cheating or Nanette helping them. I knew Jerome would keep her in check, and Carter's angelic presence was kind of a safeguard against dishonest activity. But his words struck something within me.

"Of course," I murmured. "He's just using what he's got: enhanced reflexes and senses. He's a vampire. He's physically better at everything." No wonder it didn't seem like he needed to aim. He probably was; he was just doing it really, really fast. I turned to Cody and Peter. "How come you guys can't do that?"

Silence met me.

"Cody's our best player," pointed out Hugh.

"True," I admitted. Cody had learned very quickly, and I supposed the difference in his and V's abilities made sense simply because V had been playing a lot longer. "But how do you explain Peter?"

Nobody had an answer for that, least of all Peter.

Cody actually seemed to draw inspiration from V and the realization that being a vampire should provide some natural ability. Cody's already solid performance soon improved, and I wished Roman could see him. Still, it wasn't enough to save us in that first game. We lost pretty terribly. Since Jerome and Nanette had agreed to "best of three," this meant we had two more chances for redemption. I had mixed feelings about this. Jerome's face was growing stormier, so there was some comfort in thinking we might be able to head off his wrath.

On the other hand, I wouldn't have minded ending this as quickly as possible. Maybe the Devil didn't care, but I was growing increasingly sick of the other team. I was pretty sure Tiara's outfit was getting increasingly tighter and more revealing. Although he never spoke, V's smug expressions conveyed condescension levels that words never could.

And yet, neither of them was as bad as Roger the imp. Every time he got a strike or a spare, he trumpeted his victory with some sort of money-related expression, such as "Jackpot!" or "A penny saved is a penny earned!" Sometimes they didn't even make any sense in the situation, like when he shouted, "It's like throwing pearls before swine!" When he started inexplicably quoting lyrics to "Can't Buy Me Love" at the start of the second game, I really thought I was going to lose it.

Cody nudged me. "He's getting tired. So is Tiara."

I glanced up at the scoreboard. It was a slight change, but those two were showing fewer strikes than spares and sometimes not even getting spares. Malachi remained consistently good, and V remained unstoppable. Over on our team, Peter and I hadn't changed, but Cody had continued—and was succeeding—in trying to prove his vampire skills. Hugh was also improving slightly, a phenomenon we'd seen with Roman sometimes. It was as though the imp needed to warm up in order to remember how to avoid his arm's tendency to throw curves.

I exchanged glances with Cody. "I don't know that it's enough."

"You've done better than this in practice," he told me gently. "I know you've got a bunch of stuff going on, but try to think if Roman was here. What he'd say. Then look at Jerome's face and tell me you don't want us to come out on top."

I didn't really care about Jerome keeping his pride around

Nanette, but my friends' well-being did concern me. I knew their happiness would be directly influenced by Jerome's unhappiness. Sighing, I answered Cody with a resolute nod and tried to step up my game, racking my brains for all the words of wisdom that Roman had given me over the last couple of weeks. I admit, I hadn't always been paying as much attention as I could have.

Nonetheless, something started clicking for me. I was a long way from being a pro anytime soon, but between me, Cody, and Hugh, we slowly began to keep up with Nanette's team. It was so subtle and so gradual that when we won by two points, everyone—including my teammates and me—could hardly believe it had happened. We all stared at the scoreboard in stunned silence. Only Carter was able to get anything out.

"That," he told Roger exuberantly, "is how a bird in the hand gets up before the early worm."

"That doesn't make any sense," said Roger.

Carter pointed at the scoreboard. "Neither does that, but there you have it."

Nanette's cool composure had vanished. I don't know if beating Jerome meant that much to her or if people in Portland just took bowling really seriously, but she immediately demanded a five-minute break. We watched as she pulled her team to the far side of the alley and gave them a talk. Judging from her wild hand motions and occasional expletives, it didn't sound like a very heartening talk. I glanced over at Jerome, who still kind of seemed to be in disbelief.

"Any words of wisdom for us, boss?" I asked.

He considered. "Yes. Don't lose."

Cody was already clinging to Peter's arm. "You have to come through for us here. We barely beat them just now, and you know she's putting the fear of God in them. That alone is going to give them some improvement. If you can just . . . I don't know. Get fewer splits. Do something. We can win this, but we need you."

Peter threw up his hands. "Don't you think I would if I could?"

When Nanette and friends returned, they showed us that they were adding a new strategy to their repertoire: catcalling. Every time one of the Unholy Rollers went up to play, we were serenaded with insults about everything from our appearance to our abilities to our bowling shirts. That last one really set Peter on edge, and Tiara picked up on it quickly.

"Did you pick that up at a thrift store? Oh, wait, they screen their items first. They'd never take a piece of shit like that."

"What's with that color? It's like a reject from a boy's baby shower."

"If your crappy shirts are going to say 'Unholy Rollers,' shouldn't you at least be *rolling* the ball? That was more of a caber toss."

Peter took it all in silence, but I could see him becoming increasingly agitated. Hugh grimaced and leaned toward me. "She's really not that funny. I'd expect better from a succubus."

"At least Peter isn't doing any worse," I said. "He's just getting splits in new and interesting ways."

"Which aren't going to save us, though," said Cody grimly.

It was true. We were staying even with them, but just barely. And when we were halfway through the game, it became clear we were slipping. Jerome was looking pissed off again, and Nanette's confidence had returned.

"Come on, you guys," said Carter, whom I hadn't expected to become a cheerleader. "You can do this. You're better than them."

It wasn't the angel's enthusiasm that changed the course of the game, however. It was when V finally spoke. Peter had just thrown his ball and amazingly knocked down four pins, which left behind a kind of three-way split I'd never even known was possible. We were all taken back.

"You are the worst vampire I've ever seen," said V, staring at the pins wide-eyed.

I don't know what it was about those words that succeeded where our encouragement and Tiara's bad fashion taunts had failed. But suddenly, Peter became a vampire. And not just any vampire. A vampire who could bowl.

From that point forward, everything he threw was a strike. And much like V, Peter didn't even deliberate it. He just walked up and threw, letting his vampire reflexes do the work. He quickly surpassed everyone on our team in skill, even Cody. Really, the only person who could match him was V.

But it was enough, and somehow, against all odds, we won the third game. Hugh, Cody, and I erupted into cheers and traded high fives with Carter. Peter remained much more stoic, however, and regarded the other team coolly. "Don't count your chickens before they're hatched," he told Roger. To Tiara, Peter said, "That shade of red makes you look like you have jaundice." He paused. "And like a whore."

To V, Peter said nothing.

Nanette and Jerome promptly got in an argument, most of which involved her making outlandish claims about how unfair it was to have two vampires on one team and how best of five would be the real determining factor. Jerome bantered back with her cheerfully. He was so smug about our victory, you would have thought he had thrown every ball himself. Seeing her consternation was just icing on the cake for him.

"Well," he said at one point, "we could do two more games, but your team seems terribly worn out. Perhaps once they have some time to recover mentally and physically, we can—"

Jerome stopped and cocked his head, like he was hearing music the rest of us couldn't. A strange look came over his face.

"Shit," he said.

"What?" asked Nanette. She seemed to realize something

other than bowling had caught his attention. Near me, Carter had gone perfectly still.

"I have to go," said Jerome.

And he went. Just like that, the demon vanished. I glanced around quickly, but no humans seemed to have noticed, thanks largely to our part of the bowling alley being deserted. Still, teleporting out like that in a public place was pretty irregular behavior for a greater immortal. Even irreverent demons generally knew enough to be discreet among humans.

"Well," said Nanette. "I guess there's no such thing as good winners. Sportsmanship is a lost art."

I thought that was a stretch coming from her, particularly after her team's verbal tirade. In fact, they soon all degenerated into arguing amongst themselves, each one making a plea to Nanette about how the loss had been someone else's fault.

"Georgina," said Carter, drawing my attention back. The smile he'd worn at our victory was gone. "I think it's a good idea if you go home."

"Why?" I asked. "We should celebrate." For the first time since the fallout with Seth, I actually felt like having fun with my friends. "We need to call Roman too."

"Let's go to my place," said Peter. "I can make up a meze platter in no time."

"Fine, fine," said Carter, casting a glance over at Mei. She was still in her seat, trying to observe all conversations at once. "Let's just leave now. I'll teleport you when we're in the parking lot."

I tried to protest that, but Carter was too insistent on simply getting us all out of there. Minutes later, my teammates and I were headed out to the parking lot, still crowing over our victory and how Peter was the undisputed hero of the night.

"Georgina?"

I came to a halt. There, standing near my car, was Seth.

Even in the harsh light of the parking lamps, everything about him seemed soft and inviting. The messy hair. The way he stood with his hands in his pockets. The Flock of Seagulls shirt that I could just make out underneath his flannel coat.

"What are you doing here?" I asked, taking a few steps forward. My friends had come to an uncertain stop behind me. They all knew about my rocky state of affairs with Seth and watched me nervously.

Seth glanced at my backup and then at me. "I . . . I wanted to talk to you."

"That's not what you said the last time we talked," I said. The harsh words were out before I could stop them. I knew I should jump on the chance to talk, on Seth's willingness to talk at last . . . but some hurt place in me responded first.

"I know," said Seth. "I probably don't deserve it. But . . . I've been thinking about a lot of things, and then there's all this weirdness going on I don't quite understand . . . like, my mom moving in with you? And do you know why all these toy ponies keep showing up on Terry's doorstep?"

"Why don't you come over to our place and have your heart-to-heart there," said Peter. "It'll go better with hummus and wine."

Staring at Seth, I felt my heart ache. This could be it, just like Carter had said at New Year's, about how Seth and I still managed to come back to each other. I swallowed, both scared and anxious. "Maybe I should meet you guys later," I said. "Seth and I can go somewhere and talk first."

"Georgina," said Carter anxiously, "you really need to—"

The car seemed to come out of nowhere, and, considering the way things worked in my world, it might literally have done so. All I knew is that one moment we were all standing around in the dark parking lot, and the next, a car was speeding toward us. Or rather, toward me. I couldn't discern any make or model and certainly not the driver. I probably wouldn't have known him or her anyway. All I saw were rapidly approaching headlights, heading toward where I stood alone, out in the open between my friends and Seth.

When the car hit me, there was an intense moment of pain that radiated through my whole body. Then I felt nothing. My sight shifted, and I had the surreal sense of looking down on my sprawled body while my friends hurried to me and the car sped away. Some were trying to talk to me, some were calling 911. Some were talking to each other.

The scene began to dissolve in my vision, fading to black. And not just the scene. Me. I was dissolving. I was losing all substance. I was becoming nothing.

But as I faded away, as the world faded away, I heard a few last words from my friends before their voices also faded.

"Georgina! Georgina!" That was Seth, saying my name like a prayer.

"She's not breathing," said Cody. "And she doesn't have a pulse. Hugh! Do something. You're a doctor."

"I can't," Hugh said softly. "This is beyond me. Her soul . . . her soul's not here."

"Of course it is!" said Cody. "Souls stay with their immortals."

"Not in this situation," said Hugh.

"What are you talking about?" exclaimed Seth, voice cracking. "Carter! You can fix this. You can fix anything. You have to save her."

"This is beyond me too," said Carter. "I'm sorry."

"There's still one thing you can do," said Hugh. "One thing you have to do."

"Yes," agreed Carter, voice full of sorrow. "I'll go get Roman. . . ."

And then they were all gone.

I was gone.

Chapter 18

The blackness began to lighten into swirls of color, colors that eventually resolved into lines and shapes around me. I gazed around as the world formed and soon felt solidity beneath my feet. My own body was taking on substance again, the light and hollow sensation disappearing. Feeling and movement returned to me, and for half a second, I thought I had imagined everything that happened in the parking lot.

Then I was struck by a sudden and overwhelming sense of *wrongness*.

First off, as I blinked the world into focus, it became obvious that I was no longer at the bowling alley. I was inside a room with vaulted ceilings and no windows. It appeared to be a courtroom, complete with a jury box and judge's stand. All the décor was black: red-veined black marble on the walls and floor, black wood trim, black leather chairs. Everything was very sleek and modern, clean and sterile.

The next thing I noticed was that I wasn't in the body I'd just been in. My perspective on the world was from a greater height. The weight of my limbs and muscles felt different too, and I wore a simple linen dress instead of my Unholy Rollers shirt. Although I couldn't see myself straight-on, I had a good idea which body I was wearing: the first one. My mortal one. The one I'd been born to.

Yet it was neither the body nor unfamiliar room that felt so wrong. They were surprises, yes, but nothing I couldn't adapt to. The wrongness came from nothing tangible. It was more a feeling in the air, a sensation that permeated my every pore. Even with the vaulted ceilings, the room felt stuffy and tight, like there was no air circulation whatsoever. And even though there wasn't any actual odor, I just kept imagining stagnation and decay. My skin crawled. I felt smothered by hot, humid air—yet was also chilled to the bone.

I was in Hell.

I had never been there, but you didn't really need to have been to know it.

I was sitting at a table on the left side of the room, facing the judge's bench. Behind me, separated by a railing, was the audience seating. I squirmed around to peer at it. Right before my eyes, people began to materialize in the seats. They were wildly different in appearance: male and female, all races, various states of dress. Some were as prim and neat as the courtroom around us. Some looked like it had been quite an ordeal for them to get out of bed. There was no uniformity to their appearances. There weren't even immortal auras to tip me off, but I was willing to wager anything that they were all demons.

A murmur of conversation began to fill the room as the demons spoke to each other, a droning almost more frightening than the silence that had originally met me. No one talked to me, though plenty of sets of eyes studied me disapprovingly. I didn't recognize anyone here yet and felt vulnerable and afraid. There was an empty seat next to me, and I wondered if someone would be joining me. Was I entitled to a lawyer for this . . . whatever it was? It had all the trappings of a regular courtroom, but I could hardly expect Hell to be reasonable or predictable. I honestly had no clue what was about to happen. I knew it had to be about my contract, but Hugh hadn't gone into a lot of specifics when he'd said that my case would eventually "be reviewed."

There was a table on the right side of the courtroom, one that mirrored mine in size and placement. A man with iron-gray hair and a handlebar mustache sat down at it, placing a briefcase on the table's surface. He wore an all-black suit—

including the shirt—and looked more like a funeral director than a prosecutor, which is what I assumed he was. As though sensing my scrutiny, he glanced over at me with eyes so dark, I couldn't tell where pupil ended and iris began. They sent a new chill through me, and I changed my assessment of him. Funeral director? More like an executioner.

Once the gallery was nearly full of spectators, a side door near the front opened. Twelve people filed out toward the jurors' box, and I caught my breath. I still couldn't sense any immortal auras in this room. Maybe it wasn't necessary in Hell or maybe there were just too many immortals in here for it to be comfortable. Regardless, just as I'd been certain all the spectators were demons, I could tell that half of the jurors were angels. It was in their eyes and their disposition. There was a way they carried themselves that differed from everyone else, even though the angels were dressed no differently. Also, the angels seemed to be conscious of the wrongness I'd felt in here. They kept glancing around, small looks of disgust on their faces. At first, it seemed kind of crazy that angels would be in Hell, but then I realized that, unlike Heaven, there were no gates or barriers to keep anyone out. And unlike mortals, angels had the ability to leave here when they chose. I suppose it made it easy to do business visits like this. Still, I found myself heartened by the sight of the angels. If they were going to be involved in deciding my case, then surely they would be sympathetic.

"Don't count on any help from them."

It was the prosecuting demon with the dark eyes, leaning across his table and addressing me in a low voice.

"I beg your pardon?" I asked.

He inclined his head toward the jurors. "The angels. They've got a nagging sense of justice, but they also don't have a lot of sympathy to those who sold their souls. They figure you made your bed, you have to sleep in it. Pretentious bastards, the lot of them."

I turned back toward the jury and felt a sinking in my stomach. Some of the angels were watching me, and although there wasn't open disdain on their faces, like the demons, I could still see condescension and scorn here and there. I saw no sympathy anywhere.

With so much chatter in the now-crowded room, it was hard to imagine being able to single out any one voice—but I did. Maybe it was because it was one I'd grown so familiar with in the last ten years, one that I had fallen into the habit of jumping to whenever it spoke. Tearing my gaze from the jury, I peered around until I found the voice's owner.

Sure enough, Jerome had just entered the courtroom. Even in Hell, he still wore the John Cusack guise. Mei was with him, and it was the sound of their conversation that had caught my attention. They made their way to some seats near the front, on the opposite side of the room from me, that I presumed had been left open for them. A pang of relief shot through my chest. Finally, familiar faces. I opened my mouth to speak, to call out to Jerome . . . just as his eyes fell on me. He paused in his walk, fixing me with a look that pierced straight to my heart. Then, without any other sort of acknowledgment, he looked away and continued his conversation with Mei as they went to their seats. The words died on my lips. The coldness in his gaze left no question that all the laid-back ease at the bowling alley had been a scam.

Jerome was not on my side.

And, if my empty table was any indication, no one was on my side.

A guy in a much more cheerful suit than the prosecutor walked to the front of the room and called the court to order. He announced the entrance of Judge Hannibal, which would have been a hilarious and absurd name in other circumstances. Everyone stood, and I followed suit. The show of respect kind of surprised me. The adherence to procedure did not.

Judge Hannibal entered through a door opposite the jury's. For a moment, I simply thought, *He's so young*. Then, I remembered I was thinking like a human. No one in this room—except me—wore their actual form. All of them were beings of incalculable age, and the twenty-something, blond surfer appearance of Judge Hannibal was just window dressing.

He flashed everyone a big grin, perfect white teeth standing out against his tanned skin. He riffled through some papers in front of him. "All right," he said. "So, what . . . we have a contract dispute with a succubus? Letha?" He glanced around, like there was some big mystery about who I was. His gaze landed on me, and he nodded to himself. "Who's prosecuting? You? Marcel?"

"Yes, your honor," said the dark-suited demon.

Judge Hannibal chuckled. "This is even less fair than it already was." He glanced back at me. "You got a lawyer, honey?"

I swallowed. "Er, no. I don't think so. Should I? Do . . . do I get assigned one?"

He shrugged. "We could dredge some imp up if you don't want to defend yourself. Or we can summon someone, if you've got anyone in mind."

At the mention of an imp, Hugh's name immediately popped up in my head. I wouldn't have even cared about the defense aspect. I just wanted to see a friendly face here. Was it that easy? I could just ask, and they'd bring Hugh here . . . to Hell? As soon as I had the thought, I dismissed it. Hugh had already risked so much for me. How could I ask him to stand against our superiors, to defend me against all those cold, glaring eyes? And what good could come of it? He'd probably get in more trouble if I actually won—which didn't seem likely, judging from Hannibal's earlier comments.

I was on the verge of telling them I'd just defend myself when there was an explosion of light in the aisle beside me. I leaped to my feet in fear and wasn't alone in doing so. A cyclone of silver and white light slowly coalesced into a familiar and very welcome form: Carter. Like everyone else, a day in court appeared to make no difference for how he dressed—save that he was wearing the cashmere hat I'd gotten him last Christmas. Glancing up at the judge, Carter took off the hat and held it before him in an attempt at respect. I wanted to throw myself sobbing into his arms.

"What is this?" demanded Judge Hannibal. Those who had been startled slinked back to their seats.

"Sorry," said Carter amiably. "I would've come in the normal way but didn't know how else to get her lawyer in."

Was Carter going to be my lawyer? Hope sprang anew within me until another burst of light erupted beside him . . . and Roman appeared.

Chaos of a different sort broke out, and suddenly, I was a sideshow. Outrage shone on angel and demon faces alike. Half the room was on its feet. I hadn't been able to sense any immortal auras, but I could feel the swell of power bursting from nearly every individual as they advanced on Roman.

"Nephilim!"

"Destroy him!"

We were on the verge of a full-fledged mob attack when Hannibal banged his gavel on the desk. It made a sound like thunder, hitting hard. A palpable wave of power radiated out from him, nearly knocking a few people off their feet. The growing magic in the room dissipated.

"Sit down," he snapped. "This is hardly the time or place for everyone to start playing hero."

"There's a nephilim in the room!" protested someone in the back.

"Yes, yes. Thank you, Captain Obvious," said Judge Hannibal. "And I daresay the hundred or so of us can take him if he gets out of line. That's not in question. What is, however, is *why* he's here and shouldn't be immediately smote." That was directed to Carter.

"He's her lawyer," said Carter.

Hannibal's eyebrows rose in true surprise, with no sign of his earlier smugness. "A nephilim?"

"There are no rules against it," said Carter mildly. "Any immortal can serve, right?"

Hannibal glanced uneasily at a woman seated at a corner desk who had been typing away steadily on a laptop. I'd taken her for the court reporter, but she was apparently some sort of consultant too. She made a face.

"Technically, he can serve," she said. "Our laws don't specify."

"But they do specify that anyone the defendant chooses is exempt from punishment," said Carter, as cagey as any lawyer.

A cruel smile played at her lips. "Whoever is summoned to serve as lawyer is exempt from punishment during court and afterward when they return to their normal jobs. I'm guessing this . . . creature is not in our personnel files."

With Hell, the devil really was in the details. Hugh had always warned me to be careful with even the smallest wordings because Hell would use them to its advantage. It took me a moment to fully get why she was so pleased. Any immortal could serve as a lawyer in a case like this, it seemed. And, going on the first part of what she'd said, no one could do anything to Roman while he was my lawyer, despite the normal immortal reaction to promptly destroy all nephilim. There would be no mass smiting in the courtroom. It was the second part of her words that was tricky. Those drafted as lawyers allegedly couldn't be punished for their legal performances when they returned to their regular duties, which would've been good to know when I was considering summoning Hugh (though I knew there were a million subtle ways a disgruntled demon could still get back at someone on the sly).

But Roman didn't have any regular duties for Hell, aside from an unofficial deal with Jerome that I had no doubt my archdemon would disavow all knowledge of. Roman couldn't be protected when he "went back to work" because he didn't work for Hell. The instant this trial ended and he was out of the role of lawyer, he was subject to the whims of Hell.

"Well," said Hannibal. He looked down at me. "At least it'll make this case more interesting. Sure, whatever. You want the nephilim as your lawyer?"

I wanted to say no. Some part of me half hoped that if I refused and Roman never became my lawyer, he would be free of the retribution that awaited him afterward, that he could simply escape now. Except, as I glanced between him and Carter, a terrible certainty settled over me. It didn't matter if Roman became my lawyer or not. He wasn't getting out of here. It was reflected in Roman's eyes as they met mine. When Carter had brought him here, it was a one-way trip. If I didn't accept him as my lawyer, I was simply speeding Roman to his death.

I nodded and felt my heart lurch as I sealed his fate. "Er, yes. Yes, your honor. I'd like him as my lawyer."

There was a murmur of disapproval throughout the courtroom. Carter slapped Roman encouragingly on the back and then went to find a seat in the gallery. Roman took the empty chair beside me. He was a sharp contrast to Marcel. Roman had no briefcase, not even a single piece of paper, and was still wearing the clothes he'd had on earlier: jeans and a sweater.

"What are you doing?" I hissed to him, grateful for the cover of the other voices. "This is suicide!"

"You didn't really think I'd abandon you to them, did you?" he asked. "And who knows your case better than me?"

"They'll kill you when it's over, whether I win or lose."

Roman gave me a lopsided smile. " 'It is a far, far better thing that I do—' "

"Oh, shut the fuck up," I said, afraid I was going to start crying. "You're an idiot. You shouldn't have come here."

"You remember our talk about purpose and meaning?" he asked me, the smile disappearing. "Well, I think this might be mine. I think this is what I was meant to do, Georgina."

"Roman—"

But there was no time for any more conversation. Judge Hannibal was banging the gavel—this time, sans thunder—trying to calm everyone down. They were still worked up about the idea of a nephilim walking freely in their midst.

"Enough, enough," Hannibal said. "I know we're all

shocked and awed, but get over it. We'll deal with him later. If there's no more drama in store, do you mind if we get started?" He glanced between the lawyers.

"I'm ready when you are, your honor," said Marcel.

Roman nodded. "Let's do this."

Chapter 19

And so began my day in court.

Despite Hannibal's call for order, it was obvious that everyone was still fixated on Roman's presence. I'd known nephilim were despised among greater immortals, but it wasn't until today that the full scope of it hit me. It shed new light on why Roman and his kind were often so obsessed with getting back at the powers that be. I wondered if it was good to have some of the attention taken off me or if I'd just doomed myself further by association.

"So," said Judge Hannibal. "You've got some kind of gripe with your contract. Join the club." Low chuckles from the demonic spectators rumbled around the room.

Roman cleared his throat, silencing the chuckles. "Your honor, we have more than a 'gripe.' We have evidence that Hell not only violated her contract but also drew up another under false pretenses."

"That's absurd," said Marcel. "We can't examine everyone in the world's contract. If someone else has a problem, they can have their own trial."

"The other contract is for a human who's still alive," said Roman. "He's in no position to file a claim, and his was tied in to the paperwork that brought hers to court."

Hannibal waved his hands dismissively. "Well, we haven't even proved there's anything wrong with hers, so let's settle that before we start doing favors for others."

"Can we see her contract?" asked Roman.

"Doris?" Hannibal glanced over at the woman with the laptop. She produced a heavy, metal box from underneath her desk with what appeared to be a numeric lock. After first consulting her laptop, she punched in a long series of digits. Smoke seeped out of the edges of the box. A moment later, she opened it up and produced a long, ornate scroll. She glanced at the judge.

"Copies?"

"Yes, please," he told her.

Doris repeated the procedure a couple more times, and I leaned toward Roman. "How does this work?" I whispered. "Isn't there some kind of order? Doesn't the prosecution go first?"

"Maybe in an American court of law," he whispered back. "Here? Everyone just gets out their argument when they can, and it's up to the judge to keep order."

It surprised me. Considering the obsession with details around here, I would've expected a certain amount of pain-staking procedure. Then again, a survival-of-the-fittest method of pushing your case wasn't that out of line with Hell's ide-ologies either.

Scrolls were obtained for the judge and lawyers. Even though it was a copy, I was still a bit daunted when Roman spread the scroll out before us on the table. This was it, the contract that had bound my immortal soul. One small deci-sion with centuries of consequences. It was written in Eng-lish, and I supposed Doris's magic scroll copy box must have the powers of translation since the original had been in Greek.

"May I direct your attention to section 3A," said Roman loudly. In a softer voice, he added to me, "The rest is pretty much standard Hell legalese."

It was true. The scroll was so big, we couldn't open it in its entirety. From what I could see, most of it was a painfully de-tailed description of what it meant to serve as a succubus and give Hell the lease on your soul. In their defense, there wasn't much they'd left out. I hadn't read the full contract at the time. Niphon had summarized the high points for me, but it was impossible to say they didn't let you know what you were in for. Fortunately, those technicalities weren't our concern today.

Roman read aloud:

"In exchange for ownership of the aforementioned soul (see sections 1B, 4A, 4B, 5B part 1, 5B part 2, and appendix 574.3) and services detailed below (see sections 3A, 3B, 6A-F, 12C) as performed by the contractee (henceforth called 'the Damned'), the almighty Kingdom of Hell and its representatives do agree to the following:

1. Granting to the Damned of succubus powers described in sections 7.1A and 7.3A.
2. All mortals who were acquainted with the Damned in her human life shall have all knowledge of her erased from their memories, never to be regained, in accordance with standard memory loss procedures (see appendix 23)."

Roman looked up at the judge when he finished reading. "Now," said Roman. "I can read appendix 23 if you want, but the point is that Hell did not honor part of their agreement. Someone she knew when she was human—a mortal—remembered her."

"Why wasn't this raised back then?" asked Hannibal.

"Because it happened a couple months ago," said Roman. "The person in question is someone with a reincarnation contract who was alive then and today."

"If this person was reincarnated, then the point's irrelevant," said Marcel. "It's not technically the same person anymore. Therefore, the contract stands."

"Not according to addendum 764 of the *Treatise on Humanity*," said Roman. "According to it, all individuals—humans and lesser immortals—are defined by their souls. No matter what shape that being takes, the soul remains constant, as does the individual's identity. I'm sure Doris can produce a copy if we need it."

Doris looked at Hannibal expectantly. "Don't bother," he said. "I'm familiar with the *Treatise*. Okay. Operating under the assumption that souls are constant and individuals are defined by their souls, what proof do you have that this reincarnated individual remembered the petitioner here?"

I expected Roman to say something and then realized he was waiting on me. It was still hard to wrap my head around the idea of everyone just jumping forward and speaking.

"He called me by my name, your honor," I said. "My first human name from the fifth century. The one he knew me as back then."

"Had he ever heard it before—in this lifetime?" prompted Roman.

"No," I said.

"Did anyone witness this?" asked Marcel.

"No," I said.

"I see," he said, managing to make me feel very small with those two words. His tone implied that it was a miracle we'd even made it this far on such flimsy evidence.

"It's okay," said Roman. "Because we have more. This same reincarnated subject revealed under hypnosis remembering her in several other lives."

"Are there witnesses to *that?*" asked Hannibal.

"We both witnessed it," said Roman. "As well as an imp employed in Seattle. Hugh Mitchell. He was the one who actually performed the hypnosis, if you wanted to summon him."

I tensed. Hugh was certainly an airtight witness—seeing as he wasn't the petitioner in this case or a creature despised by both Heaven and Hell—but my earlier apprehension for him returned. I didn't know if he could get in trouble for providing key evidence.

"We don't need him," said Marcel. "You and he witnessed the same thing?"

I nodded.

Marcel glanced over at the jury. "You can tell if she's lying. Is she telling the truth?"

Six heads nodded. I was surprised I hadn't thought of this earlier. Angels could tell if mortals and lesser immortals were telling the truth. That was handy in a trial like this. I was also surprised Marcel was helping me out like this.

"There you have it," he said. "She thinks she heard the subject remembering her under hypnosis. We can assume this imp would believe it as well."

"Hey," I argued. "There's no 'thinks' about it. He *did* remember me."

Marcel shrugged. "If you say so. We can only take your word for it and what you *think* you heard. There's no objective evidence to show that he remembered, therefore calling our part of the bargain into dispute."

"Oh, we can find the evidence," said Roman. "The subject in question is also under contract. And the very nature of his contract contradicts hers. Can you bring it up, Doris?"

Hannibal nodded his consent, and she turned to her laptop. "Name?"

"Kyriakos," I said, trying not to stumble over the word. "That's what it was in the fifth century, at least. In Cyprus. Today he's Seth Mortensen."

The judge arched an eyebrow. "I like his books. Didn't realize he was one of ours."

"Well, he's not yet," I muttered.

Doris meanwhile was typing away on her laptop, putting in the appropriate criteria. She must have found the right case number because she soon turned to the smoking metal box and produced three more scrolls. The copies were distributed, and a strange feeling crept over my skin as Roman opened this one, stranger even than when we'd viewed my own. Here it was. Seth's contract. Kyriakos's contract. It had existed unbeknownst to me all these years, subtly influencing my life. It had been made because of me. Roman again jumped to section 2, which was apparently consistent across contracts as far as what "the Damned" received.

" 'The Damned shall be granted a total of ten human lives, of which one has already taken place. The subsequent nine reincarnations shall occur in such times and places that he may be in proximity to the lover he believes is missing from his first life, in the hopes of reconciliation. Upon completion of the tenth life, the Damned's soul will become the property of Hell, in accordance with sections 8D, 9A, and 9B.' "

Roman fell silent, a frown on his face. I too felt dismayed but didn't think we shared the same reasons. Without Seth confirming anything, we'd been unsure if his soul was damned or not, regardless of his success in finding me. I'd half hoped that Hell had given him some fairy-tale challenge, that if he could find and reunite with me, his soul would be restored to him. That apparently wasn't true. Hell had only offered him the chance to be with me. They'd given him no more than that. If we made amends, his soul belonged to them, the same as if we didn't. Our romantic outcome made no difference. I wondered if he had bargained for more or had been so desperate and grateful for the chance to simply be with me again that he hadn't even asked for more.

Marcel smiled. "I see Letha mentioned nowhere in here. There was no violation of the terms of her contract."

"But obviously someone knew," said Roman. "You must have a record of all of his lives. He's encountered her in each one of them. So someone, somewhere made sure that part of the contract was fulfilled—his reunion with the missing 'lover' from his first life. Her. Whom he was supposed to forget, per the terms of her contract. They contradict each other."

Roman spoke confidently, laying his points out reasonably, but I could sense the uneasiness within him. I knew what the hanging point was—the same point Marcel had promptly jumped on. I wasn't cited by name here. Somewhere, there had to be a record of it if Hell had managed to let Seth be reborn near me each time, but we didn't know what that was. Hell certainly wasn't going to help us find it.

"It could be a coincidence," said Marcel. "Maybe he met someone else in his first life whom he fell in love with, someone whom he lost young and continued to seek in the following centuries."

"Someone else who was immortal and would be alive for the next fifteen hundred years?" asked Roman. "That's an awfully big coincidence."

Marcel looked smug. "Be that as it may, Letha is not mentioned anywhere in his contract. Everything's circumstantial at best, with no proof that Hell entered into this under false pretenses."

A thought suddenly occurred to me, and I began attempting to unroll the scroll, seeking a very specific piece of information. There were so many sections, subsections, articles, and clauses, however, that I couldn't make any sense of it.

"Who drafted this?" I asked Roman. "Shouldn't whoever brokered the deal be listed?"

"Section 27F.," said Roman automatically.

I paused to give him an incredulous glance. "How do you know that?"

"What do you think I've been doing for the last week?" he asked, by way of answer.

He helped me find the appropriate section, and I breathed a sigh of relief when I saw the name I'd been hoping for. Just to be sure, I found the matching section in my own contract. Roman, spying what I had, immediately ran with it.

"Your honor, these contracts were brokered by the same imp. Niphon. He had to have known they conflicted with each other. He had to have known that Letha was the lover Kyriakos was seeking."

"He didn't 'have to have known' anything," countered Marcel. "It could be a coincidence."

"Well, let's get him in here and find out," said Roman.

Hannibal considered this for several seconds. I got the distinct impression that he most definitely did not want to summon Niphon, but some of the angels in the jury were regarding him expectantly. If this were truly a fair trial, with evidence laid neatly out, then there was no reason not to bring in a key witness like Niphon.

"Very well," said Hannibal. He looked over to the guy in the nice suit, the one who'd opened proceedings. I'd taken him for some kind of classy bailiff. "Go get him. We'll call a ten-minute recess while you do." Hannibal banged his gavel, and conversation buzzed as the bailiff hurried out of the room.

I leaned toward Roman. "Niphon knows. He has to know. Did I ever tell you the full story of when he came to visit last year?"

Roman had heard some of it but was very eager for a recap as I told the tale again. Niphon had shown up, ostensibly to deliver Tawny as our newest succubus. During his stay, however, he'd caused no end of trouble for me and Seth. He'd tried to drive a wedge between us, and indeed, some of his actions were what had led Seth to believe a breakup was better for us in the long run. Niphon had also tried to broker a contract with Seth in order for us to be together without the harmful succubus effects that occurred during sex. The cost would have been Seth's soul, of course.

I paused, thinking that over. "I understand the rest . . . him wanting to keep us apart. Hugh had said it was the sign of an imp trying to cover for some mistake—and this is a pretty big one. It makes sense he'd want to split us up and avoid discovery of the conflict. But why bother to make another deal if Seth's soul was already under contract?"

Roman's eyes were alight with thought. "Because he could've done an amendment to the old contract and cleaned up the contradiction. Seth's soul would have been rese-cured."

We had no time to analyze it further because the recess soon ended. Hannibal brought things to order and the bailiff returned—with Niphon.

My stomach twisted at the sight of him, just as it had last time. Niphon always put me in mind of a weasel. He wore a gray suit, looking business-ready like all imps did, but had heavily pomade-slicked hair that took away some of his cred-ibility. He had thin lips, small eyes, and an olive complexion. He also looked like he'd bolt if given half the chance. The screwup he'd tried to conceal was now being laid out. His es-cort led him to a witness stand near the bench. Niphon gin-gerly sat down, sweating visibly. I'd worried about Hugh being dragged into this, fearful of the consequences he'd face. Niphon was probably afraid of the same thing: being pun-ished for helping my case. The difference was that Hugh would at least take some satisfaction out of assisting me. Niphon had no gain in any of this.

"State your name please," said Hannibal.

The imp licked his lips. "Niphon, your honor. At your ser-vice."

"You brokered these two contracts?" asked Hannibal, in-dicating the scrolls Doris had just placed on the witness stand.

Niphon made a great show of studying them. "I suppose so, your honor. My name's on them, but it's been such a long time. Makes it easy to forget."

I scoffed. "You seemed to remember last year when you were scrambling to cover your ass."

"Let's keep this civilized and fair," said Hannibal mildly. Really? I was the one being chastised for civility and fairness?

"Did you know when you drew up Kyriakos's contract that Letha was the one he was seeking?" asked Roman. See-ing Niphon squirm, Roman added, "And be careful about saying you 'don't remember.' The angels in the esteemed jury will know you're lying."

Niphon swallowed and cast an anxious look at the jury box before returning his gaze to Roman. "I . . . yes. I knew."

"And since you'd drawn up Letha's contract, you knew that her terms required all those who knew her as a human to forget her. The fact that he was seeking her at all was a sign her contract had been broken. You weren't able to keep him in a state of forgetfulness."

Niphon made a face. "He didn't mention her by name. He only remembered that she was gone."

Roman smacked my contract hard. "The contract doesn't specify to what degree she can be forgotten, just that she is. Period."

Sweat was practically pouring off Niphon in buckets now. He jerked one of the scrolls toward him and scanned it with his twitchy eyes. " 'All mortals who were acquainted with the Damned in her human life shall have all knowledge of her erased from their memories. . . .' " He glanced up. "This is a translation. I think the original Greek makes it clearer that only those from her human life forget her. Therefore, if he re-membered her afterward, there would be no violation. Can we get a Greek copy in here?"

"It wouldn't matter," said Roman. "Even if it does say that. We've already established that a soul defines a person's identity across lives. Even now, he's still technically someone from her human life, and he remembered. You were unable to uphold the contract."

"That's hardly my fault!" Niphon exclaimed. It was un-clear now if he was speaking to Roman and me or to superi-ors in the audience. "I made the arrangements for standard memory loss with her contract. I don't know why it didn't work. Yes, I knew he was her husband when I set up his con-tract, but I didn't think of this in terms of contract violation. I was just securing another soul."

Marcel addressed the jury. "Is he telling the truth? He made the second contract out of ignorance and not malicious intent? By which I mean, no more malicious intent than is normally called for in these situations."

Some of the angels nodded, looking reluctant to do so.

"It doesn't matter if it was in ignorance," said Roman. "That's never an excuse for breaking the law. You messed up, and in doing so, you've invalidated both contracts."

"Come now," said Marcel. "It's not as though either of the Damned were that wronged. This technicality aside, she really was wiped from the memories of all she knew. And he got nine more lives. Nine more lives! We all know how rare reincarnation deals are. He got exactly what he asked for. He was even reunited with her. Hell has fulfilled these contracts as nobly as possible, and you can't hold everyone responsible for one underling's mishap that no one else even knew about."

"Oh," said Roman, a predatory note in his voice. "I think others knew about the glitch. Others in much higher positions. Your honor, may I call another witness?"

"Who?" asked Hannibal.

"My father," said Roman. "Jerome, Archdemon of Seattle."

There was a collective gasp among some, but whether that was from Roman acknowledging Jerome as his father or simply the summoning of such a high-ranking witness, I couldn't say. Hannibal nodded.

"Granted. Niphon, you may step down. Jerome, please join us up here."

Niphon couldn't get out of there fast enough. He practically barreled into Jerome when they passed in the aisle. For his part, Jerome was sauntering along casually, as though all of this were beneath him and it was a great concession on his part to even show. He sat down, crossing his hands neatly in front of him and affecting a bored look.

"Jerome," said Roman. "Isn't it true you knew about the connection between Seth and Georgina? Er, Kyriakos and Letha?"

Jerome shrugged one shoulder. "I knew they were both contracted souls."

It was an answer worthy of an angel. Some of the truth,

but not all of the truth. I half hoped some angel would call him on it until an unfortunate fact hit me. Demons could lie without detection. There was no way to prove he was telling the truth or not.

"Did you know the terms of her contract?" asked Roman.

"Of course," said Jerome. "I do for all my employees."

"So you knew that the contract allowed her to be wiped from the minds of all those who knew her when she was human."

"Yes," said Jerome.

"And you knew that Seth was once her husband, with a contract that involved her."

"No," said Jerome flatly. "I most certainly did not."

A lie, a lie, I thought. But there was no way to prove it.

"If that's so," said Roman, "then why did you use Seth Mortensen to help retrieve Georgina when she was captured by Oneroi last year?"

"I don't remember the specifics of that incident," said Jerome delicately.

"Well," said Roman, "if you need your memory refreshed, there's an angel here who witnessed it all who can give us a recap. One I'm sure the jury won't question."

Jerome's features went perfectly still as Roman's trap sprang open around him. Jerome might be immune to angelic truth detection, but anything Carter swore to seeing Jerome do or know would be held as gospel. Carter couldn't lie. If he said Jerome had used Seth to rescue me, then everyone would believe it, regardless if Jerome continued to deny it. Seeing the futility of more cover-up, Jerome came clean.

"Oh," he said. "Those Oneroi."

"You used a human psychic to help retrieve her," said Roman. "He had the power and the ritual but no way to actually find her in the void where the Oneroi were holding her. You suggested using Seth as a way to find her soul, and it worked. Why? How did you know that?"

Jerome shrugged. "They were always mooning over each

other. I figured if ever there was any merit in that true love nonsense, then we could use it to help us."

"That's not what Mei said." I took advantage of the conversational nature of the proceedings, my mind spinning with a long-lost memory. "Mei said it defied the odds and that no matter how in love we were, it shouldn't have worked."

Jerome's dark gaze flicked to something behind me, and I was guessing Mei was now enjoying the full force of his glare.

"Georgina was trapped in the vastness of the dream world," added in Roman. "One soul lost among dreams. For someone else to reach her and call her back required a staggering connection, two souls with a tie that's bound them through time."

"Please don't get sentimental," said Jerome. "It's nauseating."

Roman shook his head. "I'm stating facts. Everyone here knows it's true. Their souls had to have been bound for him to get to her, and *you* knew it, which is why you suggested using Seth. You knew about the contracts and their history. This wasn't one small error confined to a bumbling inferior. You knew about it. And you knew there was a problem."

"Which is why you had Erik killed and initiated a transfer for me!" I exclaimed. Seeing Jerome sitting there so coolly, so uncaring . . . it drove home the truth. He had known all along what was transpiring with Seth and me, and what it meant. I'd never thought Jerome and I were friends, but it was startling to really accept just how much he'd been working against me in order to further Hell's goals.

"Oh, Georgie," he said. "Always you and the melodrama."

"It's not! We can get proof—"

Roman put his hand on mine. "Not easily," he murmured. "There'll be no paper trail, I guarantee it. And it's not relevant to this case right now."

I thought about kind, generous Erik, bleeding to death before my eyes. "It's relevant to me."

Jerome let out a long-suffering sigh. "Is there anything else? Can I return to my seat, please?"

The judge glanced between Roman and Marcel. Both men shook their heads.

When Jerome was gone, Roman pushed the case. "Your honor, esteemed jury . . . we've provided more than enough evidence to show that her contract was not fulfilled. Through whatever mishaps, those from her human life did *not* stop remembering her. Per article 7.51.2 of the *Soul Chronicles*, Georgina's contract is invalidated. She's entitled to her soul back and the remainder of this life, free of Hell's employment, per the section on damages and reparations in article 8.2.0. Likewise, Seth Mortensen's contract is also invalidated because it was made under false pretenses. The imp who drew it up knew that it violated hers and knew that the very conditions of Seth's—finding her and making amends—included a degree of remembering. It's impossible for his to exist without contradicting hers. He too is entitled to the restoration of his soul."

"Your honor—" began Marcel.

Judge Hannibal held up his hand. "Silence. I'll make you a deal."

There was a restless shifting in the courtroom, an undercurrent of excitement. Demons *loved* deals and bargains.

"Go on," said Roman.

"I'm willing to dismiss the case without a jury vote and grant that Letha's contract wasn't honored. I'm willing to give her all of the restorations outlined in article 8.2.0."

Gasps surrounded us. My eyes widened, and I turned to Roman questioningly. Was it as easy as that? I didn't know all the details of 8.2.0, but by my understanding, if the contract was invalidated, I could return to Earth and live out the rest of my days as a human. *In possession of my soul*. It seemed too good to be true.

"However," continued Hannibal, "I don't see enough evidence to support the releasing of this second soul. Your argument for it will be thrown out for being groundless."

"But it isn't!" I cried.

"If we don't accept, then what?" asked Roman.

Hannibal shrugged. "Then the jury can vote on the question of both contracts."

Roman nodded thoughtfully. "Can I have a moment to confer with my, um, client?"

"Sure." Hannibal banged the gavel. "Five-minute recess."

The spectators didn't need to be told twice. This was huge. A soul getting released was not something that happened every day, nor was a deal like we were being offered.

"What's the catch here?" I asked Roman softly.

He narrowed his eyes. "Well, I think Hannibal thinks he's in danger of losing two souls and is trying cut his losses. Your evidence is pretty solid. Seth's is too, though not quite as good—especially without Seth actually here. Still, Hannibal would rather let you go easily and ensure that he still keeps one soul in this mess."

"But if the evidence is there, then we should let it go to the jury. You just said it's solid for Seth too."

"It is," agreed Roman. "But here's the thing that Hugh told me about these juries. All contract disputes are judged by half angels and half demons—for the sake of fairness. The angels will honestly vote with what they feel to be right. If the evidence was flimsy, they'd vote against you. It's not worth it to them to get a soul free if the conditions aren't honorable. The demons have no such morals. Jerome and Niphon could both openly confess to a conspiracy of conflicting contracts, and every demon on that jury would still vote against you."

"That's not fair," I said.

"Georgina," he said simply. "We're in Hell."

"So what happens if it's split? Do they go by the same hung jury procedures we know?"

"A tie-breaking vote is produced. A thirteenth angel or demon is called at random, who then casts the deciding vote. If it comes down to that, then your chances simply fall to a 50-50 luck of the draw."

"Hence the bargain," I murmured. "If I abandon Seth's soul, I'm guaranteed my freedom."

Roman nodded. "And if you don't, you may be consigning both of you to Hell."

Chapter 20

I thought about it for half a heartbeat, and even that was too long. There was no question what my decision could be. Seth and I were bound together. Even if it had been for Jerome's convenience, Seth had found my soul across the incredible reaches of the dream world. Seth and I had found each other, life after life, and continually fallen in love. Even if we didn't consciously remember each other, some inner part of ourselves had connected. I remembered Roman's words.

Over and over, you find each other and lose each other, you bicker and fight, throw it all away on mistrust and lack of communication. Are you going to let that continue?

No, the cycle was going to end. On my terms. These lives we'd lived . . . the pain we'd suffered . . . it wouldn't be for nothing. It didn't matter if Seth hated me and never wanted to see me again. I wouldn't abandon him—not now, not ever.

"No deal," I said to Roman. "Seth and I are doing this together, whether he knows it or not."

Roman didn't try to talk me out of it. He simply said, "You understand what's at stake?"

"I do." If we failed here, I wouldn't just lose my soul. I would also be looking forward to an eternity in Hell's service, with superiors none-too-pleased that I'd shaken up the status quo. I didn't doubt that there was some article or clause somewhere that said I couldn't be penalized for this, but as I'd noted before, Hell had plenty of ways of punishing people off the record. The Las Vegas position would probably no longer exist, forcing me to relocate to some truly terrible location.

Hannibal called the court back to order, and Roman relayed my decision.

Hannibal clicked his tongue disapprovingly. "Risking it all for the new car, eh? Well, ladies and gentlemen of the jury, it falls in your hands now. You've heard the evidence—and lack thereof. Do you believe there is enough 'proof' to support the petitioner's case? Should both contracts—that these individuals willingly signed—be invalidated?" So much for justice being blind.

The jury cast votes anonymously, which I found interesting. It was a small nod toward impartiality, theoretically providing protection to those who voted against their side's best interests. From what both Roman and Marcel had told me, I could see it happening among the angels. But did it ever happen with demons? Even if they knew the right or wrong of a situation, their ultimate goal was to accrue souls for Hell. Would any of them be moved by a case enough to go with their conscience? Was it possible that some spark of goodness could still endure in the darkness of this place? Judging from the quick way everyone scrawled their responses on the pieces of paper given, it didn't look like it. There was no hesitation. The demons wore cocky, self-assured expressions. Angels and demons came from the same stock, but I'd been told that once they spent enough time in Hell, that angelic nature was eroded away. These demons weren't going to lose any sleep about what became of my soul.

The votes were collected by the bailiff. He sorted them into two suspiciously similarly sized piles and handed them to the judge. Hannibal did a quick count and nodded to himself before addressing us. A new stillness fell over the room.

"Here we go," murmured Roman.

"The jury has spoken," said Hannibal. "Six to six. We have a tie."

There was a collective exhalation in the room, and then

the tension ramped back up as everyone waited for the next step. I shouldn't have been surprised by the tie, but some part of me had been hoping maybe, just maybe, a wayward demon would've voted in my favor. I had my answer. There was no spark of goodness here. It couldn't survive in Hell.

"In accordance with article . . . fuck, I don't know . . . article something-or-other, we'll be going to a tiebreaker vote," said Hannibal. The bailiff returned with an ornate vase, which he handed to the judge. Hannibal dumped out the contents, revealing a white marble and a black marble. "In this case, it really is as simple as black and white. If the black one's drawn, a demon casts the deciding vote. If it's white, an angel will." He paused, looking bemused. "That's so clichéd. I don't suppose we could switch the colors around? Just this once? No? Okay, let's get on with it." He scanned the jury and pointed to an angel with curly red hair and long-lashed blue eyes. "You. You'll do the draw."

She nodded her acceptance and approached the bench gracefully. Again, another attempt at justice. If Hannibal had drawn the marbles, I would have been suspicious of the outcome. The fairness of the matter was future solidified when he made her swear to draw fairly, without using her powers to advantage.

"I swear," she said, placing the marbles in the vase. She shook them up and reached her hand in, casting a brief and—unless I was mistaken—sympathetic look at me. Her hand emerged, closed in a fist. When she opened it, no one could see the marble right away, but her face told the story.

"Shit," said Roman.

The angel's palm revealed a black marble. She handed it to the judge who made no pretense at hiding his joy. He thanked her as she returned to her seat and then held the marble up for all the room to see. There was a murmur of excitement among the demons, delighted at having won the gamble he'd laid before us.

I had a moment of regret, but only a small one. I could've walked away from here with my soul and life intact. I could've never brought this up and continued my life as a succubus undisturbed, living out the dream scenario in Las Vegas. Instead, I'd risked everything for the chance to free myself *and* Seth. And I'd lost for both of us.

Had it been worth it?

Yes.

" 'Fate' has spoken," said Hannibal, still admiring the marble. "Per the rules, the decision now falls to a thirteenth juror, who will be randomly selected from a pool of Hell's illustrious servants. Doris?"

Doris began clicking away at her laptop. After a few moments, she gave a nod toward the bailiff. He walked toward the back exit, presumably to escort in the thirteenth juror.

My heart felt heavy and leaden, and I was startled when Roman again placed his hand on mine. "I'm sorry," he said in a low voice. "I should have fought harder. Or pushed you to take the deal—"

I squeezed his hand back. "No. You were perfect. The only thing you shouldn't have done was get involved with this mess." It was impossible to believe, but whatever fate awaited me after my suit was denied wouldn't be half as bad as his.

He gave me a playful smile. "What, and miss the chance to laugh in the face of Heaven and Hell? Besides, there's no way I could leave you to—"

The courtroom had given way to chatter when the bailiff left, and now silence resumed upon his return. Whatever sentiments Roman had been about to say were lost, as he joined me in looking back to see the demon who would cast the last condemning vote on me. When I did, I had to do a double take.

It was Yasmine.

I almost didn't recognize her. It had been a year since I'd seen her, a year since I'd watched her fall from grace, transforming from an angel to a demon. Yasmine had committed a number of grave sins as an angel, starting when she'd fallen in love. That alone was forbidden for her kind, but it had gone one step further—she'd fallen for a nephilim named Vincent. Vince was a great guy, but like Roman, the standard reaction from angels and demons alike had been prompt destruction. One angel had finally acted on that impulse, and Yasmine had rushed to defend Vince—killing the other angel in the process.

And with that, she had been condemned to Hell.

I had seen it. It had been terrible. One angel's death, another's fall. It had all gone down the night Nyx had been found and recaptured. Vince and I had been in the cross fire of it. I'd done what I could for him, but there was nothing I could do to stop Heaven's punishment.

Before leaving town, Vince had told me that it didn't matter what I thought I knew about Yasmine. He'd said that once she had spent enough time in Hell and around other demons, she'd become like them. It was what happened to all of them, how someone like Carter could become someone like Jerome. I hadn't believed it at the time but could understand it better after being surrounded in the despair and wrongness of this place. And when I studied her now, I could see it had happened to her too.

I remembered a smiling, laughing young woman with sparkling dark eyes and shining black hair. The hair and eyes were ostensibly the same, but there was no light or laughter in them. Her eyes seemed fathomless, dark and cold as she stared straight ahead and walked to the front of the courtroom. She was wearing a gauzy black dress, reminding me of some Goth courtesan, and her long, flowing hair blended into the silken fabric. Even if I'd never met her or known her history, I would have instantly identified her as a demon. Just like the others in the room, there was something in the way she looked and carried herself.

I was about to be condemned by someone who had once been my friend.

Yasmine reached the front of the courtroom and was gestured toward the witnesses' table. She sat down, gazing around the room with an unreadable expression.

"You've been following the trial?" asked Judge Hannibal.

"Yes," she said, in a voice as expressionless as her face. How she'd been watching, I couldn't say. With Hell, it could've been closed-circuit TV or a magic mirror for all I knew.

"And you understand your duty?" asked Hannibal.

"Yes," she replied.

Hannibal was trying to maintain some semblance of formality and procedure, but the self-satisfied smirk on his face was kind of negating that. He was too goddamned pleased with himself and this turn of events.

"Cast your vote then, based on the evidence and arguments you've witnessed. If you believe the two contracts are both sound and have not contradicted each other, then cast your vote against the petitioner."

When silence followed, Roman spoke up. "And if she thinks the two contracts aren't valid?"

"Yes, yes." Hannibal made a dismissive gesture, annoyed at this obvious waste of his time. "If you believe the contracts do contradict each other, then cast your vote for the petitioner."

Yasmine was given a piece of paper and pen, just like the other jurors. And just like the others, she wasted no time in writing her vote, her markings swift and certain. When she finished, she looked up serenely, no change in her expression, no sign that we'd ever once known each other. As terrible as I felt about my own fate, I couldn't help but feel nearly as bad for what Hell had done to someone as good and kind as her. No, I thought. Not just Hell. Really, Heaven was just as guilty. What kind of group could advocate goodness and not allow its members to love?

Hannibal took the paper from her with a flourish and held it out before him to read. "In accordance with the laws of this court, and the infallible Kingdom of Hell, the jury finds—" There was a pause, and the next part came out as a question. "In favor of the petitioner?"

A spark of goodness in the darkness. . . .

For a moment, nothing happened. The courtroom was silent, frozen in time. Then, several things happened right on top of each other.

From behind me, I heard Jerome say, "Shit."

Yasmine winked at me.

Roman hugged me.

Hannibal reread the slip of paper, looked at Yasmine, and then swallowed before speaking. "Both contracts are declared invalid, null and void."

Most of the room was on its feet, voices raised in fury. I had no time to process what they were saying, though, because I was disintegrating away.

"No, not yet!" I exclaimed.

I reached desperately for Roman, whose arms had been around me, but couldn't get ahold of him anymore. I was becoming nothing, a will-o'-the-wisp, unable to grasp anything of substance. I tried, though. I tried to grab him and take him with me because there was no way I could leave him here, not in the midst of a bunch of demons pissed off over having just lost two souls. I even tried to say his name, but it didn't work. I had no mouth, no voice anymore. I was leaving this place, and he was staying.

The last thing I saw was his sea green eyes regarding me with both happiness and sorrow. I thought I heard him saying something about "a far, far greater thing," and then I perceived nothing. I would have screamed in fury if I could have, but I was gone. I was nothing.

Only darkness.

Chapter 21

You would think the first moments of my new life, with a soul, would be magical and wonderful. Mostly, they just hurt.

"Ow."

"Not quite the same without immortal healing, eh, sweetie?"

I squinted into Hugh's grinning face. He stood in front of a huge window, backlit into blinding radiance. Turning my head, I slowly assessed the rest of my surroundings, taking in the familiar signs of a hospital room. I was lying on a bed, an IV in my arm, next to some beeping machines with indecipherable readouts.

I glanced back at Hugh. "Can you close the curtains? Or move to the other side of me?"

He shut the curtains partway, still keeping the room lit but no longer to eye-searing levels. "Better?"

"Yeah. Thanks." I shifted slightly, trying to assess my body's injuries. There was soreness in my ribs, a feeling of constriction when I breathed. Part of that was from whatever hurt they'd sustained and the rest was from the bandages tightly wrapped around my torso. All the better to keep me from making things worse, I supposed. "How . . . how long have I been in here?"

Recent events were still kind of a blur. In some ways, the trial felt like it had happen seconds ago. Yet it also had the dreamlike quality of something that had occurred last century. It was hard to wrap my mind around.

"Well," said Hugh, "your *body*'s been here for about four days. 'You' on the other hand . . . oh, you came back to us about two days ago."

"You could tell?" I said.

His smile grew wry. "You forget what I do for a living. When you were in Hell, you didn't have a soul."

"I didn't have a soul before then," I pointed out. "I mean, technically it belonged to Hell, right?"

"Yes, but even if you don't own it, you still possess it. You can't function or exist without it. Our souls are like . . . oh, I don't know. It's like they're encased in amber. They're there, and I can see them inside us. They're just inaccessible, in a way that's different from humans. When you were gone, you had nothing. Not even a tagged soul. There was just kind of a . . . hollow darkness within you while you lay here."

I shivered, not liking the image. "And now?"

"And now?" Hugh's face softened, taking on a look of wonder that I'd never before seen on the usually gruff and snide imp. "Oh, sweetie. When you came back, I was here . . . and it was like . . . fuck, I don't know. I'm terrible at similes. It was like the sun, after an eclipse. You think that's bright?" He nodded toward the window. "That's nothing. You have your soul back, unfettered and unrestrained . . . and it's amazing. It's beautiful, so beautiful. I've never seen anything like it."

"Is it . . . is it tainted? I mean, I've done things . . ."

"You get it back shiny and new. That's in clause 13.2.1. It's a sign of how confident Hell is about never having to give souls back. Don't worry," he added. A goofy grin had started to spread over my face. "Even the best people have a few screwups. You'll break your soul in in no time. It's like a car. Loses its value when you drive it off the lot."

"Just hopefully not to the same degree as before," I muttered. A new, panicked thought came to me. I was pretty confident of the answer, but I had to ask. "And my body? Which one is it?"

"The same Georgina we all know and love. There are also

stipulations about that, for succubi freed of their contracts. It would get messy giving you back your original body and figuring out what to do with you as far as location and time. So, you're simply reinstated with your soul into whatever body and location you were last in." He paused. "I'm fairly certain it's never happened to any succubus before."

"Thank goodness I wasn't in the kind of body Tawny was when Jerome was summoned," I remarked. She had been wearing a truly horrendous shape, but since we were all cut from our powers until Jerome's restoration, she'd been stuck in it. Although, to be honest, if it meant having my own soul, I would've taken that body. I would've taken my original body. I would've taken anything. The physical trappings were nothing.

"Carter gave us a recap," Hugh said. He shook his head, smiling. "I can't believe you gambled on both contracts. I would've run off with the sure thing."

"I couldn't," I said, thinking back to the events of the courtroom. "Even if he hates me, I couldn't abandon Seth. I couldn't have enjoyed the rest of my life, knowing he was damned."

"He doesn't hate you."

"But he—"

"I know, I know." Hugh wouldn't let me finish. "I know what he said, but he was still in the throes of grief from that fucked-up hypnosis. That was too much for anyone to handle. Carter talked to him when you got back—explained what happened."

My heart lurched. Was that a good or bad thing? I was beginning to gain some glimpse of just how invested Carter had been in my situation (and Seth's), but had the angel really been able to fix everything so easily?

"Did . . . did Carter change Seth's mind about me or something?"

Hugh shrugged. "I don't think he needed to. If things hadn't panned out like they had that night—with the car—I think you and Seth would've had a very interesting conversation. I think he'd started to come around. It's why he was there."

"No," I said, disbelieving.

"I talked to him, sweetie. Do you really think all that love could have just been thrown away so easily? And he was here, you know. He was by your bedside until . . . well, yesterday, actually. Then he had to leave for his tour."

"His tour . . ." I vaguely remembered Andrea mentioning that, how it had become a possibility with her recovery. Speaking of Andrea . . . if my contract was off the table, Hell would have no reason to continue messing with her. She could be left in peace to heal on her own. "He went yesterday?"

"Somewhere on the East Coast," said Hugh. "I'm sure you can find it on his Web site. You were the one who always encouraged him to update it, after all."

I smiled at that, thinking of how reluctant Seth had been about the digital age. I gestured vaguely at my prone body. "Probably just as well that he's gone. I need to heal up. Maybe . . . maybe we'll talk when he's back."

Hugh eyed me, staying silent.

"What?" I demanded.

"He's going to be gone two weeks," said Hugh. "That much I know. You sure you want to wait that long?"

"I've waited a long time already," I pointed out dryly.

"Exactly my point. Look, I don't have any delusions about my soul. I made my choice and am content with fate. But if I were you? If I had my soul and the potential for a new life? Fuck, Georgina. I'd go after Seth, wherever he is, the instant I could hobble out of my bed. You're mortal now. It's easy to 'wait a little longer' when you've got all of eternity on the line. You don't anymore. You've wasted the time you have playing Hell's games, bickering back and forth with Seth and who he's been. End it. Go to him, as soon as you can, and fix this."

"You sound like Roman." As soon as I said his name, a

million memories came crashing down on me. "Oh my God. Roman. I can't believe what he did."

"I know," said Hugh sadly. "Carter told us that too."

"Why would he do that?" I asked, knowing I'd never have a satisfactory answer. "Oh Lord, Hugh. I left him there. I abandoned him."

"You did no such thing," scolded Hugh. "You had no choice in it. And it's not like he was conned or tricked. He knew for a long time he wanted to do this. After we filed the petition, he grilled me constantly about contract details and Hell's legal procedures. He wanted to do this. He prepared for it. He was just waiting for the chance."

I squeezed my eyes shut, afraid I would cry, as I remembered him defending me in Hell. A vague memory came to me, the night before the game. . . . Roman had had something to tell me but had held off. And when I'd floated above my body, just before I'd faded away, Carter had said he had to go get Roman. They'd planned on all of this. Roman had known what was happening and had been ready to depart. Hugh was right. Roman had wanted this.

That didn't make it any easier.

I opened my eyes. "What do I do?"

Hugh's face was kind as he regarded me. "Don't make Roman's sacrifice be in vain. He wanted you to be happy. So go be happy, sweetie. Go to Seth."

Any response I might make was interrupted when a nurse came and discovered I was conscious. She scolded Hugh for not getting her and went to summon the doctor. Hugh gave me a sheepish look as she did. It was a carryover from being immortal, when I would've healed so fast that we could easily dismiss modern medicine's assistance. The doctor, a forty-something woman named Dr. Addison, soon appeared and performed a few preliminary tests on me, as well as giving me the rundown on my condition.

When she was finished, I asked, "How long do you think I'll be here?"

"If everything progresses like it should?" she mused. "I'd

say you can be discharged in three more days. And you're going to have to take it easy."

"Three more days," I repeated mournfully. Being human was going to take some getting used to. As a succubus, I would've recovered from this in twenty-four hours. There wouldn't have even been any taking it easy afterward.

Dr. Addison scoffed at my dismay. "Honestly, after getting hit like you did, a week total here isn't bad at all. You took some nasty hits, but really, this could've been a lot worse."

When she and the nurse left, I saw Hugh scanning his phone. "What are you looking at?"

"Seth's schedule. In three days, he'll be in St. Louis."

"Hmm," I said.

"In four, he'll be in San Francisco."

"That's close," I said. "Relatively."

"It'd give you an extra day in there to recover," said Hugh.

"An extra day, huh?" I teased. "What happened to not wasting a single day as a mortal?"

"My point about not wasting time still stands," said Hugh. He grinned. "But even I can be realistic. Take the extra day. You need it for the logistics of travel, if nothing else. But not a single day more."

"Get out and live life, huh?"

"If you're up for it."

I thought about his words, thought about Seth. I nodded, not caring whether hopping on a plane right after being discharged was crazy. I was human now. Crazy was in the job description.

"I'm up for it," I said. "Book me a flight to San Francisco."

Hugh's attention was on his phone again. "Sweetie, I already am."

Chapter 22

Flying from Seattle to San Francisco is easy, easier even than going to Las Vegas. It takes less than two hours, and tons of flights run each day. The whole trip should've been simple. I mean, there were days when I'd spent more time in traffic just trying to get from downtown Seattle to the suburbs.

But I'd never flown on an airplane *as a mortal*. I was still determined to get to Seth, so there was no question that I was going to make this flight—only a lot of fear. I sat on the plane, waiting for takeoff, noticing things I'd never paid much attention to before. Were the engines usually that loud? Was that fuel I smelled? Was that a crack in the window, and if so, would the whole thing hold when we were airborne? I'd never done much more than politely watch the flight attendants' safety demo, but this time, I hung on to every detail. I had a lot on the line now—like, my life. An immortal could survive a plane crash. It wouldn't be pretty, but it was possible. Now? Now I faced all the risks the rest of the human world did.

My fears were unfounded, of course. The flight was smooth and easy, just as fast as I'd expected. Flying really was the safest form of travel. That hadn't changed. Only my perceptions of the world had. I made the trip white-knuckled and breathed a deep sigh of relief when the plane landed.

By the time I'd rented a car and was settled into my hotel room, I still had a couple hours before Seth's signing. My hotel was only a couple of blocks from his store—I'd planned it that way—and there was little for me to do except wait. Wait and obsess. A lot of that time was spent agonizing over my appearance. Even when I could shape-shift, I'd always prided myself on my ability to do my own styling. Of course, when Jerome had been summoned and I'd lost my succubus powers briefly, I'd discovered that I really wasn't quite as adept as I'd believed. I'd been cheating without realizing it all along, making small corrections with my powers. Stripped of them, I'd found all the little details I'd missed with blending eye shadow, straightening my hair, and myriad other grooming tasks.

Now was no different. I would never have that guaranteed perfection again. There would always be flaws in my appearance. I was going to start *aging*. How long until that set in? Staring at myself in the hotel bathroom's mirror, I searched out all the little things I thought could be improved upon and then tried to fix them. When I was finished, I was so frustrated that I didn't know if I'd come close to my previous perfection or not. The only thing I was fairly certain of was that it probably didn't matter. Seth's decision to forgive me wasn't going to have anything to do with how my bangs fell or if my makeup brought out the gold flecks in my green eyes.

I showed up ten minutes before Seth's event started, thought it was obvious people had been arriving for some time. A bit of nostalgia for Emerald City hit me as I gazed around and took in the efficient bookstore staff as they worked to accommodate the crowd. A podium had been set up in front of a large seating area, though no chairs were left empty. Staff shifted what furniture they could to improve the view for those of us who were standing, and I had to stop myself from offering to help. I ended up purposely staying near the back of the standing crowd. I could still see the podium and hoped my spot would keep me semiobscured. All around me, excited readers clutched copies of Seth's books, some even carrying huge stacks.

Their excitement was electric, and I found myself getting caught up in it when Seth finally emerged to thunderous applause. My heart leaped. How long had it been since we'd last spoken? A week? It felt like an eternity, maybe because I'd pretty much lived one in the trial. He was wearing a *Brady Bunch* T-shirt, and though it looked like he'd brushed his hair, I could already see parts of it starting to go unruly in that way it had. He didn't appear to have shaved in a couple days, but the scruff looked adorable and added to his carefree writer appearance. I felt a smile spreading on my face as I watched him and was reminded of the first time we'd met, when he'd come to Emerald City for a signing and I hadn't recognized him.

"Hey, everybody," he said into the microphone, once the applause had quieted. "Thanks for coming out tonight."

Thinking about that first meeting with him also made me realize how much he had changed in the last year and a half. He would never be entirely comfortable in front of a crowd like this—especially since they kept getting bigger—but he was certainly more at ease than that first meeting. He grinned at their enthusiasm and made eye contact where he could, something he'd had trouble with in the past. There was confidence even in the way he stood and spoke. It made me love him that much more, something I hadn't believed possible.

Sometimes he would open by reading aloud from the new book, but this time, he jumped straight into questions. Hands went up everywhere, and I found myself ducking against a shelf as he scanned the audience and called on people. I wasn't quite ready for discovery yet. I just wanted to watch him and drink him in.

I was amused that the very first question he was asked was, "Where do you get your ideas from?" That had been a joke between us, at that first meeting, because it was one of the most common questions he received. I'd commented, back then, that it must get tedious answering the same things, and Seth had told me no. He'd said that the question was always new for the person asking and that he treated it as such. It didn't matter how many times it came up. He took joy in their excitement for the books.

More questions came, both broad and specific, and Seth answered them all with friendliness and good humor that his fans loved. A lot of people especially wanted to know about the next book, the last book in his Cady and O'Neill series. My heart grew and grew the more I watched him, and I felt like I was getting away with something by being able to observe him without his knowledge. Our last few encounters hadn't exactly been friendly, and it was a balm to me to observe all the warmth and kindness that had made me fall in love with him.

It went by too quickly. I was so caught up in watching and listening to him that I was barely aware of the time flying by. It wasn't until I picked up on the subtle movements of the staff that it hit me that this portion of the event was about to wrap up. They would go into signing soon, and the crowd around me would become a massive line that would take hours to get through. Then what? I was suddenly at a loss. Why had I come here? To see Seth . . . and then? I wasn't sure what. I hadn't had much of a plan, short of the preparations needed to get here. Somehow, I had been thinking that would be enough, but of course it wouldn't be. If I wanted to do something, I had to do it now, before this turned into the machine of signing.

My hand went up, and inexplicably, Seth's eyes went instantly to me. I don't know how it happened. Like me, others had realized their chance to ask questions was running out, and eager hands were up everywhere, some waving eagerly in the hopes that they might draw his attention. How I—standing in the back and shorter than most of those around me— pulled it off was a mystery. Maybe it was like the time Erik had used Seth to rescue me from the Oneroi. Maybe after everything that had happened, we were still bound.

Seth's eyes widened when he realized it was me, but his hand was already pointing in my direction, giving me permission to speak. He faltered only a little. "Y-yes?"

I felt like the eyes of the world were on me. The eyes of the universe, even. So much rested on the next words out of my mouth.

"Are Cady and O'Neill ever going to get together?"

I don't know where it came from. When Seth and I had first met, this was the other common question he and I had discussed, and I had mocked it as well. Surprisingly, no one had asked it tonight, but judging from the intense way everyone turned to Seth, you could tell it was on a lot of people's minds.

Those amber brown eyes weighed me heavily, and then he answered my question with a question. "Do you think they should?"

"Well," I said, "they've been through an awful lot together. And if there's only one book left, it kind of seems like they're running out of time."

The ghost of a smile flickered over his lips. "I suppose you're right." He thought about it a heartbeat more. "I don't know if they will. I guess you'll just have to read the next installment."

That was met with disappointed groans, and the bookstore staff used that as an opening to segue into signing and hurry Seth off to a more comfortable table. He watched me a few moments more before he moved, the faint smile still on his face. He looked thoughtful.

Meanwhile, my heart was beating in double time. In a daze, I allowed myself to be herded with the others into line, not caring how far back I was. Some of the aches in my ribs and the rest of my body began to nag me, but I forced myself to stay strong and ignore them. It took an hour and a half for me to reach the front, but much like the questions, I barely noticed the passage of time. Only, now it wasn't because I was so enraptured by what I saw. This time, I was simply terrified. I wanted to see Seth . . . but was afraid to.

He finished signing for the person in front of me and gave me the same smile he'd had on for everyone else. I supposed he'd had time to prepare himself for me coming through the line and was able to effectively hide his shock at my presence.

"Hi," he said. I handed him my book without a word. "You've come a long ways."

"I'm a pretty big fan," I said.

He smiled and scrawled one of his stock phrases into the book: *Thanks for reading!* When he finished signing, he gave the book back to me, and I gave him an envelope in return.

"This is for you," I said. There was nothing that weird about my action. People often gave him gifts and letters. In fact, I could see a small pile of goods sitting on a chair beside him. He accepted them with good grace all the time, but then, they weren't usually from people who had the kind of history we did.

He held the envelope for a moment, and I suddenly worried he wasn't going to take it. Then, he set it down and said, "Thank you." It went next to him on the table, not on the chair.

Unsure what to do now, I murmured my own thanks and then hurried off to let everyone else have their chance with him. Mine was gone. I'd played my cards and wouldn't know for a while if anything would come of it. The envelope had had a number scrawled on one side, and inside was a key to my hotel room. It was a silly, clichéd thing to do, but I knew how these types of events worked. If I'd openly asked Seth to meet me somewhere, I would have likely gotten the unwanted attention of the bookstore staff and their security. I knew because I'd hurried a fair number of zealous fans off after book signings myself.

At least back in the hotel room, I was able to sit down. I didn't realize until that moment just how much I'd been asking of my battered body to stand for that long. Hugh had been right about one thing: being mortal changed everything. I couldn't shrug off getting hit by a car now the same way I could have as a succubus. My doctor had given me a prescription for Vicodin, but I was pretty sure I didn't want to be strung out on drugs for my grand reunion with Seth. I settled for ibuprofen and began the agonizing process of waiting.

I'd actually dozed off when I heard the room's door click open. I sprang up from the bed, only getting half a glance at myself in the mirror before I moved toward the door. Seth entered, freezing when he saw me. The door swung shut behind him, and I too came screeching to a halt, too stunned to move. Part of it was that same wonder and rapture of seeing him, just as it had been in the bookstore. Only, now he was right *here,* alone in the same room with me. It was almost too much to handle. The rest of my inability to react came from simply forgetting what I'd wanted to say. I'd rehearsed a hundred speeches and apologies earlier, and all of them abandoned me now. I fumbled for something—anything—to say that would fix all of the hurt between us.

"Seth—"

I never got another word out. In the space of that breath, he crossed the distance between us and wrapped his arms around me, nearly lifting me off the ground in a giant hug.

"Thetis," he breathed against my neck.

"Ow," I squeaked.

He instantly set me down and opened his arms, staring curiously. "The car? But it's been . . ." Curiosity changed to wonder. "It's true, isn't it? You're really . . ."

". . . human," I supplied, catching hold of his hand. Even if that hug had been quite the test of my ribs, I hated to lose all contact with him. After the chasm that had stretched between us recently, even that small touch of his fingers was like magic to me.

Seth nodded wonderingly, drinking me in. "They told me . . . they tried to explain it. I understood, but somehow I just couldn't . . . I just couldn't wrap my mind around it. I'm still not sure I can. You look the same."

"I got to keep the same body," I said. "Parting gift."

"Yeah, but it's just as perfect . . . just as beautiful. I don't know. I thought as a human you'd look . . . ordinary."

"Stop," I said, feeling flustered. I ran a nervous hand over my hair. This conversation wasn't going how I expected. "I probably have bedhead." My makeup had probably smudged while I slept too.

He grabbed my other hand and—gently—drew me near. "You look perfect."

I shook my head, still needing to summon one of my well-prepared speeches. "Seth, I'm so sorry. Sorry for everything that I—"

"Shh," he murmured. "Thetis. Georgina. Letha. It's all right. You have nothing to apologize for."

Now I stared in wonder. "I have everything to apologize for. What I did to you—"

"—was a lifetime ago," he said.

"But it was still me," I argued. "Still this life."

"What, and you can't be forgiven for that? For something you did when you were still in your teens?"

I wasn't sure how I'd switched from apologizing to trying to condemn myself, but there I was, doing it anyway. "We were still married. Or, well, I mean . . . I was to him. I broke my vows. It was wrong."

"And I was wrong—or he was wrong, whatever—to have been so oblivious to how you were feeling. We were both at fault, Georgina. We both screwed up—many times." Seth released my hands and gently cupped my face in his. "And I daresay we've paid for it a hundred times over. How long do we have to be punished? Are we beyond forgiveness?"

I had to look away then, for fear of tears forming in my eyes. Last year, not long after I'd met Seth, I'd discussed some of these same things with Carter. He'd told me that no one—not even a succubus—was beyond forgiveness and redemption.

"But what you said . . . I hurt you so much. . . ."

Seth sighed. "I know. And I'm sorry. It was all such a shock, the hypnosis . . . I still remember it all, but it's taken on kind of a dreamlike quality now. Like it's something I saw on TV rather than something I experienced. It was all a long time ago, and we've both changed. I was coming to you that night at the bowling alley to talk about it. I was still confused but knew enough to realize I'd acted rashly. Then, when you were hurt, and they told me you could actually die . . ."

He trailed off, and I dared a look upward. "Oh, no. Please don't tell me that this is one of those situations where it took a near-death experience to realize how you felt about me."

"No," he said, with one of those small, amused smiles I loved. "I knew long before that. The injuries of the past will always be a part of me, but I've grown from them—just like you have. You're the same as you've always been . . . and yet you're not. You faced me, even though you wanted to run away. You kept trying to help my family, even when I was telling you to go away. We've both changed . . . both taken the best we could of the bad. I just didn't see it right away." He sighed. "Like I said, it was the reason I came that night. Seeing you hurt only drove home what a fool I was. And then when Carter told me what happened . . ." Those warm brown eyes searched my face. "Is it true? You had a clean getaway and risked it all for me?"

I swallowed. "It wouldn't have been a clean getaway without you."

Seth tipped my head back and kissed me, his lips warm and soft. The sensation swept my body, love and desire both threatening to overwhelm me. There was no more succubus feeding, no more peering into his soul. I no longer knew his thoughts, and I didn't need to. I knew my own, knew that I loved him. And I also suddenly knew with certainty, in that same way all humans deduce such things without that benefit of succubus powers, that he loved me too.

"Is it that easy?" I whispered, when we finally broke apart. "Kiss and make up?"

"It's as easy as we choose to make it," he murmured, pressing his forehead to mine. "At least, this decision is. Nothing's truly easy, Georgina. Love and life . . . they're wonderful, but they're hard. We may mess up again. We have to be strong and decide if we can still go forward, even when things aren't perfect."

"How'd someone so young get so wise?" I asked.

He brushed a lock of hair from my face. "I learned from this woman who knows a *lot* about love."

I scoffed. "Hardly. I think I'm still learning more about it every day."

Seth's lips found mine again, and I forgot my worries for a moment, simply losing myself in him. With as ardent as he'd been earlier, I was kind of surprised when he was the one who stopped the next kiss.

"Easy there," he said, with a small laugh. "You feel too good. We don't want to get too carried away."

"Don't we?" I asked. "I mean, I gave you my room key, and you went right for me as soon as you came in."

"Well, yeah," he agreed, "but that was before I remembered you were hit by a car a week ago."

I tightened my arms around him and drew him toward the bed. "I'm still alive, aren't I?"

"Yes," he admitted, letting himself be drawn along. "But are you sure you don't want to just wait?"

Hugh had said something after booking my flight. *Everything changes when you're mortal. You don't know what tomorrow will bring.*

"I've waited long enough," I told Seth, just before kissing him.

And that was the moment I knew what it was like to have my soul back.

It sounds kind of sappy, I know. But to be able to kiss someone you love when you're fully and completely in control of yourself and know who you are . . . it's exquisite. How we love others is affected by how we love ourselves, and for the first time in a long time, I was whole. I knew who I was and in turn was able to appreciate just how much I loved him.

And of course, the whole experience was affected by the

fact that I no longer had succubus powers to contend with. I didn't have to worry about stealing his life energy. I didn't have to wrestle with the guilt. I didn't have to split the desires of my heart with my predatory supernatural nature. All I had to do was touch him and exalt in the experience of being together.

We fell onto the bed, having a care for my still-bruised body. Strangely, I'd also been recovering from injuries the first time Seth and I had made love. Then too, we'd had to balance our passion with caution. It hadn't been difficult then, and it wasn't difficult now. We peeled each other's clothes away, tossing them into a careless heap on the floor. When Seth saw the bandages around my torso, he gently kissed all around them, his lips softly grazing my hips and breasts.

Through some unspoken understanding, I rolled him onto his back so that I could lower myself onto him. I positioned my hips over his, resting my hands on his chest, and slowly brought him into me. We both cried out, from pleasure and also the sheer *rightness* of being together. He fit like he'd been made for me, and I suddenly wondered if I should have been so quick to always scoff about divine plans. Because surely, if ever there was something that seemed to have been guided by a higher power, it was the crazy path of our relationship . . . one that always kept bringing us back together.

Over and over I rode him, overwhelmed almost as much by the way his gaze held mine as I was by the heat spreading through my body. I wanted to stop, to freeze that moment in time, but my human flesh and its desires eventually won out. I increased my pace, taking him harder and deeper until I crossed the edge and could handle no more. Ecstasy shook my body as I came, and a joy so intense I nearly forgot my surroundings flooded me. There was no succubus satisfaction here, only the simple bliss of taking pleasure in the one I loved.

Seth came soon after, the look on his face causing me joy of another sort. There was such an easy, unguarded happiness in it, mingled with all his love for me. He hid nothing. It was all there on display, his affection and his bliss.

Afterward, we lay in each other's arms, both of us floating in our own emotions as we basked in the experience we'd just had. I could hear Seth's heart beating as I rested against him and was aware of the pounding of my own heart—my mortal, human heart—as well. This was what it was like to truly be alive.

"I'm almost afraid to move or speak," he said at last. "Part of me is certain this must be a dream or a spell. I'm afraid I'll ruin it."

"It's neither," I said. Then, I reconsidered. "Well, it might be a dream."

Nyx had taunted me for a long time with her dream-vision, refusing to tell me who the man in it was. When Seth had finally been revealed, I'd been certain she'd lied to me. I hadn't seen how any of that future could become a reality, and yet . . . here I was.

"A dream, huh?" asked Seth. "Does that mean I'm going to wake up to cold reality soon?"

"No," I said, snuggling closer. "Because our dream's come true. The only thing you're going to wake up to from now on is me. For as long as you want me."

"I want you forever. Is that too long?"

I smiled. "After what we've seen? I'm not sure it's long enough."

Epilogue

We were married at sunset.

Some might not consider that an auspicious time, but for me, it was a perfect compromise. I had wanted to be married in the daytime, outdoors, with sunlight streaming everywhere. Seeing as Cody and Peter wanted to attend, however, the sun presented a little difficulty. And since Peter had essentially acted as wedding coordinator for me, it seemed kind of mean to exclude him. So, we held the ceremony at sunset, and the vampires were able to show up for the reception the instant the sun sank below the horizon.

The wedding was held on the grounds of a beachfront resort on Puget Sound. We stood on a grassy hill, facing west toward the water. It was high summer, and everything was bathed in orange and gold. The bridesmaids (all Mortensen girls) wore red dresses that looked as though they'd been designed with the sunset in mind and carried white clusters of stephanotis. Our only nod to decorations was an ivy-strewn arch that the officiant stood in front of. With so much beauty around us, nothing else had seemed necessary.

I repeated my vows while holding Seth's hands. Each word I spoke was infinitely powerful, and yet I wouldn't really remember any of them until later. For those minutes, my whole world was focused on his face, on the amber gold of his eyes and the way the light played off his hair. Love burned within me and between us, making everything else a fog of indistinct details. There was only Seth and me. Me and Seth.

There was a dreamlike quality to it all. The moments seemed suspended in time. And yet, afterward, when I looked back, it was as though the entire ceremony had taken place in the blink of an eye. We had a couple hundred people who had gathered to watch us. They all rose from their folding chairs and clapped when we kissed, and I found myself unable to stop grinning when I looked out into that sea of happy faces.

The reception was held on the same grounds, just a little ways from the ceremony. We'd gone to a bit more work with the decorations here. The tables were draped with white linens and bedecked with flowers and candles that created little twinkles of light in the evening shadows. Large torches were set up along the boundaries as well, their flames flicking rapidly as wind picked up from the water. A jazz band set up nearby and began to play, providing background music for dinner. They had a space for dancing afterward too, though I didn't dance nearly as much as I'd expected to at my wedding. There were too many people to see, too many people to thank for their support. So Seth and I walked around hand in hand, going from group to group of those we loved.

"I knew those Asiatic lilies would be a good call," Peter told us conspiratorially, admiring one of the table arrangements. "The Oriental ones are bigger, but I feel like these complement the roses so much better."

"You're a regular flower whisperer," said Hugh, knocking back a drink. He held up his glass to Seth and me in a mock toast. "Honestly, your best bit of planning was the open bar."

"Because it certainly wasn't the band," remarked Doug, strolling over to where my little group was standing. "Geez, Kincaid—" He paused and reconsidered. "Geez, Mortensens, why didn't you hire me? Nocturnal Admission could've totally rocked this place out."

I smiled, happy that Doug had come. I honestly hadn't been sure if he would. "Because I wouldn't want to burden you guys with the strain of playing family-friendly music for three hours."

"Very considerate," he said. He glanced around, nodding grudgingly. "Aside from that—and the fact that the bridesmaids are all under eighteen—I gotta admit, you put on a pretty good spread."

"Thank you," Peter and I said in unison.

"I kind of agree with Doug about the band," said Cody. "I asked them if they'd play 'The Chicken Dance,' and they said no."

"I could've done a *bitchin'* cover of that," said Doug solemnly.

"It's not so much a failing on the band's part as it was a request of ours to not play it," said Seth.

"Sad," said Doug. He slung an arm around Cody. "Want to go make a bar run with me?" When Cody nodded, Doug glanced at the rest of us. "Refill anyone?"

"No, thanks," I said.

Doug shook his head. "Married for an hour, and you're already picking up his good habits." He and Cody walked off, having an intense discussion about "The Chicken Dance," judging from their pantomimes.

I leaned my head against Seth, content with everything and everyone in the world. "You did a beautiful job, Peter," I said. "Seriously. It all turned out great."

Considering how underappreciated Peter always felt, I would've expected him to revel in the praise, but he actually turned modest. "Ah, well. You guys are the main attraction. I just provided the—"

He stopped speaking, and as one, he and Hugh glanced off beyond the edge of the torches, into the darkness.

"What is it?" I asked.

They exchanged looks. "Carter," said Peter.

I followed their gaze, unable to see anything beyond the lit perimeter. It had been very easy to become human again, but there were still a few things I had trouble shaking. The loss of my immortal senses was one. Even now, it was weird to be standing with Peter and Hugh and not *feel* them. Their night vision was no better than mine—well, actually, I supposed Peter's was—but it wasn't their eyes that had alerted them to Carter's presence.

"I think he wants to see you," said Hugh gently.

I stared off at where they indicated, uncertain what should I do.

"Go," said Seth softly. "You should talk to him."

I looked up at him, into those eyes so full of love, and forgot about Carter for the space of heartbeat. It was still too unbelievable to accept sometimes that this was my life, that Seth was my husband. I pressed my lips to his in a quick kiss.

"I'll be right back," I said.

I picked my way through my guests, finding it difficult not to stop and talk to the many well-wishers. When I was out of the safety of the tents and tables, the wind hit me, whipping my hair and veil around and playing with my skirts. My dress had a sweetheart neckline and full skirt with many tiers and layers. I'd wanted a princess dress for my wedding day and had gotten one, though it made this walk a little awkward. I soon spotted Carter, standing so perfectly still among some trees that he might have been one.

"Mrs. Mortensen," he greeted me, when I reached him. "Congratulations." He wore worn gray suit pants, a long-sleeved white shirt with the first couple buttons open, and loosely knotted gray and pink silk tie. A jacket matched the pants and looked like it was two sizes too big. I nodded in approval.

"Nice of you to dress up," I said. "I don't think I've ever seen you in anything so formal."

"I should've checked with Peter to find out your colors," said Carter, running a hand through his hair. It didn't look like it had been brushed for the occasion. "Sorry if I clash."

I smiled. "You look great. Thank you for coming."

"Well," he said. "We left off kind of abruptly."

"That we did," I murmured. This was the first time I'd seen him since the trial. "Jerome's not with you?"

"No. You won't be seeing him anymore. Well." Carter paused a moment. "Let's just say, I *hope* you won't be seeing him anymore."

"I plan on staying off Hell's radar," I said honestly.

He nodded, turning serious. "That's good. That's kind of why I'm here. I've got two gifts for you. Gifts of information."

"You were checking my registry," I said. "How sweet."

We didn't have much light, but I swore, I could see his gray eyes twinkle. "You said you'll stay off their radar, but believe me, they're going to still have their eyes on you. Hell doesn't lose many souls the way they lost yours. If they can get it back, they will. They'll try. I know how close you are to them. . . ." His gaze drifted back toward the reception. "To Hugh, Peter, and Cody. But it'd be better for you—and for them—if you stayed away from them. If you moved away from them, to someplace where you don't know any of the local immortals."

I stared in astonishment. "Are you saying one of them might try to get my soul? They're my friends."

"I know, I know. And I don't think they would, exactly, but it's an ugly position for them to be in. You should really think about leaving Seattle. You'll make it easier on everyone if you just remove that temptation."

"I love Seattle," I said, turning back to look across the dark water. "But I love Seth more. I'll talk to him. Andrea's been doing better, so we can go. I don't know where, but we'll figure it out." I sighed and looked back at him. "Is your other piece of information less depressing?"

The smile reappeared on his lips. "Yes. It's a big secret." He leaned toward me and said in a stage whisper, "You're going to have a baby in December."

A matching smile came over me. "That's no secret. Not to me, at least." Seth and I had known for a little while and had decided to keep it under wraps until after the wedding. We weren't going to be able to hide it much longer. I was three months pregnant, and without shape-shifting, I was subject to the rules of nature. It was a wonder I still fit in this dress.

"Okay," said Carter. "Then try this: it's a girl."

I felt my smile grow. "That I didn't know."

Or did I? A sudden flashback to the dream Nyx had shown me played through my mind. I hadn't thought about it in a very long time. Why did I need to? I was living my own dream. But in a flash, I saw it again, me holding a small girl as we waited outside for her father to come home. And it was snowing. . . .

You should really think about leaving Seattle.

"What are you thinking?" asked Carter, studying me.

"I'm thinking there might be a short list of places I'll be moving to." I shivered, both from the cold and the memories, and he draped his worn suit jacket over my bare shoulders.

"I'm moving too," he told me.

I blinked away from my memories. "You are? Where? Why?"

He chose to answer the last one. "Because my job here is done. Time to go on to another."

It took me a moment to follow. "You don't mean . . . I was your assignment? I'm why you came to Seattle?"

He answered with a shrug.

"But . . . no," I protested. "There must be other things you do here, right? Other angelic tasks?"

"Weren't you enough?" he teased.

I was still in disbelief. Carter had been in Seattle for as many years as me. Surely there must have been more to it. Admittedly, no one in Hell ever really understood how the angels worked on their assignments. They didn't have the same level of micromanaging as my former employees. "I'm just one person. One soul. All your work and energy . . . I mean, it can't all have been just for one soul. An angel can't be solely dedicated to that."

"Well," he said, clearly enjoying my confusion. "It was actually for two souls, since you and Seth were both saved. But even if it wasn't, it still would've been worth it. Do you know the price of one soul, Georgina? It's beyond rubies and diamonds, beyond any mortal reckoning. If it had taken me centuries, if it had taken a dozen more angels to help me, it all would have been worth it."

I lowered my head, feeling tears come to my eyes. I thought about how often I'd disparaged Carter, how many times I'd scoffed at the silly, hard-drinking persona he put on. Yet, no matter how much I dismissed him, Carter had always been there in the background, always showing interest in Seth and me. He'd protected me and given me advice, and I spent most of my time mocking him.

"I'm not worthy of that," I said. I might be human now, but I understood how powerful a heavenly creature Carter was. "I don't deserve that much regard."

He reached out and tipped my chin up. "You do, Georgina. And if you don't believe me now, then strive to be. Live your life. Be kind. Love those you know. Love those you don't know. Be worthy of your soul."

A tear escaped, rolling down my cheek and probably messing up my mortal mascara. "Thank you, Carter. Thank you for everything."

"There's nothing to thank me for," he replied. With a sigh, he glanced up at the starry night. "I should be going. And your guests are probably looking for you. I'm sure they've been banging on glasses with their spoons this entire time."

"Wait—before you go . . ." I hesitated. Carter had already told me so much, but I had to know one other thing. "What happened to Roman? Is he dead?"

Carter's amused expression faded. "Ah. I don't know."

"Carter—"

"I mean it," he said. "That's the straightest answer you'll ever get from an angel. I don't know. I don't think his outcome was good, but I don't know for sure."

I swallowed back more tears. "He shouldn't have gone."

"It was his choice, Georgina. He wanted to make a point to Heaven and Hell . . . that, and well, there's more. He did it out of love, and that's no small thing. A sacrifice born of love is almost as powerful a thing as a redeemed soul. Both of them are blows to Hell."

"I wish . . . I wish I could've said good-bye. Told him how grateful I am."

"I think he knows," said Carter. "I think he knew exactly what he was getting into and deemed it worthwhile. The best way to thank him now is to do what I said. Live your life to its fullest. Take care of your husband and daughter, and let your soul shine."

I nodded. "I will. Thank you." I almost asked about Yasmine too but had a feeling the answer would be the same: she'd made her decision. I could only be responsible for my fate, not everyone else's.

"Bless you, daughter of man," Carter said, his eyes luminous and almost silver now. He leaned down and kissed my forehead. I closed my eyes and caught my breath. His lips were both burning hot and icy cold. A sense of peace and power flooded me, and for a moment, it was as though I were right on the edge of comprehending all the beauty in the world. I opened my eyes.

He was gone.

I stood alone on the windswept hill, with the moon starting to shine on the water. In the distance, I heard the laughter and chatter of those I loved and sensed the warmth they held. Picking up my skirts, still wearing Carter's jacket over my shoulders, I headed off toward my husband and the rest of my life, off to be worthy of my soul.

RICHELLE MEAD

If you love Richelle's sensational 'Succubus' series, why not try her fast and fun 'Dark Swan' novels, featuring shaman-for-hire Eugenie Markham who's got her hands full binding and banishing creatures from the Otherworld.

Here's the opening chapter of *Storm Born* to whet your appetite . . .

STORM BORN

Chapter 1

I'd seen weirder things than a haunted shoe, but not many.

The Nike Pegasus sat on the office's desk, inoffensive, colored in shades of gray, white, and orange. Some of the laces were loosened, and a bit of dirt clung around the soles. It was the left shoe.

As for me, well . . . underneath my knee-length coat, I had a Glock .22 loaded with bullets carrying a higher-than-legal steel content. A cartridge of silver ones rested in the coat's pocket. Two athames lay sheathed on my other hip, one silver-bladed and one iron. Stuck into my belt near them was a wand, hand-carved oak and loaded with enough charmed gems to probably blow up the desk in the corner if I wanted to.

To say I felt overdressed was something of an understatement.

"So," I said, keeping my voice as neutral as possible, "what makes you think your shoe is . . . uh, possessed?"

Brian Montgomery, late thirties with a receding

hairline in serious denial, eyed the shoe nervously and moistened his lips. "It always trips me up when I'm out running. Every time. And it's always moving around. I mean, I never actually see it, but . . . like, I'll take them off near the door, then I come back and find this one under the bed or something. And sometimes . . . sometimes I touch it, and it feels cold . . . really cold . . . like . . ." He groped for similes and finally picked the tritest one. "Like ice."

I nodded and glanced back at the shoe, not saying anything.

"Look, Miss . . . Odile . . . or whatever. I'm not crazy. That shoe is haunted. It's evil. You've gotta do something, okay? I've got a marathon coming up, and until this started happening, these were my lucky shoes. And they're not cheap, you know. They're an investment."

It sounded crazy to me—which was saying something—but there was no harm in checking, seeing as I was already out here. I reached into my coat pocket, the one without ammunition, and pulled out my pendulum. It was a simple one, a thin silver chain with a small quartz crystal hanging from it.

I laced the chain's end through my fingers and held my flattened hand over the shoe, clearing my mind and letting the crystal hang freely. A moment later, it began to slowly rotate of its own accord.

"Well, I'll be damned," I muttered, stuffing the pendulum back in my pocket. There was something there. I turned to Montgomery, attempting some sort of badass face, because that was what customers always expected. "It might be best if you stepped out of the room, sir. For your own safety."

That was only half-true. Mostly I just found lingering clients annoying. They asked stupid questions and could do stupider things, which actually put me at more risk than them.

He had no qualms about getting out of there. As soon as the door closed, I found a jar of salt in my satchel and poured a large ring on the office's floor. I tossed the shoe into the middle of it and invoked the four cardinal directions with the silver athame. Ostensibly the circle didn't change, but I felt a slight flaring of power, indicating it had sealed us in.

Trying not to yawn, I pulled out my wand and kept holding the silver athame. It had taken four hours to drive to Las Cruces, and doing that on so little sleep had made the distance seem twice as long. Sending some of my will into the wand, I tapped it against the shoe and spoke in a sing-song voice.

"Come out, come out, whoever you are."

There was a moment's silence, then a high-pitched male voice snapped, "Go away, bitch."

Great. A shoe with attitude. "Why? You got something better to do?"

"Better things to do than waste my time with a mortal."

I smiled. "Better things to do in a shoe? Come

on. I mean, I've heard of slumming it, but don't you think you're kind of pushing the envelope here? This shoe isn't even new. You could have done so much better."

The voice kept its annoyed tone, not threatening but simply irritated at the interruption. "*I'm* slumming it? Do you think I don't know who you are, Eugenie Markham? Dark-Swan-Called-Odile. A blood traitor. A mongrel. An assassin. A murderer." He practically spit out the last word. "You are alone among your kind and mine. A bloodthirsty shadow. You do anything for anyone who can pay you enough for it. That makes you more than a mercenary. That makes you a whore."

I affected a bored stance. I'd been called most of those names before. Well, except for my own name. That was new—and a little disconcerting. Not that I'd let him know that.

"Are you done whining? Because I don't have time to listen while you stall."

"Aren't you being paid by the hour?" he asked nastily.

"I charge a flat fee."

"Oh."

I rolled my eyes and touched the wand to the shoe again. This time, I thrust the full force of my will into it, drawing upon my own body's physical stamina as well as some of the power of the world around me. "No more games. If you leave on your own, I won't have to hurt you. *Come out.*"

He couldn't stand against that command and the power within it. The shoe trembled, and smoke poured out of it. Oh, Jesus. I hoped the shoe didn't get incinerated during this. Montgomery wouldn't be able to handle that.

The smoke bellowed out, coalescing into a large, dark form about two feet taller than me. With all his wisecracks, I'd sort of expected a saucy version of one of Santa's elves. Instead, the being before me had the upper body of a well-muscled man, while his lower portion resembled a small cyclone. The smoke solidified into leathery gray-black skin, and I had only a moment to act as I assessed this new development. I swapped the wand for the gun, ejecting the clip as I pulled it out. By then, he was lunging for me, and I had to roll out of his way, confined by the circle's boundaries.

A keres. A male keres—most unusual. I'd anticipated something fey, which required silver bullets; or a spectre, which required no bullets. Keres were ancient death spirits originally confined to canopic jars. When the jars wore down over time, keres tended to seek out new homes. There weren't too many of them left in this world, and soon there'd be one less.

He bore down on me, and I took a nice chunk out of him with the silver blade. I used my right hand, the one I wore an onyx and obsidian bracelet on. Those stones alone would take a toll on a death spirit like him without the blade's help.

Sure enough, he hissed in pain and hesitated a moment. I used that delay, scrambling to load the silver cartridge.

I didn't quite make it, because soon he was on me again. He hit me with one of those massive arms, slamming me against the walls of the circle. They might be transparent, but they felt as solid as bricks. One of the downsides of trapping a spirit in a circle was that I got trapped too. My head and left shoulder took the brunt of that impact, and pain shot through me in small starbursts. He seemed pretty pleased with himself over this, as overconfident villains so often are.

"You're as strong as they say, but you were a fool to try to cast me out. You should have left me in peace." His voice was deeper now, almost gravelly.

I shook my head, both to disagree and to get rid of the dizziness. "It isn't your shoe."

I still couldn't swap that goddamned cartridge. Not with him ready to attack again, not with both hands full. Yet I couldn't risk dropping either weapon.

He reached for me, and I cut him again. The wounds were small, but the athame was like poison. It would wear him down over time—if I could stay alive that long. I moved to strike at him once more, but he anticipated me and seized hold of my wrist. He squeezed it, bending it in an unnatural position and forcing me to drop the athame and cry out. I hoped he hadn't broken any bones.

Smug, he grabbed me by the shoulders with both hands and lifted me up so that I hung face to face with him. His eyes were yellow with slits for pupils, much like some sort of snake's. His breath was hot and reeked of decay as he spoke.

"You are small, Eugenie Markham, but you are lovely and your flesh is warm. Perhaps I should beat the rush and take you myself. I'd enjoy hearing you scream beneath me."

Ew. Had that thing just propositioned me? And there was my name again. How in the world did he know that? None of them knew that. I was only Odile to them, named after the dark swan in *Swan Lake*, a name coined by my stepfather because of the form my spirit preferred to travel in while visiting the Otherworld. The name—though not particularly terrifying—had stuck, though I doubted any of the creatures I fought knew the reference. They didn't really get out to the ballet much.

The keres had my upper arms pinned—I would have bruises tomorrow—but my hands and forearms were free. He was so sure of himself, so overly arrogant and confident, that he paid no attention to my struggling hands. He probably just perceived the motion as a futile effort to free myself. In seconds, I had the clip out and in the gun. I managed one clumsy shot and he dropped me—not gently. I stumbled to regain my balance again. Bullets probably couldn't kill him, but a silver one in the center of his chest would certainly hurt.

He stumbled back, half-surprised, and I wondered if he'd ever even encountered a gun before. It fired again, then again and again and again. The reports were loud; hopefully Montgomery wouldn't do something foolish and come running in. The keres roared in outrage and pain, each shot making him stagger backward until he was all the way against the circle's boundary. I advanced on him, retrieved athame flashing in my hand. In a few quick motions, I carved the death symbol on the part of his chest that wasn't bloodied from bullets. An electric charge immediately ran through the air of the circle. Hairs stood up on the back of my neck, and I could smell ozone, like just before a storm.

He screamed and leapt forward, renewed by rage or adrenaline or whatever else these creatures ran on. But it was too late for him. He was marked and wounded. I was ready. In another mood, I might have simply banished him to the Otherworld; I tried not to kill if I didn't have to. But that sexual suggestion had just been out of line. I was pissed off now. He'd go to the world of death, straight to Persephone's gate.

I fired again to slow him, my aim a bit off with the left hand but still good enough to hit him. I had already traded the athame for the wand. This time, I didn't draw on the power from this plane. With well-practiced ease, I let part of my consciousness slip this world. In moments, I reached the crossroads to the Otherworld. That was an easy transition; I did it all the time. The next crossover was a little harder, especially with me being weakened from the fight, but still nothing I couldn't do automatically. I kept my own spirit well outside of the land of death, but I touched it and sent that connection through the wand. It sucked him in, and his face twisted with fear.

"This is not your world," I said in a low voice, feeling the power burn through me and around me. "This is not your world, and I cast you out. I send you to the black gate, to the lands of death where you can either be reborn or fade to oblivion or burn in the flames of hell. I really don't give a shit. Go."

He screamed, but the magic caught him. There was a trembling in the air, a build-up of pressure, and then it ended abruptly, like a deflated balloon. The keres was gone too, leaving only a shower of gray sparkles that soon faded to nothing.

Silence. I sank to my knees, exhaling deeply. My eyes closed a moment, as my body relaxed and my consciousness returned to this world. I was exhausted but exultant too. Killing him had felt good. Heady, even. He'd gotten what he deserved, and I had been the one to deal it out.

Minutes later, some of my strength returned. I stood and opened the circle, suddenly feeling stifled by it. I put my tools and weapons away and went to find Montgomery.

"Your shoe's been exorcised," I told him flatly. "I killed the ghost." No point in explaining the difference between a keres and a true ghost; he wouldn't understand.

He entered the room with slow steps, picking up the shoe gingerly. "I heard gunshots. How do you use bullets on a ghost?"

I shrugged. It hurt from where the keres had slammed my shoulder to the wall. "It was a strong ghost."

He cradled the shoe like one might a child and then glanced down with disapproval. "There's blood on the carpet."

"Read the paperwork you signed. I assume no responsibility for damage incurred to personal property."

With a few grumbles, he paid up—in cash—and I left. Really, though, he was so stoked about the shoe, I probably could have decimated the office.

In my car, I dug out a Milky Way from the stash in my glove box. Battles like that required immediate sugar and calories. As I practically shoved the candy bar into my mouth, I turned on my cell phone. I had a missed call from Lara.

Once I'd consumed a second bar and was on I-10 back to Tucson, I dialed her.

"Yo," I said.

"Hey. Did you finish the Montgomery job?"

"Yup."

"Was the shoe really possessed?"

"Yup."

"Huh. Who knew? That's kind of funny too.

290

Like, you know, lost souls and soles in shoes . . ."

"Bad, very bad," I chastised. Lara might be a good secretary, but there was only so much I could be expected to put up with. "So what's up? Or were you just checking in?"

"No. I just got a weird job offer. Some guy— well, honestly, I thought he sounded kind of schizo. But he claims his sister was abducted by fairies, er, gentry. He wants you to go get her."

I fell silent at that, staring at the highway and clear blue sky ahead without consciously seeing either one. Some objective part of me attempted to process what she had just said. I didn't get that kind of request very often. Okay, never. A retrieval like that required me to cross over physically into the Otherworld. "I don't really do that."

"That's what I told him." But there was uncertainty in Lara's voice.

"Okay. What aren't you telling me?"

"Nothing, I guess. I don't know. It's just . . . he said she's been gone almost a year and a half now. She was fourteen when she disappeared."

My stomach sank a little at that. God. What an awful fate for someone so young. It made the keres' lewd comments to me downright trivial.

"He sounded pretty frantic."

"Does he have proof she was actually taken?"

"I don't know. He wouldn't get into it. He was kind of paranoid. Seemed to think his phone was being tapped."

I laughed at that. "By who? The gentry?" "Gentry" was what I called the beings that most of Western culture referred to as fairies or sidhe. They looked just like humans but embraced magic instead of technology. They found "fairy" a derogatory term, so I respected that—sort of—by using the term old English peasants used to use. *Gentry*. Good folk. Good neighbors. A questionable designation, at best. The gentry actually preferred the term "shining ones," but that was just silly. I wouldn't give them that much credit.

"I don't know," Lara told me. "Like I said, he seemed a little schizo."

Silence fell as I held onto the phone and passed a car driving 45 in the left lane.

"Eugenie! You aren't really thinking of doing this."

"Fourteen, huh?"

"You always said that was dangerous."

"Adolescence?"

"Stop it. You know what I mean. Crossing over."

"Yeah. I know what you mean."

It was dangerous—super dangerous. Traveling in spirit form could still get you killed, but your odds of fleeing back to your earthbound body were better. Take your own body over, and all the rules changed.

"This is crazy."

"Set it up," I told her. "It can't hurt to talk to him."

I could practically see her biting her lip to hold

back protests. But at the end of the day, I was the one who signed her paychecks, and she respected that. After a few moments, she filled the silence with info about a few other jobs and then drifted on to more casual topics: some sale at the mall, a mysterious scratch on her car . . .

Something about Lara's cheery gossip always made me smile, but it also disturbed me that most of my social contact came via someone I never actually saw. Lately the majority of my face-to-face interactions came from spirits and gentry.

It was after dinnertime when I arrived home, and my housemate, Tim, appeared to be out for the night, probably at a poetry reading. Despite a Polish background, genes had inexplicably given him a strong Native American appearance. In fact, he looked more Indian than some of the locals. Deciding this was his claim to fame, Tim had grown his hair out and taken on the name Timothy Red Horse. He made his living by reading faux-Native poetry at local dives and wooing naive tourist women by using expressions like, "my people" and "the Great Spirit" a lot. It was despicable, to say the least, but it got him laid pretty often. What it did not do was bring in a lot of money, so I'd let him live with me in exchange for housework and cleaning. It was a pretty good deal as far as I was concerned. After battling the undead all day, scrubbing the bathtub just seemed like asking too much.

Scrubbing my athames, unfortunately, was a task I had to do myself. Keres blood could stain.

I ate dinner afterward, then stripped and sat in my sauna for a long time. I liked a lot of things about my little house out in the foothills, but the sauna was one of my favorites. It might seem kind of pointless in the desert, but Arizona had mostly dry heat, and I liked the feel of humidity and moisture on my skin. I leaned back against the wooden wall, enjoying the sensation of sweating out the stress. My body ached—some parts more fiercely than others—and the heat let some of the muscles loosen up.

The solitude also soothed me. Pathetic as it was, I probably had no one to blame for my lack of sociability except myself. I spent a lot of time alone and didn't mind. When my stepfather, Roland, had first trained me as a shaman, he'd told me that in a lot of cultures, shamans essentially lived outside of normal society. The idea had seemed crazy to me at the time, being in junior high, but it made more sense now that I was older.

I wasn't a complete socialphobe, but I found I often had a hard time interacting with other people. Talking in front of groups was murder. Even talking one-on-one had its issues. I had no pets or children to ramble on about, and I couldn't exactly talk about things like the incident in Las Cruces. *Yeah, I had kind of a long day. Drove four hours, fought an ancient minion of evil.*

keres was dead. He wouldn't be telling any tales.

Two hours later, I finished the puzzle and admired it. The kitten had brown tabby fur, its eyes an almost azure blue. The yarn was red. I took out my digital camera, snapped a picture, and then broke up the puzzle, dumping it back into its box. Easy come, easy go.

Yawning, I slipped into bed. Tim had done laundry today; the sheets felt crisp and clean. Nothing like that fresh-sheets smell. Despite my exhaustion, however, I couldn't fall asleep. It was one of life's ironies. While awake, I could slide into a trance with the snap of a finger. My spirit could leave my body and travel to other worlds. Yet, for whatever reason, sleep was more elusive. Doctors had recommended a number of sedatives, but I hated to use them. Drugs and alcohol bound the spirit to this world, and while I did indulge occasionally, I generally liked being ready to slip over at a moment's notice.

Tonight I suspected my insomnia had something to do with a teenage girl . . . . But no. I couldn't think about that, not yet. Not until I spoke with the brother.

Sighing, needing something else to ponder, I rolled over and stared at my ceiling, at the plastic glow-in-the-dark stars. I started counting them, as I had so many other restless nights. There were exactly thirty-three of them, just like last time. Still, it never hurt to check.

After a few bullets and knife wounds, I obliterated
him and sent him on to the world of death. God,
I swear I'm not getting paid enough for this crap,
you know? Cue polite laughter.

When I left the sauna, I had another message
from Lara telling me the appointment with the
distraught brother had been arranged for
tomorrow. I made a note in my day planner, took
a shower, and retired to my room, where I threw
on black silk pajamas. For whatever reason, nice
pajamas were the one indulgence I allowed myself
in an otherwise dirty and bloody lifestyle.
Tonight's selection had a cami top that showed
serious cleavage, had anyone been there to see it. I
always wore a ratty robe around Tim.

Sitting at my desk, I emptied out a new jigsaw
puzzle I'd just bought. It depicted a kitten on its
back clutching a ball of yarn. My love of puzzles
ranked up there with the pajama thing for weirdness, but they eased my mind. Maybe it was the fact
that they were so tangible. You could hold the pieces
in your hand and make them fit together, as opposed
to the insubstantial stuff I usually worked with.

While my hands moved the pieces around, I kept
trying to shake the knowledge that the keres had
known my name. What did that mean? I'd made a
lot of enemies in the Otherworld. I didn't like the
thought of them being able to track me personally. I
preferred to stay Odile. Anonymous. Safe. Probably
not much point worrying about it, I supposed. The